THE  DROWNED MAN

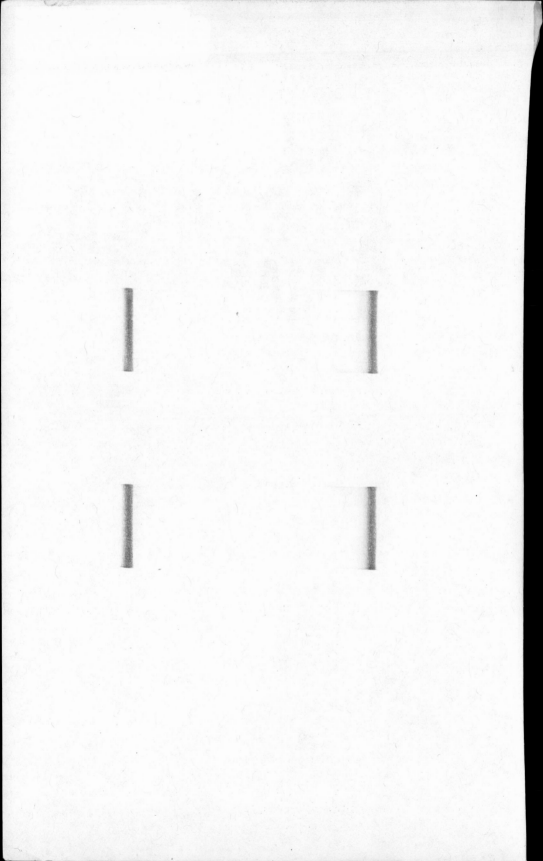

THE DROWNED MAN

**DAVID
WHELLAMS**

A PETER CAMMON MYSTERY

ECW Press

Published by ECW Press
2120 Queen Street East, Suite 200, Toronto, Ontario, Canada M4E 1E2
416-694-3348 / info@ecwpress.com

This is a work of fiction. Names, characters, places, and incidents either are the product of the author's imagination or are used fictitiously, and any resemblance to actual persons, living or dead, business establishments, events, or locales is entirely coincidental.

LIBRARY AND ARCHIVES CANADA CATALOGUING IN PUBLICATION

Whellams, David, 1948–
The drowned man / David Whellams.

(A Peter Cammon mystery)
ISBN 978-1-77041-148-7 (BOUND); 978-1-77041-043-5 (PBK)
ALSO ISSUED AS: 978-1-77090-366-1 (PDF); 978-1-77090-367-8 (EPUB)

I. Title. II. Series: Whellams, David, 1948– Peter Cammon mystery.

PS8645.H45D76 2013   C813'.6   C2012-907518-3

Cover images: Stain © Panupong Roopyai / iStockphoto.com,
    man illustration © 4x6 / iStockphoto.com
Cover and text design: Tania Craan
Author photo by Jennifer Barnes JB Photography
Printing: Friesens 1 2 3 4 5

MIX
Paper from
responsible sources
FSC® C016245

The publication of *The Drowned Man* has been generously supported by the Canada Council for the Arts which last year invested $20.1 million in writing and publishing throughout Canada, and by the Ontario Arts Council, an agency of the Government of Ontario. We also acknowledge the financial support of the Government of Canada through the Canada Book Fund for our publishing activities, and the contribution of the Government of Ontario through the Ontario Book Publishing Tax Credit. The marketing of this book was made possible with the support of the Ontario Media Development Corporation.

Canada Council for the Arts — Conseil des Arts du Canada — Canadä — ONTARIO ARTS COUNCIL CONSEIL DES ARTS DE L'ONTARIO — Ontario

In memory of my parents,
who loved books

PART ONE

Twenty Ten

*The 2010th year of the Common
Era. The tenth year of the Third
Millennium. The first year of the
current decade.*

CHAPTER 1

"There's nobody else for the job," Sir Stephen Bartleben said from his side of the massive thumping desk.

Body duty. Any other senior detective would have recoiled in outrage, perhaps even stood up and stalked out of the office. It happened from time to time that a Scotland Yard officer was needed to accompany the corpse of a British national homeward, in this case a Yard colleague who had been killed in Montreal. The assignment was a distinctly secondary one, usually handed off to a junior officer.

But Peter Cammon, veteran chief inspector, retired, though he considered leaving the office, stayed in place on his side of the big desk. He was in a sour frame of mind, ready to provoke his former boss, and sometimes the best way to throw Bartleben off his conniving game was to wait him out. Oh, bolting would be justified, Cammon reasoned: Bartleben hadn't called in eight months, and now was throwing him the most meatless of bones.

Peter Cammon decided to give it two more minutes. Then he would turn down the job.

They let three minutes go by. This, in fact, was not a long silence by Cammon-Bartleben standards. Because he knew that Sir Stephen had more to disclose, Peter stifled his impatience. The sheer routineness of the assignment mildly intrigued him. There had to be something more critical at stake for the Yard, and the boss was holding back. Why? Bartleben's gambit had been two-headed: did he mean that no other officer *wanted* the task or that only Peter was *capable* of doing it?

Peter had come up to London on a drizzly summer morning. Out of habit he had worn his black suit and black brogues, but had left his black bowler at the cottage. If Sir Stephen took this as a sartorial sign that Peter was open to returning to work, he was mistaken. Peter had fully retired. But the root of his hostility was Sir Stephen's bad form: he had failed to attend the funeral of Peter's brother, Lionel, several months back. Sir Stephen had sent a card of condolence, nothing more. In his general depression, Peter considered this a betrayal of almost fifty years of hand-in-glove trust. At least, that was what he told himself was the reason for his mood. Even if Peter was being unreasonable or muddling the causes of his depression, Sir Stephen was in for a rough time.

Peter continued to stare across the ridiculous desk. They had had no contact in all these months. Did Stephen believe that a simple turnaround trip to Montreal was enough to revive Peter's taste for crime? The tension in the room could not have been higher. Peter watched as Sir Stephen fussed with a small snow globe that housed Machu Picchu. Stephen seldom travelled anywhere and Peter guessed that it was a gift from his grandson. He resolved that if the boss turned the toy over and started shaking the snowflakes over Machu Picchu, the gesture would confirm that he was holding back something crucial.

He could easily read Bartleben's uncertainty. A take-it-or-leave-it offer would result in Peter telling him to bugger off. The boss shot a glance at two file folders on the desk, as if they might contain the seeds to foster Peter's curiosity. A fifth minute passed.

Peter wondered why Bartleben had failed to mention that he was no longer deputy commissioner of New Scotland Yard. Shunted aside. Superannuated. *Just like me*, Peter thought. Of course, if

Bartleben truly was on the shelf, what gave him the authority to send anyone across the Atlantic? There were rumours percolating that open scandal was about to hit the Yard on more than one front — the phone-hacking fiasco involving the *News of the World* seemed the most imminent — yet Bartleben's departure four (was it five?) months ago apparently had insulated him from most political and bureaucratic scrutiny. Bartleben always thought ahead of his rivals. He had jumped — though perhaps not too far from centre — and hadn't been pushed. Now he was a special adviser of some kind. Yet Bartleben had acknowledged none of this.

Peter understood that he had the advantage. There were no old times to revive and it appeared that Bartleben was no longer formally in charge of any part of the organization. He had no staff, save his beautiful young assistant, positioned outside the cavernous office. Was Montreal the best assignment he could winnow out of Whitehall? He needed Peter more than Peter needed to be back in harness. Clearly he had expected Peter to be intrigued by the Carpenter murder and had hoped to be congratulated on his own retirement, so that he could assert common ground in their shared status as retirees. All this was pitiful and, in his mood, Peter resolved to concede nothing. *Does he really expect me to join him in some troubleshooting caper on the premise of mutual impotence?*

But there had to be some discussion before Peter registered his definitive no. On the phone, Bartleben had mentioned only that a New Scotland Yard employee, John Fitzgerald Carpenter, had been brutally slain in Montreal. Peter recalled young Carpenter from a case four years ago. He worked in the Customs unit supporting Scotland Yard's criminal and anti-terrorism files. He had helped Peter out briefly, searching out a killer's alias on a flight manifest. Was this why Bartleben had summoned him to London? Peter decided to ask an aggressive question.

"Why do you think Carpenter was murdered?"

Bartleben paused for effect, then said, "It involves rare documents related to the assassination of President Abraham Lincoln."

Peter refused to be impressed by this melodramatic pronouncement. "Let me see his file, Stephen."

Bartleben handed over the larger of the files, a standard personnel dossier, not all that thick given Carpenter's seven years with the Yard. It was dog-eared and tea-stained, much of the wear and tear recent, Peter estimated. He took the folder and opened it to the dead man's photograph.

"Is the face familiar?" Sir Stephen asked with excessive cheer, appearing to believe that Peter was warming to the assignment.

"I've never seen his face before."

Bartleben was nonplussed. "I thought . . ."

"Carpenter? No. Who told you that?" Peter said, without blatant hostility but with a flat tone meant to reinforce his indifference to Stephen's plans for him. "I talked to him once on the phone, four years back or so. That problem with the husband in Dorset."

Peter returned to the folder. The heading read: "JOHN FITZGERALD CARPENTER b. 1976." The straight-on photo showed a handsome face, ageing well. Clean-shaven. But Peter wavered. The portrait gave the death a poignant humanity. His mood shifted slightly. He decided to take his time, having nothing to lose given his firm decision to reject the mission.

"Why do you want me for this? The case in Dorset four years back?" Peter said.

"Not really. It's just that Carpenter is one of ours," Bartleben offered, feebly trying to take the high road. "Decent performance record."

Peter settled back in his chair, deigning to skim the highlights. Or at least, he tried to lean back. The big desk was absurd enough but Peter's guest chair was equally pompous, straight-backed, like an unplugged electric chair, more proof of Stephen's manipulative nature: the guest was privileged to a regal audience.

Peter looked again at the photo. A stamp on the obverse showed that it had been taken one day after Carpenter's thirty-fourth birthday. His hair looked freshly cut in anticipation of the session.

For some reason, he had tried to appear youthful and rakish, which wasn't always the aim for ambitious young men at the Yard.

"Is it possible that Carpenter has a moustache now?"

"Why, yes, he does . . . did."

It was a parlour trick on Cammon's part. The black-and-white portrait drew out Carpenter's beard, a pentimento shadow, even though he must have shaved that particular morning. His face was inclined to Nixonian swarthiness, and likely someone had told him that he should present an open, clean-razored face to the camera. Peter guessed that a moustache would be more his style and that the young man would grow one soon after the photo shoot. Peter's wife, Joan, would say that the young man had "matinee idol looks." Carpenter had died in his prime.

Peter noted two fresh documents lying loose on top of the file; the rest, except the official photo, were pinned at the corner with a brad made of brass. A pristine U.K. death registration, actually a stamped official copy, was first. The consulate had inserted it as recently as a day ago, Peter guessed, and delivered it overnight by diplomatic pouch. This form established that Canada, or more probably the Province of Quebec or the municipality, had settled on a cause of death and handed down its own coroner's pronouncement. There it was, next in the file; it was a prerequisite for the U.K. form. With Canadian clearance, the corpse had been released for shipment to Britain. Peter understood that none of this changed the right of the host nation to pursue the criminal investigation. As well, the coroner in the young man's home county in the U.K. might choose to launch his or her own inquest.

The second document derived from the Quebec coroner's office. It was in French but the "Cause of Death" read the same in English: *homicide.*

"The Sûreté du Québec has carriage of the investigation," Bartleben said. "The provincial coroner signed off on the death certificate. Foreign obtained the complementary approval at this end and we're cleared to bring the body home. Heathrow has its own mortuary . . ."

"Not so fast," Peter snapped. He wouldn't be rushed. He glared across the Victorian hulk of a desk. You could transport prisoners to Australia in it, he thought. He spied a second manila file on the blotter, this one a brand new, unlabelled folder. He could see the airline ticket slotted inside. Here was another presumption on Bartleben's part: his efficient young assistant had already booked Peter's flight to Montreal. Peter turned back to the Carpenter file and continued to read, masking his emerging curiosity with a frown.

"It's a jurisdictional quagmire," Bartleben threw in.

"How so?" Peter said, still focused on the dossier. He began to read through the autopsy report, written in French.

"Carpenter was a British national killed within the city limits of Montreal. That's normally a matter for MUC police — Montreal Urban Community. But one of our people abroad on official business is an Internationally Protected Person under those Vienna Conventions signed a few years ago. That could mean the RCMP — the federal police in Canada — could try to assert preemptive jurisdiction."

Peter shot him a look of mild contempt. Not only did Bartleben have it wrong in terms of jurisdiction, Peter was sure, but these things had a way of sorting themselves out. Peter presumed local competence. If Bartleben weren't such an armchair manager, he would know that most policing responsibility in Canada rested with the provinces. Although Peter had visited Canada only once, and that a mere few hours spent in Niagara Falls, he had dealt with the Royal Canadian Mounted Police on several occasions. He knew the sensitivities of federal-provincial politics and that the Mounties would by no means rush to displace the local police. For its part, the Quebec Government, given the sovereigntist movement within its borders, would be careful to avoid unnecessary friction with a foreign state (perhaps especially Britain). Finally, whether the provincial Sûreté or the Montreal police force took the lead made little difference. The British High Commission in Ottawa would show due deference to the province. In Canada, the provincial attorney general had clear authority over the prosecution of *Criminal Code* offences. There was no quagmire.

He took his time with the pathologist's findings. His French was good; he knew that Stephen's was not. The report was embossed with *apostilles* from the Province of Quebec and from the consulate in Montreal confirming that the autopsy results had been accepted by both governments. The autopsy report followed the standard layout but Peter did note an admirable thoroughness in the pathology testing. He remarked again on the confident assertion of criminality, *homicide*. Many jurisdictions would never allow a coroner or a pathologist to go that far. Even more intriguing was the word appended to the summation: *noyé*. Death by drowning.

Peter realized that a document was missing. Foreign and Commonwealth Affairs supported a consul general's office in Montreal, so where was the interim report from British officials?

"What happened, Stephen?" he prompted, still trying to sound unmoved.

Bartleben adopted a disgusted look. "Both Carpenter and the consul general in Montreal, neither of them did their jobs." He hoisted a crisp, three-page document and dropped it back on the desk. "I'm embarrassed to show it to you."

Peter knew that Bartleben wasn't in the least embarrassed about sharing the consul general's statement, which bore an elaborate seal on the cover. The former deputy commissioner revelled in the world of diplomats, loved the game. Peter smelled politics. Someone in the High Commission had fouled up. The potential for scandal was evident and if Peter went to Montreal, he would likely face the spillover from the murder of a British official. What Bartleben characterized as simple could easily become complex. *Am I supposed to be grateful for being asked back into the Yard to do a minder's task, a delivery man's job, on the false pledge that I won't have to get my hands dirty with diplomats and careerist scoundrels? Such puppetry, such arrogance.*

Peter fixed his boss with an unforgiving gaze. "Why don't you just tell me what's in the file, Stephen."

"Nicola Hilfgott, consul general. Ambitious. I've never met her but, oddly enough, I've encountered her husband, Tom. Made his money in golf courses and retired at fifty-five. Anyway, she called Frank Counter in Special Projects a few weeks back and asked for assistance. Frank knows her from previous lives. Turned out she'd already consulted with National Archives and convinced them that she was in a position to acquire several rare documents that they would love to have. The Heritage people got on board and so did our High Commissioner in Ottawa. But Nicola wanted to 'protect the government's investment,' she said. Frank agreed to help. Who knows what Nicola really did or said."

"Why wouldn't this be an above-board purchase-and-sale? Why did she need security?" Peter said.

"Let's face it. Hilfgott was freelancing. The transaction had nothing to do with her regular duties. The dealer in Montreal, who had possession of these three rare letters, insisted on a cash transaction, the exchange to be effected at his shop after hours. Hilfgott suggested to Frank that because there was government money in play, a Scotland Yard officer would be helpful for security." Even Sir Stephen looked embarrassed this time.

"How much cash?" Peter said.

"Hilfgott made a deal for ten thousand Canadian for all three letters."

That was prevarication, Peter thought. You don't bring in the Yard for a paltry ten thousand. He at once guessed that Nicola Hilfgott, the consul general, had been trying to validate a shady deal by drawing in New Scotland Yard, and by extension co-opting Home Office headquarters. His mood soured further. *Why doesn't Bartleben see this?* he thought. *Or does he?*

Sir Stephen regrouped. "Peter, what do you know of the assassination of Abraham Lincoln?"

Peter had had enough of this dance and was tempted to burst out with: "Officially an American problem."

Instead, he merely stated what everybody knew. "Shot by John Wilkes Booth at Ford's Theatre in Washington."

"The assassination occurred on April 14, 1865. Did you know that Booth visited Montreal exactly six months earlier?"

"Why would he do that?" Peter said.

"His original plan, I gather, was to kidnap Lincoln and carry him south to Virginia as a hostage. Booth, who was a mere twenty-six years old, had contacts in Montreal, spies and blockade-runners who, in turn, could give him letters of introduction to potential helpers in Washington and Maryland."

"Did the authorities in Montreal try to arrest him?"

"Not at all. He did nothing to justify detention, and they ignored him. He was just a semi-famous actor at this point. Besides, he deliberately kept a low profile in Montreal, or so everyone thought until recently. Then Mrs. Hilfgott made her discovery. Or rather, someone made the discovery and contacted her."

Evidently, John Wilkes Booth had been up to more mischief than historians had believed. Peter understood that the three letters had historical value, perhaps enough to justify the Yard's involvement in the transaction, and so he allowed Bartleben to finish the tale.

"It appears that Booth was a loudmouth and a braggart who soon let everyone in the city know where he stood on the secession of the Confederate States. The Confederate government was desperate for official recognition by Britain and had already sent officials to Montreal to stir up trouble—for example, by launching raiding parties across the U.S. border to free Confederate prisoners-of-war. They hoped to draw Britain into a clash with the Lincoln government by provoking an incident. Young Booth travelled to Canada to make contact with these Confederate officials. It now appears that he also made contact with *British* authorities while there.

"Booth wrote a letter to the commander of British troops in Canada stating that he was authorized by the Confederate cabinet in Richmond, Virginia, to treat with the British administration.

However, there is a second letter, this from the official Confederate commissioners in Montreal to the head of British forces denying this authorization. There is apparently also a reply, a third letter, from the British commander rejecting Booth's entreaties."

"And why are these letters so valuable to Hilfgott? More important, are they really historically significant?"

Bartleben sighed. "I don't know, but Hilfgott and our Heritage friends say they are, and now the documents have disappeared."

Peter's antennae detected Nicola Hilfgott's agenda. A pampered diplomat with a hobby had paid $10,000, likely her own money, for documents that Peter gave even odds were forgeries. He suspected that senior people were already considering ways to push young Carpenter's death to the background. The murder would be left to the locals but the theft of the letters, even if they were forgeries, was shaping up to be an embarrassment for the British government. Bartleben wanted his own man in Montreal, not only to retrieve the body but also to sound out local police on their progress in the murder investigation. Fair enough, Peter thought, but the boss would also expect him to size up the errant consul general while in Canada. *No thanks*, Peter repeated to himself. Let the Serious Fraud Office deal with the letters. Obviously Stephen coveted the assignment, otherwise the SFO would already be working the file. He grunted and recalculated the odds of forgery at eighty-twenty.

Peter remained resolute. And where the Booth saga might once have captivated him, in his current mood it seemed a dry and faded drama.

Bartleben was thinking along the same lines, for he said, "Why anyone cares about such a long-gone sideshow to a long-ago war is beyond me."

Peter could see no plusses for Bartleben in any of this, no career glory, and that in itself intrigued him. The wise move was to let Frank Counter handle his own mess with the ample resources of Special Projects, whatever that was.

"The letters have vanished?" Peter said.

Bartleben nodded. "And now young Carpenter is dead. Murdered."

Noyé, Peter might have added.

Both men settled into silence again. It was Bartleben's move.

"Okay, Peter," he said, "there's a *small* obstacle to bringing the body home efficiently. The corpse, which has been embalmed and prepped, has been cleared for shipment back to Heathrow as early as the day after tomorrow. As you know, protocol requires someone be on the plane carrying the coffin. Whoever goes over should touch base with the police in Montreal, a courtesy call only."

"Why can't a member of Carpenter's family do the shipping?" It was a painful trip for any loved one but that was the typical arrangement. Alternatively, the family hired an international funeral service to transfer the body.

Peter expected the usual speech about shepherding the fallen comrade home but instead Bartleben replied, "The family is agitated. They question why it's taking us so long to bring their son home."

"What do they expect?" Peter said.

"There's a mother and a sister but the brother is the volatile one. He still lives in the family's hometown, a village called New Bosk up in Lincolnshire. He's threatening to sue us, though Lord knows for what. He wants to be the one to accompany the body to England."

"Then let him."

"No."

Peter stared across the desk. Bartleben wanted too much. He was holding back important details of the case, Peter was sure, yet he expected full cooperation. Peter knew the boss well. His clipped and reluctant answers told Peter that a scandal was about to metastasize. The bottom line remained the same: Peter didn't want the work.

"What do you expect from me, Stephen?"

"I'd like you to talk him out of it."

Sir Stephen sat back in his throne-like chair. His approach had been deliberately crude, disclosing just enough to make Peter contemplate the obvious questions. Why, for example, hadn't Nicola Hilfgott been recalled from her Montreal posting? And who had granted young Carpenter the time to fly to Canada for such frivolous reasons?

But Peter didn't voice those questions. In his morbid state, his brother's ghost haunting his skull, he fixed on a different worry: *Who from the Yard will speak at John Carpenter's funeral?*

"Do you have a room I could use?" Peter said.

"Yes. Basil Wilton's office is free, he's on holiday. Down the end of the hall."

An hour later Cammon came back to Stephen's sanctum.

"Okay, I'll drive up to Lincolnshire and see the family. But I won't go to Montreal."

Sir Stephen nodded and Peter left. Sir Stephen picked up the little glass-domed souvenir, turned it upside-down and back again, and watched the swirling Peruvian snow.

CHAPTER 2

Bartleben's strategy had failed to tip the balance. Peter left the big office still determined not to fly to Montreal, no matter how Sir Stephen tried to cajole or guilt him into it. But Peter would have to tend to a few logistical matters regarding his brief mission to New Bosk, Lincolnshire. With luck, he could get his old partner, Tommy Verden, to drive him up from London in the morning. Peter would stay in town tonight, and he needed to call home to arrange for his wife, Joan, to mind Jasper, the family dog. Finally, he decided to call Frank Counter in Special Projects for some background on John Carpenter. Without being aware of it, Peter had begun to fall back into a detective's way of thinking.

Bartleben's sleek assistant saw him hesitate in the anteroom, and she flashed him a smile in which, had Peter been more attentive to Sir Stephen's planned seduction (and Peter was always dazzled by beautiful women), he might have read her true motives. She was Sir Stephen's proxy and knew how to prod Peter's curiosity. She held out a slip of paper.

"Are you going to visit Mr. Counter?" she said. "I have his personal number."

Peter wasn't the only one capable of parlour tricks. He smiled back and took the note.

"He's not in his office today, or most afternoons," she continued. "In the far reaches of Whitehall, I believe. The Home Office is a strange world these days."

She was alluding to both Bartleben's and Counter's current status, Peter knew, although she did not go on to explain Sir Stephen's role as a floating executive, even though she must know that Peter was curious. The Metropolitan Police organization chart formed a quilt of abstract job titles — Specialist Crime Directorate, Specialist Operations, Counter Terrorism Command. Peter would have been content with everything lumped under an expanded Special Branch, but the bureaucratic universe had been transformed in 2001 because of terrorism. Special Projects had gathered about itself extraordinary resources (which would be sustained at least through the 2012 London Olympics), and had spat out plum assignments for ambitious men like Frank Counter. As for Stephen, he wouldn't have been the first executive to retire because the organization chart made his eyes ache.

And so, in part to learn how Counter and Bartleben were placed inside the new Home Office, he made the call.

"Tell me about Special Projects."

They were sitting in a grotty pub called the Feather. Its velvet banquettes and oak tables needed refurbishment but Scotland Yard people were known here, and the proprietor gave them a private booth. There were few other customers. More important to Peter, the pub stocked beers he liked.

Frank Counter smiled. He was a veteran of the Yard, and although they hadn't collaborated in more than five years, Peter had worked with him often over the decades. He was fleshy, his face ruddy at the extremities of cheekbones, nose, and fingertips; Peter noted a tremor of his right hand as he raised his glass.

They had always maintained friendly relations, in part because

Frank shared the field experience lacking in Bartleben. Six years from retirement himself, Counter appeared to have fashioned an ideal job for himself.

"Peter, we're busier than a regiment of typing chimps." A touch of defensiveness entered his tone. "It's the ideal job. We get the cream of the exciting cases. Oh, it's all political, but it's an opportunity. Life's good for career officers like us. My shop's kind of a flying squad for the high-profile cases."

"Do you have the resources you need for these big investigations?" Peter said blandly.

Frank smiled again. "Lots. Unless the counter-terrorism people start poaching our funding again." Frank quickly downed his first pint and prepared to fetch a second. "I understand what you're coming to, Peter. Where does *Bartleben* fit in the new groupings? Well, my old friend, he has no mandate at all except what the minister assigns to him. No people and no funding. I don't report to him."

Frank thumped the table and left for the bar, giving Peter time to kill his impulse to respond that Bartleben's ad hoc mandate sounded precisely like . . . Special Projects.

Frank returned with two more pints. Peter had been polite but now he wanted to get to the point. "I understand you flew to Montreal about John Carpenter."

"Yes. I made contact with an Inspector Deroche of the Quebec police. Spent most of a day with him. Very cooperative and quite eager."

"Did you view Carpenter's body?"

Frank recoiled; his face turned red. "Oh, no. But I reviewed the pathologist's photographs. Face was bruised, scarred. Stomach-turning."

"The photographs aren't on Carpenter's file. Why is that?" Peter said, trying not to be too confrontational.

"I really don't know."

Bartleben and Counter kept piling up the evasions, Peter thought. Counter was treating this case as a nuisance, but John Carpenter's murder was too nasty to be glossed over like this. "Who's the lead suspect?" he said, edgier this time.

"The book dealer, original owner of the mysterious letters. Name of Leander Greenwell. Deroche has put out a Canada-wide warrant for him."

Peter moved to the interesting part of the coroner's ruling, the dual cause of death. "The report says Carpenter was struck by a hit-and-run driver, then somehow made it to the canal's edge, fell in, and drowned. How did your inspector explain that?"

"The driver deliberately ran him down, then Carpenter crawled to the water."

"There's mention by the pathologist who authored the report that a local man, a Professor Renaud, tried to rescue Carpenter in the water. Any chance he took the money or the letters?"

Counter frowned, as if Peter had posed a flippant question. "Jesus, Peter, you're pushing a bit hard."

Peter continued, "I've read Madam Hilfgott's report but I'm no clearer on why she contacted you in the first place."

This was a none too subtle way of asking why Counter had responded to Nicola's request at all; it could easily have been handled without any Yard involvement. Peter's instincts told him that Frank should be worried for his career.

"I know, I know, too much skulduggery. But I confess, it seemed routine. It wasn't all that much, only ten thousand Canadian dollars. Nicola told me it was a steal, that the three letters were worth much more than that. Archives agreed. That won me over. And the High Commission in Ottawa approved."

A pleading look came into his eyes.

"You realize, Frank, that volunteering our services as, what, couriers or bagmen, immediately shifted the accountability onto us?"

Counter winced. Peter saw that he had gone too far.

"Do you believe her?" Peter said. "Are the letters valuable?"

Counter sipped the head on his beer, as if to fortify himself for the next disclosures. "I know what you're really asking, Peter. Nicola argued, with some support from Archives, that the letters technically belong to us, since in 1864 Canada was still under British rule and all three letters either derived from, or were sent to, the head of Her Majesty's Forces in the colony."

No wonder Sir Stephen appeared concerned, Peter thought. This was the thinnest legal argument for ownership he had heard in a long time. Sometimes the Mother Country forgot that its former colonies took pride in their heritage, too. At minimum, Peter estimated, Nicola was guilty of receiving stolen goods.

Counter looked sheepish and quaffed more beer. "How the hell do you explain Nicola Hilfgott? Her older brother and I went to school together, Cambridge, and she kept in touch with me over the years. The call came out of the blue. She wasn't apologizing for asking my help, she said. Typical Nicola. She said the High Commissioner needed reassurance and could I assist with an officer to make sure everything stayed above board."

"Hundred-dollar bills in a brown envelope at midnight?" Peter said.

Counter grimaced and Peter changed the subject. "What was Carpenter like?"

"Moderately ambitious and moderately talented," Counter said. "He was good at his assignments, did a lot of complex customs investigations in his time. I have to say, there was something callow about him. I dunno . . . He had the aura of always wanting to be somewhere else, doing something else. Tended to think too far ahead."

"A dreamer?" Peter prompted.

"An aggressive dreamer, I'd phrase it. Always ambitious for something. Fancied himself a ladies' man, too."

"Why did you pick him?"

"Ah, Jesus. I scouted around my group and he simply volunteered. He asked for two weeks' vacation while he was in Canada, and frankly, no one else wanted the job."

Echoes of Bartleben, Peter thought.

"But you said, Frank, that you're bustling with work. Carpenter wasn't in Customs anymore, was he? What files was he on?"

Counter sat back and stared into his glass. "We seconded him to my group from Customs a year ago. Carpenter was on the task force looking at the alleged tapping of cell phones and text messages by the *News of the World*. The hacking scandal. You read about that one?"

"I'm retired, not brain-dead," Peter fired back.

Counter looked startled, but proceeded. "You read, then, the allegations in the *Guardian* of massive phone-hacking of British nationals by Rupert Murdoch's people."

Those British nationals had included the royal family. Peter stared coldly into Counter's bleary eyes. "Did Carpenter work full-time on the hacking dossier?"

"Let me catch up," Counter said. "The Commissioner of the Met, that was a year ago, publicly declined to relaunch the investigation."

"And now we're about to pay the price of procrastination?" Peter suggested.

Frank Counter wiped sweat from his hairline.

"The *Guardian* was right," he continued. "There were thousands of incidents. Celebrities, crime victims, the royal household, maybe even Prince Harry. Peter, we expect the House of Commons will announce a formal parliamentary inquiry sometime in the next six months. The mandate will encompass the Yard's conduct in this matter and its cozy dealings with *News* staff. The Commissioner could look like a fool."

Peter had a sudden thought. The hacking allegations weren't new. Why hadn't Sir Stephen borne the brunt of the cock-ups back then? He had detected no unease from Bartleben that afternoon. "Tell me, Frank, why hasn't Sir Stephen been tainted by this?"

Frank shook his head in grudging admiration for Sir Stephen. "Bartleben was lucky. Some time ago, the powers that be decided to assign the hacking investigation to Counter Terrorism. CT! Lord knows why. That suited me fine, Stephen too. CT was glomming onto all the resources anyway. But then, for equally obscure reasons, they shifted the hacking business back to my unit, and it's all landed on my shoulders. Sir Stephen dodged all responsibility."

Peter understood it was more than luck that had saved Sir Stephen. The boss was a master at bureaucratic games.

Frank continued. "If they do a parliamentary inquiry it will keep me fully occupied for the next year or more. That's why I can't spare an officer for Montreal now."

"But you could spare Carpenter. I'm confused," Peter said.

"That's a huge irony. While the hacking scandal was over at Counter Terrorism, John Carpenter served as our liaison. But frankly he wasn't all that busy. We were all waiting for the techies to process more of the taps."

Peter could sense Frank rehearsing his testimony before the Commons committee.

"In fact," Counter said, "six months before he left for Montreal I had assigned him another file involving football and cricket match-fixing. My unit has the lead on this one as well. Huge problem in Asia with the betting syndicates corrupting the game. Some £280 million wagered last year on the Indian Premier Cricket League alone. Something of an issue in England, too, as you might expect. Carpenter was maintaining a watching brief on the file."

Counter shook his head, this time in open consternation.

"What?" Peter said.

"Don't tell anyone, but sooner or later the cricket thing is going to blow up, too, and my section will wear it if we don't lay charges. Charges by the ton."

"Shouldn't the sport betting problem reside with, say, the Serious Fraud Office?"

"The issue has become prosecution. The best hope we have is to follow the betting money, and that should be the SFO's bailiwick. But the money is hard to trace, and until we trace it, we rely on bribery offences, suborning officials, criminal charges of that nature. You see how 'Special Projects' can be a catch-all, a curse?"

Peter suspected that the Yard would continue to walk the devil's tightrope on both the betting scandal and the phone-hacking outrage. On the former, he knew that the Yard had largely handed off discipline of the gambling syndicates to the regulatory bodies for international cricket. Prosecutions under the U.K. *Gambling Act* were notoriously problematic. Frank's best strategy might be to delay.

Peter reminded himself why he was here. His brief was very simple: drive up to Lincolnshire and talk to the Carpenter family. He returned to Carpenter's strange assignment.

"So, Carpenter could be spared?" he repeated.

"I asked the staff and he volunteered, and I agreed to vacation time."

"Have you been able to chart his movements in Montreal?"

"Hilfgott's chief assistant in Montreal, name of Neil Brayden, has done that for us. Carpenter was booked for four days in a downtown hotel. It's confirmed that he stayed there the three nights before his death. Carpenter told me before he left that he was going to do some gadding about. He said he hoped to go up to Ottawa to see the Parliament Buildings and over to Quebec City to take the view from the Plains of Abraham. I confess, I don't know my Canadian history."

Peter tried a last ploy to draw Frank out. "Were you convinced the letters were real in the first place?"

Counter smiled. "That's the old Peter. Sly like a badger. Well, Nicola swore they were real. Of course, preserving her credibility in this fiasco requires her to maintain that. I have no idea, to be honest. But I admit, our confidence that Foreign would wear the stains from any blunders led us to minimize the effort we should have brought to bear. Young Carpenter not only said that he knew Montreal, having been there with his mother once, he had also taken courses in American history. The icing on that cake was his expressed hope to take a fortnight of leave. If we would pay the airfare and the first week of hotels, he would cover his other expenses."

Peter wondered if Frank Counter knew what he was admitting — that he had played bureaucratic games, colluded with Nicola, and taken a flutter without knowing whether another department would "wear the stains" of failure. Now the only escape from his lapse of due diligence was a cover-up, and that's what he was trying out on Peter now. Frank should have known better, Peter thought.

Counter sat back in his chair. "We underestimated the risks. But now we've lost one of ours. I'm glad you're on this, Peter. We want our man back."

They sat in silence. And then Peter — out of impatience, or perhaps indignation — pulled off his second parlour trick of the day.

"Frank, Bartleben showed me Carpenter's personnel file, the original. It was tea-stained. The stains are recent."

"You are a Sherlock," Counter said.

"And you've been poring over the file. No one spends time on a personnel dossier unless there's a secret in there somewhere."

"Human Resources will be pissed at me."

"You were trying to figure something out. What was it?"

"Ouch. That's harsh, Peter. The Quebec police have everything from us. It's their baby. The inspector impressed me as being on the march, quite capable."

Peter was unforgiving. "But you say you've no idea — not only who murdered Carpenter, but why your man would have wanted the assignment in the first place. Deroche may have the inside track on the killer, but you sloughed off the case in only one day, Frank. That smacks of containment, not commitment."

Peter had gone too far and Counter bristled. "There's *every* reason to think that the book dealer went back and killed Carpenter for the documents. Ran him down with his car and dumped him in the river."

Peter couldn't stop himself from sneering. "Do you know if he even had a driver's licence?"

That ended the meeting. As Peter walked down past the Houses of Parliament, quiet at this hour, his old detective's brain began to understand what Frank had been looking for in the file. He had been searching for evidence that John Carpenter had been in on the scheme to steal Nicola's ten thousand Canadian dollars.

Peter reached Joan on her mobile. She often didn't answer at once, since she spent so many hours in hospitals, which frowned on cell calls.

"Hello, Peter. Where are you?" Joan's voice was weary.

"I'm in town. I have to go to Lincolnshire tomorrow morning."

"That's fine," his wife said. They fell into an awkward silence, Joan's family tragedy hanging in the air, as it did over all their conversations recently. He understood that his wife deserved more than his forbearance now as she lurched between distant points across England giving comfort to her dying siblings, and seldom sleeping at the cottage two nights in a row. Joan had a high sense of the dignity of life and her treks had become a double vigil, a regimen to ensure that her brother and sister passed on in a cloud of warmth and compassion. None of this gave her any opportunity to apply her clinical nursing skills, but her mere presence ennobled her family. Her brother Nigel had late stage lung cancer, and although her sister Winnie's surface memory had been obliterated by Alzheimer's, Joan got through to both of them by her touch and tone. Peter struggled to find ways to contribute more but his own brother's death had lately hamstrung his will.

"Do you want me to come up with you to Birmingham tonight?"

"No, stay in London."

Peter tried again. "I could get to Birmingham tomorrow afternoon." It was technically possible to jump from Lincolnshire to Birmingham in a few hours, though it wasn't much of a plan.

"No need," Joan replied. "I'll go to the cottage tonight, off to see Winnie late tomorrow in Leicester. Do you need the car?"

"Tommy will drive me up, then back home."

It was like this, logistics substituting for communication, scheduling details for confidences.

"Can I make a suggestion, Peter? Why don't you and Tommy take a jaunt? Not Lincolnshire. Go back to some exotic spot you worked a case together. Check in with some foreign police people you worked with. Paris. Vienna."

Peter jumped in too fast. "I never worked a case in Vienna."

That killed the chance of connection. Peter could sense her giving up.

"Okay. I'll be home to feed Jasper and take her for a walk," Joan said. "I don't leave till eleven o'clock tomorrow and if you're home by late day, she'll be fine. I'll be back by evening."

Logistics. He would have to find a better way to become part of her grieving.

CHAPTER 3

Tommy Verden picked up his old friend in front of the hotel at 8 a.m. The hotel stood only a few streets from Scotland Yard Headquarters, yet Tommy had to navigate multiple right-hand turns, as mandated by London traffic planners and enforced by cameras that, he always imagined, were set off by the dozen in trip-wire fashion.

As Peter got into the front seat of the Mercedes, Tommy sputtered, "Effing cameras. It's like a hundred paparazzi provoking you with flashbulbs. Gives new meaning to 'reflex lens.'"

"Good morning to you, too," Peter said.

Yet the day was sunny and held the irresistible promise of a new adventure. Peter fastened his seat belt and Tommy eased out into the rush-hour stream. Having not seen his friend for six months, Peter looked Tommy over with curiosity, noting without criticism that his age had finally caught up to his features. This was overall a good thing. He had always had a craggy face with the crow's feet of experience radiating out from the corners of his eyes, but now the cragginess had turned distinguished, layering extra gravitas on top of a brawler's grit. Peter thought he resembled the actor Michael Rennie. But Tommy took pains not to appear to step up in social class; he wore his hair shaggy and he retained his tweed jackets and heavy detective-issue wingtips.

"So, Lincolnshire," Tommy began.

"A town called New Bosk."

"Never heard of it. All these years, we've never been to Lincolnshire on an assignment."

"I expect they have the same roster of perverts, picklocks, and gunsels as any other place in the U.K.," Peter said. But it was a light-hearted comment, and Tommy laughed. They both loved Hammett, Chandler, and early Graham Greene.

"So, John Fitzgerald Carpenter. Full disclosure, Peter. I told Bartleben I was picking you up, but we didn't discuss the case, except his saying be careful around Carpenter's brother."

Peter understood that Tommy was notionally attached to Special Projects, Frank Counter's group, but frequently took on assignments for Sir Stephen Bartleben. But there were no divided loyalties here. Tommy would never be Bartleben's conduit to Peter's thinking. In return, Peter would never place Tommy in a position where he would have to prevaricate to Bartleben about Peter's actions. Besides, decades of partnered casework by the two field men shifted Tommy's primary allegiance Peter's way, if the test were to come. Tommy was clear-eyed about his duty to the boss, but duty and loyalty could be different things. Soldiers in battle primarily fought for each other.

The first signs for the motorway appeared. "It'll take a while to get there," Tommy said casually.

Peter reached for the road atlas in the door pocket but Tommy waved him off.

"A man's reach should exceed his grasp, else what's Sat Nav for?" Tommy said, and accelerated.

The morning light was cheering and they tacitly agreed to approach this trip as a lark. Carpenter's murder might hover on the horizon, but so far neither of them had invested much in the case. They were veterans; after a half century of mayhem, they were entitled to enjoy themselves on a minor assignment. Peter slid the reports out of his briefcase and began to relate the travels of John Carpenter, chronicling his arrival in Montreal, the time of his sign-in at the hotel, the exchange of cash for documents, and ultimately his death at the Lachine Canal.

"A lot of gaps," was Tommy's reaction. "Why doesn't Frank Counter know more? I mean, he went all the way over there."

Peter agreed. "Only spent a few hours with the locals. And barely a summary of his meeting on the file — unless there's a case folder they haven't shown us. Counter owes the file a full report."

Tommy showed his amusement. Here was Peter Cammon insisting that he had no intention of flying to Montreal, yet griping about the shortcomings of an investigation he claimed to be shunning.

Peter paraphrased at length from the coroner's report, translating as he went. "The car hit him hard enough to kill him, but not imme-diately." Peter felt an urge to call the intrepid pathologist and discuss these findings. "The report states that he was conscious enough to crawl a hundred feet across the grass to the lip of the Lachine Canal. There's a sidewalk — pavement — running parallel to the waterway. I wonder how long he lay there on the cement."

"And why wasn't this an accident?" Tommy mused.

They were speculating but at this point it wasn't important to get everything right.

Peter read on. "The doctor says the blow from the car would have been fatal eventually but the pathology leaves no doubt that Carpenter was alive when he fell into the canal."

"Water in the lungs," Tommy said.

"Right."

"So, for the sake of argument, the hit-and-run might not be homicide in the strict sense," Tommy persisted. He paused, recon-sidering. "You have to admire that medical examiner. He could have written 'cause of death unknown' to play it safe. Let's see. Carpenter was mortally injured and he knew it but he scrabbled across a hun-dred feet or more of dew-covered grass, and over an asphalt path. He was fleeing his killer as best he could. That's what the forensics told our doctor."

Peter let this scenario hang in the air while he went on to read selectively from Hilfgott's brief report on the Civil War letters. Finally, Frank Counter's pitiful note confirmed that the Sûreté du Québec had issued warrants for the vanished book dealer, Leander Greenwell. Peter circled back to the victim.

"Tommy, I have to ask: Why did Carpenter book 'up to two weeks in Canada'? Frank Counter said that he had the vacation credits, and August made sense for a holiday. But Frank also told me it was all last minute, that he 'jumped at the chance.' Carpenter made a big deal of the trip but there are no signs he had relatives in Canada."

Tommy turned off the motorway where the Sat Nav instructed, the female voice an intrusion into their male domain. Peter looked over at his friend.

"Tommy?"

"Oh, sorry. Just thinking. I don't know what Carpenter had in mind but I was just reconsidering the cause of death. The violence of a murder can tell you a huge amount about the killer. We've both seen cases where the murderer goes too far. For example, he fires off a full clip when the first shot achieved the kill. Or he sticks around to slice and dice for no good reason. Things like that reveal a nasty perpetrator, or maybe something about motive. Peter, there's real perversity at work here. That's why the pathologist, that Dr. Lowndes, made the double-barrelled judgement. Sorry, don't mean to run on."

"And what do the facts tell us about Carpenter's death, bottom line?" Peter said.

"Easy. They tell us that he was murdered twice."

The town of New Bosk lies a few miles south of Lincoln. The detectives were able to avoid the county hub by Tommy's clever programming of the Sat Nav, which took them onto circuitous back roads. The town may have qualified as an adjunct of Lincoln but none of the larger city's smokestacks marred the bucolic horizon here. Instead, New Bosk offered an array of church spires and its own small factory towers, including the chimneys of a large brewery.

"This is a long way from Canada," Tommy declared.

They passed farmland carpeted with maturing wheat, barley, sugar beets, and other vegetables. Peter knew that immigrant workers from Eastern Europe would soon arrive by the hundreds to harvest the crops, but for now the countryside remained sedate. He recalled from his long-ago studies of Old English — or was it Old Norse? — that "bosk" meant "a grove of trees"; perhaps so, but the forests had been cut back for tillage centuries ago. There was little new or leafy about New Bosk.

They decided that in the interest of keeping interaction with the Carpenters low-key, Tommy would leave Peter to deal with the family alone. Nonetheless, Tommy gave him a pointed look as they entered the town.

"We're all right, then?"

Both policemen knew that the brother, Joe, had threatened Frank Counter and Bartleben's aide over the phone. Tommy Verden was armed. Peter Cammon wasn't, but he had handled a thousand difficult witnesses in the past and he felt no worry.

"I'll need a Batemans ale afterwards," he said as he climbed out of the Mercedes in front of the Carpenters' address.

Tommy drove off. They had their plan. Tommy would circle back for Peter in exactly one hour. Another hour after that for lunch, and they could make it back to Peter's cottage by nightfall. They would manage their report to Bartleben from the car.

The house was part of an undistinguished row of red-brick units, their front doors only a foot or two from the paved lane. There was no one about, the sun having beaten everyone indoors. N. 628 had no knocker. Standing out on the street, Peter rapped on the door panel before noticing a sign that read: "ENTER BY BACK LANE," with an arrow pointing to the right. Peter waited, baking in the sun. The lace curtain in the front window parted and a woman held up a palm to hold him there. A few seconds later — as if the woman had rushed to head him off from knocking again — the front door opened on silent hinges.

She was about twenty-eight, maybe a year or two older, and gave off an efficient, if downtrodden, impression; Peter's mother would have called her "one of those buried beauties" (although that had been one of his mother's sly ways of slandering the Irish). The woman wore a black skirt and crisp white blouse, as if she knew a guest was coming; her skin was pallid and she wore her hair in a tight bun. Her smile was tentative. She clearly understood that he represented the police.

"I'm sorry, sir," she said. There was nothing to be sorry for and Peter hastened to reassure her.

"Pardon me, I'm a colleague of Jack's. Chief Inspector Cammon. I didn't mean to interrupt you, I didn't see the sign in time."

This was the younger sister. She had manners, in the way that the supportive junior child taking care of a parent usually does; Peter knew that the father had died twenty years ago and that the brother, age thirty-two, lived in the house as well. She opened the front door wide and welcomed Peter inside before locking the door firmly behind her.

"Please come in," she said, hesitating on the entrance mat. The front room was dark and still, and Peter was forced to move farther into the space. "My name is Carole, with an 'e.'"

Carole turned and tapped superstitiously on the door. She spoke in a lilt that was as much Irish as Lincolnshire. "Do you know the tradition, Chief Inspector?"

Peter was happy to keep everything friendly. "No, I haven't heard it."

"Now then, the Lincolnshire tradition is to only use the front door for a new baby, for a new bride, or for a coffin."

Peter smiled and came farther into the living area. The mention of coffins might have hung heavily in the musty room but old Mrs. Carpenter entered at that point and immediately took the talk in another direction. She was thin and creaky but self-propelled, and

29

she crossed the Persian carpet to place her hand on Peter's arm before Carole could waylay her.

"Montreal!" the old woman burst out, and with that single word answered one of the questions about John Carpenter's travel planning. She took what was evidently her regular seat on the sofa. A cup of tea waited beside her on a souvenir saucer from Cleethorpes and Peter understood that if Carole failed to keep the cup filled, her mother soon would call out for more. He introduced himself but her attention at once drifted away.

"Montreal!"

"My mother is a bit more lucid than she seems, once you get used to her style," Carole said.

"I trust my colleagues have conveyed their condolences," Peter said. "Let me add my own. Does she know?"

Carole sighed but remained upbeat. "A lot would label her, without shame, as having the Alzheimer's, but she's more complex than that. Like I say, she tunes in and out. Can be quite funny, actually."

She meant that Peter should make an effort, and so he did. "Have you been to Montreal, Mrs. Carpenter?"

"Oh, definitely! I had an affair of the heart with a Montreal man. He took me away to the Colonies for a time."

This was a well-honed fable, but then Mrs. Carpenter surprised him with the punchline. "But then the cad brought me back!"

Peter had to laugh. He checked the snow globe sitting close by her teacup with MONTREAL etched in script on the base; the glass dome encased a cross on a mountaintop. He turned to Carole Carpenter but she gave him a look that held him in place. Without warning, the old woman raised herself from the sofa and declared, "Nap time, I think."

Peter stood as the daughter guided the woman behind a beaded curtain into a back room that now must serve as a bedroom. Soon she was asleep, allowing Carole to come back and sit where her mother had been.

"Would you like tea, Inspector?" She seemed glad of company.

"No thanks. Just to be clear. How much does she know?"

The question was abrupt but they had already established a rapport, he felt, and Carole did not appear discomfited. It was Peter who was suddenly derailed. A small black wreath hung over the old woman's bedroom doorway. Melancholy swept over him like a wall of fog. The blue devils, his mother might have said. He raised his eyes to Carole's and for a skipped beat drew a complete blank, a white page without jots or hints of what he wanted to say. Fifty years of interviewing witnesses, and nothing kicked in. His brother's death had snatched away his mind, and this house of mourning, curtained and hushed, triggered a rush of fears in him.

Carole pretended not to see his distress. "No, she doesn't know and there'd be no point. She confuses my brother, Joe, with Johnny a lot."

Peter fought to recover his composure. The woman waited primly, expectantly.

"I thought he was called Jack," Peter managed to say.

"What he's called in London may not be his nickname at home."

Peter liked the kind, well-mannered young woman. "Is Joe expected, Carole?"

"Joe could be anywhere in the town, but you can be sure he's *in* the town."

Peter rubbed his eyes, as if to massage away black thoughts. "I'm sorry, I missed your point."

"I'm sorry, too. I wasn't implying that he's a ma's boy or anything. I'm meaning to say that Joe told me the other day that he never plans to leave New Bosk. He grew up here and has a good job here. He seldom goes anyplace else, I meant."

"What does Joe do for a living?"

"He's a Level 3 mechanic. Has a half interest in a choice garage."

Peter had been told that Joe Carpenter had demanded to fly to Montreal to retrieve his dead brother. He did not sound like much of a traveller. Peter was already gaining a sense of a deep anger in the brother.

Joe did not show up for the balance of the hour. Peter accepted the offer of tea, although he craved a pint, and he and the young woman talked easily. As he had surmised, Mrs. Carpenter had been to Montreal once as a girl but never on a lover's tryst. The snow globe — Carole turned it over to demonstrate — restored her imagined memories every time. Peter tried not to read too much into it — it was a harmless talisman, a mnemonic device — but pathos existed in the fact that John Carpenter had yearned to see Montreal since his boyhood because of this souvenir. In his pitch to Frank Counter, John Carpenter had spoken with enthusiasm about Canada. He had likely done research on Google and had expanded the trip into a major vacation. It seemed innocent enough.

Although the Mercedes was tuned to a smooth hum, Peter caught the idling motor out front. Carole apologized for Joe's absence but suggested that Peter return in a couple of hours. Peter had hoped to be gone from New Bosk by then so that he could get back to the cottage and his dog. Carole walked him out the rear door and around to the street. Primroses and hawthorn bloomed in pots along the towpath. She presented a final wan smile and turned away.

CHAPTER 4

Peter and Tommy swung by the garage in the centre of New Bosk but Joe Carpenter had left for the noon hour. The mechanic on duty didn't think Joe intended to return home for his lunch.

They decided to stop at the first restaurant in the high street that advertised Batemans ale, and then do another round of the garage and the Carpenter residence. They ordered the ploughman's lunch: Stilton cheese, pickle, chutney, and Lincolnshire plum bread.

Although Peter spoke admiringly of Carole Carpenter, Tommy judged that the meeting with the sister hadn't changed his partner's mind about going to Montreal. In fact, Peter's debriefing was perfunctory and Tommy noted the cloud that had descended on his old friend. He remained watchful as Peter ordered a second cask ale.

Peter eventually spoke. "So, Tommy, what's the story on Bartleben's retirement? Frank thinks Sir Stephen may be vulnerable. The phone hacking thing."

"The phone hacking thing? The boss is *not* vulnerable at all. He left his old position, shall we say, in a timely fashion, making him no longer accountable for the messes in Special Projects or anywhere else. Good sense of self-preservation, our man."

"But he has no power from his spot on the shelf. What does he have to gain by staying on the sidelines?"

"His title is special adviser. Think of it, my friend. The title is open to further definition. He intends to be the one to define it."

"So he wants back in?" Peter's speech was slightly slurred.

"Yes, he does."

"Wants Frank's territory?"

"When the timing is right."

They decided on a quick tour of the town. Turning off the Sat Nav, Tommy drove them through the old central marketplace, which aside from a few parked cars was as barren of humans as a Mexican town in a Sergio Leone western. A signpost on the far side of the square pointed to various compass points but Tommy ignored it in favour of exploring the town. It did not take more than five minutes to reach the true countryside, with its ordered farms and dirt roads. A few sheep were scattered picturesquely across the far hillsides but they still saw no sign of the forest that gave the place its name. The fields stretched to infinity, only a few pinwheel wind turbines marking the vista.

At the edge of town Peter spied an ancient church and forced Tommy to slow down. The spire of All Saints Catholic did not provide much of a landmark against the afternoon sky, for it was a Romanesque structure and its architects, and all subsequent tinkerers, had kept its profile low, maintaining its stunted towers and hunkered-down personality.

Peter at once said, "Let's stop. We have time."

Verden had all the time in the world but he was an impatient man by nature and couldn't see much profit in investigating this dusty and currently empty church. He edged down the unpaved lane and parked by the small cemetery.

Peter was immediately pleased to note that the church, after most of a millennium, still stood apart from the town, a place of sanctuary for pilgrims. Near the building an effort had been made to dredge out a pond, which was now overgrown with duckweed. The sexton, or perhaps local volunteers, had scythed the yellow grass around and inside the cemetery; all the gravestones stood upright in precise rows. Peter got out of the Mercedes.

"I'll pick you up," Tommy called through the passenger window.

"I won't be long," Peter said. "I'm guessing that Carpenter's funeral will be held here. But I won't dawdle and if Joe isn't back home yet, we'll simply head for the cottage. Fifteen minutes."

Tommy drove off, leaving Peter to admire the exterior of the much-amended Catholic church. A plaque told him that All Saints had risen in Norman times on a cruciform foundation; the lack of flying buttresses and other Gothic innovations had kept the outside stocky, the wings of the cross short. The cornerstone had been set about the year 1150. The small building was wonderfully preserved. In terms of the local superstition Carole Carpenter had described, brides and candidates for baptism or burial had no choice but to enter by the main door at the base of the cross and proceed up the centre aisle.

Within, the diocese had maintained the original stonework and the immense font in the nave, and that in itself was a triumph of preservation, Peter saw. The nearby pulpit had been added much later. Although the outer stone walls were thick, the church interior was laid out in three rows and two aisles, in the Romanesque style. Norman arches, which always reminded Peter of an archer's bent bow in some movie version of *Henry V* (wrong era, he knew), set the confident character of the interior. Stained glass scenes enlivened the path up the aisle. The clever early churchmen had appropriated the best of the pagan era, with carvings placed at the capitals of each pillar, water-leaf and animal masks etched everywhere. Discreet plaques explained that major renovations had been implemented in almost every century. From the entry, the eye was drawn inevitably forward to the small altar, which was in its own room, separated from the main space by an iron gate that was more like a fence. Today the gate was open and Peter came forward, curious about the altarpiece, which backed against the stuccoed end wall.

He wasn't surprised to find few paintings — Henry VIII would have taken care of these — and likewise the candlesticks were new and undistinguished. What did catch his attention was a cross perched high above the altar and affixed to the wall. It had double horizontal arms. Peter recognized it right away as a reliquary cross, by far the most valuable single item in the building. Any wayfarer in the Middle Ages visiting All Saints Church for the first time would know from the multi-armed crucifix that the church possessed one or more venerated relics from a saint. Perhaps fewer would know that the body part — a finger, a lock of hair, a vial of blood (Peter had once encountered a reliquary box asserted to contain a saint's foreskin) — would always be held sealed inside the horizontal arms of the cross rather than the vertical.

The altar room was silent, remarkably cool in the August afternoon. He craned his neck to see the golden cross better. Peter was determinedly agnostic and his interest was secular. In *Casablanca*, he mused, the Cross of Lorraine is the signal used by the underground in the Nazi-occupied city, a double cross to outwit the double-cross. But today he found the reliquary and the church as a whole morbid. It felt like a museum and he wasn't particularly curious about the Church's prized relic. He almost walked out.

Instead, he stood by the altar and ruminated on the cross. He was still determined to turn down the Montreal assignment. Sir Stephen, and perhaps Tommy Verden, were hoping that the trip would bring him back to his old self. But there would be no revival of his old self, Peter reflected. Not yet. For now, he was all too aware that the gold cross above his head was a false icon — not that it wasn't actual gold or that the silver inlay and stuck-on amethysts and garnets weren't real, but that the relic inside held no curative powers for him. His brother, a devout Catholic convert, had died suddenly and alone of a massive stroke, giving no one the opportunity of intercession, with or without magic relics. The air in the chapel was cool but stuffy and he felt delirious, although not in any religious way. Whatever the forces in play in Peter's mind, they were earthly and ultimately depressing to him: at that moment he didn't care to speculate on what miracle-spinning body parts were encased in the arms of the cross. He had lost his taste for exploration.

Without warning, he began to weep. He pounded his fist on the last pew, causing the chalice and the candlesticks on the altar to tremble. His brother had left without warning, perished of a stroke on the Persian carpet in his library. The housekeeper had found him ten hours later lying in gouts of his own blood and vomit; the telephone lay on the rug beside the body, proof that he had struggled to call for help. Peter wondered if Lionel had been trying to call him. The police were requested; they had even called Peter in as a courtesy, but there was nothing criminal about it. The death had been a cheat, in Peter's view. His brother was a civilized man and a loyal older brother. He shouldn't have died alone. That wasn't their fraternal deal.

The chalice toppled. The clatter jerked Peter out of his self-pity, at least for the moment. Since the cup stood at the back of the altar, he could hardly reach it, even when he took the final step up to the dais where the presiding priest normally would have stood. He stepped up and stretched to his full height of five-foot-six to reposition the cup. Wiping away his tears, he looked higher and noticed that the reliquary cross had shifted off the vertical by a couple of inches. This was a small miracle in itself, since he was sure it must be anchored by screws to the wall. He descended the two short steps, picked up a stiff-backed wooden chair, and carried it up, so that by standing on it he could just reach the base of the cross. It centred easily. Peter paused in mid reach to read the inscription below the crucifix. It had been fashioned by Lucas di Vieri, a Sienna goldsmith, in 1347. It held the index finger of St. Jerome.

Peter was still standing in this ludicrous pose when Joe Carpenter came up behind him. He had nabbed Peter in the posture of a snoop, a thief, and a desecrator.

"Now then, what the fuck is this?" Joe Carpenter said.

Peter tried to stay calm. In his personal turmoil, he might have given out a gallows laugh in response to the man, but when he turned the fellow was pointing a gun at him.

Peter recognized the dark eyes and broad forehead of the Carpenter line. His face was ruddy, from sun rather than drink, Peter estimated, and he sported an elaborate but scruffy fringe of beard; his black hair flopped over his eyes. John Carpenter stood five-foot-ten according to his file, and Peter had the impression he had been lean and thin-boned, but Joe was stocky and not much taller than Peter. He held the battered carbine pointed at the detective's chest. Peter deduced that he kept the weapon permanently in his car; but why carry a cumbersome weapon around in one's vehicle? The point was moot; the rifle was quite real.

Peter wasn't worried. He decided that he wouldn't explain himself, whatever the provocation; he was in that kind of mood. He would not be aggressive, either. He stepped down and replaced the wooden chair. Joe Carpenter's gun tracked him.

"I'm Chief Inspector Cammon. Please lower your gun. You were told I would be coming down."

"Well, here we both are. What are you doing in our church?"

"Is this the family church, then?" Peter continued, alluding to the impending funeral of John Fitzgerald Carpenter.

"Yes, but you won't be attending the doings."

Right. A misstep. No more probing, Peter decided.

Joe continued, "If the funeral ever gets done. You represent the Scotland Yard? Well, where would be my brother's body?"

"That's what I'm here to talk to your family about."

"Never mind that. My ma's in and out and my sister's not making the decisions."

"Please put down the rifle." Joe lowered it a few degrees.

"My brother will be lying there just where you stand. The pastor will say the Mass and splash water on the coffin. Let the rotting process begin. Walnut."

"What?" Peter said.

"Walnut, the coffin. It's bought. Lies empty in the funeral home as we speak. What do you suppose they ship him home in from Canada? Cardboard? Pressed board?"

"It's something they've done many times before," Peter said. "They use metal. The paperwork has been signed off at both ends. I've seen the papers."

"I'll see to it when I get there," Joe said.

He had been waving the short-barrel rifle about with each response from Peter. A veteran of gun confrontations, Peter knew to move slowly and choose his moment, but for now he still had hopes of talking Joe out of shooting. The detective wasn't afraid or angry.

Peter saw Tommy enter silently from the back of the church. He was carrying a Glock 17 in a two-hand grip pointed at the mechanic. It was a bodyguard's weapon and it was entirely wrong for this job. In brandishing the powerful gun, Verden was sending Peter a bundle of signals. He was using the gun only to intimidate. One shot from the Glock would break all their eardrums and blow out windows, and if Tommy had it loaded with .40 calibre rounds, the noise and effect would be devastating. As well, the bullet would pass right through Joe Carpenter and shatter the altar. No, Tommy wouldn't be firing the big pistol.

"Would you put the carbine on the floor by the step, please, sonny," Tommy said. "One move, one twitch and that'll be a sacrificial altar for you."

Joe Carpenter turned. Although he (unlike Peter) could have no doubt that the tall detective would use his gun, he did not lower his own weapon completely. "I could take your eye out."

Tommy held his stance. "You might put his eye out, but not mine. I can take you down easily, lad, no problem. By the way, one shot will blow out that lovely stained glass and generally fuck up the tourist potential of this institution. The sacred meets the profane. You've lived here all your life? You want to die here?"

Quite the speech, Peter thought. The melodramatic language was designed to scare and befuddle the mechanic, and to signal to Peter how they would play this through. No one was going to get shot, unless Joe Carpenter lost control. Peter had a vision of Joe joining his brother in a twin walnut coffin right where they now stood.

But it wasn't Peter's move. No one changed position for a full minute. Joe then lowered the rifle but held onto it, as he considered whether to place it on the marble floor or prop it against a pew.

Tommy held his aim. Peter sensed his indignant anger. "Why don't you lay it on the altar, if that suits you, lad?"

Joe turned to Peter, his voice petulant. "I want my brother brought home this week. And I want your promise to find his killer. Full effort by Scotland Yard."

Peter knew that he could not make that promise. Tommy knew it, too.

"Tommy," Peter said, "leave us for a minute.

"Give me the gun and I'll leave you two to sort it out."

"It's okay, Tommy," Peter said.

Verden frowned, utterly opposed to leaving the mechanic anywhere near the carbine. The tension binding the three men in place was becoming too much, and Peter knew that Joe might raise the rifle again. Peter reached for the gun. Joe held it by the barrel, safety on, and Peter took it and propped it against the wooden chair. Tommy lowered the Glock and backed down the central aisle and out the church entrance. Peter turned to the young man. "We'll bring him home with dignity. There are forms to sign and we're in the best position to get it all done smoothly. The consulate is experienced in such matters. It will work with the funeral home on the shipping arrangements."

Joe paced to the far end of the altar and turned. "Oh, yeah? What do they do to the body?"

Peter understood that the picture of his brother's coffin obsessed Joe Carpenter. Peter wasn't exactly sure how international air carriers shipped bodies in this post-9/11 era. "As dignified as you'd hope."

"Do they refrigerate the body and all?"

"I don't think that's needed, Joe. The embalming will be done in Quebec, part of the rules."

"Frenchies."

Peter was starting to wonder if he had made an error. The carbine was in easy reach.

"They prefer 'Québécois.' I believe. Let's talk in there."

Peter led Joe into the main church and they halted by the middle row of pews. Something about Joe Carpenter was chilling even now, without the gun. Something in the way he refused to focus on the other person's eyes. Peter wondered if Johnny had shared that sinister aura.

"Tell me about John."

Joe Carpenter took a deep breath and ran his hand over the carved top of a pew. "Have you ever met a person who spent his life trying to live up to his name? Literally, I mean. Like, I'm a 'Joe Carpenter' if ever there was one. Mind you, I like being a local fellow. But Johnny always had this obsession with his name. Ma was the one who named him after the American president. Our da didn't care, said long as we don't name him Lyndon. You get the idea how funny my family *wasn't*. But Johnny had this thing about the Kennedy 'style.' He collected pictures of JFK ever since he was a sprat. I noticed one day he bought a suit that looked like one of Kennedy's in one of those photos. Johnny even smiled all the time, like Kennedy in his campaign pictures."

Peter was surprised by Joe's candour and tried to keep him talking. "His file says he went to Leeds University and read American history."

"Is that important? Yeah, he got his degree in history, but that was just one of the subjects he was into. He'd come home at breaks and we'd talk all about his latest courses. Passion-of-the-month, all the time. He was dead keen with everything he tried, though he jumped all over. Ambitious, he was. Funny, everything he attempted he found a way to say 'Jack Kennedy would approve, I bet.' Carole and I hoped he'd become rich like the Kennedys. Ma just wanted him to marry a girl from Boston."

Peter saw how devastating John Carpenter's murder had been to the family. He was the boy who left for the broader world and now he was coming home to lie in a walnut casket that the family probably couldn't afford. Joe's resolve to guide him safely to the All Saints graveyard was understandable, even admirable, though bringing a gun inside wasn't. In that moment, Peter felt his own bitterness about his dead brother start to recede.

"I'm curious, Joe. Did John approach his police work with the same enthusiasm?"

"Terrific, he was, yeah. He wouldn't talk about particular cases but he loved the investigations. Grand puzzles, he called them. He was a wiz with computers, forensic stuff. You should have heard him."

"Forgive me for asking this, but did he explain why he was going to Montreal?"

"Just vague talk about a negotiation, something like that, for the British ambassador in Montreal, a woman. Easy job. A frolic, really."

"A frolic?"

"Sure. He booked two weeks' vacation. Didn't you know that?"

"Did he have plans to tour around Canada, then, and hire a car? Because his assignment wouldn't have taken much time."

"Sure. At least I think they did. That bitch."

"Who? You don't mean the British consul? Who do you mean?"

"What? No, of course not," Joe said.

"So, you mean he was hooking up with a girl in Montreal?"

"What? No. He took his new doxy. From London. That was always the plan, though they hadn't known each other more than eight weeks. He booked his trip just a few days before they left."

"You met her? In London?"

"No! Don't you know nothin'? They came down to New Bosk. Johnny introduced her to me ma."

"What was her name?"

"The wog bitch called herself Alice."

CHAPTER 5

"Of course you're going," Joan said, no equivocation in her tone. They sat at the dining room table. She flipped pages in her day-timer, back and forth, red notations for Leicester and blue for Birmingham, and grunted at her frantic schedule. This only served to emphasize that she was the busy one and Peter was fully retired, with no need for a scheduler.

"I'll go with you to Leicester tomorrow," he said, recognizing at once how lame he sounded.

They had finished dinner and now they lounged at the big table, the veranda doors open to the summer evening air. Jasper sat out on the porch, idly monitoring the night creatures. They had finished a bottle of claret and had agreed not to open a second.

"I don't want you there. There's nothing you can do for my sister. She doesn't recognize any of us at this point. Do your chore."

"It's a nonsense assignment. A rookie's job." This came across as whinging.

"Don't make me say it, Peter. You love nonsense. People pulling guns in a church. You revel in it. And why complain about Stephen's playing Machiavelli? After how many years, you don't know his method?"

Peter had recounted to her his uncomfortable phone call to Bartleben from the Mercedes outside New Bosk. Bartleben had exploded, launching into a tirade against Frank Counter.

"Counter told me he sprang for one tourist class ticket. Why didn't he know about the girl? Why didn't Carpenter inform his manager he was bringing along a tart?"

Everyone looked incompetent, Peter thought. "Why, for example, didn't Nicola Hilfgott or her people know about the girl?" he replied.

Tommy and Peter had debriefed Bartleben from the car, but there had been little to debate. They could only speculate about "Alice." Bartleben agreed to have Counter track down John Carpenter's co-passenger through the British Airways flight manifest and find her passport file, on the double. The important question hung in the air, until Stephen had finally said, "Will you do it? Will you take on the Montreal trip, Peter?"

Peter had looked across at Tommy, who shrugged.

"I'll do it," Peter had eventually said. "A turnaround. Only that. And subject to Joan giving it the okay."

Joan stood up from the table and began to gather the dishes. "I won't be back by tomorrow night. You'll have to arrange a drive to the airport. Maddy's off this week, so she'll take the dog if you call her." Maddy, their daughter-in-law, was always willing to mind Jasper, and was a full member of the family. She and Michael lived in Leeds.

She paused at the entrance to the kitchen and turned. "It'll shake you out of your retirement doldrums."

He stayed in the dining room, not eager for an argument. He waited five minutes, then got up and lifted Jasper's leash from the hook by the door. The dog stirred but her fealty was to Joan this time and she trotted into the kitchen. *The dog is smarter than I am*, Peter thought. He followed.

Joan was at the sink and Peter went over and put his arms around her.

"Winnie won't recognize you, and as for Nigel, you don't want

44

to sit in some stinking hospice room with a man with no lungs, and watch him disappear before your eyes," she said.

"I know," he said, as she turned to him.

"An inquiry into murder most foul," she said, with a slight lilt in her voice. "It's what you do best, Peter. Go."

In the morning, Peter awoke to find Joan ready to climb into the car for her wearying trek to Leicester. They kissed and muttered good-byes, and he agreed to call her on his first night in Montreal. He watched the car until it disappeared down the lane beyond the field of sunflowers.

Peter had bought Jasper, the dog, in April, just four months ago. The silence in the cottage had been driving him batty and he reasoned that a gentle, passive mutt would be good company on his long walks along the nearby country lanes. All this was the typical resolve of a man who had formally announced his full retirement and convinced himself that self-discipline would both fill his days and stem mortality. He had no objection to a recycled dog, although he was dubious about the older pets abandoned at the local shelter. He had an image of the dog he needed, hoping for a long-haired retriever, its mouth in a perpetual smile. It would have to be good with children, since Michael and Maddy planned to try again to conceive, although they had lost a boy in childbirth.

It was a small miracle that he found what he needed and wanted. Her name was Jasper, and unidentified owners had dumped her at the shelter the week before; she was a purebred golden retriever but without papers. Peter did not mind the broken provenance but, to preserve some continuity in her history, he decided to keep her decidedly masculine name. She seemed copacetic with the new life he promised through the bars of the holding pen. The two must have appeared to be a perfect match, for with a little cajoling the staff agreed to waive the waiting period. He took her home at once, off-lead, in the back of his car.

He worried the first month that Jasper would run away if he let her off her lead but she heeled like a trained hunter, which she may have been. Her thing was sticks and she brought back every limb and sprig she came across on the downs and roadways. Soon a bonfire's worth of branches had grown beside the garden shed. Their walks became legendary in the area, and the neighbours took note of their morning and afternoon schedules. After a month, she stopped collecting sticks and somehow this change established that she was Peter's dog, settled in for the long run.

Peter took Jasper for an hour's walk along familiar country roads and returned with a mental list of tasks to fill his day. He ensconced himself on the veranda in an Adirondack chair, coffee and a bagel at hand, while the dog wandered in the long grass by the potting shed. First, he called Sir Stephen's assistant to arrange a ride to Heathrow on the morrow. She promised to courier him the ticket, and verified his return booking, three days hence, with the body on the overnight Air Canada flight. She informed him in her efficient tone that "Alice's" last name was Nahri, and that she was sending a copy of the girl's British records in the packet.

He called the funeral service to introduce himself and to confirm that they would position themselves at Heathrow Freight to accept the coffin from Montreal. A junior official with the agency assured him that the paperwork was in place but he would have to sign off on the shipment at the delivery point.

The funeral director came on the line. "Chief Inspector, I can confirm that the Carpenter family, the sister and brother, gave their permission last night for us to transfer the body to our counterpart in New Bosk." There was a rueful note in his voice. "The forecast is for sunny weather in Lincolnshire this week." This was a non sequitur. *Then again*, thought Peter, *he's in the non sequitur business.*

Peter stayed on the veranda to finish his coffee before going upstairs to pack. Although he knew very little about the murder in Montreal, he was sure he would need no more than three days to do his bit by touching base with the local police and compiling a few impressions of the investigation for Bartleben's use. He resolved to come home and give Joan a lot more help with her dying siblings. He would also find the time to sort through his dead brother's papers, which now sat in plastic boxes in the old air raid shelter out by the shed.

His mobile trilled, causing him to jump. He had the ring tone set to Big Ben chimes, which now struck him as annoying; he would change it to something more anodyne before flying to Canada.

"I hear you're off to discover America," his daughter said before he could even say hello.

"Sarah!"

Peter sometimes had trouble connecting with his daughter, though since she helped him out on one of his bloodier cases a few years ago she had begun to treat him with a little more understanding. Perhaps that was why she was the most convinced among the family that he would never embrace retirement.

"Where are you?" he asked.

"Off in the Hebrides. Small island with mostly undisturbed fauna. Don't avoid the subject. I'm glad you're back at work. Mum told me about it."

A good detective would have queried *when* Joan had found time to tell her. A good father knew not to ask. "It'll be routine." The assertion rang hollow.

"Let's see," said Sarah. "Forty-six years you've been a chief inspector. You haven't given up the title, have you?"

"No. Why would I give it up?"

"They wouldn't send one of their top men across the Pond unless they needed a senior detective and wanted to make use of your forty-six years of blood and glory. Let me guess. It's murder!"

"Well, yes. But murders happen every day."

"Not here in the Hebrides. What are you talking about, Dad? Of course you'll solve this one, too. This is a fresh challenge. We'll call it 'Gunfire in the Vestry.' By the way, Grant works down in Massachusetts. If you happen to be down that way . . ."

Peter was reminded that he and Joan had never exposed the kids to the U.S. or Canada. America was both a promised land and *terra incognita* for Sarah. Her latest boyfriend, Grant, was a marine biologist like her, and he worked out of the Woods Hole Oceanographic Institution. But knowing Sarah, this was not a formal bid to have Peter meet him. In her frame of reference, Massachusetts was just down the road from Montreal.

"I'll be back in three days, possibly four, if you need me to pick you up at Heathrow," she said.

Sarah exhausted him. "That's okay," he answered. "The office will make themselves available. Besides, I'll have a dead body with me."

"Yeah, that's pretty routine, Dad."

Sarah merrily rang off.

Peter called Jasper in. As he was debating what clothes to take — the Weather Channel reported that Montrèal in September was as hot as everywhere else — his daughter-in-law called on the cottage line.

"Hi, Peter, it's Maddy."

He took a beat to absorb this; he had been expecting Bartleben. He liked his son's wife and appreciated that she always treated him with respect, although he inferred that she found him reticent and formal. Since she lost the baby, Peter hadn't known how to approach her pain, let alone the subject of trying again. But he found himself yearning for a grandchild. Whenever he was away from the cottage for more than a night (it had happened only three times since January) and Joan was shuttling around England, Michael and Maddy cared for Jasper. They welcomed the dog every time but Peter wondered if she reverberated a sadness for them, reminding them of their loss. They knew that he had shopped for a child-friendly dog. His son, Michael, ever pragmatic, insisted that Jasper was a comfort to them.

"Peter, are you there?"

"Yes, dear. Sorry. Are you keeping well? Is it any trouble to take Jasper?"

"Jasper's never any trouble. Listen, I thought I'd drive you down to Heathrow tomorrow. Head to the cottage this afternoon, stay the night if that's okay, and she can come back with me after I drop you off."

Her breezy conversation was intended to give him the option of saying no. In fact, he was delighted that she wanted to keep him company, even if he had never had a long conversation with her.

"I hope it's no inconvenience," he said.

"Nope. I look forward to it, but I'm afraid I won't get there before late afternoon. I'll bring supper. See you then."

And that was that.

CHAPTER 6

Sir Stephen called just after noon. "The girl is Alice Ida Nahri," the boss began. "British passport. Born April 1978 in Bihar, India. Father a local businessman, deceased, but nature of business uncertain. Mother is Ida Mabel Nahri, born in Britain, and still alive, we think. I'm surmising the mother was either a governess or a lower-level diplomatic functionary, or the daughter of one, who fell in love with a local. My money's on the former. But I'm speculating. We know so little at this point." Stephen's ramble carried a note of chagrin. Peter understood that this derived from the bald fact that Bartleben hadn't trusted Frank Counter to make this routine call.

"Very little on the mother," the boss continued. "She does not Google well. If she held a Foreign Office posting, we'd find her name on something, you'd expect."

Peter would have wagered that Stephen's gorgeous assistant had done the Googling. "Do we have pictures of the daughter?"

"Yes. Passport only. She's a stunner."

"And if she was born in 1978, she qualifies as a woman more than a girl."

"Either way, she's unforgettably beautiful."

"All right, Stephen. My flight is midday tomorrow. Your exec arranged a courier, I am told. Can you send along the photograph, a copy of Alice's documents and anything else relevant? I'll report back when I get to Montreal."

It was wise to keep it brief with Bartleben; open-ended speculation just dragged Peter further into his web.

"Okay, Peter. Tommy'll pick you up in the morning."

"No need. My daughter-in-law will drop me off." The note of pride in Peter's voice surprised them both.

"Okay, then."

"What's the story on Carpenter's hire car?"

"Nothing yet. We know that the hotel in Montreal didn't arrange one, and no rental agency has called about an overdue unit. Nicola's office says they're in the dark. She reluctantly agreed to have her people ring up the various auto outlets. Her man, name of Neil Brayden, will pick you up at Trudeau International Airport."

Peter guessed that John Carpenter had hired a vehicle. He could imagine a half-dozen ways to track down the rental — had anyone thought to search the parking lot at Trudeau International? A morbid thought popped into his mind. Was it possible that Carpenter was run down by his own car? But he said nothing. Let Bartleben worry about what he would or would not delve into in Montreal. Peter felt his resentment returning and could not resist declaring himself with a last dig.

"And Stephen, we can talk when I return, but let me liaise with Frank Counter while I'm over there. After all, it's just a dead body."

Maddy arrived at four o'clock in her Saab — a sensible car, but for its cherry-red paint job. She worked in women's services in Leeds and travelled frequently to poor neighbourhoods to visit abused women and local shelters. The bright red sedan let the men know she was coming, she said.

Smiling broadly, she got out of the car with two plastic sacks stuffed with groceries, and immediately took them to the kitchen and began to unpack. Peter and Jasper traipsed in from the veranda; he had forgotten what a whirlwind of energy Maddy was. She was taller than the Cammons and her long, thick black hair held a reddish undertone that glinted in the afternoon sunshine.

She patted Jasper and pecked Peter on the cheek, and within minutes laid out the components of supper on the counter in a logical sequence. Accepting his offer of a drink, she joined him in a beer rather than wine; she knew that he preferred the former. She insisted that they eat at the dining room table and that he help with the preparations, which meant that he had to root out a table cloth, napkins, and the silver. Like Sarah, Maddy had joined Joan's cabal to manage him in his retirement.

They continued to drink beer through supper. Afterwards, they remained in the dining room. Peter noted that Jasper stayed close to Maddy throughout the evening. Every few minutes, Maddy rubbed the ears of the gentle retriever. Peter was pleased that she liked the dog. Although he had bought her in part for Benjamin, the loss of the child had not distorted Jasper's place in the family. The turns of old age astonished him. The two old survivors, Peter and his dog, sat at the family table with a young woman he hardly knew. The angled sun from the west highlighted Maddy's hair and the golden ale she swirled in her glass. The harmony of the moment sparked an emotion in Peter.

"It may not be appropriate but I want to tell you directly how sorry I am about Benjamin," he said.

She smiled. "That's okay. We're all right. You know, Peter, we called him Benj, even for that short time. Always Benj."

"I know."

"But you've always called him Benji or Benjamin."

"I am sorry. I didn't mean . . ."

"No, that's not a problem. I only mean that it shows your obsessive-compulsive side. 'Benj' is rarely used, I know. You figured the normal would be Benji and Benjamin, so you kept using it." She saw that he was upset. "I apologize. Profusely. I'm not criticizing you, really, Peter."

She leaned over and patted his hand, and sat back in her chair.

A mischievous look came across her face. His detective's neurons told him that not only did she have something on her mind but that she would take a while to get there.

"Why are you headed for Montreal?" she said.

"An officer with Scotland Yard has died. It's customary for one of us to accompany the body back to England on the plane. That's me." Peter had kept his reply casual, planting a dead body in the conversation while not disclosing any inside information. He waited for her reaction.

She wasn't put off by the image of the corpse, he could see, nor was she impressed by the idea of Peter riding in the passenger cabin with a coffin stored a few feet below.

"It'll be great for you!" She smacked the table. Her conviction startled him. She made the assignment seem a Boy's Own adventure. Evidently she had been consulting Sarah, and probably Joan. Before he could speak, she said, "You don't want to cut out a major part of what defines you."

"I don't?"

"Mum tells me you see this as a very limited job."

"Joan does? Oh, yes. I've no interest in going back full-time. This lets me stay on the outside."

She stood up and fetched two more bottles from the refrigerator. "Peter, you are a force to be reckoned with."

"Nobody's said that to me before. What do you mean?"

"You're trusted. Detective emeritus. You could throw your weight around, if you chose to. You have the chance to define the task the way it suits you."

"I think I've done exactly that."

"Fair enough. You've defined the *limitations* of the case but what about the larger challenge? What's the positive, important part of the case?"

"Important? I don't know yet. To be honest, I don't intend to find out."

If he hoped to shut down this line of discussion, he failed completely.

"Joan told me once over lunch that you always find the moral centre of your cases. You come across as unemotional and methodical — all good, by the way — but you see the humanity, the poignancy of the victims and criminals. My words, not Joan's. Sorry to be baroque."

"I certainly don't know what this case is really about," Peter said.

"Okay, but none of us kids think you're ready to give it all up. *I* don't want to see you slide into retirement."

"What does that mean?"

"A vocation that puts humanity on display? Can't be quick to chuck all that." She had exceeded a daughter-in-law's privilege, and knew it. "I'm sorry. I deal with battered women. I see humans at almost their worst every day, and I want to toss it sometimes. You have every right to retire. Every right." She scratched the top of Jasper's head.

"Tell me, what would be the opposite of sliding?"

She perked up. "Maybe you'll get shot."

"A bang and not a whimper?" Peter immediately said.

Just then Jasper, lying under the dining room table, whimpered in her dream, a keening sound. Peter and Maddy laughed, breaking some of the awkwardness.

"You're an extraordinary woman, dear," Peter said.

"Michael told me you've killed six men."

"Lord, that's blunt . . . Maybe seven. And I'm not proud of any of them. For the record, I didn't expect to shoot anyone on any of those occasions. I was thinking about that the other day, in fact. Four of those times I wasn't originally carrying a weapon. I was handed a gun at the scene."

Anyone else would have demanded the gory details but Maddy held back, even though she looked curious. She was indeed an extraordinary woman, Peter thought.

The extinguishing night was closing in now and only a guttering candle on the dining room table and the standing lamp behind the television lit the room. A pair of headlamps came silently down the lane. Maddy turned and looked at him inquiringly; Jasper raised her head with only the mildest interest.

"Delivery from London," Peter said, and got up and went out to the front garden.

"Invite him in for a drink. London's a long way."

"He won't stay."

Peter stepped down from the porch and walked out into the darkness. Three minutes later, he came back in with a large envelope, which was covered in striped tape and "confidential" labels. He had already opened it to check the girl's passport. Maddy was visibly impressed.

"Well, we should call it a night," Peter said.

She didn't budge. "You're kidding."

"What?"

"No hints about what's in the envelope?"

Peter sat down at the table, as if merely to finish his beer. Maddy waited, pretending to listen to the crickets as he examined the shipment from London. He darted a look at her. She was right: it was time to redefine his relationship with the Yard, although he thought he had done that by retiring. He knew that he couldn't work the same old way and that he had to shake up his stale detective's habits, but what did this minor assignment mean to a seventy-one-year-old copper who was stuck halfway between his old mindset and complacent retirement?

The documents lay on the tablecloth between them. He knew Maddy wouldn't press any further tonight; it was up to him.

He made a decision that would have been unacceptable to him only hours before.

"Dear, you asked about the assignment in Montreal. I don't know the 'essence' of this case and I doubt that I'll find out while I'm there. The moral centre, as you call it, is far out of sight. But let's agree on a starting point: the mystery is real enough and the solution isn't self-evident. I'm going to show you something that would certainly earn me a reprimand. So keep this between us."

She nodded.

"I'm only asking for your reaction, your visceral response, if you will," he said.

Peter was pleased. He liked Maddy. She found his profession intriguing and she hadn't asked any stupid questions so far. He was willing to test her — he was still hesitant — but the urge to run through the evidence with her was very strong. There was the gender factor, too, he rationalized; she might see a dimension to the woman that he would miss. His instincts told him that there was something strange about Alice Nahri.

He slid the photocopy of the face page of Alice's British passport across the table, along with the computer records of her passage through British passport control. When he saw that Maddy had finished one run-through, he looked her in the eye and said, "Here's what we know about Miss Nahri. She sat in the seat next to the victim, who is a Scotland Yard officer, and according to the victim's brother she was his girlfriend. I talked to the brother yesterday up in Lincolnshire, where the family lives."

"How long had she been his girlfriend?"

"Not known at this point. Neighbours and coworkers will be interviewed and we'll narrow it down. Good question, though. I'm guessing not longer than three or four months. The brother thinks only two months."

"But serious enough that he took her home to meet his brother."

"And his senile mother, but not his sister. He didn't introduce them."

"Why? Do you think he was ashamed of Alice?" Maddy said.

"No one at work seems to have met her. I think he agreed at her request to keep their relationship secret. On the other hand, he insisted on at least introducing his brother. The mother, who is close to senility, posed no danger to Alice, since she would certainly forget all about the visit," Peter said. "But I'm not sure about Carole, the sister. The family's name is Carpenter."

For the next half hour he briefed her on John Carpenter's background. At the end of his account, he pointed back to Alice's picture. "Impressions?"

Maddy took her time, examining the photos of the Alice and the dead man by the candle's light. "It says she's thirty-two but she does look younger. Beautiful. Portrait is well lit, flattering. Shows she paid well to have the picture taken. God knows, the rest of us should follow her. This is a British passport but she was born in Bihar . . . I actually know a couple of women from Bihar. Dirt poor, that place. She could be a naturalized immigrant but I'm guessing one of her parents is British by birth. Just from her face, she looks mixed."

"You're right about the mother. Notes from headquarters indicate Mrs. Nahri may still be alive, but no address known. No information on the father, except that he's deceased."

Maddy turned to the list of border crossings appended to the passport face page. "There's a notation showing she entered the U.K. from Pakistan six months ago, and several times before that. Wouldn't an Indian-born woman have trouble getting in and out of Pakistan?"

"Perhaps, but a British passport would have eased the way. We lack a full picture of her travels. My impression is that she moved around a lot more than indicated. We'll check with customs in Pakistan and elsewhere. She may have both Indian and Pakistani papers."

Over the next twenty minutes he expanded the briefing to cover the elusive Civil War letters and the disappearance of both the documents and the cash. He did not over-theorize, except to mildly disparage Nicola Hilfgott's erratic behaviour. He showed Maddy the autopsy report and translated the French where she faltered. Still, at the conclusion, he realized that his narrative, with its deliberate and unintentional gaps, formed a threadbare tale.

Maddy said nothing for a long time. She understood the strictures on what he could disclose. She also seemed aware that he was testing her.

He put the papers to one side. "I can only give you limited details, and as a result this may sound like half a puzzle. Can you make any sense of it?"

She finished the dregs of her beer. "Okay. Some would conclude that John Carpenter didn't tell his employer that he was bringing his girlfriend, in case the Yard didn't approve. It was already a bit sketchy, the whole holiday thing, right? Plus, he didn't want to give the impression he wasn't available to put in the hours in Montreal if the consul general demanded it. He kept Alice under wraps with *everyone*. Still, there seems little harm in introducing the sister."

"A racial thing, perhaps?" Peter said.

"No!" Maddy rapped on the table. "It was the *woman's* plan. He insisted on introducing the mother and brother but she balked at the sister, who would perhaps see through her wiles."

"You're right," Peter said. "Same approach in Canada. Never met Nicola Hilfgott."

"Right. And she could have visited the morgue in Montreal after John's murder but I bet she didn't. She's a secretive one. I wonder if anyone remembers her at the hotel they stayed in."

Maddy would have stayed up all night debating every shred of the investigation but she saw that Peter was winding down. She stood up and collected the beer bottles.

"Sorry to bore you, Maddy," Peter said.

"You didn't bore me and you know it. I'm interested. I'll start the coffee in the morning. I'm an early riser."

"So am I."

On the way up to the master bedroom, Peter found himself nodding in agreement. Maddy's scenario about the woman felt right. And his daughter-in-law's fervour had paid him the greatest compliment she could have delivered: she reminded him of his old self.

CHAPTER 7

Maddy was first downstairs in the morning, and although Peter was only thirty minutes behind her, she had already fed Jasper, let the dog out into the front garden, and installed herself at the computer station. Her flying fingers had launched her on multiple Google probes of distant realms.

She turned, bright and carefree. "I didn't try to crack your Scotland Yard password."

Peter cleared his throat. "When they started giving out secure email hook-ups, they had to advise employees to stop using variations on 'Moriarty' and 'Mrs. Hudson.'"

"There's coffee in the kitchen." When he returned, she said, "Well, I've scored a goose egg on 'Alice Nahri.' No one by that name. Most people don't stay anonymous these days. There are Nahris in the state of Bihar but nothing to lead us to this woman. I've blanked. Why do you think that is?"

"I don't think. It's too early."

Undeterred, she continued: "Do you think she's using a pseudonym?"

"I have no idea. Let's get going."

A half hour later, with Jasper and her chew toys in the back seat and Peter's Gladstone bag in the boot of the Saab, they left the cottage. They fell into the previous night's rhythm, Peter beginning: "You don't manage to get a British passport without a real birth certificate. We know her mother's name and that's probably how London will track down her whereabouts. Info from the airlines will also tell us whether Alice booked her own travel."

"You said you met John Carpenter?"

"Spoke with him just once," Peter said. "I was trying to bird-dog a killer through an airline passenger list from a flight bound for Manchester from Barcelona. Carpenter did a good job, figuring that the fugitive had changed passports in mid-flight, and thus arrived in Britain with a new identity."

"How did Carpenter figure it out?" Maddy asked.

"He noted the mismatch of passenger names between the departure manifest and the arrivals processed through British customs."

Traffic proved lighter than expected and it was not long before several aircraft flying up from Heathrow came into view. As Maddy and Peter wound their way onto the airport access road, she channelled the conversation towards next steps.

"Do you think anyone made good copies of the letters, the ones supposedly written by John Wilkes Booth? Somebody thought they were important."

"I'll find out," Peter said. "But I know what you're getting at. Why would anyone kill to get hold of them?"

"Such a waste." Maddy's sympathy was genuine but there was girlish excitement there as well. "Alice's flight to Montreal?"

"What about it?"

"It would interesting if she booked only a one-way ticket."

Peter unloaded his gear at a drop-off stand by Departures and said goodbye to Jasper, now in the front seat, through the passenger window. Maddy leaned across, and with a mischievous look, said, "Peter, do you have a gun in your suitcase?"

He leaned back in through the window, and Jasper tried to lick him. "Not on your life. And keep it down, my dear."

60

He tried to walk away but she called him back. She got out of the car.

"Peter, about the woman. She's the essence that we were talking about, the essence of this case. I'm certain."

"Why's that?"

"For one thing, she's clever. We need to track her movements. She'll raise your game, Peter."

"*Our* game, dear," he said, smiling as he strode off to Departures.

Bartleben's aide had booked him in first class, and so he had room to spread out. He needed it. He had trawled the airport bookstore for anything relevant to the Lincoln assassination but the closest he came was a general history of the U.S. Civil War and an epic biography of Honest Abe. The trip would take six hours or more and he had no interest in watching Air Canada's in-flight offering, which was *Avatar*, on a tiny screen. Eight hundred pages of densely packed historical prose sat on the table beside him. He levered his seat backward, ordered coffee, and prepared to read.

His instincts told him that Maddy had it right on at least one point: the girl was at the centre of the case. The convolutions of Alice's self-concealment did not add up, and therefore, in his preliminary reasoning, she sat near the top of the list of suspects. Greenwell, the book dealer, headed the list. But there was no self-evident link from the girl to the Civil War letters, and he put her aside for the moment and turned to his purchases.

The two massive histories intimidated him. He had no real idea where to start but, of course, that was the investigator's lot in life. And so, he began with an investigator's question: Was there a threat to Canada from the Civil War? Peter had a vague cartographic impression of Canada sitting atop the American behemoth, one-tenth the population, liable to be shrugged off at any minute or, in the mid-nineteenth century, to be swallowed in one gulp.

He turned to the index of the survey history. The tome addressed

John Wilkes Booth's plot in the last two chapters, while Canada was referenced a mere five times at scattered points in the historical record; Montreal did not earn a mention. Peter thought it worthwhile to try to absorb the main themes of the war, and so he opened the volume to the first chapter and began to read.

As an Englishman, he found the conflict distant — though not abstract, since the war was bloody, having claimed 623,000 lives. Above all, the struggle had been senseless. Armies mired in outdated Napoleonic tactics had crudely battered one another for four years and robbed the growing country of a generation of young men, all for a cause, emancipation of the slaves, that had been settled in Britain decades before. Even he knew that the classic question for American schoolchildren was "What were the causes of the Civil War?" Slavery refracted the growing pains of the economies of the North and South and the settlement of the West. Slavery distorted all of American society, earning it the label of the Peculiar Institution.

When it came to the Lincoln assassination, the general history expended few words on John Wilkes Booth, and less on Canada. The author charted the recognition of Southern independence by Britain as a key objective of the Rebel government early in the war but said nothing about any anxieties of the Canadian colonists. The turn of fortunes at Gettysburg in 1863, a Confederate defeat by any measure, pushed Southern hopes into the background, but late in the conflict, as a Union victory seemed assured, British and Canadian fear increased that the million-strong Northern army might decide to pivot a hundred and eighty degrees northward.

Peter's first reading of Nicola Hilfgott's three-page report and her recollection of the stolen Booth correspondence had given him little comprehension of how the letters could have made any difference to the endgame of the war.

The Lincoln angle proved more useful, although again, the index made no reference to Montreal. Throughout his time in office, old Abe was hectored by the British Question, first when the Confederates threatened to cut off cotton shipments to England's textile mills, then more ominously when Confederate diplomats began to lobby Parliament in London for official recognition. The European powers sat on the sidelines initially, but after early Southern victories began to expect decisive victory for the secessionists. England and France waffled a few more months but apparently only needed one more major victory by General Robert E. Lee to tip the balance. Gettysburg stalled that juggernaut. Peter had no doubt the issues were far more complex, but the Lincoln biography did a good job of showing the brilliance of the president in avoiding incidents that might have incited Britain to recognize the breakaway regime — or worse, tumble Britain and the Union into a second war, a war for Canada.

Vague as the text was in both volumes, it was evident that the American-Canadian border remained active throughout the Civil War, with slaves escaping to Ontario and Quebec along the Underground Railroad and Confederates using Montreal and Quebec City to ship goods to, and weapons from, Europe. The Union built prison camps in upstate New York and near the Great Lakes, and Johnny Reb prisoners often escaped to Canadian sanctuary. Peter guessed that young Booth would have had no difficulty with the authorities when he crossed the St. Lawrence River. His ambitions while in Montreal — apparently to provoke England into a military clash, and to forge alliances with sympathetic Canadians — still rang hollow to Peter, even when he took out Hilfgott's report and reread it. Her passion for the letters, whatever they might say, eluded him. The additional notion, referenced by the consul general, that Booth tried to stimulate an uprising of French-Canadian nationalists in conjunction with the enfeebled Confederate States of America, seemed even more tenuous.

He took a break from the Civil War histories. Every first class passenger had been provided with a copy of that day's Montreal *Gazette*, and Peter had retrieved a copy of yesterday's *Telegraph* from the magazine rack. He scanned the British headlines. The world was churning away and there was hardly enough room on the front page to clock the quirkiness of the week's news. British Petroleum hoped to choke off the oil spill in the Gulf of Mexico using something called a "static kill" device. Reports offered little hope for a rescue of thirty-three trapped miners in Chile. Floods had hit Pakistan, drowning hundreds, while Maoist rebels had launched attacks in Pakistan's Swat Valley. Peter, who had fond memories of Washington, D.C., and had briefly considered a side trip to see old colleagues, noted that he would be missing a monster rally of American Tea Party supporters that afternoon on the Washington Mall. It was to be convened in front of Abe Lincoln's statue. The last article he read, and wished he had not, chronicled the bitter debate over the building of an Islamic cultural and prayer centre near Ground Zero in New York.

He turned to the Montreal paper with no pretence of gleaning profound insights into life in Quebec, but one article did catch his eye. Reportedly, Montreal prosecutors had announced that they hoped to lay charges in the gangland murder of a member of a local mafia clan known as the Rizzuto Family. The *Gazette* furnished a helpful chart of the organization, which had ruled the city's criminal element over three generations and was now under attack by forces unknown. One patriarch was in jail, while assassins had eliminated two scions of the family and several bodyguards in the previous eighteen months. According to the article, gangsters were being pulled from the streets on a regular basis and "disappeared" by their abductors. From his experience with U.K. gangs, he calculated that the attacks were about to reach a crescendo with a really big — and public — hit. He was sure of it. At least, he mused, he would have a tidbit of conversational material for his meeting with Inspector Deroche at the Sûreté du Québec.

For the dozenth time, Peter reminded himself that he was only here to retrieve a body.

CHAPTER 8

The plane landed at two thirty in the afternoon, on time, at Pierre Elliott Trudeau International Airport. Peter wound his way across the customs area, scanning for a fast-track lane, or better yet, his pick-up. That was Neil Brayden, whose elevated title was chief of protocol, but whose functions, no doubt, encompassed every kind of errand and enforcement duty in the consul general's office. Peter had asked that he not be greeted by a sign with his name on it.

This left the question of how Chief Inspector Cammon would be identified, which the consulate solved neatly by sending a policeman to recognize a policeman. A lean, six-foot-tall man in a black suit stood to one side of the customs processing hall and at once caught Peter's eye with a quick nod. He wore a white shirt and a narrow black tie, and had cut his hair short with an electric trimmer. He wasn't a mere chauffeur; the suit was unmistakably Savile Row and the attitude was don't-mess-with-me.

"Neil Brayden, chief of protocol with the consulate." They shook hands and the fellow smiled. Peter recognized the type. The Foreign Office and Scotland Yard itself often placed retired policemen in these positions.

"You're staying at the Bonaventure," Brayden said, guiding Peter towards the luggage carousel. "Have you been to Montreal before?"

"No. I've spent more time in the States."

"Ever work with the Sûreté?"

Peter understood that the man was making an effort to find common professional ground. He saw no reason not to be responsive.

"From a distance," Peter said. "You're liaising with them on the investigation?"

Brayden hoisted Peter's Gladstone off the rack and headed for the parking lot, Peter in tow.

"Yes, though Nicola considers them unresponsive." Brayden would say no more. They reached the consulate vehicle, a black Mercedes, recently washed and detailed. Out on the traffic circle, Peter blinked against the sun while Brayden cranked up the air conditioning.

"I'll let you book into the hotel and, if it's okay with you, I'll wait while you settle in, then we'll drive to Nicola's. It's close by. She's invited you for an early meal at her residence up in Westmount."

"Everything is close together, I gather."

"Yup. The core of the city used to be called the Square Mile, where the rich merchants built their first mansions up from the river. Your hotel is down by the edge of Old Montreal and the harbour. Nicola is a real Quebec history buff, and she's got me into it. Watch it or she'll get going on the history of the place and lecture your ear off."

Peter spoke as non-confrontationally as possible. "And the Civil War, too?"

"More than you want to know. The damn letters. Nicola will talk to you about it at supper and I can fill in the rest. She's very keen to meet you."

"As long as she knows that I'm here for no more than three days," Peter said. He sounded waspish, he knew.

"Understood. But she wants your views on the job being done by the local police." Brayden himself did not express a desire for his views. Peter suspected that Sir Stephen had oversold his acumen, and his whole assignment, to Hilfgott but Brayden, an experienced policeman, wasn't so easily impressed.

Brayden slipped through the traffic, clearly in a downtown direction. "As requested, I made an appointment with the chief pathologist, Dr. Lowndes, for 10 a.m. tomorrow. He's lodged in the same police building as the Sûreté, so you can connect with Deroche there, if that suits you."

By now the Mercedes had diverted from the highway and was sweeping downhill on narrow streets. Brayden eased around the circular drive in front of the Bonaventure and let Peter off at the entrance.

Peter climbed a set of steps and the doorman held the big glass door open. An elevator took Peter to the lobby level, where a sign pointed him to the reception desk. Carpenter had stayed here for five days; he must have been known to the staff, but Peter had no intention, at this point, of bracing the desk clerk about his colleague's habits. The local police would have done that, and he was fairly sure that Brayden had made his own inquiries on instructions from Nicola. Peter was given a room towards the lift and down a smaller corridor on the main floor; he declined the bellhop's offer to carry his bag and his briefcase. Once in the room, he decided to unpack later. As he turned to go, he noticed the red phone light blinking, signalling a waiting message.

The voicemail system had recorded the message at noon. "Chief Inspector, this is Inspector Deroche, Sûreté du Québec." The voice was bright and forceful, like a man shouting against the wind. "I'm very sorry that I will be unable to greet you on your arrival. I look forward to meeting you tomorrow. Your reputation precedes you. I know that you will be very interested in the reason I am unable to meet you today. I would love to see you tomorrow at ten o'clock at Headquarters. I have planned a very special tour."

Deroche finished by stating his phone number, twice, although he did not request a confirmatory call-back. Peter hung up and said to the empty suite, "My reputation precedes me?"

When he exited the hotel he saw through the side window of the waiting Mercedes that Neil Brayden was agitatedly talking into his phone. Peter hurried in but the conversation was already over. Brayden slapped the phone shut.

"Goddamn! Heads will be rolling. Specifically, the kid back at the office who finally got around to remembering that the consulate booked Carpenter's hire car several weeks ago, and now at last he's found the paperwork. I hope he enjoys his next posting in the Ivory Coast." It was odd, Peter immediately thought, that Carpenter had asked the consulate for assistance with the car rental. He had done all his other bookings himself, so why not the car hire? Alice Nahri had persuaded him to keep his other arrangements, including her airline ticket and co-residence in his hotel room, off Scotland Yard's books. Carpenter had likely gone ahead and asked for the car hire without informing her. Peter mused on whether Alice had been listed as a second driver.

"Funny the rental company hasn't been phoning for the overdue vehicle," Peter said.

"Blue Ford Focus," Brayden stated. "Not an expensive rental." But then he smacked himself on the forehead. "I don't suppose that idiot clerk forgot to check his messages!"

Brayden was an expert driver and they made progress in spite of the building rush-hour flow. He drove intensely, aggressively. Peter detected an additional note of watchfulness in his manner. Clearly there was something he wanted to know. Finally, the younger man said, "Can I ask, Chief Inspector, how far your brief extends on this visit? What have you been brought in to do?"

Peter had been idly gazing out the window, trying to form an impression of the city. He shifted all his focus onto the question. "My duties are confined to making sure Carpenter's body gets home. I'll be leaving two nights, three days forward. My session with Deroche is an exchange of courtesies. I'm not here to assess their handling of the case — that's Frank Counter's brief — only seeking an assurance of ongoing cooperation with Scotland Yard. I'll talk to the pathologist, too; the report I have isn't labelled 'final,' so he might see his way to sending us more test results. And, of course, touch base with the funeral people."

Neil Brayden turned to Peter again. "Aren't you a tad elevated in rank merely to retrieve the body?"

Peter did not take offence. He smiled. "I've been asking myself that question all week."

Peter and Brayden shared no more theories or confidences on the drive to the consular residence. They headed in what Peter guessed was a northwesterly direction, generally uphill, although he had no idea if they were heading towards the mountain, with its famed neon cross. But Brayden turned west and began to negotiate a grid of streets, crossing from urban to suburban neighbourhoods.

"Can you point me to the mountain, Neil?" Peter said.

"Yes, Mount Royal is up and to the right. Surprising how little you see of it from the city core, but try it from your hotel, as high up as you can get. Or go south across one of the bridges; you can see it from there clearly. It must have been a sight for Champlain and other explorers coming up the river. Perfect spot to place a cannon or two, they must have thought. Of course, the enemy had to fight his way past an even tougher obstacle first, the Citadel at Quebec City. Wolfe and Montcalm, the Plains of Abraham, and all that."

They penetrated Westmount, an enclave comprising winding avenues of elegant houses, many qualifying as mansions. As they neared the consular residence, Brayden pulled over.

"Peter, I understand that you're only here for the body. But be careful of Nicola. She wants a lot more from you."

Peter felt no need to argue with Brayden, and merely said, "For the record, I won't be changing my flight."

"Her husband is named Tom," Brayden said. This was meant as a word of caution, as Peter soon found out.

As the Mercedes rolled into the driveway of the stone-pillared mansion, and Peter and Neil exited the car, the Hilfgotts emerged onto the front landing, hand in hand. In one look, Peter absorbed the judgement behind their grins. *Oh, shit. They think I'm ancient.*

It was a lot to assign to one look and Peter, surprised at his own recoil, resolved to be diplomatic. Nicola Hilfgott was a dozen years younger than Tom. She was thin and elegant in a sinewy, Duchess of Windsor way, and displayed the practised elegance of a woman who had walked up and down a lot of red carpets, though her face was a bit too horsey for a professional model. She wore a floral print dress of fine Cambodian silk; Peter thought it a bit much for a casual early dinner, but then diplomats had their own rulebook. It was her hair that was most striking: black, upswept on the sides like the bonnet ornament on a luxury car, with white accents swooping back from her temples; she echoed Elsa Lanchester in *The Bride of Frankenstein*. She looked predatory but Peter understood her strategy. The hard-edged first impression set you back, but her warm and fervid welcome would pull you in, thereby throwing you off balance. He hoped she wouldn't kiss him on both cheeks.

There was family money here — Tom's. The Foreign Office subsidized a consul general's rent, but not to this level. He guessed that they had leased the robber baron estate as much for its façade as for its appointments inside, but it all cost a bundle. By the time Peter gained the top step two hands were stretched out towards him. Tom Hilfgott wore a knit cardigan sweater, pale blue, and Peter noted that it had Arnold Palmer's signature stitched over the left breast. It must have been oppressively warm. Then he saw that Tom was also wearing a chef's apron underneath the sweater. Peter struggled to keep an open mind as he shook hands.

"May I present Nicola Hilfgott," Brayden said. Knowing his station, he quickly retreated from the introductions and went back to the driveway to put away the car. Clearly, Peter understood, he had seen the Hilfgott team at work many times before and had chosen to disappear.

"Tom Hilfgott. Not spelled quite like the character in *Shine*, the Geoffrey Rush pianist," Tom said.

"My husband is retired Army," Nicola said. Her smile broadened, giving Tom his next cue.

"You can call me Major Tom. Most people do."

Okay, then, Peter thought. There was no irony in Tom's statement. He seemed unaware of the David Bowie song, a retro favourite of Sarah and Michael.

Inside the house, the first noteworthy feature was the frigid air conditioning. Peter understood why Tom wore a sweater. Nicola led the parade straight along the hallway, and Peter could already see the back patio where the skewering and grilling would take place. Not bothering to stop, Nicola proudly swept her hand to the right, indicating the entrance to the massive dining room. Peter saw that there were no place settings on the mahogany table; they would be eating al fresco. He noted several pleasant oils and watercolours in the dining room, rural scenes of sleighs and people wrapped in furs; he guessed that they were authentic and valuable.

"We're having barbeque," Nicola announced as they reached the sliding door out to the patio. Tom smiled even more broadly as he moved towards the drink cart. The patio was well equipped for back-yard dining, including an eight-foot-long grill and a round glass table that was set for three. Neil Brayden wouldn't be joining them for dinner.

"Let's have a drink first," Tom said.

"Your department," Nicola sing-songed.

"Gin, scotch? Or perhaps a rum Collins?" the husband said. He turned to the trolley, which contained every tool of mixology needed for any drink in the *Bartender's Guide*. Peter looked for what he really wanted, and pointed to a plastic cooler by the cart.

"I don't want to be impertinent," he said with deference, "but is there beer in there?"

Tom Hilfgott brightened. "Yes, there is beer in the bucket. Nicola didn't think you'd want any but I packed a few in the cooler anyway." He opened it and pulled out two brown bottles of something called St-Ambroise. "I'll join you."

71

He uncapped the bottles and handed him one conspiratorially.

It was plain to Peter that they weren't "having BBQ." The term had special meaning in the U.S., and Peter had indulged in plenty of it when he was assigned to Quantico in the mid-nineties. In Virginia and points south, "having BBQ" meant ribs and pulled pork and murderous hot sauce. It was a competitive sport, full of raucous boasting and overstatement. This occasion would be more restrained, the middle-class version called "having *a* barbeque."

Tom began to lay out his tools, like a surgeon or a three-card monte dealer setting up his trick. Nicola, after asking if Peter wouldn't rather have white wine, poured herself a glass. Tom took off his cardigan and revealed his barbeque apron, which proclaimed: "Someone is killing the great chefs of Europe. That's why I'm cooking."

"That's our cue, Inspector," Nicola said. "Let's snatch a talk inside, shall we? Tom, call us when the steaks and shrimp are ready."

Nicola led the way through the patio door. Tom caught Peter's eye and mouthed "Rare?" Peter gave him a thumbs-up. He wondered if Brayden might be monitoring all this from somewhere near the house. He followed Nicola to a small but lavishly decorated library across the corridor from the vast dining room. The room had no windows but a round central skylight hovered over them in a cupola ceiling. The walls were panelled entirely in dark wood and a Tree of Life Kashan rug covered most of the oak floor. She ushered Peter to a wing-back chair and took a seat opposite him. To one side, a small round table held two pads of lined foolscap, two manila file folders, and a half dozen books.

"Welcome to Montreal, Chief Inspector. Where shall we begin?"

"It would be best if you started at the beginning. The documents?" Peter said.

Nicola immediately slipped into diplomatic mode, laying elbows to wrists on the arms of her chair in a pose that conceded nothing. Her smile remained full but enigmatic. But Peter, watching her, found that he could read her mind. She was disappointed in him. She was thinking, *Why should I recount the full story to an octogenarian policeman who is only in town for the purpose of retrieving a dead body?*

He barged ahead, quite aware of what mattered most to her in this scenario. "Tell me about the Booth Letters." He knew from her three-page report that she labelled them this way.

"They are authentic, I assure you," she said, her voice rising. "I have seen all three. Leander Greenwell showed them to me on two occasions, and I subsequently undertook my own research."

Peter softened his tone to draw her out. "I'm intrigued. How did you do that?"

"Tom and I did the researching."

"Your husband?"

"Oh, yes. Tom is assistant regimental historian for his regiment. He has a graduate degree in history from Cambridge."

So did Guy Burgess, Peter thought.

She continued. "Tom and I thoroughly enjoy delving into local history whenever we have a new placement. Now, this is important, Chief Inspector. Important. The Quebec Archives here in Montreal have no record at all of the letters. Yes, that could mean they are forgeries but I don't believe it. They *are* authentic. And if the provincial archives have nothing on their document registry, we are out in the clear."

"So, you are confident Greenwell did not steal them from the archives here, or elsewhere?"

"Quite. Tom and I also checked the Maryland Historical Society collection in Baltimore. We have contacts in Washington who helped us search the National Archives. Booth's visit to Montreal is well established but these letters are something brand new. They are British documents."

"But the Americans must have been excited about the discoveries," Peter said.

Nicola paused, hinting at indignation. "We did not feel we had to disclose the precise contents to them. The Americans have no claim on the letters."

"Do the police here have a theory of what has happened to them?"

"The police are incompetent. They don't believe there are any letters at all. That Deroche isn't taking the investigation seriously."

"I'm meeting with the Sûreté tomorrow."

"I know. I would appreciate your pressing them on the search. Obviously, Greenwell stole them back from your unfortunate colleague."

"And killed Carpenter?"

The woman betrayed no sympathy for the British citizen she had lured into a killing zone. "That's obvious, too, isn't it?"

Peter glanced at the two manila folders, making sure that Nicola noticed him do so. She handed him one.

"I have been doing my best to reconstruct the letters from memory," she said. "I've only managed parts of the first two and tidbits of the third."

Peter had honed his interrogation methods on tougher characters than Nicola Hilfgott. He wasn't about to let her seize control and he pressed her on the details. "The first letter chronologically, you mean."

"Of course. One flows to the next. The first letter was signed by John Wilkes Booth, the assassin. It's short but I'm snookered if I can remember the first paragraph."

She wasn't apologizing. Peter took one of the files and read the first page. Her reconstruction was little more than a sample of the full text. If the correspondence was so significant, why was her memory so thin? The foolscap was covered in strike-outs, arrows, and insertions. The date and salutation, however, were cleanly set out in letter number one:

October 23, 1864
To: Sir Fenwick Williams
British Commander, North America

Dear Sir:

My sincerest Regards . . .

At once, Peter wanted to quibble with the text. The commander of British forces in Canada undoubtedly carried initials of his honours, befitting his status and career. Had Booth not known them, or had he ignored them? Had Nicola forgotten them?

Peter read the first letter to the end, such as it was. Booth employed melodramatic language to denounce the Union, and declaimed on the virtue of the Confederacy. Even with his minimal knowledge of the Civil War, Peter fixed on two rhetorical gems that leapt out from the butchered text. Booth, referring to the "oppressors from the North," adopted an urgent tone: "There is yet time for Britain to honor its common ground with the Confederate States." The actor asserted that he was authorized to represent Jefferson Davis and the Richmond government but failed to explain how lecturing Sir Fenwick should endear him to the British government. In the final paragraph, as sketched out by Nicola, he made his motives overt: "My reasons for this disclosure are honorable. The goal of the South is not to undermine the stability of the Canadas, rather mine is to alert you to the impending threat from separatists in your midst."

Although there were two more letters to go, Peter already felt sickened. A man was murdered for this? For a dusty artifact of questionable origin?

Nicola handed over her draft of letter number two. "The three have to be read together," she said.

Jacob Thompson purported to speak for the other two official Confederate commissioners to Canada from Richmond. His letter, as reconstructed by Nicola, made it clear that Sir Fenwick Williams had contacted him about Booth's claims within a day of receiving the first missive. Thompson — her notes were especially spare on this point — denied that Booth was an agent of President Jefferson Davis, and called upon Sir Fenwick to ignore the fanatical actor. He went on, in fawning prose, to denounce the alleged activities of "Separationists" aimed at drawing "Europeans" into "such factionalism."

The third letter consisted of the salutation and a final paragraph, with a blank middle, and reminded Peter of the redacted text of a disingenuous response to a Freedom of Information request. Williams replied to Booth in a note sent care of St. Lawrence Hall, Montreal, and dated October 26, 1864. Nicola appeared to have devoted extra effort to the last paragraph, in spite of her disclaimer of a poor memory. The letter seemed little more than a half-hearted thank-you note, but Sir Fenwick had added a gratuitous flourish, stating:

Her Majesty's Command will not tolerate the insurrectionist actions of French radicals in Canada at any time. Without commentary on the merits of your cause, which I feel compelled to say is in a state of military decline, I can assure you that I will oversee the suppression of the French cause here.

"I'm sorry they aren't complete," Nicola said.

You should be sorry, Peter thought. The recreations were no better than fragments, and who knew what spin she had added. "How did Greenwell get hold of the letters?"

A waft of meat-scented air invaded the study from outside. Peter understood that he had to move faster.

"Greenwell's a shifty character but extraordinarily well connected in the rare books community," Nicola said. "On this point, I believed him. He tracked down the letters over a period of three years. He found two of them in family collections in Montreal. Serendipitously. The other he got through a dealer contact in Virginia, or somewhere. The chain of ownership was clear, nothing nefarious."

She protested too much, Peter reasoned. He still doubted their provenance. He decided to provoke her.

"And they were worth only $10,000?"

Her hesitation was momentary. "Between you and me, Chief Inspector, Leander was fearful of a lawsuit from the Quebec Government. It isn't always easy to prove you haven't committed theft. He wanted to sell."

Peter found that he enjoyed prodding the consul general. "So you weren't afraid of a similar challenge in the courts?"

"These letters are part of British colonial history. They belong to us. Archives is satisfied of their provenance, and I intended to ship them at once straight to London."

"Yes, but . . ."

Her voice rose. "A claim from the Quebec Government? Yes, and the Americans and possibly the Booth family, too. But Canada East and Canada West were under undisputed British supervision at the time, until three years later when Canada won its independence. The head of British Forces was a party to all three letters. Williams was in charge of all military units in Canada and he frequently acted for the governor general. Montreal served as headquarters for both the Army and the GG. The letters belong to us. The Queen is the head of state here and we are acting legitimately."

This was the moment when Peter lost all sympathy with Nicola Hilfgott. The only exemplar in her saga was herself but whatever the merits of her constitutional argument, she couldn't deny that she had put a Scotland Yard officer at risk. Peter had no doubt that Archives, the High Commissioner, and everyone else at Foreign and Commonwealth Affairs had demanded she take a formal approach to the purchase of the letters and had not expected British officials to be skulking about at midnight with pockets stuffed with cash. Peter had the nauseating feeling that John Carpenter had died for her hobbyhorse.

He changed direction. "Did you have Carpenter over to the house?"

"Oh, yes. It's in my report. But you're asking about this girl, aren't you? Frank Counter called me this morning, warned me you would be inquiring about her. We never saw any female companion at any time. Hadn't a clue." Her smile turned chillier, something Peter had thought impossible.

"So, he never alluded to bringing a date. Never *asked* to bring her along? Didn't talk about taking off for a jaunt with someone?"

"Never. He did have a lot of free time while he was here but I never sensed that he was desperate to get away to meet some girl."

"Did Greenwell ever mention a young woman?"

"Never."

"By the way, do you know the man who tried to rescue Carpenter from the canal?

"Just some professor at the Université de Montréal. A separatist, I am told."

Tom Hilfgott had a knack for ill-timed entrances. He came in with a spatula in one hand, Peter's glass in the other. He wore a chef's hat.

"Supper, then?" He scuttled out.

They got up from their chairs. Peter turned to her. "The money was yours personally, wasn't it?"

She wasn't fazed. "Yes, but I planned to get reimbursed. I had authorization from the High Commission in Ottawa. Think about it this way. The Booth signature alone makes his letter valuable. The $10,000 was a bargain."

The dinner conversation, and the smoky barbeque, bored Peter to tears. The comparison of Tom Hilfgott with Denis Thatcher was almost too easy. When irked by a case, Peter sometimes amused himself by conjuring up one-off connections. He recalled that Margaret Thatcher was born in Lincolnshire, not far from the town of New Bosk. Had anybody asked he would have conceded that it was a pretty meaningless coincidence.

Tom drank gin-and-tonic and told amiable stories. He cooked Peter's steak to order, expertly rare. At one point he said, "Do you play golf, Peter?"

"I've always thought that I was too short for golf," he replied.

"Not necessarily. Ian Woosnam is only five-foot-four."

Peter had no idea who that was.

The steaks might have been suitably rare, but Tom had over-spiced them and insisted on garnishing them with tiger shrimp. Peter tried not to drink too much beer, knowing that his jet lag and the time zone shift would soon catch him up. When Tom carried the dinner dishes into the house, Peter took the opportunity to say to

Nicola, "Have you thought of giving your notes on the Booth correspondence to Inspector Deroche?"

"I don't see why," she snapped. "He doesn't seem in the least inquisitive."

Nicola made a show of walking over to the gigantic grill and retrieving a pack of cigarettes from a niche. She lit one up and exhaled with a flourish. *Smoking has been reduced to a confessional intimacy in our society,* Peter thought.

"Tell Deroche what you like. Show him the reconstructions. Only, can we agree to meet here tomorrow night for drinks and dinner again and a debriefing, Peter?"

Peter nodded politely, although he was determined to avoid any more of these occasions. But he understood her plan. If Bartleben and Counter did not see fit to assign anyone full time to the case, she would enlist Peter as her proxy — and scapegoat-in-reserve. Could they blame her for making the tough decisions when no other British officials were making an effort to hunt down the artifacts?

"Peter, I look forward to working with you. And getting your feedback on your session with Inspector Deroche."

Peter was startled by the arrival on the back patio of Neil Brayden, who silently materialized in the uncanny way that aides-de-camp have.

"No wish to rush you, Chief Inspector, but you said you needed a lift back to your hotel."

Peter was grateful for the interruption. They all said their goodbyes. As Brayden led him towards the car, Nicola called out, "I hope that you can stay on, Peter."

At this point, Peter wasn't sure whether Nicola was more avid to retrieve the Booth letters or the money. She had the temperament of the fanatic and she wouldn't leave Peter alone for the duration of his visit. He also guessed that it had cost the consul general a lot more than ten grand of her husband's fortune to buy the Booth letters.

CHAPTER 9

At first, back at his hotel, Peter was relieved to be alone. His room faced west, leaving him a poor perspective of the mountain and the river as touted by Brayden. He would have liked to have caught the illuminated cross atop the hill before going to sleep. For a while he lay on the cool bed with the lights off and watched the oblique beams from the setting sun play on the ceiling. He knew nothing about the city but he would like to get to know it. The tourists and locals were enjoying the perfect summer weather, and he wanted to join them.

He sat on the edge of the bed and wished that the phone would ring. It was the middle of the night in England and too late to call Joan, even though he had promised to check in with her his first night in Montreal. Maddy? Tommy? Now that he had met Nicola Hilfgott, he pondered a call to Bartleben. For Sir Stephen and Nicola, it was becoming clear, this was about the network to which they both belonged, and the network demanded a cover-up. Yes, the High Commissioner in Ottawa would see to Nicola's quiet removal for her bungling. Meanwhile, the investigation of the death of John Carpenter would be sloughed off to the locals. Any sympathy the senior bureaucrats had for Carpenter himself was quickly fading, Peter was sure. At this point, a conversation with Sir Stephen would likely be unpleasant.

Stephen needed a little more against Nicola, and Peter was his evidence-gatherer. The consul general remained unrepentant in the face of all attacks, and it occurred to Peter that Bartleben might no longer have the clout to have her cashiered. She was a survivor — a bit like Stephen in that regard. Peter had landed in the middle of the turmoil, just the kind of conflict he despised. He was fast becoming everybody's favourite canary in the coal mine. But he would soon be well out of the nastiness. He remained stoic: two more nights and then he would head home.

He hadn't drunk enough at the Hilfgotts, although Major Tom had overfed him with steak and vile potato salad. Considering the Hilfgotts as a couple, he guessed that they were happy enough together, having worked out the game plan for her career. Peter supposed that Montreal was a good posting, usually a stepping stone and never a banishment. Tom Hilfgott had dropped a hint, with her smiling approval, of an anticipated embassy appointment in some former Soviet republic. If anything, they had too much money, although they went out of their way to avoid "displaying the large bills," as Tommy Verden would say. Major Tom made sure that Peter knew of his stint in the Falklands, a record that carried much weight in military circles in Britain. Peter wasn't all that impressed; sometimes it seemed that every male of a certain age had been there. Tommy Verden, who had gone to the Falklands and killed Argentinians, might have met Major Tom. Peter resolved to check with Tommy.

He couldn't sleep. A beer in the bar seemed a depressing prospect. He took the lift down to the hotel entrance and nodded to the doorman, who high-signed the single taxi waiting out front. Peter had no idea what it would cost to reach the Atwater Market but he didn't care.

He instructed the cab driver to let him off as close as possible to the Lachine Canal. The cabbie pulled up behind a large market shed and pointed to the canal a few yards off. Peter could make out the dark line of the waterway. Where he stood, young couples and tourists spilled out onto the patios on either side of the long building.

John Carpenter had partied here, he was certain; the coroner's report had revealed an alcohol reading of .11 in the dead man's bloodstream, well over the legal driving limit of .08. But there was no point in questioning the waitstaff about Carpenter or Alice Nahri; they were simply too busy.

He crossed the asphalt fringe to the old canal. A locked chain stretched across the steps that led down to the water, where a Parks Canada sign promised boat tours of the canal and an additional plaque informed him that the Lachine had opened in 1825. It ran only fourteen kilometres but, in bypassing the rapids on the St. Lawrence River, had revolutionized shipping to Canadian ports upstream. Now it endured as an artifact, a pleasure spot for boaters and a backdrop for condominium developers. Yet for Peter the canal reverberated with boyhood stories of *coureurs de bois* with their canoes laden with furs, and oak ships filled with New World rarities. Stereotypes are a colony's revenge on the colonizer.

Thirsty though he was, Peter first walked in a wide circle around the lively market building. Thus anchored, he headed for the cluster of condominiums in the darkness away from the lights and clamour. He had little hope of pinpointing the spot where the automobile had hit Carpenter but he knew that the young man, with or without help, had struggled an agonizing distance after being struck.

He started at the canal's edge in a dimly lit spot that he calculated to be a hundred feet from the avenue, where a street lamp pooled light on the crime scene. A strip of pavement ran along the canal; the section where he stood lacked a safety railing. One strange addition to the landscape was a short railway line that paralleled the canal and then turned inland, where it disappeared through the gate of a chain-link fence into a factory. It appeared to be a train to nowhere but Peter noted that the rails were silvery from recent traffic. The factory didn't bustle with activity but neither was it decrepit. A single flood lamp illuminated the gate.

He paced to the roadway. He found no skid marks, and did not expect to, and if there was any blood it had been scrubbed away.

But Peter felt the sudden thrill of being back on a case. He wished that Tommy Verden was with him. Crime scenes were always Peter's starting point. Give him a foaming lunatic drenched in blood and cordite and Peter would ask to view the crime scene first. The trick here, if it was a trick, was point of view. By kneeling down and sighting towards the canal, he imagined the line of flight of the dying man. He wanted to see what panic saw. The laughter and music floated from the patios, reminding him of his urge for a cold drink. He crouched down. The fertilized grass smelled of chemicals and chlorophyll. With a broken foot and a cracked pelvis, Carpenter could not have made it alone to the edge of the canal.

"A sad place to meet your maker."

Peter thought at first that he had heard the surge of a movie soundtrack emanating from one of the condo units across the way. The dialogue was delivered with almost a Wild-West accent typical of a movie.

He saw the male figure standing near the light from the factory flood lamp. He strained to make out the face but only discerned that the man was bald on top, with shaggy hair at his temples. He stood motionless, exactly half in and half out of the light, cut in two by shadow. This was odd, Peter reflected: people choose to stand all the way under the light, or entirely in the dark.

A sad place to meet your maker, the man had said.

Peter thought he heard a wisp of a laugh, a chuckle.

"Come closer. A few metres over this way." Now the voice had a French-Canadian flavour, the baritone level the same as a cowboy's — if the cowboy were Yves Montand.

"What will I find a few metres that way?" Peter said. He wasn't afraid.

The man came out of the circle and now he was backlit, but it was still difficult to make out his features. "The place where the young fellow crawled to his death."

Peter wasn't annoyed at the melodrama contrived by the man. He had spent the afternoon and evening dealing with evasions. Now, at least, he might have a potential witness or suspect in front of him. Peter moved closer. The man lit a cigarette, a Gauloise by the smell; now they were into *The Third Man*, with a canal for a Viennese sewer. Peter decided to play along. He had an idea who this was.

His senses heightened by the echoes of tragedy surrounding him, Peter said, "Are you Professor Renaud, by any chance?"

The figure came up to him and held out his hand. Peter saw no reason not to shake it. "Peter Cammon."

"Pascal Renaud. I think you are either a relative of the poor man who died here, or you are a British police officer."

"Good deduction. I'm with Scotland Yard. I'm here simply to escort Mr. Carpenter back to England for burial."

Renaud crossed himself and shook his head. "Scotland Yard. Please tell me that you hold the rank of inspector."

"Chief inspector."

"Fantastic! All my expectations have been met."

Peter could see the man clearly now. His demeanour was friendly, his expression affable. Peter realized again how much he missed the companionship of Tommy Verden. Having experienced Nicola and Tom Hilfgott, he was ready to make a friend — or at least an ally of convenience.

Renaud laughed, though not so loudly that anyone in the nearby condos could have heard. "I will show you where it happened," he said simply.

He tossed his cigarette butt on the grass and led Peter to the asphalt roadway. Although there were no marks on the road to identify the point of impact, Renaud was sure and precise. "Here . . . the edge of the car hit him. It threw him onto the grass . . . here. He crawled, or stumbled, straight that way."

"At a ninety-degree angle to the road, exactly?" Peter said.

"Not quite. He got a few feet, then I think he fell. Keep in mind, Inspector, I did not *see* him at the instant. I looked at the grass after the police left. I think he got up and changed direction, but only ten, twenty degrees. I am sure he fell again. I will show you where he toppled into the canal."

They returned to the tracks and continued to the brink of the waterway. Peter considered the vertiginous drop into darkness.

"Monsieur Renaud, do you mind if I ask you a few policeman's questions?" he said.

After a pause in which he sized up Peter, the professor said, "Certainly. Call me Pascal."

"What made you come out of your house in the first place?"

Peter's probe was gentle. He sensed that the man had a lot to say. At this point, a witness often threw back, "The other policeman already asked me that," but not Renaud.

"I was smoking on the front steps of my house. I was *not* at an angle to see the place where the accident happened" — he pointed back to the street — "and I had finished my cigarette and just gone inside when I heard the brakes of the car. So, when I came out again, I was not sure what had happened."

"How long before you figured out where Carpenter was?"

"I am ashamed to say, it was several minutes. I went in the wrong direction at first. You see, the sound from the bars bounced off the houses, confusing me."

"When you reached here, by the canal, how much could you see?"

"Wait, Inspector." Renaud turned one way, then the other, trying for exactitude, orienting himself to his surroundings. "It was frustrating. I could not find the injured man but I was sure I had heard a painful sound. I retraced my steps towards my house. I heard a car moving fast and I turned to the canal again. I saw a small blue car racing for the access road to the canal bridge down there."

To the east of where they stood, a small bridge led to the far bank of the Lachine Canal.

"Did the blue car stop?" Peter said.

"Yes, yes it did. But it was dark and anyway too far to see the licence."

"I have to ask this, Monsieur Renaud, but how did you know to look *in* the canal?" The single spotlight by the factory gate did not illuminate the canal rim, nor did the distant lamps on the bridge.

Renaud was a quick study. "There wasn't enough light for me to follow the man's trail from the street to the edge. I did that afterward. I *heard* him."

"Heard what exactly?"

"A cry. And a splash."

Peter looked in. It was one thing to follow a noise but another to spy anything in the stygian canal.

"It was brave of you to jump into the water," Peter said.

Pascal Renaud could have responded to this compliment in several ways but he merely shrugged. Even in the blackness by the canal, Peter detected the professor's chagrin.

"I did not save him, did I?"

"I fancy a drink. The market?" Peter said.

"May I suggest my apartment? A townhouse just over there."

"Are you sure? No imposition?"

"I jumped into the canal. Your compatriot is *noyé*. That surely requires a discussion."

They abandoned the damp grass and crossed the street to a row of houses that stretched at a right angle to the waterway. Renaud started up another Gauloise, creating a penumbra of smoke. Peter got a good look at the professor for the first time. His smoking habit suited his lean form and narrow, weathered face. He belonged on a dust jacket with Camus.

On the stoop of Renaud's house, Peter turned and stared along the quiet avenues of the condo development. Other units blocked any view of the crime scene, whether the street or the canal rim. The professor had indeed operated by sound.

They entered and Peter followed his host into the kitchen. He immediately felt comfortable in Renaud's presence, able without offence to ask the non-sequential, lambent questions that were the hallmark of his interrogative style. He immediately said, "Did you hear Carpenter cry out a second time, after you jumped in?"

"Yes, I did. That's how I knew where to look for him in the water."

"Still, it's intimidating to jump into water that you cannot see." As well, Peter thought but did not say: *The sides of the channel are perpendicular, impossible to climb out of with a body, unless the rescuer reaches the dock on the far side, or makes it to the base of the bridge pillars farther along.*

"I'll tell you my story when we have glasses in our hands," Renaud declared.

The condo served a bachelor professor's needs, with books everywhere and stereo speakers positioned around the big living room. He had set up his desktop Mac in the room; stacks of notes teetered next to the computer and sprawled unapologetically onto the adjacent work table. When Peter stated a preference for beer, Renaud showed him a half dozen Quebec brews in the fridge and explained each one's provenance. They agreed on a dark ale from the Gaspésie region. They returned to the living room, where Renaud displaced piles of books from two stuffed chairs near the fireplace and gestured for Peter to take a seat. Renaud stubbed out his Gauloise; he did not smoke again for the rest of the evening.

"You have an expression in English, 'Don't speak ill of the departed,'" he began. "I believe in granting the dead their dignity. The young man deserves my best accounting of the details. I heard him say something after the first time he called out. He said, 'Oh, God!' Undoubtedly, you have been told that I followed him in to save his life. Sure, but the thing is, I knew he was almost dead when he said those two specific words. It was like his *cri de coeur*, his . . ."

"His death rattle."

"Yes. Very sad."

"On behalf of Scotland Yard, Professor, thank you," Peter said.

"Chief Inspector, you would not want your worst enemy to die alone in a dark, stinking canal." Renaud paused. "The canal doesn't go anywhere. If I ever romanticized the old Lachine, I think I've lost my illusions because of Carpenter's death. I am sorry, I have to confess my sentimental nature. In fact, I moved here because of the canal. Yes! I am a romantic. Lachine. The Canal to China. I loved that. Otherwise, my friend, this is a yuppie place to live and not a politically correct spot for a *vrai Montréalais* to reside."

"You teach Canadian history. Where?"

"Université de Montréal. And it is advisable in the present atmosphere to call it *Quebec* history, my friend. For the record, I am a card-carrying *péquiste*, a separatist."

The professor smiled. He punctuated his admission with a long swig of his beer, and continued. "Do you know the significance of the Lachine Canal in our history?"

"I've hardly seen any of the city," Peter said, "but I did read the official plaque."

"The canal was a big deal. It allowed the big ships to move farther up the *Grand Fleuve* to Lake Ontario and Toronto. Inspector, the symbolism for Quebec separatists of a canal that had its destination in English Canada is irresistible. But at first, the word 'China' evoked a vision of the exotic Far East. The Québécois in Montreal saw a rosy future. After that, Montreal became the most important harbour for trade, the centre of commercial life and shipbuilding in the east. But the vision was doomed. The English already dominated trade here, and now they shunted the Québécois to the fringes of the economy. Children of the French began to enter the law or the Church, or local politics, no longer favouring commerce or manufacturing. The canal was, pun intended, a watershed for the French."

Peter had little time for the politics of resentment — whether in Quebec or Scotland — but he did recognize the academic's need to deliver a lecture before the discussion could rebalance itself. He eased the conversation back to his mission.

"Can you tell me about Montreal during the Civil War period?" Peter said.

Renaud reached behind him and pulled a shiny-jacketed hardback from a bottom shelf: *The American Civil War and Quebec*, by Pascal Renaud. He prestidigitated another, thinner book and handed it over, too: *L'Histoire du Canal Lachine*, also authored by him.

"Half of the city was pro-Confederacy, half pro-Union," he began, "with the newspapers split about evenly. Some of the French feared Uncle Sam while others took encouragement from the spirit of the breakaway Confederacy. Shall I continue? When the North won, there was no appetite for turning the victorious armies against the Canadas. That left the way clear for Canada's national independence in 1867. The Anglophones swept aside all hopes for Quebec self-reliance, as they always have. A dead end, just like the Lachine Canal out there. Our history inscribes circles of frustrated ambitions."

Peter tolerated the dogma, and the professor's tone was benign enough. But his next statement took Peter by surprise.

"The Booth documents?" Renaud said, and smiled.

How did the professor learn about the letters? Nicola had emphasized the secrecy underpinning her negotiations. The strong beer and Peter's jet lag sent his thoughts whipsawing. He had to admit that he had little idea of the motives of Hilfgott, Greenwell, or even the High Commissioner in Ottawa regarding the letters. And then there was the elusive girlfriend. *Where do you fit in all this, Professor?*

Peter jerked back to the surface. "Does *everybody* know about the letters?"

"The police have interviewed me several times," Renaud said. "First while I was soaking wet." He shrugged. "The second time, the next day, they asked if I had seen any papers floating in the canal. The Sûreté detectives vaguely mentioned documents from the Civil War period. An academic community is like a small village. I had heard rumours of the letters, but I said nothing to the detectives. The third time, it was a call from the presiding pathologist but he never mentioned the papers."

"That night, you called the police from . . . where?"

"I swam with the young man to the bottom of the bridge and got him onto the platform at the base of the pillars. I knew Monsieur

Carpenter was dead but I tried CPR. He did not respond. I had my cell phone with me and called 9-1-1. Then I tried to revive him again."

Peter was sorry for the opprobrium implied in his next question, but he asked anyway. "You carry your mobile with you when you go walking in the middle of the night?"

"I am a university lecturer. Believe it or not, I have to be on call, like a doctor. Or a policeman."

"I'm sorry. I wasn't insinuating anything."

The academic continued. "They pulled me out of the water and asked me a bunch of questions. Only then was I allowed to change my clothes. When I returned they had already placed the body on a stretcher and put out the *rubans*, the yellow tape. Inspector Deroche asked me a couple more questions. Not very astute questions, either. After they finally left, that was when I came back and was able to retrace the route Carpenter took from the curb to the canal."

"That's useful," Peter said in a coaxing tone. "Was it your impression that he crawled across the grass, or that he stayed on his feet?"

"I am no expert, but it was pretty clear, *tiens*, that the car tossed him onto the grass. But, you know, I think he got up and walked, with great difficulty, towards the canal. The way the grass was disturbed. He may have been trying to get to the sidewalk. Why would he do that?"

Peter knew that Carpenter had been trying to get to the false safety of the shadows, but he simply stated, "Because he was fleeing the driver of the car."

Renaud's grandfather clock in the hall chimed eleven o'clock, and the cross-Atlantic time shift suddenly caught up to Peter. Much as he was enjoying Renaud's company, he needed to take his leave. He thanked his host for the books, which he promised to read.

"What is your schedule for the next few days, Peter?" Renaud said.

"Visit the Sûreté tomorrow, then I fly home with the body the day after that."

"It's too bad you aren't staying longer, to get to know the city."

"You're not the only one who wants me to stay on, but I have to leave."

"How about tomorrow? I can show you the Montreal of John Wilkes Booth. I have a class in the morning but a late lunch?"

"I would like that. Should we meet here?"

"I'll come to you. At the police station?"

Peter fished out a note from his wallet. "The morgue is in the Sûreté Headquarters building."

"Rue Parthenais. I will meet you out front about 1 p.m."

But Peter recalled the other squib of paper in his wallet, and took it out. "I forgot, I want to drop by the funeral home and make sure the shipping arrangements are in shape. But I should be all done by one o'clock."

He showed Renaud the address, and Renaud nodded. "Okay. I'll pick you up there instead. It will give me the opportunity to pay my respects as well."

Renaud walked Peter over to the market to hook him up with a taxi. They shook hands. Peter turned to his new friend. "Did you see a young woman near the canal at any point that night, Pascal?"

"A woman? No, not at any time."

CHAPTER 10

Peter returned to the Bonaventure and collapsed on the bed, not bothering to pull back the comforter. As his eyes adjusted to the gloom he noticed the blinking red light again. He turned on the overhead and pressed a button on the phone console. A message had been recorded at 11 p.m.: "Chief Inspector, it is Inspector Deroche again. Once again, I am sorry to have missed you. Exciting times, and I am glad you are here. I do hope that you will join me for our excursion."

None of this made any sense, right down to the slightly British inflection of the last phrase, "I do hope that you will join me." Peter killed the red light and set his wristwatch alarm for eight o'clock in the morning, Montreal time.

The phone chimed again a short twenty minutes later. Peter knocked the receiver onto the carpet and when he answered heard the same resonant baritone. "Inspector Deroche."

"Inspector?" Peter managed to say. "To what do I owe . . . What time is it?"

"One thirty-three."

"Give me a minute," Peter said. He got up, poured himself a glass of water, and returned to his bedside. "Inspector, where exactly are you calling from?"

"Monsieur Cammon, I can't actually tell you the address. I'm in a police vehicle."

Peter was tired and wanted nothing more than to end the conversation. "Are you working a stakeout, Inspector?"

"Very good, sir. Yes, one of our local biker gangs. I wish you were here."

Peter suddenly understood. Frank Counter had mentioned that the Sûreté policeman was obsessed with organized crime, in addition to having the Carpenter murder on his plate. For unknown reasons, Deroche expected him to participate in a stakeout — not the current one, but the following night. Did Deroche ever sleep?

"So you are calling me . . . why?"

"I'm just sitting here watching a warehouse. Thought I'd verify your availability for tonight's stakeout. Chance to discuss the Carpenter affair, and other interesting things." ·

"Aren't we scheduled to meet at ten at the Dr. Lowndes's office?"

"Yes."

Flummoxed, Peter could only say, "Is there a particular reason you want me to join you on the stakeout tomorrow . . . tonight?"

"Mr. Counter tells me you knew the Krays. I want to hear all about that."

So that was it. Frank Counter had dropped a reference to the Kray twins, the notorious East End gangsters. *My reputation precedes me,* Peter thought. There were plenty of fetishists out there, civilians and cops too, who romanticized Reggie and Ronnie Kray, both dead now, and found them as charismatic as Dillinger and as mysterious as Jack the Ripper. Tell people you knew them, or worked with the Murder Squad that brought them down, and you might as well have said that you knew Bonnie and Clyde or the Wild Bunch.

"I'll see you tomorrow, Inspector," Peter said.

"No, I'll see you later this morning."

A minute after Peter arrived at the morgue in the Sûreté building on Rue Parthenais, the chief pathologist himself came out to greet him. It was never a good idea to keep guests waiting too long in a morgue, Peter supposed. Dr. Lowndes was tall and white-haired, and underneath his lab coat he sported a striped pink shirt and navy blue tie. They shook hands and introduced themselves.

"I expected Inspector Deroche to join us," Peter said.

"Ah," said Lowndes, "the young inspector is a busy man. Out chasing various Rizzutos, I imagine."

"Rizzutos. The crime family?" Peter said.

The pathologist raised an eyebrow, surprised at Peter's familiarity with the local mob. "That's right. They keep dying and Deroche keeps watching the coffins go by."

"Why does the body count stress him?" Peter said, trying not to sound gossipy or judgemental.

"Because the procession never stops! He's distressed because there seems to be an unlimited supply of mafiosi in this city. How do you measure progress when the challenge is Sisyphean?"

The man's a philosopher, Peter concluded. Lowndes ushered Peter into his office. Peter recognized the Carpenter autopsy analysis in the clutter on the desk.

"Deroche takes the burden of organized crime on his own shoulders," the doctor continued. "That's all he is interested in. A nostalgist. Thinks he's Eliot Ness. The Cosa Nostra factions in Montreal are currently battling for control and, for now, the Rizzutos are on the receiving end. I personally have dealt with five on the slabs in the back, though a few others have just disappeared. Deroche leads a task force on the killings. You understand?"

"Young Inspector Deroche has ambitions?" Peter said.

He nodded. "Deroche feels responsible for the entire mob in his hometown. Me, I say the only thing worse than a bureaucrat who does too little is one who does too much."

Peter moved quickly to address the double-barrel cause of death asserted in Lowndes's autopsy report. "Why did you put down both homicide and drowning in the report?"

At that exact moment, Inspector Deroche rushed in. He was all smiles. He had a round, boyish face that gave a first impression of immaturity, although his caramel baritone rendered him older and more authoritative.

"Chief Inspector! We finally meet." He at once turned to Lowndes. "Did I hear homicide and drowning?"

Lowndes clearly wasn't intimidated by policemen, not in his own domain of the dead. He hefted the John Carpenter folder, like a butcher might present a cut of steak, and addressed Peter directly, almost as if Deroche weren't present. "You and I have been at this game many years, Mr. Cammon. Most of the time our task is to simplify. What finished off the victim? Was there intent to kill? But sometimes the reductive approach won't do." He threw a conciliatory glance at Deroche. "We agreed that hit-and-run wouldn't suffice."

"I wanted to keep our options open for later charges, crim neg, for example," Deroche stated.

"Future charges aren't my concern," said Lowndes. "But I certainly supported 'homicide' and 'drowning.' At least we didn't settle on 'death by misadventure.'"

Peter suppressed a smile. Every student of British criminology loved that ancient term, which coroners and constables could always agree on: what could be a better catch-all than "death by misadventure"?

Deroche suddenly seemed to lose interest, even though his smile did not contract a millimetre. He came over and shook Peter's hand.

"So! I will pick you up at midnight in front of your hotel." With that, he rushed out.

Lowndes grinned and shook his head, but remained unruffled as he turned back to Peter. "If my assessment of cause of death is wrong, I'll put the blame on the Rizzutos. 'Mafia hit.' Deroche might like that."

Peter was glad to have the pathologist to himself again. "Tell me what you can about the car. Deroche hasn't found it yet."

"First, notice that Carpenter was struck by the automobile from behind. It arced him forward, face down onto the grass."

"Squarely in the back?" Peter asked.

"Back of the legs and buttocks. There are lateral impressions on his thighs that show the grill of the car hit him squarely. There were no paint flakes on his clothing, though they might have washed off in the canal."

Peter imagined Carpenter's agony. *You were hit square on, with heavy force. Speed. You had no time to turn, because you didn't hear it coming. Look for a well-tuned, i.e., late-model car. A rental.*

At the risk of repeating what's in your report," Peter continued, "would the initial blow have eventually killed him?"

"His pelvis was cracked — ischium, sacrum, and coccyx. He was catapulted onto the grass — hard. Grass stained his chin. But adrenaline and panic are powerful stimulants."

"Could he have stayed on his feet all the way to the canal?"

"The damage to his internal organs would have proved fatal within minutes. But he did get to his feet, briefly. He crawled most of the way."

At first, you were fleeing your killer. The driver took a minute, or two or three, to stop, turn off the engine, walk towards you. He was after you.

Peter pointed a finger at a description in the file. "What do the abrasions on his hands tell us?"

"He clawed his way for some distance, but not the full way. It was fear that drove him forward. Broken nails, raw pads on his fingertips. Inspector, I contacted the witness, Professor Renaud. He heard Carpenter call out before hearing a splash. When Carpenter cried out again in the water, Renaud was able to find him. Otherwise, it was pitch black in the canal and he wouldn't have seen Carpenter from above." Lowndes seemed to grow weary. "Yes. He did drown. His lungs were full. Full of blood and filthy water."

Who helped you into the water, Johnny?

The interview was winding down.

"Just for the record, Doctor, I talked to Professor Renaud. He described the drowning man as trying to say something."

Lowndes shook his head. "Blood and water, Inspector. He was in the process of drowning. Little chance of forming words. And his rescuer would never have been able to revive him. In fact, Renaud tried and failed."

"May I ask why you called Renaud directly to confirm this, rather than relying on Inspector Deroche's notes?"

"Ah, Inspector," Lowndes said, "I don't trust Deroche. Renaud is a separatist and the young inspector hates separatists."

Peter arrived by taxi at the funeral home exactly on time for his appointment with Monsieur Parrish, the director. He counted on a quick visit to confirm that the coffin and paperwork had been straightened away. He looked forward to lunch with Pascal and a tour of the old city.

He sat down in the waiting room and fished out the professor's history of Montreal during the Civil War. He was still at the first years of the conflict, 1861 through 1862, when the urbane Monsieur Parrish entered.

"What are you reading?" Parrish said, proffering a manicured hand. Peter looked up and saw a very old man, who smiled with warmth and sincerity. The mortician exuded smartness, his black suit as much the stockbroker's as the body broker's. Peter had dealt with many undertakers and they fascinated him, with their specialized knowledge of death and its final indignities. Morticians were great sources of insight into foul play. Peter displayed the cover of the history and Parrish responded with an unimpressed murmur.

"Everything is ready, Chief Inspector, but I regret that I cannot show you the body."

He conducted Peter down the main hallway of the funeral home to a wide set of stairs to the basement. At the lower level the air became cold and infused with the inextinguishable residue of formalin. Parrish kept the storage room brightly lit. The dead man's coffin lay on a gurney, amongst a mah-jong array of empty coffins. The consul general's office had paid for the mid-priced burnished mahogany model. What stood out was the ugly blue, ribbon-like tape that had been laid across the lid. Worse, it was sticky tape, Peter noted, and removing it would certainly lift some of the mahogany polish from the lid. In a way, the desecration of the lacquer finish was a moot issue, since John Carpenter, as Peter knew from Joe, would be transferred at Heathrow into a new walnut coffin. Peter nonetheless experienced a queasy feeling at this wasteful expense. (He must have been more jet-lagged than he knew, for he had a sudden vision of the walnut box floating empty on the ocean, like Queequeg's coffin.)

Parrish pointed out a mechanism that looked to Peter like just another latch. On closer view, he saw the misshapen keyhole in the coffin lid.

"Regulations require special sealing procedures for shipping outside the country. The tape is mandatory. We should lock it, too. Few people know that a casket lid can be locked. They think, Why bother? But the Egyptians did it and we certainly can, too."

He held up an elbowed metal bar with a six-sided head, similar to an Allen wrench. Even though it was only a few inches long, Peter pointed out that airport security would never allow him to carry it on the plane with him.

"You're right, Inspector. Forget the wrench. No need to lock it under the circumstances. Most often, believe it or not, these days no one accompanies the body home, and I thought I'd entrust a key to you. But I don't want a minimum wage security screener with his cattle wand refusing to let you through at the gate."

Peter liked the older man but he was venting unnecessarily. The shipping would be routine. Peter was confident that no one would need to open Carpenter's coffin.

"Listen, I want to thank you for coming, Chief Inspector," Parrish said.

"Why do you say that?"

"It is helpful to us that you are taking the documents to the airport. It will help avoid last-minute hiccups with the officials at Air Freight. Sometimes we give the package to the relatives, but they usually become upset. Confronted by the bureaucracy of death."

"I'll stay with the body at Freight until it is loaded," Peter stated.

"Not strictly necessary," the mortician said.

"I owe it to my colleague."

The mortician placed his palm on the lid of the coffin and held it there for a long moment. He began to hum "Abide with Me." It was a gesture of respect for the deceased and for Peter's role as Charon to the dead. And it was Parrish's benediction.

"I do have a few questions," Peter said gently.

Parrish's smile turned mischievous. "Was Lowndes unable to answer them?"

Peter hesitated, but only because what came next implied a mild criticism of the pathologist. "No. Lowndes got it right — unless you tell me different. Carpenter died by drowning in the canal but would have perished from his injuries anyway. Internal injuries. What interests me now is how the young man struggled all that distance. It was a hundred feet to the water."

"And Lowndes's explanation has not satisfied you?"

"His report describes 'abrasions' and 'bruising' around the neck and face. Also, there was scraping of the pads of the fingers. I don't need to see the body. But you restored the face. I assume you also attended to the hands."

Parrish appeared to agree with everything Peter said, happy to have someone empathize with his challenges. "Yes, we do that. Especially in cases like this, when we are shipping a body overseas. The law requires us to perform the full embalming in Canada, in order to be able to issue the final burial permit. We never know what customs prevail in the receiving country, or how the grieving family wants the body displayed at the funeral rites. It would be a shock to have the family open the coffin and find residual markings on the corpse. In the case of Monsieur Carpenter, an open coffin will be suitable, if the family wishes it."

"Tell me about the face," Peter said. "That very much interests me. Tell me about the bruises and the scrapes you had to cover up."

Cammon and Parrish stood by the long mahogany chest as they talked, Carpenter a haunting presence inside the case.

"By the time I get to the cosmetics, the face and its wounds have evolved. Not swelling, though everybody thinks of that. In fact, the draining of the blood and the embalming process reduce bloating. But the body has aged just that much more when I get it. We work closely with the coroner to understand the trauma to the deceased but, frankly, his needs and ours are a little different. After the autopsy, there was a delay of only two days before the body reached me. *Néanmoins*, I could discern that someone had applied fingertip pressure around the neck. Not all the way around the neck, but on both sides."

"As if someone choked him?"

"The bruising originally was subcutaneous. Lowndes saw it, yes, but the separate finger marks emerged more visibly after an extra two days. I cannot say for sure that he was choked. It could have been someone was trying to help him. Perhaps the Good Samaritan who pulled him out of the water."

"But someone gripped him around the neck, probably before he died."

"Yes."

"What about the fingertips of Mr. Carpenter. Did you see anything unusual?"

"The fingertips, *oui*."

"In what respect?"

"The long fingers on both hands were *éraflés*. Scraped. Some of the abrasions were *on top* of the grass stains, if you know what I mean."

Peter was confused. "He tried to crawl up the sides of the canal?"

"No, no. I think the sad Mr. Carpenter made it to the sidewalk by the canal, and that's where he collapsed. The scraping was from cement, not rough stones."

Peter envisioned a scenario where the killer caught Carpenter at the paved path and threw him into the canal. The young man made a last effort to resist. He — or she — really had killed Carpenter twice. Carpenter hadn't made it into the water unassisted.

But Parrish had more speculation to offer.

"There was something else unusual. How should I put it? There were small marks, a few cuts, and other small bruises that made no sense to me."

Peter let him work it through.

"It was as though the body was abused. Like someone hit him. I know, I know, he hit the ground hard and then crawled across the grass, but even so, I think he was . . ."

"Manhandled?"

"Yes. *Malmené*. Attacked in a frenzy."

Parrish furnished Peter with a bundle of documentation but retained the coffin key. The package contained an official certificate of death, a copy of the Burial Permit, the Canadian Burial Transfer Permit signed by both Parrish and Lowndes, a copy of the funeral home's *facture* — already paid by the British consulate — and the original of the conveyance report signed by the coroner.

"The coroner's statement itemizes the body parts provided by his office to me," Parrish said. "When the coffin reaches the Air Freight office at Trudeau tomorrow, they will place the body in what they call an air tray, labelled 'human remains.'"

"I assume that container will be locked," Peter said.

"Yes. They know what they're doing."

There was little more to discuss. They moved back up to the main office and prepared to say goodbye. Parrish placed the stack of documents in a plastic portfolio that had the funeral home's logo stamped on the side.

"I'll walk you out," Parrish said.

Upstairs, as the two men exited into the early afternoon sun, the ancient mortician turned to Peter. "Did you know that they once used lead coffins for international shipment? They sealed them and pumped out the air. The coffins were incredibly heavy but they did the job. Homeland Security ended the practice after 9/11. Crazy Yanks."

Parrish seemed reluctant to end the conversation. He led Peter down the front steps. The architecture of the Parrish Funeral Home was restrained and dignified but the director pointed along the avenue to a much different building three blocks away. Peter could make out its white pillars and a pastel-blue domed roof. It belonged in a fantasy of ancient Athens, or on the Las Vegas Strip.

"Chief Inspector, do you see that edifice down there? It is another funeral home, the Caparza. Much favoured for mafia funerals."

Parrish smiled. But he saw from Peter's raised eyebrow that his statement might be misinterpreted. "No, Monsieur, I am not a competitor for its trade. I only mention it because of Inspector Deroche's obsession with la Cosa Nostra. He has spent much time at the Caparza Funeral Home. Or, at least, outside watching it."

Peter now suspected where he would be sitting most of the night.

Renaud had not yet turned up, and Peter was content to wait for him in front of the building. Parrish was in no hurry. Peter thanked him again and reiterated his promise to take good care of Carpenter.

"Chief Inspector," Parrish said. "I know nothing about the American Civil War but do you know of General Wolfe?"

Peter registered the allusion to Renaud's book. He also remembered from school days the death of General James Wolfe, victor at the Battle of the Plains of Abraham over the French General Montcalm at the climax of the Seven Years' War. And he recalled the lurid novels of G.A. Henty from his boyhood. Both Wolfe and Montcalm had expired in the battle. He acknowledged the reference.

Parrish smiled. "They shipped him home in a pickle barrel. Preserved the body nicely."

Pascal Renaud pulled up to the entrance. He got out of the car but remained at the driver's side. He kept his sunglasses on and merely

102

nodded to the funeral director. He smiled when he saw the portfolio with the logo stamped on it. In his own black suit, Peter might have been the mortician.

Parrish held out his hand. "Good luck, Chief Inspector. I hope that you find Mr. Carpenter's killer."

Both men were conscious of the likelihood that some clues remained locked inside the mahogany coffin with the body of John Fitzgerald Carpenter. Peter hoped that they did not include a letter signed by John Wilkes Booth.

CHAPTER 11

"Let's have lunch in Old Montreal and I'll show you John Wilkes Booth's itinerary from 1864," Pascal Renaud said as they entered the flow of midday traffic downtown. Renaud seemed hyper to Peter and he suspected that the professor had consumed a drink or two already. But Peter was content to sit in the passenger seat and enjoy the old city. Renaud parked and led the way through the cobbled streets of Old Montreal. They had almost passed an old church when Pascal gripped Peter's shoulder and turned him around.

"No! Let's do the church first, then we'll eat." As he turned, Peter caught the view down the adjacent alley all the way to the waterfront; the church would have been visible to sailors a long way up and down the great river. Peter stopped by the main door to read an inscription that identified the building as Chapelle Notre-Dame-de-Bonsecours; it had been in continuous use since 1655. The inscription further described it as the "Sailors' Church." A statue of the Virgin Mary presided in a niche above the central door; she was identified as Our Lady of the Harbour. Above her, a narrow spire with a modest bell tower stretched high into the summer sky. Peter was eager to enter, recognizing that the church had provided refuge for thousands of seamen who had landed in Montreal over a period of five centuries.

Before he could open the heavy door Renaud stopped him for a brief history lesson. "There is no evidence that Monsieur Booth actually went into the chapel during his ten-day visit, but he must have seen this church. Booth was on the lookout for Confederate sympathizers in Montreal to help him with his kidnapping plan, and he would have found them in this area. They all lived in this neighbourhood. We know for certain that he stayed at the St. Lawrence Hall Hotel over on Great Saint James Street. Unfortunately, it no longer exists. The old Donegana Hotel, also long gone, served as another hangout for Confederate agents in Canada."

They entered the quiet chapel. A few women knelt in the pews and prayed silently. The atmosphere was subdued. At various points flanking the central aisle along the nave, lamps in the form of small sailing ships hung from the ceiling. Booth might have come here, Peter agreed, but he doubted that the assassin stayed long. It was not a place for men consumed by hatred.

Out on the bright street, Renaud gestured vaguely ahead and stated, "I want to take you to the site of the St. Lawrence Hall, where Booth stayed, and the Notre Dame Basilica nearby, but first let's have lunch."

In the rich gypsy gloom of a Russian restaurant in a basement on Crescent Street, surrounded by scarlet velvet and oak carvings, they were welcomed by the rotund owner in his sash and embroidered outfit, possibly a Cossack uniform. It seemed an odd place for lunch. Only one other customer inhabited the restaurant and he merely anchored the bar. Even so, the flamboyant Russian gave them a secluded booth at one end of the room. They knew Pascal here and he drank down the complimentary vodka shot almost before the glass could touch the table.

"I am feeling guilty," Renaud stated, fussily straightening the cutlery and making room for the booze that Peter had no doubt was coming.

"I don't understand why," Peter said.

"I want to show off my city, give you a tour of what Booth saw, but it would be under false pretences to continue unless we first finished discussing the letters."

Peter nodded. He certainly wanted Pascal's expert views on the documents. As long as the letters remained hidden, their mythical effect grew. They had become Nicola Hilfgott's Grail; she appeared far too exercised about the letters as historical treasures. Saddest of all, the theft of the documents seemed to him a feeble motive for killing Carpenter.

They toasted their health with tumblers of Ruskova.

Renaud adopted the Socratic method, which had never been Peter's favoured mode of interrogation. "Why do I believe Booth didn't write that letter?"

"Tell me," Peter said.

"Because he was a loser. *Un raté.* The Confederate commissioners and all those others were losers too. None of their schemes had a chance of changing the direction of the war. I confess that Booth was full of sly, nasty ideas, including kidnapping the president, but had neither the sophistication nor the interest to approach the British commander about a French insurgency."

"I've seen fragments of the letters," Peter said.

"From what I have heard, Peter, and what you have told me, the letter signed by Booth claims that he was authorized by Jefferson Davis to deal with the Canadians. There has been recent scholarship showing that Booth was more connected to the Confederate spy network than previously believed. It was called the Confederate Signal Service. Booth came to Canada to make contact with agitators and spies who could help him carry the kidnapped President Lincoln through the swamps of Maryland towards Richmond, the Southern capital. So, Booth was well connected to the South. but there is no evidence that President Davis ever met the actor."

"Maybe he simply bullshitted in his letter to Sir Fenwick Williams."

Pascal's voice rose. "Ah, but there is another reason to believe that John Wilkes Booth would not have contacted the British governors in Canada. Booth had his eye on only one prize, the taking of Abraham Lincoln. Booth was unstable. He was his mother's favourite — had vowed to her never to join the army. Lonely and bitter, he was searching for a dramatic gesture to prove his manhood. He was indeed a fanatic, as the histories have portrayed him, and his mania only got worse over the six months after Montreal. Booth would have despised old fellows like Jacob Thompson, the primary Southern rep in Canada. He would not see any merit, this late in the war, in trying to stir up the British or the French-Canadians."

Renaud paused to sip his vodka. "There is one more reason to believe that he didn't compose that letter to Williams."

Peter had to laugh. Renaud conducted an argument like a military campaign. "Okay, let's hear it."

"You have the expression 'a perfect storm'?" Renaud continued. "*Bien*, Mr. Booth came to Montreal at the moment when many forces were converging. The tragic raid on St. Albans, Vermont, by Confederate soldiers happened the day he arrived, and the newspapers were full of headlines accusing the Canadians of supporting treason. It was a good time to keep your mouth shut. The constitutional talks among the Canadian colonies were going on that week in Quebec, and Montrealers were excited about playing host to the delegates the following weekend. And guess where the banquet would be held?"

"The St. Lawrence Hall?" Peter suggested.

"Yes. Everyone was too busy to listen to the rants of an out-of-work thespian. He stayed here for ten days before folding up his theatrical costumes and going home. He had no inclination to wait for replies to your phantom letters. His trunk was later recovered from the bottom of the St. Lawrence River and handed over to his brother, the actor Edwin Booth. We know that the trunk contained some costumes and a sword, but no letters. Another reason to believe that the letters are forgeries, *non*?"

As much as Peter wanted to continue his friendship with the ebullient professor, he wouldn't allow Pascal to forget that he was a policeman. Renaud remained a key witness, though perhaps not a suspect.

"Were the letters ever offered to you?" Peter asked, finishing his second tumbler of Ruskova, while Pascal worked on his third.

"No."

"Did you try to find them?"

"No. You forget, Peter, I do not believe they are real."

"It occurs to me that the letters, at least the Booth one, could be quite valuable," Peter persisted. "Enough for Greenwell to kill for?" The question was half rhetorical and Pascal did not reply.

The moustachioed Russian kept the vodka and the seven dinner courses, including borscht and "pre-Bolshevik" delicacies, flowing to their table.

Renaud continued his history lesson. "The Civil War did little to encourage those who hoped to win Quebec's separation. In fact, Confederation in 1867 was not entirely a disaster; we gained official status for the French language and some provincial powers over culture and our economy. No, the French never supported the Confederates for long. Quebec leaders already knew the downside of societal isolation, and the Confederacy, it became evident, was an example of a government heading nowhere. Also, the evident strength of the modernizing, industrial North showed us that we French had to change to keep up with the rest of the world and do it in spite of, not because of, the great British Empire."

The Russian food proved messy, replete with pickled dishes and many sauces, but Pascal ate everything without getting a drop on his clothes. Such was Gallic elegance, Peter mused.

"Ah, Quebec independence! Jump ahead a hundred years, Peter. My book will bore you enough without my telling it all now. The Quiet Revolution of 1960 was accurately named. After two centuries of complaining, we finally did something for ourselves. For the first time, the *indépendentistes* saw hope. The newly elected premier had promised 'national liberation' for the province. By the way, it is significant that we Québécois use many different terms to describe our utopia. You know the cliché that says the Inuit have a hundred words for 'snow'? The Québécois have a hundred words for 'independence.' You will hear 'sovereignty,' 'sovereignty association,' 'distinct society,' even a 'conflict of races.' We have our militants, who talk about '*pure laine*.' We are no less isolated than we ever were, my friend, but we have more terms to justify it. The desire for purity for our little province reminds me of the expression popular in the Civil War: a 'last ditch stand.'"

Renaud paused in his drunken narrative to check that Peter wasn't drowsing off, and to slide another oyster into his mouth. Peter watched him. There was a bit of the voluptuary to Pascal, a male Scheherazade.

"Then came 1970 and the FLQ Crisis . . ."

He looked up. Peter indicated that he was still interested.

"You know about James Cross?" Pascal said.

"Some," Peter answered. "Scotland Yard was called in — discreetly — on the kidnapping. Cross was our man."

"Yes. James Cross was the British trade commissioner in Montreal, kidnapped by the FLQ. And don't think Nicola Hilfgott ever forgets it."

Peter was quite willing to explore Nicola's perspective on the FLQ affair but he was far more interested in getting Pascal to follow through on the events of 1970. He detected something personal lurking in the background.

"The Front de Libération du Québec was a radical group that openly admitted to being terrorists. Some of them were students at UQAM, the Université du Québec at Montreal. The FLQ were true radicals, with all the confused thinking that goes with being a *soi-disant* revolutionary. John Wilkes Booth would have fit in nicely. Anyway, by 1970 these radicals had placed bombs in mailboxes and maimed and killed innocent people. You see, by detonating the mailboxes, they were attacking an institution of the Federal Government. That gives you a picture of their mentality. It all hit the fan on October 5, 1970, when a cell of the FLQ kidnapped Mr. Cross. The FLQ were

Marxists and Cross lived on Redpath Crescent; I always look for small ironies in history.

"He was held under brutal conditions for fifty-nine days before being released. There was no real reason for taking Cross, since he personally had done nothing to offend the nationalists. But, you see, he was a symbol of British oppression and his abduction ensured the Feds would get involved. It has recently come to light that the FLQ planned to abduct the consuls of Israel and the United States as well. Peter, I don't know what role your Scotland Yard played in the crisis but those are not the secret services I would have chosen to offend."

Peter smiled to signal that his companion had hit the mark. The discussion remained genial but Peter was growing concerned about the professor's vodka intake.

Pascal continued. "The FLQ then took a Quebec cabinet minister hostage, Pierre Laporte. The Feds and the Provincial Government declared the *War Measures Act* in force and martial law was imposed, though the Federal Government refused to call it that. Suddenly there were tanks in the streets of Montreal."

Renaud paused and Peter noticed a decline in his confident voice. Peter knew the bare bones of the rest of the story, at least the official one. The FLQ operatives murdered the cabinet minister and left him in the boot of a sedan on a side street. They eventually released Cross in exchange for the government allowing a few of the kidnappers to find asylum in Cuba. Peter had met some of the Yard officers who debriefed the trade commissioner; he had been lucky to survive. The police and army detained hundreds of FLQ members and sympathizers. It was a sad tale in which all the players overreacted.

The professor suddenly fell silent and leaned back in his chair. Peter sensed a decline in the man's spirits. The Russian, though he was standing on the far side of the shadowy room, seemed to notice it too and he took the opportunity to bring over coffee — to replace the flow of vodka.

"Pascal, were you living in Montreal at the time?" Peter said.

Pascal sat back. "I was only a first-year student in Quebec City way back then. Not everyone was sympathetic to the kidnappers. I stayed where I was and watched it all on television."

The follow-up question was so obvious that Peter did not dare pose it: If he had skipped the crisis in Montreal, how did his conversion come about?

Another pause followed. The professor leaned forward. A tear emerged on his cheek. He looped his right index finger through the handle of the coffee cup, as if to steady himself, and he stared blearily at Peter. The Russian, watching from afar, looked concerned.

"The Anglos like to say that no one was injured when the troops took over Montreal. They detained four hundred people without warrant but at least no one was shot or killed, they always said. It isn't true, Peter. My sister was killed."

"My God, Pascal. What the hell happened?"

"Not by a bullet," Renaud continued, as if his dinner companion hadn't spoken. "She was protesting with the UQAM students in the streets, not very far from here, and she got too close to an armoured vehicle, not a tank but what do you call it?"

"An armoured personnel carrier?"

"Yes. Used by all fascist governments for crowd control. The crowds hadn't been violent. My sister never attacked anyone. Anyway, I did not take it well. I was studying politics at the time, a traditional Québécois obsession, but I immediately moved to Montreal and changed my studies to history." Renaud looked up and tried to smile. "And that is how I ended up here with you, Peter."

Peter knew when to stop pressing a witness. He wanted to ask so much more about Pascal's sister but the man was drunk and mired in his despondency.

Changing angles, he asked in a quiet voice, "Where is the liberation movement headed now?"

"There have been referendums. There is a separatist representation in the Canadian parliament and the provincial Parti Québécois occasionally gains power inside the province. I don't know. There are two theories regarding our recent history."

Renaud recovered and fell into his lecturer's cadence. "One is the grand theory hinging on trauma, the belief that progress is only made by upheaval. The strategy here is to win a referendum and declare sovereignty. The second is the theory of evolution, though Darwin would never recognize it in its present state. Quebec will gradually, inevitably gain more powers and move towards independence, negotiating its way out."

"Which theory do you belong to?"

"I believe in the theory of exhaustion, Peter. Canada will get tired of Quebec. There will be an accretion of powers — *agrandissement* is a word the French like — taking over areas of legislative jurisdiction. It started with economic powers during the Quiet Revolution, then culture and language. The final break will eventually be seen as inevitable. Did you know that, in French, 'inévitable' also can mean 'nécessaire'?"

Peter was reluctant to say goodbye, knowing that he would likely never meet Renaud again. And so he skipped the farewell. He paid the bill; the Russian took the other side of the professor and they shuffled up the stairs to the street, where a cab was already waiting. Renaud fell asleep at once in the back seat. The restaurateur gave the driver an address and granted Peter a moment to lean into the passenger window and say to his friend, though he might not have heard, "Thanks for everything Pascal. I'll be in touch."

CHAPTER 12

Peter wasn't psychic but this time the blinking red light on the bedside phone could only mean Nicola Hilfgott. He called up the message and deleted it without listening to the end. It was past 6 p.m. and he had planned to nap until eleven o'clock, then get up, shower, and be downstairs on time to meet Deroche. At that moment, his mobile chimed.

"Peter? It's Maddy. I'm so glad I reached you."

"Is everything all right? It can't even be sunrise yet where you are."

"I'm at home. Leeds. And Jasper's fine."

"She is?"

"She misses you. We just came back from our pre-dawn walk. Listen, shall I pick you up tomorrow?"

"It'll actually be the following day, I leave tomorrow night my time and get in early, about 5:30 a.m."

"It's okay. Can we talk now?"

Peter luxuriated in her voice. Maddy represented youth and impulse and a connection to home. There was something else there too: she chased away the cobwebs from his old brain.

"Go ahead," he said.

"Peter, I've been doing some snooping. Only on the internet.

Well, one or two phone calls. I think I've figured out where Alice Nahri's from."

"Does she Google any better this time?" he said.

"No. I tried every permutation of her name, augmented by 'India' and 'Bihar.' She simply refuses to pop up anywhere. There are 'Nahri' surnames in Bihar — Lordy, there are a hundred million people in that one jurisdiction and that may be one avenue you could pursue."

Peter had contacts in the Indian State Police, and Bartleben surely had more. Peter also had an old friend he could call directly in the Research and Analysis Wing, the Indian spy agency.

She continued. "Often, British passports for Indian-born British nationals list the capital of the province where the applicant is from. The convention makes sense: birth registrations are centralized that way. Therefore, it was no surprise that Alice Ida Nahri was listed with Patna as her birth city. Patna is the provincial capital but she could easily have been born somewhere else. And I think I know where."

Peter knew to be patient. He imagined Jasper sitting on Maddy and Michael's kitchen rug, listening contentedly.

"All right, where was she born?"

"Trivia time, Peter. What famous person was born in Motihari, India?"

He indulged her. "Kipling?" He knew it wasn't Kipling.

"Orwell."

His brain spun out what he knew about George Orwell. Born in India but became a policeman in Burma for a time. Died young — forty-eight? forty-nine? Every schoolboy read his novels and he did write an approving article about Kipling. He also wrote "Decline of the English Murder."

"Tell me," he said. He was terrifically amused by his daughter-in-law, happy that she was so happy.

"I Googled every major city in Bihar and came across several Nahris in the directory for the city of Motihari, which is up near the border of Nepal. Every website for Motihari boasts about its connection to George Orwell's birthplace. He was born Eric Blair, his father being Richard Blair, who worked in the Opium Department of the Government of India. Orwell's mother's maiden name was Ida Mabel Limouzin; Orwell also had a younger sister named Avril."

Trying not to sound impatient, Peter interrupted. "Dear, is there a connection between Alice Nahri and George Orwell?"

"Alice's middle name is Ida, just like Orwell's mother. It's a lead, at least. And Alice isn't far from Avril. By the way, Orwell's mother moved back to England when he was just a toddler. Henley-on-Thames."

"Oxfordshire."

"Yup. The husband joined her a while later. Avril was born in Henley. There you go."

"That's not quite enough," Peter said.

"It's a start. British mother, probably a governess, impressed by the only local British celebrity, clings to a famous name."

"Keep looking. I'll be back soon."

"Peter?"

"What?"

"I've opened a file. It's sitting here on the kitchen table. It contains over a hundred pages of research."

"Now I'm in trouble."

At five minutes to twelve, Peter was waiting in front of the Bonaventure. He had waved off the standing taxi and refused the doorman's offer of directions. He felt foolish standing there alone and it was still possible that he would reject Deroche's great adventure and refuse to get in the surveillance car.

Why had he accepted? From what Peter had seen, he might be getting in the car with a crazy man; he wasn't fond of obsessive-compulsive cops. He couldn't say that he was excited: he had endured many stakeouts, and they mixed tedium with too much coffee. And he had only agreed to "touch base" with the Sûreté on Frank Counter's behalf. Midnight stakeouts were beyond the call of this duty.

Peter shivered against a gust of wind and sank his hands into the deep pockets of his coat. It was the letters. The letters and the girl. *There's irony for you,* he thought. Deroche had shown no interest in either, and probably thought that the Booth documents and Alice Nahri didn't exist. But Peter wanted to know what the inspector had learned from interviewing Leander Greenwell, the book dealer, on the night of the crime. It could be the key to learning why anyone would kill to get the letters.

Deroche arrived in front of the hotel at midnight sharp and hardly waited for Peter to open the door before saying, "Welcome to the Rizzuto tour, Chief Inspector."

"You might as well call me Peter."

"Call me Sylvain."

The tour began at once, Deroche's personal story intertwining with the saga of the Rizzutos as they swept through urban and sub-urban neighbourhoods at wild speeds. Deroche offered his philosophy without any prompting from Peter: he loved his hometown, and every day fought to protect it, but a policeman with ambition needed a career strategy, and organized crime quickly became his focus. His hatred of the mob and his commitment to anti-mob tactics — always willing to stay up all night on a stakeout — had won him notice. Montreal was an old city. The Montreal Calabrian-Sicilian gang had been around less than seventy years, the Rizzuto family less than fifty. They were *arrivistes,* in Deroche's view, cancers to be excised.

The inspector had been born and raised in Point St. Charles. He had avoided cultural politics. Like Chicago, New York, or Boston, in Montreal your neighbourhood defined your youth but what turned you into a cosmopolitan adult was transcendence of the parochial and the tribal, he believed. For him, maturity for a Montrealer was achieved by giving loyalty to the city as a whole and suppressing neighbourhood affiliations. The mafia operated all across the town and respected few boundaries. He would do the same. Whoever was eradicating the Rizzutos was taking down opposing soldiers at will, often in public. Deroche wanted Peter to see the crime scenes in order to understand how abhorrent he found their heedless vendettas.

The black unmarked Chevy Malibu whirled out of the Square Mile and into a neighbourhood north of the core in only a few minutes. They soon emerged into an upscale streetscape, brightly lit, with large treed lots and mansions to match. Unlike traditional Westmount, this was a freshly built enclave for the nouveau riche, including local mafia, apparently. Deroche slowed to touring speed as they passed a particularly garish house.

"The Rizzutos have run organized crime in Montreal for three decades. Loan sharking, drug trafficking and especially protection money. They have been very successful in infiltrating the construction industry. The mafia competes in the narcotics trade with the biker gangs, in particular the Hells Angels and, until recently, the Rock Machine. Think of them as three generations of management: old Nicolo, the founder of the dynasty, Vito, his son and successor, and Nicolo, Junior. That's the patriarchal home you're looking at."

Where are we headed next? Peter thought as Deroche hit the accelerator. He idly wondered how many guns Deroche had in the Malibu. Deroche's driving called back the residue of vodka in his system and made him queasy. The inspector pulled away and they hurtled through more neighbourhoods, until Peter was completely confused about their location.

Deroche slowed down again unpredictably and jerked to a stop across the street from a small café, indistinguishable from a dozen others in a neighbourhood that possessed a distinctly Italian flavour.

"By the mid-seventies, Vic Cotroni, the boss of Montreal's drug trade, was having legal troubles, not to mention he was ageing, and the question hung in the air. Who would take over the Montreal mob? There were two rivals to succeed Cotroni. Paolo Violi was his top lieutenant. He'd managed the gang when Cotroni went to jail for a couple of years. Vito Rizzuto had ambitions himself and he was not without supporters, even though he was Sicilian. You can guess how this all got settled."

Peter played the willing acolyte. "A gang war?"

"Exactly. The bar across there? Used to be called the Reggio

Bar. Coffee and ice cream. Violi liked to call himself the 'ice cream king' and 'the godfather of Saint-Léonard.' This was the seventies, remember, when *The Godfather* was popular. But Paolo was no Marlon Brando. A shotgun blew him apart one night in 1978 inside that bar. No one was convicted of the hit. Vito Rizzuto's power in the city grew. Cotroni expired from cancer in '84."

They sped off again into the maze of streets. With the punctuation of each instalment by another headlong slalom through the city, Peter was becoming dizzy. The inspector lurched to a stop before an all-night American-style diner. Two men sat in a booth by the plate glass window but otherwise the diner appeared to be empty.

Deroche turned off the engine. "Peter, we should be getting in place soon."

Peter looked at the nondescript restaurant. If the inspector was in a hurry to position them for the evening stakeout, why were they visiting the diner? They entered and took the booth farthest from the two men, whom Peter sized up as an alcoholic and his sponsor.

Old fluorescents created a parchment glow in the diner. In this glare Deroche's face appeared older, the stress of long nights imprinted on his sallow cheeks. They knew him in the café and the waitress looked up as he signalled for his usual. The price paid by Inspector Deroche, Peter comprehended, the universal price of all zealots, was loneliness.

Deroche sat back against the corner of the booth. "It all came to shit for the Rizzutos in 2004. The RCMP and the Sûreté went after them with Opération Colisée and a hundred agents, while the Americans double-teamed them with RICO charges and prosecutions for murder in New York State. Some of the killings they investigated were mob hits allegedly committed by Vito Rizzuto in NYC years before. We nailed them with everything we had. Threw the book at them, is that the expression?"

"Why, yes," Peter said, startled. He was always careful about patronizing any of the Montrealers he met and he was deeply impressed by the self-assuredness of the Québécois. He did his best to speak

French whenever he could, yet he still did not fully grasp the sensitivities of bilingualism. Deroche was beyond fluent in both languages. Peter began to think that the key to the excitable inspector lay in this domain: he was the opposite of the *pure laine* Québécois, proud to occupy both worlds. He loved his community in all its diversity, and the city-wide infection of the gangs was his filter for surveying the state of his city. Peter decided to cut the inspector some slack.

The waitress brought bacon and eggs, but only to Deroche. Peter was still full from his Russian dinner and he nibbled on a bagel. The woman left a carafe of coffee on the table. Deroche continued his story, checking his BlackBerry as he narrated.

"Opération Colisée resulted in arrest warrants for both Vito and old Nick. First, we and the Americans collared Vito on racketeering charges, including conspiracy to commit the murder of two New York gangsters, and he was extradited two years later. He lost all his appeals and now he's incarcerated in the maximum security prison in Florence, Colorado."

"The Supermax?" Peter said, surprised.

"That's the one. He won't be out for two more years. But that's not the real story."

Peter had to smile. "No? Somebody saw an opportunity?"

"Right." Deroche held up his coffee cup in a dramatic toast. "We are celebrating, Peter. It is early September, perhaps time for the monthly payback for the Famille Rizzuto."

Peter was alert to the fact that the decline of the Rizzutos was recent, and ongoing. "Monthly?"

"Absolutely. Almost every month over the last twelve someone has bumped off a Rizzuto or one of their close associates. It started in August a year ago with Frederico Del Peschio, a Rizzuto captain, getting himself shot to death in La Cantina, his own restaurant. I didn't bother taking you there: shall we say, it would be an uncomfortable dining experience."

Peter had to laugh again. At that moment, unprompted, the waitress delivered a stack of cinnamon toast to the table. It seemed that all of Montreal existed to punctuate Deroche's protracted stories in the middle of the night.

The inspector enumerated the many assassinations and shootouts that were reducing the clan. He might have been dictating an affidavit. Peter waited for the final update on the Sophoclean tragedy of the Rizzuto organization.

"And just two weeks ago," Deroche said, a touch of schadenfreude in his grin, "the U.S. courts turned down Vito's appeal for early parole."

The Rizzuto family remained under siege and Peter wondered if they had managed to strike back in any effective way. Such was the dynastic history of the mafia; regime change was vertiginous and peppered with public executions. Deroche was implying that the climax to the turf war in Montreal might not occur until Vito Rizzuto returned from prison. Meanwhile, it was clear, open shootings and strategic firebombings would continue. A September attack was to be expected but it was only the beginning of the month. Evidently, Deroche had inside information. The young policeman jumped up from the booth and announced, "I'm going to the toilet but when I get back I want to hear all about the Krays."

Deroche's bathroom break gave Peter time to think about the best way to relate the story of the Kray brothers. It was tit-for-tat: no discussion of the stolen letters until he told the story of the twins. The young inspector saw the battle with the Montreal mafia as a classic struggle and more important to the identity of his city than even the separatist movement. The war waged against the Kray gang by the Metropolitan Police Murder Squad had its classic elements too — Peter's Oxford professors would have called it minor Greek tragedy — but was difficult to understand without knowing the bizarre culture of the East End of London.

Deroche returned with the same expectant smile on his face and repeated, "The Krays. Tell me." But the command was ill-timed, for at that moment four men in dark clothes entered the diner. The waitress looked up but remained unperturbed, though Peter saw the pair in the corner booth cringe. It was evident that the four were policemen; they ignored the waitress and sized up the conversation in the other booth as innocent. They did check out Peter but, he judged, they were used to Deroche's quirky methods and were not deterred. For his part, Peter, obviously not local or a francophone, knew to keep anonymous and silent.

Deroche spoke to the men in French. Peter grabbed a few words but they used a flowing *joual* that went over Peter's head. He heard the words *"cagoule"* and *"membre en règle,"* and the Rizzutos were mentioned twice; he knew that *"membre en règle"* bespoke an initiate of the mob, a made man. The two diner patrons edged out the door. The conversation lasted several minutes, ending with Deroche issuing orders and his men nodding. After they left, the inspector slapped a ten-dollar bill on the table. They got up.

"I still want to hear about the Krays," he said.

Peter had been inside dozens of stakeout vehicles during his career. That was mostly back in 1995 when the FBI, to whom Peter had been assigned that summer, went after the Unabomber, the scruffy Luddite who had attacked targets across the United States with a series of deadly home-made bombs in an almost random pattern. No one knew where or when the Unabomber would attack next, and the Quantico wonks identified more than ten potential targets in as many states. Peter had wasted many summer nights staring at the walls of university laboratories and corporate head offices from the passenger seat of an unmarked sedan. Every one of the stakeouts had been futile, although Peter had usefully employed the long, vacant hours to develop a theory on the Unabomber's attack pattern that eventually helped the Bureau narrow down the manhunt.

As protocol for stakeouts seemed to require, the two detectives sat in silence for the first five minutes while they evaluated the sightlines and settled in for a long night. The two teams from the diner were out there somewhere, Peter assumed, with everyone focused on

121

the Caparza funeral facility across the way, where pink and lavender spotlights lit up the façade in a kind of Bellagio-celebrates-Easter effect. This was the facility Réjean Parrish had pointed out to Peter. He turned in his seat to assess his companion's mood, wondering if Deroche could sit still for the next several hours. Peter had reconciled himself to a night with no sleep, knowing he could nap on tomorrow's plane ride.

He took care in delivering the saga of the Kray gang, aware that Deroche would draw parallels with the Montreal mafia. Peter also knew that the Kray story was bound to disappoint. There was a quicksilver quality to it. The true, factual story was strung through a thousand court documents, sentencing statements, the testimony of a hundred victims and a heap of prison evaluations. The public story, distorted by the tabloids, had long ago been encased in impenetrable clichés. Even the moral lesson — the Krays were born poor and found wealth only via the most brutal pathways of crime — had been undermined, rendered problematic, by their minor-key ending. Ronnie had died in prison of a shattering heart attack, while miles away in Norfolk, Reggie rotted away in Wayland Prison until, the evil and the malice sapped out of him, he was released in 2000. He died an enervated has-been.

The funeral home distracted Peter. *Why would anyone attack a repository for the dead? Is there another Rizzuto in the basement?* Perverse, unpoliceman-like thoughts ran riot. *How precisely does one effect a breach in a funeral home? Do they leave night watchmen?*

He ran through the sordid story of the identical twin brothers who, egged on by a wilful mother, brawled their way to dominance of the East End and expanded to the West End of London in the Swinging Sixties. Peter looked for points of resonance for Deroche. He knew nothing about growing up in Montreal but the saga of criminals fighting their way out of destitution was a universal one. The Krays had been evil, not lovable or benighted; the twins were destructive hoodlums and Peter said so. He spoke for thirty minutes while the young inspector listened raptly.

"The twins were eventually taken out of circulation by a team of Met officers who came to be known, mostly afterwards, as the Murder Squad. In truth, the Yard was pretty ineffective during much of the sixties, failing to nail the brothers on the usual organized crime fiddles like extortion, skimming of gambling proceeds, drug smuggling, gold smuggling, and so on. We eventually got them on a murder charge."

"Were you a member of the Murder Squad?" Deroche asked.

"No, it was before my time," Peter said. "I met Reggie much later, in prison. Ronnie was already dead. I interviewed Reggie about the money laundering trade run by his successors. You see, we hoped he would give us inside information. He refused to cooperate."

Deroche leaned back in the driver's seat "How long have you been a chief inspector, Peter?" "Forever" was the answer. Peter wanted to be honest but as usual with Deroche he found it hard to tell what direction the younger man was coming from. But they were only reminiscing.

"A long time, Sylvain. The ranks keep changing with Scotland Yard. They asked me to take the classification 'superintendent' a few years ago but I never felt like a superintendent."

The Yard was constantly adjusting the senior grading of detectives, merging — and muddling — the detective function in with executive management. Peter wasn't sure where the classifications stood presently but he was pretty certain that "chief inspector" would be revived on some future organization chart. Evolution in the Metropolitan Police was circular.

Deroche grew melancholy. The night had turned cold but he seemed unwilling to turn on the heater. "The next rank up in the Sûreté is chief inspector."

"Of course, Sylvain, these days I have to add 'retired' to my stationery."

Deroche evidently could not imagine the concept of retirement and he jumped to another topic. "You're leaving for London tonight, Peter?"

"Yes, but I need more information from you. What happened when you questioned Greenwell the night of the killing? What did he say about the letters?"

"A colleague and I went to his shop in Old Montreal as soon as Mrs. Hilfgott informed us of the transaction. That was less than four hours after the incident. Greenwell owns the building that holds his bookstore. He sleeps in a room above the business. I agree, Chief Inspector, that Greenwell is our best suspect. But he had an alibi. When I knocked on the door of his bookshop, he came downstairs to meet me. He was not alone. We went inside. A younger man — his name is Georges — came out of his rooms upstairs. He claimed to have been there for several hours, and that earlier Greenwell was at the club where this boyfriend works."

"Did you believe him?"

"Not sure," Deroche said. "A cool customer, Georges. But Greenwell was upset."

"He was nervous, you mean?" Peter said.

"Yes."

"Did the transaction happen?" Peter said.

"According to Greenwell, it did. He met Carpenter downstairs in the store and they exchanged the money for the letters."

"Did he have the ten thousand cash? Did you examine it?"

"He showed me the bills. He kept them in a cigar box, loose. But . . ."

"What?"

"The store was a mess. He had the cigar box just sitting on a shelf beside some dusty books. A bad way to do business."

"Did you impound the money?"

"No." Deroche hesitated — both detectives knew that he had made a mistake.

Peter persisted. "But Greenwell *is* your top suspect?"

"Yes, in the sense that he is one of the few we have to choose from. But Greenwell does not possess a driver's licence, let alone a car."

"Does Georges?"

"Driver's licence, yes. Vehicle, no."

"Where is Greenwell now, do you think?"

"He asked if he was under arrest. I had to say no but I told him not to leave town. He promptly fled Montreal later that day and we believe he is staying with his cousin in Halifax. His boyfriend did not go with him. We will arrest Greenwell when he returns. Second degree murder, at least."

"What about the letters, Sylvain?"

"Greenwell swore the letters were authentic, and he never saw them again after Carpenter took them away."

"This is important. Did Greenwell or Georges mention the girl?"

Deroche shook his head. "No. Not a word. but I confirmed with Frank Counter that her particulars have been added to Interpol's database, as well as CPIC. And the rental car, too. A stolen car citation has been posted on CPIC and the FBI base, and I've notified Canadian Border Services."

Peter knew that CPIC stood for the Canadian Police Information Centre, the national criminal database.

Incomprehensible static burst from the radio. It put Deroche into manic mode. Quickly, he leaned past Peter and opened the glove box, revealing a large revolver. Peter looked in astonishment at the .357 Smith & Wesson; it was a cowboy's gun. Next to it sat a black, rectangular device with a pistol grip that Peter recognized as a Taser, a tool that he had never used or even trained to use.

"Peter, I trust you are up to date with your weapons!"

Peter said nothing.

Deroche reached in and with a flourish hefted the gun before Peter's face. Peter did not visibly react, but he was certainly confounded. He wasn't licensed to carry a firearm in Quebec. Here loomed disastrous consequences, he thought: any discharge of a gun this size in a quiet suburban neighbourhood would generate fierce outrage from the public and civic officials alike. The Sûreté hierarchy would come down hard on Deroche, and Peter had no intention of getting himself or the inspector in trouble. The weapon had a six-inch barrel and could not easily be concealed. But the most important consideration was Peter's lack of local authorization to carry a gun at all. Peter was about to point out this fact but then Deroche restored the gun to the glove compartment. Peter diverted to a different subject.

"Who do you think is attacking the Rizzutos?"

Deroche shut the glove box, though not in an angry way. "Could be the Calabrese faction. Maybe the bikers. Never underestimate the Angels. They're all over North America."

Peter read his thinking. "But you don't think so."

"No. This is a real live gang war, Peter, but whoever it is knows they will need the approval of the mafia Commission in New York, or what passes for the Commission these days. That cuts out the Angels, at least in terms of directing crime in Montreal. I think it's the 'Ndrangheta faction."

Peter knew, if vaguely, that the 'Ndrangheta were an outgrowth of the Calabrese factions within the mob. They were known for their viciousness and for their impenetrable, cell-like structure. There would be no Joe Valachis ratting on them.

"They're moving into Ontario," Deroche said. "This group comes out of southern Calabria and are a cutting edge force to be reckoned with . . ."

His account was shut down by the buzzing squawk of his radio, which he extracted from his black leather jacket. He pressed a button on the front.

"*Oui. Allo?*"

Peter missed the entire blurred response in French, except for the one word, "*camion.*"

"*Attendons. Deux minutes,*" the inspector replied, and punched the red off button.

The inspector turned to his passenger. "They spotted a panel truck, no printing on the side, coming along the street behind Caparza's. It paused two hundred yards away then drove off slowly."

"It didn't turn up our way," Peter said. There had been no traffic in the entire time they had been stationed in the alley.

Deroche eased a .45 pistol out of the inside left pocket of his coat. Peter stared at it in dismay. One shot would send a victim straight into the basement of the mortuary across the way, and if mourners were needed, the gun report would wake up every snoring resident of the surrounding streets. Deroche placed the weapon delicately on the console between the front seats.

A blast of static and the same voice said, "The van is back. We can't see it but it hasn't come out the other side of the building."

"Okay," Deroche instructed. "*Attendons.*"

Deroche opened the glove box and considered the .357, then the pastel-lit façade.

A loud *whump!* came from the area behind the Caparza facility. It rippled through the building and underground across the road towards the two men in the car. A mushroom cloud of white smoke rose from the rear of the funeral home, and as the mist climbed it was highlighted by the pink and blue floodlights shining on the front windows. The plume dissipated within a few seconds but by this time Deroche had the .45 in his right hand. Peter noted that the inspector became completely calm. A grin was on his face as he called into the walkie-talkie, "*Allez.*"

Peter did not hesitate. He reached into the glove box and took hold of the awkward revolver, as well as the Taser, which he wasn't sure how to activate. But Deroche had his door open now, and Peter, a weapon in each fist, awkwardly came out the passenger door. As he crossed the street he shoved a weapon into each pocket of his coat.

Deroche ran full tilt ahead across the empty avenue. Peter, who was fit from his expeditions with Jasper, soon caught up. He smelled fire and soot, although from his angle by the side wall of Caparza's he could not see any flames. Peter was cued in for gunfire and secondary explosions, as well as the engine noise of the van that was supposed to be there. He was unsure whether the detective on the walkie-talkie had identified a sports utility vehicle, a small truck or a minivan but he told himself to be ready for whatever came out of the back parking lot.

Instead, the two detectives heard only shouting, which became screeches of human pain. Rounding the back corner of the home, they met a scene of fiery chaos. A storm of concentrated yellow, red, and orange flames shot out from a wide back window of the Caparza facility. A man, unidentifiable in the flames that rendered him a torch, flailed against the fiery backdrop. For some reason, he did not drop to the ground and roll; rather, he flailed uselessly against what Peter could see was a gasoline inferno. One of the black-clad detectives ran into the light with a puny fire extinguisher, from his surveillance vehicle no doubt, and sprayed foam retardant on the man, who then collapsed onto the paved parking lot. The detective emptied the canister onto the sizzling body.

His partner arrived with two plastic bottles of water and dumped them up and down along the unfortunate figure. A policeman from the second team was preoccupied with another assailant whom he had trapped face down some ten yards away on the edge of the firelight. He cuffed the man. His partner arrived at that moment, a large extinguisher in his arms, and they turned their attention to the main blaze, which roared out through the back door and the broken windows. Peter noted that the first attacker, though his clothing continued to ·give off acrid smoke, was no longer afire. All the policemen now faced the flames. The one with the large tank heaved it up with both hands and launched it right into the centre of the window opening.

"Baissez-vous!" he called, and all the policemen, Peter included, hit the ground. The projectile went off and somehow caused the raging flames to implode, contracting the fire, and perhaps slowing its revival and saving the building. Already Peter could hear a fire engine approaching down the avenue.

The two teams backed off from the building; they had no choice but to await the *pompiers*. They had enough to attend to with the two prisoners on the ground. Neither was going anywhere in the near future but the need to monitor the one in handcuffs and to minister to his scorched partner distracted the detectives from what should have been an obvious threat: a third villain.

Peter had remained close to Deroche, in part to avoid being

mistaken for one of the funeral home attackers. The flames had died down, if temporarily, and he stood partly in darkness, a few steps back from the two groupings of men. Deroche had his .45 in his right hand and was barking orders into the radio held in his left.

The third assailant, big-bellied, wearing blue jeans and a dark jacket, emerged from the shadows at Peter's back. Peter sensed his presence and pivoted that way. The man held a pistol levelled at Peter but was in the process of swinging his aim towards Deroche, who himself had begun to turn instinctively. The man should have seen that his options were minimal. Certainly he was not about to single-handedly rescue his accomplices from the array of armed cops in the parking lot, all of whom had started to raise their guns in his direction.

But Peter, his thinking sharp, understood that the scene of pandemonium escalated the risk of a shootout to a critical level. Panic was in the air. The third assailant was committed.

And Peter understood that the next move had to be his.

The shooter remained fixed in position, heavy-footed and uncertain about his targets. The pistol wavered in his hand. Peter was positioned at a sideways angle to the man. He had his right hand in his pocket wrapped around the Taser, out of the line of sight of the gunman. The revolver was in his left pocket but he knew that the long barrel would catch if he drew it out too fast. He was guaranteed to lose the gunfight. There was an even better reason for avoiding the gun, tempting as it was to cut down this bastard on the spot. If Peter succeeded in killing the man, he knew that he would be stuck in Montreal for days, perhaps a week, if he, an unlicensed foreign police detective, used a firearm against a Canadian citizen, however unsavoury a specimen.

Sylvain Deroche torqued to his left to bring his .45 to bear and as he caught Peter's intentions, he gave one of his patented smiles. In some maniacal way, he was enjoying himself.

Peter grimaced back.

He guessed at the fat man's next movement, but he guessed correctly. The gunman took one measured step towards Peter, who understood that his attacker had formed some demented plan to grab a hostage. The fellow planted himself less than three feet away, the gun rising towards Peter's left temple. In a second he would be in a position to shoot both Deroche and Cammon. With no idea where the on switch was, Peter fished in his right pocket for the electronic device. From the weight of the thing, he guessed that this was one of the less powerful units. He hoped that its features would resemble those on a gun and that he could find the safety and the trigger.

But he wasn't sure and so he took the time to look down at the black Taser as he turned. He saw the safety switch and disengaged it. Now only six feet from the man, he raised the Taser and pulled the trigger. The device sparked and buzzed, launching two steel-barbed wires into the assailant's chest. The cops later told Peter it was a perfect strike.

At once, the atmosphere in the back lot changed in a strange way. Movement stopped as everyone gawked at the man on the ground. The crackling fire seemed to quiet and the fire engine siren held back for an extra few seconds in the distance. Deroche's mania, for once, subsided. The Quebec cops, who until now had ignored the British interloper, gazed at Peter with something he hadn't felt for a long time: professional respect.

CHAPTER 13

The taxi driver happened to know the direct route to the freight depot at Trudeau Airport and Peter arrived earlier than he expected. Delivery vans and semi-trailers, transferring crates of all sizes to the rows of warehouses that fronted the airport tarmac, surrounded him. Two uniformed clerks manned the desk inside the main shipping centre, checking paperwork and periodically slamming ink stamps down on multiple forms. A dozen men and one woman were queued up ahead of him at the counter. The staff knew their business, understanding the deadlines the truckers and van drivers faced, and they moved the crowd through rapidly.

Peter got out his documentation for the coffin: black-and-yellow stripes rimmed the special shipping authorization. It, and the death certificate, burial transfer permits, and *apostille* certifying that the U.K. approved of the work done by the funeral parlour — Britain would not accept a body that was not fully embalmed — would get Carpenter home to his rest. A beefy man in khaki coveralls came out from the back to consult with one of the counter staff. The man made eye contact and waved Peter over behind the counter. Without comment or query, he led him through the flapping plastic strips that hung across the entryway, and into the heart of the warehouse.

"Which one?" the big man said.

"Carpenter. To the United Kingdom on AC870."

"Yup. There he is, there."

Off to the right, the broad doors of the warehouse stood wide open and Peter was surprised to see an Airbus 360 with a maple leaf on its tail fin sitting right there on the tarmac, fewer than a hundred yards away.

They walked to the far side of the cavernous building to a fenced-in storage area. Between the diamond spaces of the wire grill, Peter saw two coffins sitting on trestles. The warehouseman unlocked the door and they entered. Peter handed his papers to the fellow, who began to check them against a bundle of documents that had been taped to the lid of the first coffin. As Réjean Parrish had promised, the steel air tray had been sealed with tape and labelled "HUMAN REMAINS." The man grunted with satisfaction. The papers were in order; one more problem off his hands.

"Hope the other one comes soon. The funeral director himself is signing off on that one. You a relative of . . . Mr. Carpenter? John Fitzgerald. Jesus. Echoes of Dallas."

"No, I'm with Scotland Yard," Peter responded, confident that this information would help to clear any last-minute concerns about his bona fides as companion to the corpse.

No beat was skipped.

"Thanks for coming early, Inspector. I recommend you stay and watch the tray go up the belt-loader. Ensures what we call chain of custody."

"I'm used to the concept," Peter stated drolly. Both men smiled, two pros at work.

"We do it over here now so as not to upset the passengers watching the bag belt from the boarding lounge. Some people get riled, especially the Chinese."

Peter watched the loading from the doorway. The veteran warehouseman handed over most of the documents, after returning to the front office to obtain a last stamp. Peter wouldn't have to be present when the coffin was unloaded at Heathrow or when the funeral people from London took possession. But he had decided to call Carpenter's brother, or maybe the quiet Carole, when he arrived, to confirm that he had shepherded John Carpenter home, from loading to landing.

He settled into his first-class seat, took out Renaud's Civil War tome, and placed it on the arm rest, along with a notebook and pen, in case he felt like starting his report to Bartleben. The flight attendant offered him a Montreal *Gazette* and a day-old *Guardian*; he had also snagged a week-old Sunday edition of the *News of the World* from the magazine rack. He was equipped for an easy flight, through most of which he would sleep, he hoped. He was exhausted.

All the news felt recycled from his earlier flight. Floods in Pakistan. A continuing vigil for the miners trapped in Chile. Vitriol over the planned Islamic Centre close to Ground Zero. And France had announced that gypsies weren't welcome any longer. An advert in the *Guardian* suggested everyone pre-order Tony Blair's autobiography; *I'm not that retired,* Peter reflected.

He took a drink of Perrier from his complimentary bottle. He missed his family and his dog and there was no reason to return to North America. His work was done. He was no longer angry with Sir Stephen, though Peter's role, as he predicted, had never been more than routine and bureaucratic. As for follow-up, until Greenwell was found there was little the Yard could do, and nothing for Peter himself. He perhaps owed more to the murdered man, but Greenwell remained the obvious suspect and the key. Far away from Montreal, Peter could do little more to aid the Canadian authorities.

Ruminating further, and without trying for any epiphanies, he noted the range of motives of the many players in this investigation. Nicola Hilfgott had turned manic about three letters from a century and a half ago, because of oblique references to Quebec revolutionaries. Pascal implied that the separatist community shared her interest in the letters, though from the reverse angle. The obvious reason for the assault was the envelope full of cash, and here Alice Nahri and Leander Greenwell topped the suspect list. Someone at the Yard would have to sort out the killer from the merely greedy.

Peter's regret focused on the victim. Young Carpenter had been displaced in all this muddle of self-serving agendas. There was little Peter could do about it. Bartleben had never intended to give Peter the authority necessary to clean up the mess.

The girl did make it interesting. If Peter were to stay on the case, he would hunt her down before attempting anything else. So far, she was a ghost, yet she must have been present, at least nearby, when Carpenter perished. Or was there ever a girl? Hilfgott, Deroche, and Renaud doubted it. Even Greenwell, in his interview with Deroche, hadn't mentioned her.

The flight attendant nudged his arm. Peter awoke from his reverie to her smile. She held out a yellow note folded in two.

"Inspector Cammon?" she whispered. "There was a call from London at the Montreal terminal. We didn't have a chance to deliver it to you in the departure lounge. I'm sorry." She lowered her voice and leaned closer. "From a Deputy Commissioner Bartleben?"

Peter took the note and the woman watched his face as he read: "Important news. Girl found in D.C. Essential you contact before departing Montreal. Sir Stephen."

As he reached the last bit, the hovering attendant said, "We apologize for not getting it to you in time. You can make a call using the seat phone." She pointed to the beige telephone implanted in his chair.

Peter smiled and waved off the woman to show that all was forgiven. He picked up the phone but took a moment to think before he dialled. Why was Bartleben still calling himself deputy commissioner? Had Alice Nahri been found dead or alive? No use speculating, he reasoned, yet the tone of the message was clear: Bartleben wanted him to stay in Montreal. Peter read the instructions on the phone and punched in the numbers for London. It would be about 1 a.m. there and Bartleben should be at home with his wife.

"Peter, is that you?" Bartleben said, having picked up the receiver on the first ring. *Does the man ever sleep?*

"I'm afraid I'm calling from the plane." Peter said. "Only got your message just now. This is an unsecured line."

Stephen's tone remained sanguine. "I see. You understand that the girl is dead?"

"No, I don't know that." The phone irritated Peter. The connection, though clear enough, felt remote and tenuous. Bartleben seemed uncomfortable, too. "How did she die?" Peter asked. "Tell me as much as you can. Let's not worry too much about the secure connection."

"All right. But no names, please. She committed suicide. Drowned in the Anacostia River three nights ago. That's in Washington . . ."

"I know where it is." Peter knew the area from his time at Quantico.

"We found the car."

"The rental?" Peter said.

"Yes. Our man's rental. Don't know how she managed to get it across the Canadian border. Rental agreements don't usually allow . . ."

"Stephen, did they find the Sat Nav?"

"I have no idea." Peter could tell that Stephen was impatient and ready to take offence: somehow it was Peter's fault that the message had missed him on the ground, and now his man was heading in the wrong direction.

"None of the documents we discussed were in the vehicle," Stephen stated.

"The Booth letters."

Peter felt Stephen recoil; he never wanted to be explicit. "Is that what we call them now?"

"What agencies are involved?" Peter said.

"The Washington Metro force, Maryland State Police and the U.S. Parkway Police, since the car was spotted at one point on the Anacostia Freeway."

"How about our friends at Quantico?" Peter asked, coding for the

FBI. "And what about the Big One?" The Big One was Homeland Security.

"Not yet. You know, Peter, I still see no national security / terrorism dimensions to this case. Do you?" There was a wistfulness in his voice.

Peter avoided the question, although he barely suppressed his scorn. From the outset, Bartleben had two bugbears: the potential political scandal generated by an intemperate consul general over in the colonies; and a cock-up that might draw in the Americans and turn this into a terrorism threat. *Maybe I'm tired*, Peter thought, *or I have an overdeveloped sense of irony.* For he knew one small fact that Sir Stephen did not. No, there wasn't a whiff of terrorism in any of this but according to a recent news report, the American security agency was about to build a massive headquarters complex in the neighbourhood of Anacostia, D.C., right by the river. Alice Nahri had drowned in the new backyard of Homeland Security.

"Tell me the story, Stephen."

Bartleben launched into the official account. "It's incomplete but three days ago the car was found in the parking area of a yacht club on the edge of the Anacostia River. The Anacostia is the eastern branch of the Potomac and the spot lies only three or four miles from the White House. Did you know they sail yachts in the heart of Washington?"

"What condition was the car in?" Peter asked, ignoring the rhetorical question. He hoped to learn how much damage the hit-and-run had caused to the front of the Ford. That would tell him a lot about the targeting of John Carpenter.

"Don't know. The vehicle sat there for three or four days, Metro Police estimate. The body was discovered in the river three days back. Almost simultaneously, someone visiting the yacht club noticed the Canadian plates and called it in. The authorities checked the outstanding Canadian warrant and a match was made on the tags."

"So, the body washed up after only two or three days?" Peter said.

"Seems so. Something about the tides, they told me. They're sending a report via our embassy in Washington."

136

They had already said too much on a public connection, although Peter had never heard of anyone hacking a phone call from an airplane. Perhaps the *News of the World* knew how it was done.

There was a weighty pause on the line.

"Well, Peter, can you turn around and go back to D.C.?"

Peter had known that the question was coming. He also knew that he had the advantage and could do exactly what he wanted. For these reasons, he did not immediately respond. Yet his thinking remained conflicted. Bartleben and everyone else had studiously ignored John Carpenter and the pain inflicted on his family. It seemed that Peter Cammon, who had the narrowest role in this tragedy, was the one who cared most about the victim.

"Stephen, let me get Carpenter home and dry, then I'll see how I feel about it. The girl will keep."

Bartleben had to be content with that much. Peter hadn't sneered at the idea. They embarked on one of their long mutual silences and it did not matter that the office was paying for every minute of the call. Peter knew his old colleague well. Bartleben was asking him to shepherd a second body across the Pond and the bizarreness of his initial assignment had just been doubled. Peter refused to acknowledge this farce, because for him it was no longer farcical. The case was turning ugly. He told himself defensively, almost saying it out loud, that he would do exactly what he pleased, to hell with London. There was more to this than a drowning suicide. A young man, ruined, lay in a metal box in the airplane hold below and now the waterlogged corpse of a girl sat in a morgue somewhere, likely headed to a grave in a potter's field. Bartleben waited. The drone of the airplane engines seemed to raise the tension of their standoff.

Peter hung up without saying goodbye and looked at his watch; they were scheduled to land in two and a half hours. He turned to the rumpled copy of the *News of the World*, a paper he seldom bothered with, blazoned with pictures of a cricket bribery sting on its front page. At least three members of the national cricket team from Pakistan stood accused of taking bribes to throw games. The story amplified what Frank Counter had told him, that the *News* had set up a sting in a Mayfair hotel, capturing on film and audio the payment of large amounts of boodle to three rising cricket stars. The exposé charted entrenched corruption in what was the national obsession of several countries. The national pride of Pakistan had been sullied, so said its prime minister. Candid photos showed players partying with sweet young things, while other shots displayed the grim faces of the named sinners. Careers had already been ruined.

Counter had mentioned that John Carpenter had worked on the file. Peter searched for any explicit reference to Scotland Yard involvement, and there it was: the bribes had been dispensed in London, and the Yard conceded that it had no choice but to press the investigation. He had no doubt that cautions had already been issued in anticipation of heavy charges. Bad luck for Frank Counter, Peter thought. He wondered how close Carpenter had been to the cricket dossier.

He beckoned to the flight attendant and asked her if it was permissible to use his BlackBerry to send an email to his wife. Ever since the crash of Swissair 111 a few years ago off the coast of Nova Scotia, Peter had been wary of in-cabin electronics when he flew. Early reports had suggested that glitches in the aircraft's entertainment system had caused a fire, which had ultimately brought down the plane. Peter was never sure if this story was true but new technology made him nervous. The attendant assured him that it was quite safe to send emails.

He opened his file and found only one relevant missive in a long list of messages: Maddy confirmed that she would pick him up at the airport, no matter that he would arrive just after dawn. He wondered how to tell his daughter-in-law that he would probably be turning around within forty-eight hours and heading back to North America.

PART TWO

Twenty20

A variant of cricket, adopted into professional play in 2003. In the first Twenty20 World Cup, played in 2007, India beat Pakistan. Pakistan won the Cup in 2009, England in 2010.

CHAPTER 14

1998

Alice crossed the Motihari Bridge in a state of contentment. She paused in the middle to appreciate the view in both directions of the Motijheel, which means "pearl lake" in Hindi. The Goddess Lakshmi had blessed her with 20/10 vision, what the ophthalmologist in Patna described as hyperacuity. It enabled Alice to see details at great distances. On a clear day like today, she might have turned around and imagined she could spy the top of Everest in the Nepali Himalayas, but she did not look back this time.

This day, she found little to impress her in the lake. Squatters and unscrupulous builders had despoiled the waterfront for years — she could see both ends of the Motijheel — and fuzzy green islands of pollution-fed hyacinth had choked the oxygen from the water.

With her sharp sight, she could make out the roof of the old cantonment, and next to it the crumbling go-down, the opium warehouse that George Orwell's father, Mr. Blair, had supervised one century ago. Orwell's birthplace, itself a decaying homestead, lay off to the west. She had visited the near-shrine the day before to say her goodbyes to the spirit of the Blairs. Alice looked forward to telling her mother back in Britain about her pilgrimage.

Alice was leaving Motihari forever and with no regrets. The city held nothing for her. She planned to join her mother in Oxfordshire; she had been accepted into university for the fall term. The famous had left, too, she noted. Motihari was a place for leaving. Orwell and his mother, Ida, moved to England when George turned four. Gandhi had launched the Satyagraha revolution from Motihari, the independence movement based on civil disobedience tactics, but the Mahatma's memory, fifty years on, was a flicker in Bihar State. Alice's own mother had abandoned Motihari fourteen years ago.

The floods had devastated the Terai, the grasslands outside Motihari, but the city was dry as cow bones, as they say. Alice passed the Shagun beauty parlour where her cousin worked, and the BSNL telephone exchange. She walked by the railway station, flanked by the bus terminal, where she planned to catch the daily to Patna. At the gupta store, she stopped for a bottle of *aam jhora*, the mango drink everyone consumed to protect against the heat.

She had said goodbye to her relatives and teachers, and offered a last prayer to Devi, the goddess of knowledge, at the Gayatri Mandir. Alice's father had taken offence at her announcement and had refused to see her off at the bus depot. Nevertheless, she headed to the garage for a final goodbye, if not for a reconciliation.

Motihari boasted two fine movie theatres and Alice's pride in this fact outweighed her regret that she would never sit in their cool darkness again. The Madhav Talkies offered Indian films from the Mumbai Bollywood factories. Just yesterday, Alice had attended the other one, the Sangeet, which showed first-run American pictures. *Titanic*, with Jack and Rose and the great ocean liner, was imprinted on her young mind forever; and today she daydreamed of a shipboard romance as she walked along the dry, rutted streets to the downtown.

She glanced at the poster outside the Sangeet, which stood across the road from the garage where her father was a partner with her uncle, albeit a junior one. Both of the city's cinemas were good-luck tokens, Alice thought. Madhav was one of the names of Lord Krishna and Sangeet meant "celestial song" but also referred to a Hindu pre-wedding celebration in honour of the bride-to-be.

Alice entered the familiar dark garage and called out, "Aamon?" She addressed her father by his first name out of habit and respect. Her uncle, Vikram, who owned the shop, went by an invented name, Raji Bosh, a pretension she had never fully understood. The room was both hot and cool; the corrugated iron roof contracted and pinged in the hammering sun, while damp air rose from the service well, sending up oil and chemical smells that she knew well. She knew the cars, too: a poky Ambassador, a Tata Sumo, an Avenger, a Blaze, and the police commissioner's yellow Scorpio, which sat astride the service pit.

No one was working. She had expected to find her father in the office but he was off somewhere. The junior mechanic, Hashi, must be at lunch, she figured. Uncle Raji Bosh was notorious locally for minding the store 24-7, in case someone tried to steal one of the cars. He often slept on a cot in the corner or night-hawked behind his beloved computer in the office. Raji Bosh had worked himself up to prosperity in the small world of Motihari.

Alice moved to the end of the garage, to the wall of tools and the diagnostic machine that was the pride of the commercial business. High on the wall hung three pictures. The first was a bright metal advert for Thums Up Cola (for years Alice had misspelled 'thumb'), red, white, and blue. The obligatory Gandhi portrait hung in the middle. Alice recalled George Orwell's ruling on the Great Man: "Saints should always be judged guilty until proven innocent."

For the first time, Alice took a close look at the third piece of garage art. A fierce soldier encased in armour rode the back of a huge bullock, prying open its jaws as if to kill it. She had always assumed the warrior was the god Shiva and the bull Nandi, who bore Shiva into battle.

"That is the god Mithra," a male voice said from behind her.

She turned to meet her uncle, Aamon's older brother. He had a ragged wisp of a beard and greasy black hair, slicked back from his forehead. He was smiling and held a plate of *thekua* pastries.

"Who is Mithra?" Alice said. She had always found her uncle sly and haughty and wondered why her father put up with his arrogance.

Raji Bosh came closer and gestured to the picture. "Zoroastrian divinity, mighty protector of the waters, and guardian of the harvest. He is slaying the bull as a sacrifice to the weather. I pray to him for a good growing season."

This revelation struck Alice as strange, since floods had devastated the plains of Bihar that fall, and besides, Raji Bosh had never been a farmer.

Her uncle approached her and offered a *thekua*. She was about to refuse when she realized she was hungry. Raji Bosh leaned around her shoulder, too close, and picked up a bottle of *thandhai*, a sweet drink of sugared yogurt and spiced fruit. Alice took two of the deep-fried snacks and chewed them one after the other. She swallowed both *thekua* pieces before the dizziness struck her.

The sugar that was laced into the coconut-and-wheat-flour treats masked the salty character of the dose of what her uncle had mixed in; gamma-hydroxybutyrate gives off a saline tang, but it is odourless, and he had added a large amount.

Raji Bosh had not eaten any of the pastries containing the drug, but he was sweating and he drooled as he tipped the bottle of sweet *thandhai* to his niece's mouth. She took a swallow to relieve the salty taste.

Her dizziness moved in phases between euphoria and nausea. The sugar in the drink and the drug-laced snacks caused her gorge to rise but she did not vomit. The GHB made her delirious and pushed her into a floating netherworld. She was aware of her surroundings; GHB, unlike most rape drugs, builds slowly and relentlessly and does not produce unconsciousness.

Nor amnesia.

Alice felt the bonds on her wrists and ankles, even though she couldn't remember her clothes being removed. She slid in and out of awareness of the assault on her body. Ropes bound her to a chair, perhaps a mechanic's trolley of some kind, the bands crossing her belly and breastbone, and pinning her four limbs. Her uncle began to move her about the garage, between the cars, and Alice realized that

142

he was positioning her for a further attack. Odd thoughts fluttered across her feverish mind, the first being that he couldn't rape her while she was strapped down this way. This idea offered no comfort.

He halted the trolley by the yellow Scorpio sedan that hovered above the below-ground work bay. The updraft of cool, oily air let her know where she was. She feared his pitching her into the hole. But Raji Bosh let her sit there a full five minutes. The drug half blinded her; it refused to weaken its grip. The man was suddenly mauling her, palming her face, scrunching her lips together and kissing them. He pinched her breast and poked his finger inside her. But Alice could sense his frustration, his immediate disappointment. She guessed that her rape would not be . . . traditional.

Raji Bosh touched cold metal to her breastbone, just above the upper strap. Next she found herself recoiling at the focused agony of the teeth of the jumper cables as he affixed them to her breasts. The metal ends refused to grip her nipples and fell onto her lap. She felt the trickle of blood down her breasts. She tried to yell. He had pinned her to this weird chair, which was flexible at the waist, like an exercise frame. The pain came again but she failed in her first attempt to scream. The alligator teeth gripped her under her breasts and held fast the second time, sending hot pain into her lungs and heart.

Her uncle did not speak but twice leaned his face against her ear and moaned. He exhaled warm, rancid spice. He did not try to kiss her again, which, in her demented panic, Alice found odd. There was a pause and then, a great distance away, a motor fired up. Simultaneously, the burn of the electrical charge coursed across her chest. It was a skittering, flaring pain that moved from the surface of her skin down into her fat cells, and worst of all, found the hard muscle and ropy tendons that make such good conductors.

But it was this flesh, the muscle and sinew protecting her chest, that saved her. That and the voltage regulator on the small sedan. Alice's scream broke through with the first jolt. Her uncle cut the ignition, came over, and tied a filthy rag across her mouth.

He turned the key again and Alice vaulted against the straps. Her wail, despite the gag, approximated her first open scream, and Raji Bosh pounded on the dashboard of the car as if to silence her. She sensed his panic and anger. He stopped the engine. The filthy cloth must have offended him but she knew that he hated her screeching more. Alice, in her distress, grabbed onto a small truth. He wanted her perfection. Her body was a chalice to Raji Bosh; at nineteen, her figure was nearly flawless. For months he had watched her and now that he had her undressed, he would make her his toy. Alice understood his plan to possess her through pain. As long as he kept away from her eyes: it was never her body that she thought of as perfect. She treasured her eyes most. Alice Nahri had magical eyes that could see from the Motihari Bridge to the mountaintop of Annapurna at the end of the great Nepal trade route.

He adjusted the claws and turned on the starter one more time. Alice screamed again but this time she knew that he would not hit her, or steal her eyesight, and with those eyes she fixed him with a look of hatred.

Unlike a Taser, which releases 50,000 to 125,000 volts, a car battery typically shoots out about twelve, and painful as the current is, human skin and subdermal tissues are efficient at dissipating the flow. The danger lies in the amperage behind the jolt, but a car's voltage regulator imposes limits on the amps that get through. Had Raji Bosh connected the cables to the ignition itself, the electrical force would have killed her.

The mechanic, perspiring and agitated, pulled off the claw grips but he did not immediately release his niece from the bendable chair. The electrocution wasn't working and Alice for the first time thought she might survive. Her uncle wheeled her over to a blacksmith's trough, a long galvanized steel tank used to cool forged metal and clean dirty car parts. It resembled a horse trough from a western movie.

But her attacker had seen other movies. He removed her gag and retied it as a blindfold. He also undid the straps from her chest. In an awkward but efficient motion, he tipped the chair forward, so that her upper body tilted into the water.

144

Had he wanted a confession — to anything — she would have offered it. Waterboarding and dunking are forms of torture because they simulate the experience of death. *Just stay away from my eyes*, she prayed.

He pushed her head into the filth. Alice's mind hooked onto every shred of survival strategy. She began to count. She told herself that he was an amateur at this. His assault had no purpose. But a subsequent thought sent a chill to her heart, even as she fought to hold her breath: if he wanted to kill her without marring her outer perfection, this was the way. She would make a good-looking corpse.

He kept her under for forty-five seconds before bringing her back. The human body's reaction to oxygen deprivation is autonomic. As she sucked air into her throat, her uncle gripped her tighter, prepared for the next dunking. Alice hoped that she could count to one hundred and twenty, a full two minutes.

A new, greater fear rolled over her, into her heart and brain. She saw the cables, the leads lying on the greasy floor, stretching back into the motor compartment of the yellow car. Twelve volts alone, she knew, would not kill her but twelve volts in water would shock her heart to a full stop.

He held her under for two and a half minutes. And when he pulled her up, and as he realized that she hadn't quite drowned, he gripped her again to ready her for a third immersion in the trough. Alice had reached her limit. It was not anger that drove her now but the grim understanding that she was done. Where was her father? He had abandoned her. She would survive one way only, and if her desperate plan fell short she would at least leave a telltale clue that even her spineless father couldn't fail to note.

Her lungs were raw. She gasped for control of her intake of air. She attempted the unexpected, the impossible. As her uncle leaned over the pool, Alice mustered a pocket of air and exploded the word "Rape!"

Raji Bosh let her fall forward. As before, her upper body tipped below the surface and her head banged on the side of the steel

145

container. But this time, all of her, bound to the chair, toppled in and she was engulfed.

Underwater, she thought clearly, while fighting the conviction that there wasn't enough time. The wrist and ankle straps held her tight. The withdrawal of the chest band allowed her to lever forward, but the motion neither loosened the waist strap nor enabled her to slip out of any of the bindings on her limbs. She hadn't stopped wondering what he'd tied her to. At first she had imagined it to be some form of mechanic's dolly, but now she realized that she was in an old-fashioned wheelchair, something colonial British, with multiple metal joints and levers and a flexible, tilting back, probably made of rattan and mahogany.

She began to roll from side to side. She had no ambition to break the chair back or disjoint the hinges. Instead, she rocked and created waves that, though she could not see, sloshed four or five inches of water out of the tank. It wasn't enough to overturn the heavy steel trough, but a piece of luck rewarded her struggle. She kicked her feet, which were not firmly fixed to the chair frame, down towards the foot props. As the left foot plate folded down, it struck the drain fitting, dislodging the bung and causing a flood onto the cement floor. It was almost not enough. She held her breath for a count of two hundred before the filthy water subsided below her nose. Her blindfold had sagged from her eyes and she was able to look down the length of the tank at her knees.

Kicking some more at the bonds on her left ankle, she broke the pinion on that side of the chair. From there, Alice was able to worm her left arm from its wrist band. She freed the rest of her body as though she were an apprentice Houdini.

Her uncle had panicked and fled. Her clothes lay over by the wall with the three posters. Gandhi and the god Mithra looked down on her bruised form. Pain tightened her ribcage; her hips and sternum ached. The wounds under her breasts were half burn and half scarring but she judged that the healed marks would each be less than an inch long.

She saw no sign of her father and she wasn't about to seek him out for any kind of solace. She would gain her revenge her own way. She dressed and fled the garage. She tried not to think of anything as she came into the light outside and began to limp away.

The water had nearly become her doom. Alice had been minutes away from leaving Motihari for good but now there was no chance of getting the daily bus to the state capital. She turned the corner into the roadway. There on the wall hung the poster of Jack and Rose, figureheads on the bow of the fated ship. Jack drowns; Rose lives. Which character would Alice Nahri be?

CHAPTER 15

For once, Heathrow Arrivals was subdued and the queues moved efficiently. Peter collected his luggage at the carousel, then returned to the Departures level, where Aviation Security kept the office he required. His Scotland Yard ID won him cooperation from the Met officer on duty, who suggested that he simply call the morgue facility rather than walking all the way over to the receiving hangar. Peter hesitated, feeling he was betraying the Carpenter family by not staying with the coffin. But he was weary and a call to the hangar confirmed that they had offloaded the body. The hearse would pick up the dead man later that day and he would reach home by evening.

But then the distortion of red-eye flying kicked in and led to an impulsive decision. One thing he could do was offer reassurance to Carole Carpenter (though he would not reveal the report on Alice Nahri's drowning).

He rang up the house in New Bosk on his mobile, and Joe answered.

Peter tried to be nonchalant. "Joe, this is Peter Cammon. We've arrived."

"*We* have arrived?" Joe picked up on the creepiness of the phrase. "My dead brother is home to be put in the ground, then?"

148

Peter fumbled through the arrangements for transfer until Joe interrupted. "Did you find the bitch?"

"Not yet. I could use some help. Any detail. Was there anything really distinctive about her, other than her good looks?"

There was a short pause this time. Joe stated flatly, "She has a bad twitch."

Joe hung up. Peter's mobile rang a few seconds later. It was Maddy. "Peter! Welcome home. We're just across the way."

Jasper yelped and danced at her leash at the sight of Peter, and he could tell with one look that Maddy was eager to brief him on her research into Alice Nahri's personal history. The news of Alice's suicide would disappoint her.

They took care of preliminaries as they pulled away from the nest of roads around Heathrow. Joan was at the cottage, trying to catch up on sleep. Her sister and brother continued to decline, with her sister not expected to last more than a month. Maddy herself was taking three days off, "because I need the time."

"How was Montreal?" she asked.

Peter could only offer the blunt truth. He summarized the police investigation and warrants put out for Leander and the girl. "Headquarters called me on the plane over. The FBI have discovered a body they think is the girl. Drowned in the Potomac River."

"Are they sure it's Alice?"

"Not confirmed. But they found the hire car on the riverbank."

Maddy contemplated this news for two minutes and then made a statement that was almost elegiac. "Johnny Carpenter drowned in a canal. Now Alice has drowned in a river. Both far from home."

"Bartleben wants me to fly to Washington."

"Are you going?"

"Probably," Peter said.

"Well, if you need a lift to the airport, give me a shout."

The cottage was silent when they arrived. Maddy helped Peter unload his bag from the Saab and he carried it to the front steps.

Jasper raced around to her familiar spots but knew not to bark when Joan was upstairs sleeping.

Maddy retreated to the car and shooed Jasper, who was ready for another ride, towards the house. "Glad you're safe, Peter," she said, almost as if she guessed that he had placed himself in danger. He had said nothing about Caparza's.

Were all the women in his life clairvoyant? "Wait a moment, dear, would you?"

Peter left his Gladstone on the veranda and went inside, intending to consult Joan. He wanted to invite Maddy to dinner so that they could review her material. There was only silence on the ground floor. Peter took two steps towards the staircase but stopped. A plastic cloth covered the mahogany dining room table. Joan rarely used anything but a linen cover. A neatly squared stack of paper, four inches thick, sat at one end of the table, a red marker and two ballpoint pens lined up beside the pile.

Peter didn't bother going upstairs to get Joan's permission. He turned and went to the Saab. Maddy and Jasper waited exactly where he'd left them.

"Come 'round for dinner. I want your opinion on a few things."

Maddy cocked an eyebrow. "Okay, good."

He blurted out the thought that had been percolating in his jet-lagged brain. "I suspect that the girl from the river isn't Alice Nahri."

Joan awoke as Peter entered the bedroom. He had the skewed feeling that he hadn't seen her in a very long time.

"Is Maddy coming back?" she said, slightly anxious.

"Yeah." Joan looked played out. His own weariness must have been obvious to her, too. Their common ground of exhaustion made them fall into making love. It promised to be a perfunctory performance but they soon found an almost desperate, mutual passion.

"You know I have to go back to Leicester tomorrow," she said afterwards, her head on his chest.

"I can go with you."

She shook her head. "Did you see Maddy's research on the table?" she said.

"Yes."

"Welcome Maddy in. It's so important to her. Finish it, dear. It's what you do."

An hour later, Sir Stephen Bartleben called.

"What's the latest, Stephen?" Peter said.

"The medical examiner at Quantico is having trouble determining the cause of death." Bartleben's frustration showed.

The boss had never seen an autopsy table in his life. Peter suspected that the ME was having a hard time with the floater's identity, not with the cause of death.

"Echoes of John Carpenter," he said.

"Peter, the whole damn thing is turning into a melodrama. The murkier it gets, the greater the likelihood of Homeland interfering."

Sir Stephen was right, even if tiresome on the issue of Homeland Security. The oddball suicide of a suspect in downtown Washington could soon draw the spooks in. The diplomatic wrangle would spread in multiple directions when triggered. Alice, Indian born, had crossed the U.S.–Canadian border in a parody of terrorist infiltration patterns, and Homeland, particularly the INS, but also the FBI itself, was already paranoid about terrorists sneaking in from Canada.

"Shall I have my aide book your flight?" Sir Stephen said.

"Yes. Give Owen Rizeman a call at the FBI HQ and let him know I'm coming. I prefer to deal with the Bureau, even if it's now a subsidiary of the Big One."

"I'll tell him we have a common interest in keeping it simple," the boss stated.

"It was hard to get a fix on Alice's mother," Maddy said to Peter at the dining room table later that evening. Joan had cleared the dishes and retreated upstairs, and now the two of them were sorting through Maddy's research. Bartleben's call had encouraged them.

"Lead me through it," Peter said.

"Alice was proving impossible to trace, almost as if she had brushed away her tracks. So I focused on the family name. I finally came across a Nahri Auto Dealer in Motihari. That was the hook."

"How did you confirm the link?"

"I did the obvious. I emailed the owner of Nahri Auto. The Indians are so polite. He emailed me back, said the founder of the business died ten years ago. The name of the shop was retained for business goodwill. But the founder, a Vikram Nahri, is dead. He was Alice's uncle and brother of Aamon, Alice's father. The current owner had lost track of the family."

"Did he confirm the mother's maiden name?" Peter said.

"Parsons. Christened Mabel Ida after Orwell's mother."

Peter smiled at the validation of Maddy's Orwell theory. At least three generations of Alice's family were connected to India. The missing girl's grandmother named her child Mabel Ida, who kept up the tradition with her child, Alice Ida. Peter guessed that Alice's mother had returned at some point in her youth to Motihari, perhaps for a visit or as governess or nurse, and married a local man named Aamon Nahri.

"I wonder how far the parallels go," Maddy said. "Did Alice's mother come back to England like George Orwell's mum did? Does Alice have a sister named after one of Orwell's? I'll start looking in phone directories."

"And is the mother still alive?" Peter said.

They agreed that Maddy would keep searching. Only two questions continued to bother Peter. Did Alice go home after Montreal, and where exactly was "home"?

If I owned an elephant, said the blind man, I'd name him Everyman, since the elephant is a different fellow each time I touch him.

Peter had rendered himself blind to John Carpenter's death by telling himself at the outset that he did not care. It was murder, he had confirmed, but he still had no stake in it. No hot vengeance, no cold satisfaction, no goal at all. There was no requirement to touch the elephant again.

But in the dream that night his finger stretched out of its own wilfulness, and he brushed against the elephant. The touching drew him in, electrically, like a jolt of painful fire. He might have touched the beast anywhere but all it took was one connection. *Murder is the story*, the beast told him, *and in the face of it, the other human stories are fairy tales. Start with the murder story, the one written in John's blood.*

Contradictorily, his fevered brain cooled as he surfaced from sleep. He was a detective. Every story had a logical ending. He had to find the key.

The young woman.

He owed John Carpenter.

He realized that he had the need again.

CHAPTER 16

The horror had begun well before dawn two days back by the canal's edge, and Alice hadn't rested since. She didn't need much sleep but she was worn through now, and all that was keeping her awake was the twitch. She opened the window and let the breeze revive her.

It took so long to get anywhere in America, even with the atlas and the GPS to help guide her along her route. But she wouldn't get far at all if she couldn't manage a border crossing somewhere. The map offered the choices of New York, Vermont, New Hampshire, and Maine, yet there appeared to be nothing to distinguish one from the other. A smaller crossing point was probably best but even there she was unsure. She faced a decision. She had traversed the Champlain Bridge across the St. Lawrence River to the south shore, just below Montreal, and the nearest American border station loomed straight ahead.

She turned into an all-night truck stop and positioned the Ford in a shadowy area far away from the gas pumps. With the overhead light on, she opened the Rand McNally atlas to the full display of North America. The map symbols confused her at first. She flipped to the list of markings and abbreviations on the first page of the atlas, and there it was: "Map Legend." *Legend*. Alice was used to tortuous travel. She recalled her many struggles up the Patna–Kathmandu Highway, carrying gems, gold, and drugs. On the Nepal Road, as it was known, she had feared, every minute, robbery, extortion by the Maoist gangs, and arrest by the Nepalese customs guards. Entering the United States of America had to be easier than that. Feeling better, she slept for the next thirty minutes.

She was lucky. The American Customs woman at the tiny border crossing into Vermont let her through, barely raising an eyebrow at the Indian birthplace on her British passport. Alice settled in for the long drive to the Maryland coast.

The atlas was a trove of useful measuring sticks: mileage counters between cities, spacing between interstate off-ramps, and alternate secondary roads. The interstates offered the obvious route to her destination of Annapolis, Maryland. They led her on a snaking path from Montpelier, Vermont, to points south. She knew she had to pull over somewhere soon to call ahead and she hoped to stop in a major city in case she had to wait for call-backs. The last thing she needed was a small-town policeman bothering her at a street-side phone booth.

At a discount store off a nondescript cloverleaf north of Springfield, Massachusetts, Alice caught sight of a sign that promised to accept Canadian dollars at par. She stopped and asked the frizzy-haired cashier lady, the only person in the store, if she could pay in hundreds.

"Hundreds are fine, darlin'. Social Security checks. Food stamps. Just about anything 'cept personal checks."

Alice filled a small shopping cart with plastic-wrapped snacks, shampoo and cheap cosmetics, five pairs of underwear, and three T-shirts. On impulse, she picked up a child's rucksack — a "knapsack," she reminded herself — with a picture of Jack and Rose on it; the thing was bright pink, but she risked it anyway. The cashier smiled (was everybody in America friendly?) and didn't blink as Alice handed over a Canadian hundred, although she did hold it up to some kind of ultraviolet light to confirm that it wasn't counterfeit.

Alice, emboldened, had the woman change another hundred for full value.

"Some of the big banking chains will change big cash bills, but they wouldn't give you a one-for-one deal like this," the woman said. Such was Alice's introduction to the convoluted world of American finance.

In the car, Alice wolfed down a pair of Twinkies — she had heard about them, but had never eaten one — and felt a little sick. Down the road she stopped at a McDonald's and ordered two Egg McMuffins and a black coffee from the counter. Giving herself five minutes to eat, she watched the drive-through lane until she thought she had mastered the procedure; from now on, she would only use take-away.

Springfield was bigger than she had expected and the interstate through the city confused her with its constantly shifting lanes. She would require a telephone soon. One exit was as bad as the next, and so she arbitrarily took a ramp into what happened to be the centre of the urban zone. The Ford eased down into a grid of darkened streets.

No one bothered to walk the streets of Springfield, Massachusetts, at this hour. At one empty intersection she turned right and drove for two blocks parallel to a giant brick building. A sign at the end of the structure read "Springfield Armory National Historic Site." She knew what an armoury was; Maoist guerrillas in Bihar had once famously raided an armoury housed in an old colonial cantonment and made off with four hundred guns. Alice drove on. She hoped for a pay phone in a quiet area but not entirely isolated from pedestrian traffic. She worked through the deserted avenues until she found a street of one-storey shops and diners; a moment later she spied a phone kiosk on a side street. Although the only human presence was a man running a street sweeper, she stopped and scouted the avenues for potential threats. She parked the Ford where she could see it from the kiosk.

Alice dropped a quarter into the slot, pressed ten numbers, and in response to the recorded prompt prepared to add a stream of coins to cover ten minutes of talk. She stood by the phone kiosk while the rings accumulated.

The professor sounded relaxed when he answered, on the sixth ring. He hadn't been sleeping, Alice could tell, for she heard the clink of a coffee cup and a faint radio voice in the background.

"Lembridge."

The voice was an even baritone, confident and maybe slightly confrontational. All this she could tell from that first word. The fact that he answered the phone with his name also interested her. Johnny had reported that Hilfgott described him as an "arrogant sod." Coming from that bitch, Alice thought, that was rich irony. But according to Johnny, Professor Andrew Lembridge was the "go-to guy" for authentication of rare documents. Alice had easily obtained his phone number, though not his address, from the university website.

A formal approach seemed best. "Good morning, Professor. My name is Rebecca Cameron and I am calling from the British Embassy in Washington. I believe you have had a conversation with Madam Nicola Hilfgott . . ."

"No call display."

"I beg your pardon?"

"No number shows up on my screen. Last time, your office displayed your number."

It had already been a long drive, with hours more ahead, and she had to restrain herself.

"We at the embassy haven't called you previously. Mrs. Hilfgott is in Montreal. In Washington these days everything is security, including an innocent call like mine."

She waited to see if he was growing impatient with this sparring. She knew she was.

But he moved on. "All right, Miss Cameron, I'm guessing this has something to do with Booth and some documents."

"Exactly, Professor Lembridge. I have two of the letters with me. May I ask, what did Mrs. Hilfgott request from you when she first inquired?"

She was taking a chance on not alerting him to her larger game.

"It was a tease," Lembridge answered. "She said she had three letters from the 1864 period, one of them signed by John Wilkes Booth himself. She claimed to have had an evaluation done by somebody local but wanted confirmation of provenance and signature authentication. Haven't heard from her since."

"And would you still be in a position to provide that service?"

Lembridge's curiosity seemed to win out over his annoyance. "As I told the consul general, yes, I can do it quickly. For a fee. I don't have a spectrometer at the house but I can do a good job with what I have. If need be, we can take it to the Archives labs over in Harpers Ferry. Why only two?"

"Two letters?" Alice said. "That's all she sent us. But the package includes the one signed by Booth. I can leave both of them with you for a few days, if needed."

This sweetened the pot and she felt him lower his guard. She counted on him inferring that Nicola Hilfgott was no longer in the picture. She was sure that she could read him: he was about to ask whether she trusted him with letters that could be very valuable on the autograph market. It was the beginning of the alpha-male flirtation dance, she could tell.

She certainly wanted to know the market value of the letters — more than anything else — but she held back. Instead, she suggested that she drive down to his house that evening. He dictated an address and invited her to dinner.

To clinch his commitment, she said, "I can stay for a couple of hours if you want to examine the papers on the spot and give me your recommendation. By the way, there is an honorarium paid by the embassy, as well as your invoicing for your authentication fee."

His voice shifted to full seduction mode. "Sure. I'll take the honorarium but forget my fee, I'm glad to do it. International comity, and all that. My wife is away but I'll rustle up some appetizers and a bottle of the local white."

Well, at least now she knew what to expect. She wasn't in the mood to be seduced but she would do whatever she had to do. Lord knew, she had done it all before.

She took down the street address, said goodbye and entered the coordinates into the GPS. The trip took her all day and even with the course set electronically, she got lost a few times. Bypassing Baltimore, she spun directly south onto the highways leading to D.C. and Chesapeake Bay.

As darkness eased through the western sky, displacing the retreating light of day, she imagined Washington big and bright ahead of her, though she failed to see any landmarks. She knew that she had entered Civil War country. It was a mark of her joy at finally being in America that she resolved to read a history or two of the devastating war. She experienced a fleeting thrill: she would like to become an American.

Unknown to Alice, the armoury she had remarked on in Springfield had been the centre of rifle and small-arms production for the Union through much of the conflict. Now, the boyhood home of John Wilkes Booth lay just a few miles off to her left. She was entering territory that a million soldiers had traversed on their way to battle. She remained unaware of these facts but did feel the presence of the battlefields around her. She understood that she was circled by ghosts.

The towns on the Chesapeake peninsula bore names like Prince Frederick and Scotland. The Brits and the Yanks had always been great globetrotters, naming their local towns after exotic foreign locations, even when the label made little sense. Her atlas showed Utica, Rome, Batavia, Syracuse, and Ithaca, and that was just in New York State.

She passed through Dunkirk and Bristol and Lothian, silent, bucolic towns. The final leg of her marathon, made in darkness on mostly empty roads, took her along the main street of Chesapeake Beach. Cheap hotels and seafood restaurants lined the route. Newer hotels had been erected right at the harbour's edge; coming closer, she understood that these were in fact residences, probably condominiums, although she didn't quite grasp the North American condo concept. She hoped to arrive at Lembridge's place well after sundown, in order to lessen the risk of being seen on the roads near his house.

Exhausted, she pulled into a broad, asphalted area by a seaside walkway that itself belonged to a new hotel. She parked and walked to the edge of the sea along a wood-slatted path. She looked out on the Intercoastal Waterway, although the far side wasn't visible from the deck, even with her hyperacute vision. On her right, a narrow dock probed out into the bay. She impulsively decided to walk out to the end, to the last tethered sailboat. As soon as she started, something extraordinary happened. Alice had always feared water; there was little of it in the state of Bihar except during the monsoon floods, but then it was a living, killing force. She had never been on a boat. When Jack saved Rose in *Titanic*, she had cried, as much from fear and nausea as joy. And, of course, there was her uncle's garage. Now, she padded along the slender quay and felt the sea calming around her, somehow granting her dominion over the water, over the slow tide that was arriving to her call. She looked up and imagined she hovered above the water, not like in the Bible story, but as a flying, ruling sea bird, not a petrel nor a heron, but Vishnu in one of her shape-shifting tricks. She reached the end of the dock, touched the last boat for luck, and turned back, ready for the next phase of her life.

CHAPTER 17

Lembridge's house stood on an upward slope off a dirt road a few miles in from the harbour, a chalet in what Alice imagined to be a Swiss style. A light beckoned in a big front room behind floor-to-ceiling windows. The house was isolated from the main road. Her first thought — a sign of her stress — was that she could kill Lembridge, if necessary, without anyone hearing from down by the entrance to the driveway.

She was sure, from his voice and her experience with men, that Lembridge would be alone.

The reliable Ford made little noise as she slid up the path onto the parking pad, the crunching of the tires blending with the background crickets. Still, Lembridge must have noticed, for his silhouette darkened the big window and she felt him looking down at her. She turned off the motor. The letters were in folders in a bag in the boot of the Ford and she retrieved them. She took her time, thinking that keeping him waiting gave her an edge. She was operating on instinct.

He waited on the top deck as she climbed the freshly painted stairs. Lounge chairs were lined up along the platform and the glowing central room inside looked inviting. Without speaking, he ushered her into the big room. A Labrador retriever lounged by the unused hearth and the professor had positioned candles, as yet unlit, across the mantelpiece. It was a cliché seduction scene.

"Miss Cameron," he said, and reached to take the folder with the letters. She let him.

He was between forty and forty-five, she estimated, a crucial time when a man tries to mould his image for mature middle age and often gets told by his ageing body that his ideal may be unsustainable. But he was doing pretty well at it. His jaw was set nicely and his brow remained unwrinkled. He razor-cut his hair and he was still lean; a jogger. The moustache should go — it made him look artificially older and close to avuncular — but he was at ease in his T-shirt and linen slacks, and he moved with the *savoir faire* of a naturally graceful man in his own home.

She had wrapped her pashmina scarf around herself before leaving the car. She hadn't worn it since Montreal. She did so now in order to give him something to hang up, and to demonstrate that she had kept her ethnic links, unashamedly. She may not have matched the image of an embassy functionary but she knew that she looked good, exotic. Her form was trim, compelling men to fantasize about unwrapping her. Her skin was flawless, except for the pair of small marks under each breast.

Alice found that she was most alluring to men when she was initially reticent, forcing them to come on to her, and she played it that way now. She kept silent in order to make him speak first.

"I am sorry to drag you all the way down here," he said. "Come in, relax."

She became business-like. "Professor, I don't claim to know much about the two documents, or the Civil War generally, but we are told that you are the man who can help us. Could you look at them now?"

This was repetitive of their phone conversation but he pretended not to notice and showed no surprise or urgency. She opened the cardboard folders in which the letters were preserved under translucent glassine covers. Food smells wafted from the open kitchen at the far end of the big room. He had prepared appetizers. He handed her a flute of white wine and took the material to the dining room table, placing the pages under the glare of the wrought-iron chandelier. The ensnarement proceeded.

"Well, first of all, these are extraordinary, it's obvious," he said almost immediately, real interest entering his voice. "They are undoubtedly from the period." He continued to read. "Besides, who would fake pieces of obscure history like this?"

In her brief exposure to Americans in England, India, and Pakistan, Alice had noticed their tendency to disparage anything that did not bear directly upon the United States, and the documents were perhaps more sacred to Canada's history than America's. She continued to wonder about the professor: would he manufacture excuses, attempting to minimize their historical import and their commercial value? She resolved to observe him closely when the question of market price came up.

But if his integrity as a historian was battling with the obscurity of the subject matter, his professionalism won out. He waved his head back and forth in appreciation.

"Extraordinary."

She smiled and tried to appear collected. It was time to make a move, to redirect his perspective onto the question of forgery. She had seen many faked religious scrolls on sale in the Patna bazaar when her father took her there as a child and she knew scepticism was a wise policy. She came to the table and leaned over the single page. "What will it take to authenticate them, Professor?"

Jasmine scent from the pashmina floated around her sleek hair. For the moment, he was too entranced by the documents to be diverted. Quickly retrieving an old-fashioned magnifying glass, he examined the Booth letter. It took him five minutes.

He stood back from the light.

"It's real. It's a shame you don't have the third piece. Consul Hilfgott told me it's from the head of British forces in Canada to Commissioner Thompson, and it references the Booth letter."

"I wouldn't know." Alice remembered bits of the content from

Johnny, and from her haphazard glances at the originals. She couldn't admit any of that to Lembridge. She changed tack again. "How much would a single letter be worth in the current market?"

Perhaps she was too eager, or mercenary, in her tone, for he gave her a wry look. "Gee, I don't know, Miss Cameron. But doesn't Mrs. Hilfgott want them for their heritage value? To complete the record, she said?"

Hilfgott's still a bitch, Alice wanted to say. But Miss Cameron said, "I'm just intrigued. I don't know what she wants. I remain a loyal servant of Her Majesty."

Alice unbuttoned the top of her blouse and retreated to an over-stuffed divan closer to the cold fireplace. The dog hadn't moved since her arrival, but now it raised its head and watched her, perhaps sensing that she hated dogs. She pretended to lose interest in the letters. She sprawled back onto the divan in a Dietrich pose from *Shanghai Express* and scanned the room with a bored look to signal she wanted him to pick up the pace. He might consider her quixotic and shallow, it didn't matter to her. Keep him off balance until he revealed his estimate of the letters' value; that was her main purpose.

She saw no downside to flirting. There was always a chance that she wouldn't do him; she told herself that she still had that option. She could walk away.

Her wine glass was empty. Six ounces of wine had almost knocked her out and her mind wandered as he still refused to move away from the table. To flatter him she shot him looks that were appreciative of his decorating taste — she bet that he would take credit for his wife's decisions — although the carved wooden ducks hanging in flying formation from the peak of the cathedral ceiling and the rough miniatures on the mantel of fishermen, complete with rods with strings attached, repelled her. The Sword had given her a taste for European Modern. She went and poured herself more wine. She wanted to leave but knew that she was locked in to her fate for the night. It wouldn't be so bad; the chalet at least provided a hiding place from the police.

"I'm right!" he said, turning to her. He walked over to the divan, took the white wine bottle from her and hoisted it like a boy with a trophy. "They *are* valuable. They add to the historical record. Your Madam Hilfgott was spot on. They're important to the history of all three countries. Aren't I the ecumenical one."

Not really, she thought. *Don't condescend to me, Professor, with expressions like "spot on."* Impatience began to overwhelm her. She hoped for a tough-minded partner for the next stage of her plan but if he didn't get to the money question soon, she would leave and take her chances — with Greenwell, maybe.

He continued. "The Booth letter shows that he had a broader view of the benefits that could flow from attacking the Union presidency itself. Scholars believe Booth only focused on his little kidnapping plot. New research has connected him to the Signal Corps, the spy network run by the Confederacy. This letter indicates he was capable of embracing innovative strategies and working with the Confederate commissioners in Canada."

I'm bored fucking stiff, Alice thought. She borrowed the wine bottle. He would get there at his own pace, she knew, although they might arrive at sex and the money answer at the same moment.

Lembridge prattled on boyishly. "The second letter is important, too. It shows that Thompson could have met Booth. That's a breakthrough. Until now, it was believed they never interacted in Montreal."

That was enough for Alice. She went over to the mantel and lit a wooden match. Lembridge fell silent as she fired the wicks of the seven squat candles. (She considered setting fire to the dog.) When she started back to her seat, the professor stood up and stopped her and lightly kissed her. She held him away with her flat palm.

Keep him off beam, that was the ticket. "Not so fast, Professor. Can you put a value on the Booth item? You said you would."

"Can I ask you a question first?"

"I would rather you put a price on the letters."

They scribed a slow dance around one another in the centre of the big room. She broke off and walked to the window, and then circled around to the divan. He backed away and began to pace parallel to the big window. He made to speak — always the lecturer — but she jumped in to preempt him and maintain control.

"You want to know my interest in these rare documents. Am I right?" said Alice.

He smiled and stopped pacing. "I want to know if you are really from the D.C. embassy," he parried.

She turned off the swag lamp that hung in the centre of the panelled room below the squadron of ducks and then did the same with the chandelier over the dining room table, leaving only the candles for light. There was a goatskin rug directly in front of the hearth; unfortunately, the dog lay on it. Didn't that curtain of fur ever move? They would have to do it on the divan.

Alice then positioned herself centrally in the big room, creating an on-stage effect, and the expectation of a performance. She stayed motionless for a long minute and looked him in the eye, fixing him in place against the giant window. She concealed that she found all this ludicrous. He was handsome enough, in a self-absorbed way, but Alice hadn't fallen in love in years and it wouldn't be this man — the professor with a wife somewhere out there in the night. She glanced at the fireplace; one of the candles seemed to her at risk of tumbling onto the dog. That would get rid of the cur, she thought. She undid all the buttons of the blouse. She slipped out of her slacks and socks. Another girl might have paused and struck a pose in her lingerie but Alice swiftly took off the last items and kicked them away. Then she did pose, turning so that the candle shadows caught her curves and perfect, odalisque proportions.

When to ask again about the money?

Her movements added up to a carefully constructed test, one she had made work before with men. How he reacted would tell her a lot about her prospective new partner in crime. If he hesitated, he would break the mood and prove himself unreliable. If he tried to imitate her blithe strip act, self-mockery would set in and he would

166

reveal himself as too adolescent, too soft to pull off the scam she had in mind.

But Lembridge went for the experienced-older-man act. He slowly disrobed and beckoned her to him, so that they ended up body-to-body in front of the window. He was backlit by the side-long glow of the postern lamp down by the driveway entrance. She gave him credit: the voyeurism of it electrified the mood, making his skilled gropings exciting.

Alice liked sex, even if she was usually selling her act while doing it. This night she was weary and, now in his arms, remembered that she had slept no more than three hours at a stretch over the past three days. But the professor knew what to do and she was grateful that he was the one to figure out how to shoo the dog from the rug. He picked up Alice in his arms and nudged the retriever away with his foot. It dutifully got up and trotted off to a bedroom almost as if, it occurred to Alice, he had been in this situation before.

The sex lasted no more than half an hour and the professor was rough. They rolled off the scratchy goat rug several times and at one point resumed screwing under the pergola at the back of the house. But Lembridge was no rougher than some cricketers and one footballer she could have mentioned, and she ended up surprisingly content and sleepy in front of the stone fireplace, the man lying parallel to her.

But money was a better aphrodisiac. Dollar signs wafted into her reverie. She got up and went to the kitchen for a Perrier, leaving the light off. He called from the main room and asked if she wanted some cold wine. She stage-whispered, "No," to keep the hushed afterglow in place, and walked silently, still naked, back into the main room. She tossed back the rest of the water, making sure that some spilled down her breasts and caught the candle shine. She came and sat next to him but he got up and retrieved a woven caftan for her, another for himself. They looked like hippies. She was lost in the robe but did her best to appear debauched.

Some men went to sleep afterwards but Lembridge was the kind who had to talk — to continue to show off. He anticipated her next question.

"So, you want me to estimate the value of the documents. On the market, that is."

"Tell me more about them first. *Why* are they valuable to someone?" she said, stroking his cheek.

"These letters will send a shock wave through the community of Civil War buffs. No one knew they existed. But it's the collectors we should concern ourselves with. On the open market, the competition will be between the private collectors and the National Archives here in Washington. By my estimate, the money value is in the Booth *signature*, flavoured by the fact that it references, obliquely but clearly, the Lincoln assassination. But for the Archives all three letters are important historical artifacts, and they'll bid high to get them. You know, the most famous rare documents in the Booth story are the missing pages from his diary, which he kept while on the run after killing Lincoln. The rumour is that the secretary of war, Edwin Stanton, later tore out the pages because they incriminated top members of the administration in the plot to kill the president. Well, if the collectors can't have the diary, this will be the next-best sensation."

"Does this mean the Canadian archives people will want to buy the letters, too? For 'historical' reasons?"

He smiled again at her. She knew then that he would try for a second round of sex.

"For sure," the professor continued, academia trumping libido for the moment. "And that presents us with a problem. Who owns the letters — and I include the third one, wherever it is — and can that ownership be traced through legitimate buyers? Does the Booth family have a claim? We Yanks are a litigious bunch. There are competing international interests. Hilfgott bought the letters but that doesn't mean she's the legit owner."

His ramble was really an invitation for her to fill in the blanks. They were at a turning point. The unasked question hung in the air up there with the hovering ducks.

"She doesn't own them now," Alice said.

"Then maybe we should find them a brand new owner," he said, recognizing that they had entered new territory.

"Private collector?" she immediately said.

Lembridge held back for a minute. "First, tell me about Hilfgott's source."

"A dealer in rare documents in Montreal. He told me he found two of the letters in an attic in Montreal. He wouldn't say where he got the third one."

Alice could tell from the professor's look that he believed that she had slept with Greenwell, too. She might have explained that Greenwell was gay but she said nothing. She looked him in the eye again. The story about the attic wasn't remotely believable.

"You want to know the value?" he said.

She nodded and let the caftan slip to her waist. He proceeded. "There are rich men out there ready to purchase an assassin's signature, even if they don't get to put the letter on public display. The Booth letter should go for $80,000, as high as a hundred, maybe. But we need to find the right buyer."

Nearly a fortune. Added to the Canadian cash in her pink rucksack, she might have enough. *This country is so big*, she realized; *I might just be able to disappear.* She cuddled up to Lembridge once more. She was pleased. He had said "we." They were partners. Co-conspirators.

As she disrobed again, she murmured, "Can you find the right man?"

"I have someone in mind."

Afterwards, she took another glass of Chardonnay and stood, starkers, by the big window. There wasn't much to see in the darkness but the insects and bats. The smell of evergreens called up her earlier imaginings. She wondered if she could disappear and take up a new life here on the Chesapeake.

"Is this a good place to live?" she said, staying by the window.

Lembridge was subdued and fell back into his patronizing

professor's tone. "It's a perfect spot to live. Maybe the most beautiful place in the country. But there are lots of other, different places. It's a cornucopia, America. Have you travelled much since you've been stationed in Washington?"

She would let him think she really was from the embassy. She turned to answer but saw that he had moved to the far end of the room and had booted up his computer. He hadn't expected a response to his casual question, and he wasn't interested in her credentials. Alice brought him his wine glass and watched over his shoulder. He was on the site of the American Academy of Forensic Sciences. She knew few academics but she knew men, and understood that another display of male assertiveness was coming. She struggled to smile; she was uneasy. She yearned to lock in the deal.

"I was just checking," Lembridge said. "If we want to keep this thing hush-hush, we shouldn't use the Archives Lab in West Virginia or the FBI labs at Quantico. But the University of Virginia in Charlottesville has what I need and they'll leave me alone with the spectrometer."

He concentrated on the screen and when the dog ambled in to be patted he ignored it. Watching over his shoulder, she found nothing comprehensible on the website home page, only references to "electrostatic detection apparatus" and "digital image processing," and the like.

Finally, he said what she needed to hear. "I know a collector in Rochester, New York. Name of Ronald Crerar."

Alice let him play online and went to her crumpled clothes by the fireplace. She took John Carpenter's phone out of her pocket and flipped it open. She hadn't dared make calls with it but now she was glad that she had held on to it. It had a sophisticated camera function — she had made sure to delete the pictures Johnny had taken of her — and, in the dim light from the row of candles, she set the flash to maximum; she hoped there would be enough light.

Lembridge exhaled dramatically and turned away from the terminal. He hummed to himself and called over the retriever. Alice came over and joined him in scratching the dog's head and muttering to it. Of all the unpleasant things she had done that evening, sucking up to the dog may have been the hardest. Her twitch had come back, and she feigned a seductive gait as she fetched another bottle of wine, hoping her tremor didn't show. Calmer now, she returned and, showing Lembridge the phone, she gestured for him to move aside. By the light of the computer monitor, she snapped two quick shots of the Labrador. She was merely testing the exposure, although she continued to coo to the animal. By the second click of the digital flash the dog had moved out of frame, but by then Alice had confirmed that she had enough light for the clear portrait she wanted.

She pointed the mobile phone at Lembridge, who was still naked. *No man likes his picture taken in the nude, unless he is a pervert,* she thought, and Lembridge was, in her dismissive lexicon, nothing but a typical horny heterosexual male with a patronizing attitude. He cringed and waved her away with a laugh. But Alice knew what she was doing. Before he could fully react, she snapped a full frontal shot of the professor. He started forward to seize the phone but thought better of it. *The son of a bitch is hoping for more sex,* Alice thought.

She knew where the professor lived and worked and the cell phone photo could reach his wife anytime Alice chose. She possessed a useful new weapon but was unsure of her next move. She was willing to leave the two letters with him, since they had to be conclusively authenticated before they could be sold, but she remained wary of him. She reiterated the arrangement, just to be clear. He would locate the buyer — the man in Rochester — and they would split fifty-fifty. Lembridge nodded his assent.

Alice wanted to put her clothes back on but nakedness was a good way to keep him hooked for a few more minutes. Instead, she asked to use the computer. He watched her as she sat down in front of the blue-lit monitor. She quickly checked one of her email accounts, the one that only her mother's nursing home knew about. She was paying a nurse attendant at the home to provide forthright reports at the end of every month on her mother's condition. The August report contained nothing alarming, only that her mother had been asking when her eldest daughter would be visiting.

Next, Alice scanned the websites of the British papers for any significant news on Bihar, or — the subject she dreaded — cricket. Nothing new about India emerged, but the cricket matches had started at Lord's among British, Pakistani, and Indian teams and she checked out the scores in the sport sections of the *Times* and the *Guardian*. She was looking for something special and ignored the match results, which held no interest. With deepening trepidation, she called up the *News of the World* site. "Cricket Scandal!" was blazoned across multiple shots of a party in a hotel room. The *News* had busted three star players. The feature ran four full pages of the tabloid. In the photos, three Pakistani players and a girl were identifiable in the foreground.

The girl was Alice.

Alice had a prepaid subscription to the *News of the World* and she inputted her account code and password so that she could read the full text of the day's news and call up past editions. She found other, smaller photos of the party room, supplemented with candid shots of the accused Pakistani cricketers in old matches, along with their Cricket Council identity portraits. Alice wasn't named anywhere in the body of the feature. The hotel, a posh place in Mayfair where she had stayed that one night, wasn't named either. The article was brutal. The scandal had progressed much further than she had expected. The three cricket stars were accused of throwing a match at a test back in April. The day the *News* released the scorching story, the Asian Cricket Council suspended the three players. A Scotland Yard spokesman stated that his office would be investigating. Alice's sense of dread increased. It would not take long for the police and the editors to determine her identity.

The betting syndicate had been suckered by the *News* sting and now they must be panicking. They would never trust Alice to keep quiet, even though she would never give evidence to the police. Alice's boss, her master the Sword, must be in a fury. In its overall impact as a news story the feature was diffuse but heavy with implications for her safety. Whatever the public scandal, which likely would result in life suspensions for the Pakistani players, the danger to Alice was disproportionately greater.

The Sword would try everything to get rid of her.

Lembridge had wandered to the kitchen to make coffee — she could smell it — and now he approached her from behind, coffee mugs exuding steam. Like her, he was still nude, and now it all seemed filthy, inappropriate to Alice, a wretched mistake. Her clothes lay across the room by the hearth. She was tempted to whirl and knock the coffee into his crotch. Killing the internet browser with a keystroke, she got up slowly, feeling completely exposed, and shook her head to the proffered mug.

He saw the change in her and he managed to restrain his ego and his erection. He watched her cross the room and knew this tryst was over. She seemed almost deadly in her coldness.

She dressed in two minutes flat and made for the Booth letters on the dining room table.

"Where the hell do you think you're going with those?" he said.

"I have to leave." She put the papers in their folders and then said, "The deal is off."

She sized up Lembridge. He wasn't stupid. It had been about money from the start. He had liked her because she was reckless and wanton, and he craved some excitement in his life. He wanted the cash as well, and she bet it wasn't the first time he had steered Lincoln memorabilia the way of a rich collector rather than to a public archive. He let her go out through the sliding door to the deck. She seemed glacial, asexual now.

Alice avoided looking at him as she rushed down the steps from the balcony. She ran to the car, aware that he was following. Realizing that she was actually leaving, he reached out to grab her. She twisted around and spat at him, "Don't. And don't tell anyone about any of this. Or your wife gets the pose with your dick at attention. Thanks for the wine."

That was her last moment of bravado. She began to sob as soon as she got into the Ford. The crickets and birds had fallen silent; the night now held only terrors. How could she have deluded herself with this fantasy of disappearing into postcard America? She had drawn a mental painting of her sanctuary, somewhere in a house on the edge of a forest but with the smell of the sea to remind her of her twisted journey to find peace.

She had imagined Rose at the end of the movie, when the RMS *Carpathia* rescued her and brought her home to the United States. Rose might have settled in a place like this: rode horses on the beach, learned to sail, started a new life. Alice possessed three passports. As Alice Nahri, British citizen, she had journeyed to Montreal. As Alice Nahri, citizen of India, she could return to Bihar, though she knew it was too late.

In her mind's sketch she had given no name to the woman on the edge of the forest. But now, as Alida Nahvi, the girl in the third passport, her reinvention of herself in America would be her final transformation.

CHAPTER 18

Alice sped north on the twisty two-lanes, homing in on Annapolis. She ignored the quaint "Welcome" plaques on the edge of each village and the billboards trying to sell her seaside bliss. Drying her tears on her sleeve she fixed her gaze and her fevered mind on the vacant highway ahead. Self-preservation conjured up a plan that arrived almost fully formed. Oh, she had always organized her calculations around a vanishing act of some kind but now it would be a Plan B disappearance, not quite the first happy ending she had envisioned. She would extinguish her British self. Alice, named for Orwell's mother but also Lewis Carroll's little girl, would die in the rabbit hole. It all made her sad; she had been running so long. But if there was a positive glimmer on the horizon, it was the chance she still had of merging with anonymity into the heartland of the America she imagined. She knew where she would go.

Her mistake was to assume that Annapolis was bigger than it was. She reasoned that a state capital positioned at the top of something labelled the Intercoastal Waterway would be a sailors' town, and sailors usually meant prostitutes. She planned to scan for street-walkers down by the docks. She wasn't using the GPS for now but the green road signs all pointed to the city core, and she hoped to use

175

the masts of ships to guide herself to the harbour. But it turned out that Annapolis wasn't that kind of port; perhaps farther up or down the coast, but not here. She cruised slowly down the quiet access streets to the waterfront and found only restaurants, T-shirt shops, and hotels, all closed down for the night. She saw no one at all. She felt stupid for fantasizing images of a whaling port out of Melville.

She pulled back from the water and stopped at the next fast-food parking lot. Even the all-night pizza joint was shuttered. Until now, she had kept the GPS turned off. She had used it intermittently to reach Lembridge's house but she knew that the device contained a complete record of her travels. Police and immigration officials would find it interesting. Employing it now, with her lethal plan forming, was sketchy but she had no choice. The solution would be to take the whole unit with her when she ditched the car; let the cops puzzle over why it hadn't been left in the vehicle.

She programmed it in now and set the centre of Washington as her destination.

Still, she had no idea where to look for a prostitute in D.C. Even more challenging was finding a girl with the requisite skin colour and body type. The capital was only an hour away on Route 50; already, signs presented alternative routes to the downtown. New panic churned in her stomach. There were few cars on the road. She had to make a decision in the next ten minutes. She pulled into a rest stop and examined the atlas; a helpful insert map of Washington showed Route 50 intersecting with something called the Anacostia Freeway at the north end of the city. With no one neighbourhood appearing more promising than any other, she reprogrammed the GPS. It offered several choices for "Anacostia" and she plugged in the "River" setting.

Her entry into urban Washington began bizarrely. The navigation program channelled her onto a six-lane "parkway" but gave no hint of the size or feel of this route. It turned out that elegant trees flanked the road and a wall constructed of yellow stones lined the edge of her southbound lane. It was all very pastoral and not what she antici-pated. Worse, she couldn't see any houses or urban avenues from the sheltered parkway. When she caught sight of an overhead sign for "Anacostia Park" she took the first exit, ignoring the complaints from the GPS voice. This was better. She took the next turn into a dense grid of streets and immediately saw that this was a poor, predominantly black area. The houses were shabby, though not totally run down, and the gritty streets held a threatening quality. She saw a pair of men exchanging packets of drugs in a side lot. A string of two-storey warehouses held promise for what she needed but she cruised the row without spying any hookers. A couple of solitary men walking fast along the pavement eyed her dusty car. She wondered if they knew rental plates from owner plates and what they would conclude if they did. She had yet to see any women at all.

She noticed the orange glow of lights at the distant end of one of the wider thoroughfares and veered in that direction. She slowed the Ford to fifteen miles per hour. The Anacostia River remained her favoured destination but she had no idea where to find it. As she wandered the undifferentiated streets, increasing her exposure with every minute, she began to understand that the neighbourhood was a self-contained square, framed by several large bridges that she glimpsed from time to time. She headed towards the bright lights, reasoning that they marked a major bridge crossing. She had to try. There would be streetwalkers there or there wouldn't.

Alice found what she wanted before she met up with the bridge. The neighbourhood had not quite degenerated to the point where there were burned-out houses or congregations of men smoking ganja on street corners, but Alice remained hopeful of finding a working girl. Turning up and around the right-angle grid in a hairpin pattern in the hope of locating the orange lights, she finally discovered a dark avenue that ran close by the river. A grassy berm blocked any view of the water but she could sense it off to the right, while ahead the street appeared to run right under the lit-up bridge. It looked promising. A streetlight four hundred yards dead ahead provided enough illumination that any hookers would be noticed by cruising johns, without it all being too blatant.

Alice stopped the Ford in the shadows, invisible. She turned off the engine, got out and opened the back. She took out the tire iron. Then she opened the rear door to verify that a snoop looking through a window wouldn't see anything memorable in the back seat. Leonardo DiCaprio and Kate Winslet smiled at her from the pink rucksack. She would have to ditch the bag soon; for now she thought, *what the hell*, and left it where it was. She got back in the car, started it up again, and drove towards the pool of light.

She made out the two mannequin shapes ahead and rolled slowly up the avenue — she wanted the girls, on her first pass, to dismiss her as a prospective client. The closest girl, who stood just out of the streetlight's circle, seemed promising to Alice — Alida, now — a typical prostitute, suspicious of eye and anxious for business. Alice watched her reaction. She checked off Alice as a stupid, lost girl, dumb enough maybe to stop and ask for directions. Alice glanced at her without slowing and moved past the second girl, who scowled from the grass fringe. This one was all wrong, chubby and dressed in a short skirt, with glazed, middle-distance eyes, indicating heavy drug use. Alice frowned. Neither woman qualified as *apsara*, the celestial consorts of Hindu myth. The *apsara* were shape-shifting beings who were associated with water and were the patronesses of gamblers. It was too much to hope for.

As she passed under the street lamp and made a sharp left turn, Alice pondered whether the first girl would do. She was darker than Alice, and wore her hair longer, but she was roughly the same height and weight. Alice sensed the night hours ebbing away.

When the car stopped next to her, the first hooker did nothing. She waited for the passenger-side window to open. Far up ahead, the second girl noted the car but it was dark and she couldn't be sure that it was the same sedan that had just passed. The first girl keyed into the fact that it was the dumb-ass woman again. Alice let the window down halfway so that the girl could not quite put her head inside the car. The hooker crossed the wet grass fringe and leaned close to the window. She saw that the driver was dark, maybe Pakistani, she thought, and she was immediately suspicious. Had she bothered to mark the Canadian plates she might have held back.

"What kind of fool are you, lady? You think some sisterhood is going to protect you on this beat?"

The girl was a better body double than Alice had first thought. She had to get the hooker into the car. Alice lowered her voice. "Hi. I'm looking for . . ."

"You looking for what, sugar?"

"Service."

She took out Carpenter's billfold, making sure the girl saw the wad. She removed two hundreds, in fact, most of her American cash; the rest was still in multicoloured Canadian bills.

The sight of the money lessened the prostitute's misgivings. She adjusted her bra and tightened the sash around her waist in greedy anticipation.

"What kind of service?" the girl said, preparing to control the transaction by naming a firm price.

Alice pressed a button to bring the window all the way down. She rubbed the two bills together and said, "You can fuck me for two hundred dollars."

The hooker gasped. This bitch was kinked out. Leaning through the window, she sized up the risk. The Pakistani bitch was a sicko — why else would this lesbo cruise Anacostia Park? — but she was no danger to anyone yet. The hooker judged that she could handle the woman. She had her gun, a Lorcin .380 that fit nicely in her clutch bag. Her pimp liked the tiny guns because they were cheap and universally available on the black market, and the girls liked them because they made a big, scary bang. The hooker had never fired her gun and was unaware of its tendency to foul and otherwise break down. She liked it, light as it was, because she had confidence that she could always get close; slap that barrel up against a client's head and the bullet would rattle around his skull like a pinball.

Alice made a move to slide the crisp hundreds into her own bra, a gesture both inviting and potentially dismissive. It told the prostitute that it was her decision to make. The hooker tried to open the passenger door but found it locked, and Alice opened it with a button in the armrest. The girl got inside and turned to look her free-spending client over. She caught sight of the pink bag in the back, with two vaguely familiar faces painted on the front panel. Was that Leo, Leonardo DiCaprio? Yes, it was! She had seen him the week before in that new movie *Inception*. Alice caught her looking and turned as if to lift the rucksack over the headrest. This move brought her close to the girl and her mint breath. But Alice never got to the bag. As she subsided back in the driver's seat, she swung the tire iron in a smooth movement against the back of the hooker's skull, with a force calculated to stun without killing.

The prostitute crumpled forward in the passenger seat, her forehead just avoiding the dash. Alice held the bar above the girl's head. She gurgled a couple of times, moaned, and collapsed against the door. Hitting her again was the wrong thing to do, Alice judged. If the hooker woke up, Alice would club her a second time but she hoped to avoid getting blood on the upholstery. If she managed to run the Ford off one of those bridges — only one of her scenarios — the blood might not matter but she increasingly had reservations about that plan. If this had been London, one or more of thousands of cameras would have caught her on any given bridge. Even though America — even its national capital — might not be so scrupulous, the bridges she had seen so far appeared too exposed.

The girl moaned again and shivered, a bad sign: she might have a messy seizure in the car. Alice knew she had to move. She eased the Ford down the avenue but turned left at the first corner, leaving the second streetwalker farther along puzzling over her rival's new client.

The side street was deserted and there were no overhead lamps, so Alice risked pulling over. It was easiest to go around to the other side of the vehicle (the shotgun seat, Johnny had called it). She centred the wounded girl so that she appeared to be looking straight ahead; Alice strapped her in with the seat belt. She had stopped moaning, and Alice pulled the cheap fringed sash from around the young woman's waist and wrapped it about her head like a hood. The hooker had coughed up some blood but no open lesions showed on the back of her neck. Alice folded and tucked the scarf in the Indian fashion and tilted back the seat to make it look as if the girl was her sleeping passenger.

Alice beelined towards the next bridge but found herself *under* it with no route onto the span. She would have to keep going and find a way to double back. But when she pulled over and glanced back, she saw that the bridge was lit by fixed lampposts every forty feet or so; it was no place to dump a body. She decided to try the next crossing and continued driving parallel to the river. A hundred yards on, she took a completely wrong turn and ended up again on the Anacostia Parkway; she could see the river receding behind her. All this driving increased the risk of detection by a night owl trucker, or worse, a bored state trooper. She decided to turn around at the next exit.

She met no one on her side of the divided road until a sedan began to pass her in the left lane. The two vehicles were alone on the parkway. As the sedan pulled up parallel to her she saw the decal on the passenger door: "U.S. Park Police." The driver looked over but, not really hesitating, pulled away.

Alice turned at a featureless exit a mile on and followed the ramp to the parking lot of a small power plant, its bulky generators sequestered behind chain-link fencing. Tread marks in the driveway showed that others had turned around here before.

She opened the Rand McNally to the expanded D.C. city map and followed the Anacostia River from the top of the page to where it joined the left branch of the Potomac just south of the capital, and continued to Chesapeake Bay. The hooker sat silent beside her. Any other driver would interpret the scene for what it was: a fellow driver losing her way. Alice moved inch by inch down the river. Her eye caught a narrow strip of white on the map on the far side of one of the bridges, hard by the Anacostia, and she considered its suitability as a disposal site. To be thorough, she traced the river down to a third bridge, where she encountered an installation labelled "Anacostia Naval Annex." Anything military in nature was to be avoided in this post-9/11 world; also, she saw that if she crossed the last of the bridges she would be forced into the city, close to Capitol Hill. She went back to the white blotch and decided to give it a try.

She examined the tiny notation next to the white spot: "Eastern Yacht Club." Most promising was its location right on the water. She might be able to organize the body in some secluded spot and roll it into the river.

The hooker didn't wake up. Alice judged that she was close to dead, or had already expired. Without employing the GPS, she found the northern entrance to Anacostia Drive and at once spotted the bridge to the far side of the river. She followed the signs onto the vaulting span. It was under reconstruction, with plastic cones lining the road, and there was no possibility of stopping to heave a body into the river. Temporary signage had been tacked up everywhere. One sign read, "John Philip Sousa Bridge, secondary access ahead." Another arrow vaguely pointed the way to Robert F. Kennedy Memorial Stadium on the far shore. A chill ran through her: he was the president — but no, Johnny Carpenter had been named after JFK, the brother, the actual president.

Yet another sign promised an efficient turnaround over to the Navy Yard, which lay downriver on her map. Alice had no way of knowing that she was on the Potomac Bridge (both branches of the river were called the Potomac in 1865) and that John Wilkes Booth had crossed it in his flight from the killing ground at Ford's Theatre.

Almost onto the far shore, she studied a last-chance sign that gave her two choices: turn around and head back to the Naval Annex, or proceed "Downtown." Moving straight ahead on the second tack she noticed a narrow construction road off to the right. She lurched onto it, the wheels grinding into the gravel surface.

And there it was. The sign she wanted, nailed to a telephone pole, beckoned her to the Anacostia Yacht Facility, with an arrow pointing ahead.

She was now running parallel to the water. Two SUVs sat by the road and she gathered that construction crewmen used this lane for parking. She would have to watch out for traffic, especially security patrols. But for now the farther section of the road remained empty and she soon found the yacht club lot, also vacant at this time of the morning. She pulled in and parked, angling the Ford towards the river.

The girl hadn't moved from her original position. Alice came around to the passenger side and leaned over the body, not certain she was dead. She hefted the iron bar, ready to strike again. When it proved unnecessary she dragged the girl out of the seat and onto the gravel, managing to turn the hooker about so that she sat leaning against the front wheel. Moving to the boot of the Ford, Alice used the key to open it. She thought about replacing the tire iron but she saw that it had blood and hair on it; she was strong enough to hurl it about fifteen feet out into the water and she did so now without hesitation. Returning to the rear of the car, she took out a plastic jug of windshield washer antifreeze. She crouched down by the girl and opened the container, careful not to get fluid on her own slacks. Pushing her left hand inside the black girl's slack mouth, Alice used two fingers to wedge open the throat, at the same time levering the head back in a crude parody of a sun worshipper's pose. The jug was full and Alice spilled half of it on the gravel. Holding the gullet open, she managed to pour several ounces down the hooker's throat. She replaced the jug in the back of the car.

A few yards beyond the parking lot stood a clapboard house, once a harbour master's residence. It remained entirely dark. The Stars and Stripes and a marine flag drooped from a flagpole next to it. She saw no sign of life in the house.

Alice Nahri's plan was all about buying time. If she created enough confusion, the police might believe that the prostitute in the Anacostia was Alice Ida Nahri and stop searching. Her greatest fear was the sunrise. It was now almost 4 a.m. but she had one more bit of misdirection to fabricate. She worked her way between the body and the car's front quarter panel, slipping her arms under the dead woman's armpits. It proved easy to lever up the body this way. She dragged the slumping corpse across the gravel and broken macadam to a section of smooth asphalt only three yards from the river's edge; the final few feet was grass, culminating in a stone retaining wall. She put down the body in a spread-eagle position on its back.

The girl coughed. Alice recoiled backwards and tumbled onto the sharp gravel. Just as swiftly she launched herself forward and fell on top of the stubborn victim. "Bitch!" she hissed.

The fringed scarf had slipped and Alice had to get up from the reanimated hooker to retrieve it, but in seconds she was back straddling the woman and pressing the sash into her throat. She held it there — three, five minutes? — until she was sure.

Dawn was emerging in the eastern sky directly across the channel. The early shift of construction workers might arrive any minute now. Alice stuffed the scarf into her *Titanic* bag in the car. She returned and without ceremony took the hooker's out-flung left arm and turned the hand over, straightening the fingers. She pressed the tips against the pitted asphalt, pushing down on all five together, and drew them across the surface towards herself. She did this several times under the maximum pressure she could generate, scraping until the fingers were grey, bloody sticks. Let the coroner figure that one out, Alice said to herself. She repeated the mutilation on the right hand.

Alice scooped out the contents of the sequined purse: lipstick, condoms, a richly embossed business card from a customer (a reckless one), a roll of American twenties, and the pistol. She couldn't spare the time to count the cash but at least $400 went into Carpenter's billfold. The rest of the junk she left in the purse. She had no use for the gun and decided to throw it into the river with the body from the end of the dock.

In order to drag the corpse the length of the quay without raising a racket, Alice had to remove the girl's spiked heels. She again gripped the corpse under the arms and heaved it backwards along the wooden pier, out to the end. It surprised her that there was no danger light there, no beacon for passing river traffic; it also seemed odd that no boats were moored in either side of the dock. She set the body down and immediately understood her mistake. The river below her was almost a mud flat, not deep enough to drown a rat. She appreciated that the Anacostia was tidal but this was absurd. She came from a dry, barren state in India and knew little about the timing of ebb and flow. How long would it take the eastern arm of the Potomac to refill itself from downriver? She sensed that the tide was rising but at an agonizing rate. And was it possible that the tide would send a body *upstream* in the morning flow?

She had little choice. Eventually the tide would rise and carry the body away, perhaps as far as Chesapeake Bay. She wanted the corpse found but certainly not right away. Five days, even three, in the water would suffice. The emergence of the woman's body in Maryland would halt the search for her in the other forty-nine states and by then Alice would have selected her new, anonymous home. With some gruesome luck, fish and crabs would chew up the corpse and the water would bleach the face and leave its features bloated beyond recognition.

The dead woman hit the muddy soup with more of a splat than a splash and, to Alice's surprise, began to float, face up, in the shallow river. She did not wait for the tide to take it away. She had seen enough burials in the Ganges.

She gathered up the clothes and the girl's purse. She decided not to risk the gun getting stuck in the river mud and put it into her rucksack for the time being. Leaving her British passport under the driver's floor mat, she checked that she had her Indian passport and her European Union papers. For the next stage, she would use her Indian identity. Everything went into the pink bag with $20,000 in Canadian cash. She tossed the car keys into the river. At the last minute she turned back to the Ford and retrieved the portable GPS unit and its dashboard stand; it went into the bag. She recapped the GPS port in the console between the front seats; perhaps they would forget that the hire car had been leased out with the device.

It was still an hour short of sunrise and she walked down the dirt road and up the ramp at the side of the massive bridge without seeing anyone. She was a student or perhaps a young charlady on her way to work. At the rise, she sighted in both directions along M Street. Instead of turning left or right she began to walk directly north. She wanted to clear the nest of elevated carriageways and bridges as soon as possible. At G Street she paused and tossed the scarf, the shoes, and the purse and its contents into a dumpster. She kept the gun and the GPS for now.

She paused to breathe in the freshening pre-dawn air. The fashionable streets were peaceful. She liked this neighbourhood, even though she could never settle in such a high-end community. Off to her right she saw a massive banner that had been strung across the side wall of a school building. In red and blue, it shouted, "Tea Party! Glenn Beck. Restoring Honor to America." She had no idea who Glenn Beck could be — one of the TV evangelists Americans seemed to dote on? — or what the Tea Party was all about, and she did not care.

She did a last check of her picture and name in her new passport. Alice Nahri / Alida Nahvi turned away and began to walk into the heart of Washington, with no fear of anything more the night could offer.

CHAPTER 19

Peter Cammon flew into D.C. in an optimistic mood that approached exhilaration. He had always enjoyed himself in the U.S. capital and had many old friends in the FBI. He took the shuttle in from Washington Dulles International and registered at the Willard Hotel (a place where Abraham Lincoln had often stayed) and quickly grabbed a taxi to the J. Edgar Hoover Building on Pennsylvania Avenue.

He still believed that the key to John Carpenter's murder was his mysterious girlfriend, Alice Nahri, and further that it was a good possibility she was alive and hiding somewhere in the maze of the lower forty-eight states. He was eager to track down the medical examiner at Quantico and review the autopsy results on the woman lying on a cold slab in the FBI mortuary. Protocol, however, required that he touch base with headquarters first and sort out the jurisdictional niceties.

From the lobby of the Hoover Building he was ushered up to the office of Owen Rizeman, a Bureau lifer well known to both Peter and Sir Stephen Bartleben.

"Peter Cammon! Thought you'd retired. Are you here for a job interview? I'll tell the others to sod off. I'll hire you myself."

He beckoned Peter to take a chair, while he positioned himself behind a desk that was covered in memorabilia from a lifetime of service.

Rizeman was sixty. His hair had turned white and he risked becoming the cliché Southern gentleman out of an antebellum movie, with the bluster to match. He ran the Office of Law Enforcement Coordination but Peter had first met him during the Oklahoma bombing case in 1995. Rizeman was the eternal optimist, a force of nature. He had sent Peter a friendly note when he retired.

"Thanks for that offer, Owen," Peter responded, "but driving around the country on the right hand side of the road, well, those days are behind me."

"So, to what do I owe the honour, Peter?" Rizeman said. He knew the reason for Peter's visit but the basics bore repeating.

"Dead body dragged from the Anacostia a few days ago. Woman. Apparent suicide. We need to confirm COD and her identity. Quebec Sûreté have formal jurisdiction over the larger case, which is murder. She's a British national and a fugitive from Canada."

"I get your point, Peter," Rizeman said, "but we need to be a bit careful. The girl died on U.S. territory. Either the Bureau or D.C. police have authority over that matter. We'll have to sort it out. I'm willing to coordinate jurisdiction and smooth the way for you. I do agree that the murder of a Scotland Yard officer within the boundaries of Canada is the more compelling issue. Let me introduce you to the special agent in charge at our end of things."

He pressed a button under his desktop.

While they waited, Peter considered Rizeman's interpretation. Unlike some of his colleagues, Peter had the greatest respect for the Bureau and he had no doubt that Rizeman would extend full cooperation. Sharing wasn't the toughest issue. There could be considerable tension between the FBI and Washington Metro, and Peter was relying on Rizeman to sort out any friction inside the Beltway.

A tall young agent entered the office.

"This is Henry Pastern from our Art Crime Team," Rizeman said.

The young man fit the FBI profile: neat blue suit, clean-shaven, perfect American teeth.

Peter instantly understood how the Bureau regarded this case. They were assuming that the girl had committed suicide. Any offences committed by Alice Nahri — crossing the U.S. border with intent to commit a crime, for example — had become moot with her death. All that remained was the disappearance of the Booth letters. Hence the delegation to Art Crime.

Rizeman rushed the discussion along. "Don't worry about bailiwicks, Peter. There are enough federal dimensions for us to assert our preeminence, if necessary. Henry will drive you over to Quantico to see the girl's body."

Pastern had said nothing beyond "Hello," and appeared nervous. Peter knew that Pastern was wondering why a senior Scotland Yard officer, even a retired one, had been dispatched merely to view a dead body. It was the question Peter had been asking since day one.

"One last thing, Peter," Rizeman said. "Is Alice Nahri an Indian subject as well as British?"

"Dual, likely. That is, two passports. She was travelling on a British passport and we should work towards repatriating her body to the U.K. Only family is her mother and perhaps a sister, and we're trying to locate them."

"Then my ruling is that we proceed with suicide, let the Sûreté take the lead on the Montreal killing, and put the mythical letters on whatever hot list seems appropriate. Nice and neat. Putting it indelicately, Peter, will you be taking the girl's body off our hands this week?"

"As necessary," Peter answered coyly. He now grasped that this was all about containment. The dead girl, it had been ruled, was not an active threat, and most important for Rizeman, never a *terrorist* threat.

Peter accompanied Henry Pastern to the basement of the Hoover complex. Peter liked his earnestness. He stood over six feet and had a distinctive shaved head. At one time, the Bureau wouldn't have allowed a cue ball cut, but anyone would have to admit that Pastern presented the proper buttoned-down image of a purposeful FBI special agent.

Yet it was strange that Pastern had chosen to make his mark in Art Crime. These agents spent their time retrieving paintings and *objets d'art* listed on the National Stolen Art File Index — not exactly pounding the pavement. As for a missing document with an unverified signature, such as the Booth note to Sir Fenwick Williams, the Bureau, like other national forces, hired experts with very specific forensics skills. Peter wondered what credentials Henry Pastern possessed, other than, perhaps, a fine arts degree. He concluded that young Henry was simply playing the angles, initially getting in the door through the Art Crime unit, and now seizing his chance to work a murder case. Street cred was everything in the FBI.

Washington was a humid city and the art of navigating it in early September depended on adroit leaps from air-conditioned office to air-conditioned transport. Retrieval of a Bureau sedan from the basement entailed signing out a vehicle and moving through several layers of security barriers. But in a few minutes the agent had them out onto 10th Street, steering south across Constitution Avenue towards Quantico. Peter was always happy in the U.S. capital and he rubbernecked like a tourist.

Any jitters Henry had from sharing a car with a Scotland Yard chief inspector did not impede his driving, and so Peter felt comfortable launching into a more detailed briefing on the murder of Carpenter. Without expressing an opinion on Alice Nahri's culpability, he emphasized the equally important goals of pursuing both the girl and the letters. Pastern nodded constantly as he wended his way through traffic. As Henry adjusted his grip on the steering wheel to make a turn, Peter discovered a clue to the young man's background. On his left hand he wore a small ring embossed with "CTR." Choose the Right. Pastern was a Mormon. Two of the most famous document forgery cases in U.S. history involved the Mormons: the case of the putative

Mormon Will of Howard Hughes, and the murders committed by Mark William Hofmann, a rare book dealer and counterfeiter of Mormon artifacts. Over the decades, the Bureau had welcomed such straightlaced Mormon recruits as this young man, assured of getting reliability and loyalty. Henry Pastern had opened a logical career door.

"Can I ask you a question, Chief Inspector?" the special agent said, his voice tentative.

Peter was in a benevolent mood. He smiled. "Ask me anything, Special Agent."

In this context, Peter knew, this was neither a right nor a wrong posture towards what was coming. Pastern regarded him as a Sherlock-Holmes-slash-dinosaur and would be hoping for pithy revelations. He must have heard that Peter had worked on the Unabomber, Oklahoma City, and Yorkshire Ripper cases. Peter wondered if Henry Pastern had ever viewed a body on the slab.

"Did you really find the Unabomber?"

"No, it was a team effort, and as you know, his brother finally turned him in and led us to the cabin in Montana."

"But you visited every crime site, *every* place he bombed," Henry said.

"Not exactly. Some of the bombs were on airplanes. Others blew up in places they weren't intended to, or got the wrong target. We tried to figure out, first, who the next target would be and what Kaczynski thought he was likely to achieve. For example, if he sent a bomb through the post, did he care who opened it? Then, when he issued his Manifesto, that told us a huge amount about his preoccupations, his targets. We ran word analysis and text extrapolations on the Manifesto, combined that with a map of both his known targets and the actual locations of the explosions, and then ran regressions to determine his pattern. Then we superimposed it on a map of the country."

The FBI academy taught the Unabomber story to all recruits. The case exemplified the classic manhunt but Peter, enjoying being chauffeured through sunny Washington, decided to add some flavour to the tale — stuff not taught to trainees.

"You know who Brin and Page are?"

"The founders of Google."

"They helped us out a bit. That was in the first year of Google, back before they became billionaires."

Peter sensed that the young agent didn't quite believe him. That was okay with Peter; he was starting to like the earnest young man.

"Chief Inspector, I heard that you worked on Oklahoma City, too."

"That was around the same time. Someone came up with the theory that the Murrah Federal Building bombers and Kaczynski might be connected."

"Well, were they?"

Peter looked off towards the Jefferson Memorial. "No," he lied.

For the first two hours the girl floated face up in the muddy swill. Her body hung up in the shallows. But with the incremental flow of the morning tide the current refloated her and she drifted to the centre of the Anacostia, to begin her fitful journey to Chesapeake Bay. A quarter moon gave some light to the river yet there was no one to see the poor girl, even as the sun rose. It was Sunday; the commuters were home asleep. The construction crews were off too, and the single watchman who came out of his hut on the middle of the 11th Street Bridge to spit over the edge might have seen her, had she not by then drifted three hundred yards farther to the south. With the tide building, her body turned over in the main stream and she continued face down through the gap between the posts of the Frederick Douglass Bridge, past the Navy Yard complex, where duels were once fought at dawn.

Her head drooped below the surface and her arms stretched down like strange seaweed. For several hours she bobbed against the shore, her sequined shirt tagging on the weeds. Branches abraded her now bloated face. Sunfish and bass nibbled at her soft tissues and macerated her fingertips, which were already raw and blanched, chewing away the whorls of her prints. Once, her right hand twitched and clutched at the weeds as if she had come alive, but it was only a cadaveric spasm. She drifted in a toxic pool of boat slick and chemicals, and after another two tidal cycles her corpse was coated with oily residue. On the second night, just before sundown, the tide rose and carried her farther on her journey. The warm water attracted live diatoms — algae — to her orifices, but they failed to force an entry to her throat, which had been sealed by strangulation and was further defended by the methyl alcohol in her stomach.

For a while, her clothing increased her buoyancy and carried her smoothly along the flow of the river but on the third day her body sank. Immersed, her flesh began to decay faster. The fish were all over her, eating at the pulpy skin and coring out the punctures left by hypodermic needles in the fat around her waist. The weak brine of the river leached the blood out of these wounds. The different specific gravities of her bodily fluids and the methyl alcohol, still not metabolized, caused her stomach wall to swell.

By the fourth day, the putrefying gas in her corpse raised it again to the surface. The last section of the Anacostia, before it merged with the Potomac at Buzzard Point, was twenty feet deep in the central channel, and she might have made it many miles farther, but for the new creatures. They swarmed her body, lacerating her face, legs, and shoulders. There were so many that two shoreline residents sailed out to take a gander, and they were the ones who found what was left of the prostitute.

CHAPTER 20

Dr. Robert Ehrlich worked inside a large bureaucratic onion. Surrounded by a Marine Corps base in Virginia, the Bureau coexisted happily with the military. The FBI kept laboratories here but Quantico was perhaps most noted for its training facility. As Peter Cammon and Henry Pastern moved through the layers of security to the morgue, they met dozens of earnest young men and women. "High policing," the shaping of broad policy to protect the nation, might be the preoccupation of the executive cadre at the Hoover edifice downtown but Quantico was the place that excited every recruit and stayed in the memory of every graduating field agent.

A smartly dressed young trainee called the medical examiner out to the reception room to meet Cammon and Pastern. Owen Rizeman had been lucky to get them an appointment in Ehrlich's crammed teaching schedule. Ehrlich was short, about Peter's height, and with a bald pate, though not as smooth as Henry's landing-strip skull. He sported gold-rimmed glasses and a fresh Brooks Brothers shirt and silk tie, and his manner was Old-World gracious. Peter knew that this formality was his way of showing respect for the dead. Lowndes was a bit like that, too.

If the pathologist seldom made eye contact, it was not because he was shy; rather he was used to explaining his work while looking down at a body. Rusty blood stained his lab coat. Ehrlich introduced himself but did not shake hands. He didn't appear to find the detectives an odd pair, the tall Mormon and the shorter Brit.

"Thank you for receiving us on short notice," Pastern said.

"I want to thank *you*, Special Agent, Chief Inspector," Ehrlich responded. "Finally, someone has taken an interest. This is the damnedest autopsy. I'm on my fourth straight day. Actually, three evening sessions and today."

"Is there a particular problem with this one?" Peter said. His tone was sympathetic; he wanted Ehrlich to know that he had seen many an autopsy table.

"Come with me," Ehrlich said, and led them through a short passageway. Cold air and the odour of formalin flooded from the doorway as they entered the examination room. Three steel tables stood in parallel in the centre of the room, only one occupied and it covered by a plastic sheet. He led them over to the draped body and paused to allow Henry Pastern — he wasn't worried about Peter — to compose himself for the unveiling.

"Gentlemen," Ehrlich began, "I am saying that I've been having trouble with cause of death. That is not an easy admission to make."

He drew the sheet back from feet to skull to reveal the remains of a woman who might or might not have been Alice Nahri. There wasn't a lot left to interpret.

Peter was surprised by the sweeping trauma to the body. He expected the head to be swollen and battered, but not like this. Much of the facial skin had been eaten away by fish or some caustic chemical, and the rest of the forehead and every feature not protected by the girl's black hair had turned dark purple. Peter bent over closer and noted a pearly sheen just beneath the remaining purple skin on the chin and cheeks. He looked along the surface of the body, naked except for a sheet of muslin covering her excavated chest and stomach. This was a dark-skinned woman, African-American, he concluded from the less damaged surface of her upper thighs.

"How long in the water?" Peter said.

"Not more than four days," Ehrlich said, exhaling loudly. "At first, I thought more than a week, but the pearlescence you see under the facial skin is not adiposia. That usually takes a month or more. The fatty layer of the body starts to turn to soap as it decays."

"What accounts for that effect, then?" Peter said.

"A lot of things going on that accelerated the rot and putrefaction. There's evidence of strangulation. Her oesophagus was crushed pre-death, or at least damaged. That accounts for the unusual swelling of the face, and that was compounded by three or four days in filthy water. There are other problems in determining both cause of death and how long she was floating in the river. Take a look at her stomach. Prepare yourselves . . ."

He pulled back the square of muslin to reveal a gaping stomach wound. Peter understood that the opening was not entirely the result of Ehrlich's excavations. The remaining fat around the midriff had the pearly sheen, and odd puncture wounds had been stitched horizontally into the fat.

"How did *that* happen?" Peter said. "I've never seen that. Was this woman a drug addict?"

"That was my first thought. As it turns out, she was diabetic. The injection marks for insulin would be less conspicuous than smack injections, and if you take insulin daily then the stomach roll is a convenient spot. Nonetheless, the original puncture locations were wide enough to let in sea lice to feast, leading to coring out of the belly fat and the enlargement of the holes you see here."

Henry threw up on the floor. Ehrlich raised an eyebrow and nodded to the perfectly good sink a few feet away. He went to a cupboard and took out a mop and rags.

The pause gave Peter a chance to scan the entire corpse. The body was a mess. It left so many questions. He quickly reached at least one conclusion: to pin down the woman's identity they would have to employ every available tool, from fingerprinting to dental impressions to DNA tests. For now, he returned to the fundamental riddle of how she died.

But it was Henry, having cleaned off his face with a towel, who asked the essential question. "Did she drown, Doctor?"

"No," Ehrlich stated.

"Oh," Henry said. He felt stupid, though the query wasn't.

Ehrlich was a tolerant man, no more so than when instructing students, and he hastened to say, "No, no. At first I wondered if she might have entered the water with a spark of life still in her. It is usually easy to tell. The drowning victim ingests water, possibly debris. But she was dead when she entered the river."

The pathologist turned the head to one side. The area at the top of the spinal column was darker than the rest of the swollen head. He looked to his guests for comments.

Emboldened, Henry leaned in. "Skin is ruptured. Blunt force blow?"

"That blow in itself would have proved fatal, may have been, in fact," Ehrlich said. He straightened the head and pointed to the throat. "But the crushing of the oesophagus is what fully dispatched her, in my view. It's a shredded mess now, but I can tell you that her throat was destroyed by massive pressure. It made it impossible for silt or other detritus to enter her stomach, even if she had been alive."

"Done by someone in a frenzy?" Peter asked.

"Quite possibly, considering the ferocity of the other wounds. I'll show you her extremities."

Peter walked to the end of the table and looked at the girl's scarred feet. Ehrlich meanwhile turned over both of her hands.

"Look at the hands. Fish and sea lice have been at the fingertips. They're so bad, I can't get prints from them. I may be able to draw images off them with fluoroscopic and chemical processes but I haven't succeeded yet. But what I did find was signs of scraping on all the finger pads. Often, if a person falls into the water still alive, she will claw desperately at anything solid, a bridge footing, for example, or a tree floating in the current. I did find some weedy material in one hand, but that was post mortem, a reflex."

"But?" Peter prompted.

"I found the scraping on all the fingers, every one. Somebody tried to destroy the fingerprints. I can't see it being self-inflicted. And I think it was done after the girl expired. Just one more confusing element. Gentlemen, this was never a suicide."

Peter considered the evidence. The girl could have died in any of three ways: the blow to the back of the head; the violent crushing of her breathing passage, from the front; or, a series of traumas to other parts of her body. Now there was the desecration of her fingerprints.

And he expected there was more to come.

Ehrlich had covered the stomach hole again out of consideration for Henry. Now he flipped back the cloth. "Her stomach exploded."

"From what?" Henry said.

The ME looked up. "Methanol. Can you guess the form it was in?"

"Windscreen antifreeze," Peter said. "What you call windshield washer fluid."

Ehrlich, smiling, said, "Chief Inspector, how *ever* did you know that?"

"The girl was murdered. Probably finished off out near the spot where she entered — was dumped into — the river. The killer first knocked her out. Then he or she crushed the victim's breathing passage by pressing both hands straight down with considerable force. But the victim ingested the antifreeze before that moment. Likely she was strangled outside the car, where the vehicle was found. You can't put pressure straight down on someone sitting in a small car. Next, the scraping of the fingertips must have been done outside the car. It strikes me that it was inflicted at the last minute. We need to examine the ground. Most of the manic aggression occurred in the few minutes before the murderer dumped her. If all this was accomplished in the parking lot of the yacht facility, there was only one last-minute source of methanol."

Henry Pastern was now sure that Cammon was the reincarnation of Sherlock Holmes. Ehrlich let a minute go by. The girl's body, all three men were thinking, could not possibly seem any more gruesome.

The ME picked up the thread. "The Ford is parked out in the FBI compound. I found a plastic jug in the trunk contained several ounces of washer fluid. Methyl alcohol is highly toxic. In living people it attacks the optic nerve and causes blindness very quickly. It's one of the reasons they're moving to ethylene glycol. This was the old kind. The stomach was one of the things that initially drove me nuts. Literally *exploded* after only three or four days. I at first thought ethanol, which is the basis for booze, but no. Methanol metabolizes fast, causing metabolic acidosis. Too much acid built up in her bodily fluids. Combined with the leaching of blood from her system over the four days, the acidosis imbalance grew even faster, to the point where swelling of the stomach blew out the stomach wall. To make it even faster, the girl suffered from diabetes, and diabetic acidosis was already in progress."

"You *are* saying the methanol was ingested before death?"

"Before she was strangled?" Ehrlich said. "Have to be, wouldn't it? At gunpoint, perhaps? It couldn't have been much before the point of death, since there was no optic-nerve damage, and it would be devilishly hard to open the throat cavity after death."

Peter concluded that they might never have the answer. But now he understood that the girl might have been terminated a fourth way.

"Did you perform blood tests?" Peter said, already aware that serology tests were standard procedure.

"You're asking about race, Peter?" Ehrlich said.

The race of the victim would have been evident in most cases but Peter did not apologize for his question. The woman appeared to be African-American but her head, hands, and feet were so abraded and torn that he could not be sure. Her arms and legs showed lacerations that had swollen and discoloured the epidermis layer. He approached the racial issue delicately.

"We know that Alice Nahri was half-Indian with a white, English mother. We hope to get more pictures of Alice but I can't tell just from her passport how dark she was."

Ehrlich went to a shelf by the wall and took an object from a cardboard box. He returned and, respecting Henry Pastern's status as lead investigator, handed Alice's passport to him.

"Neither can I," the ME said. Henry looked from the passport photo to the mutilated face and back again. Did Peter see a tear in the corner of his eye?

Ehrlich launched back into his forensics. "Blood testing for race remains controversial. It may seem offensive to test for characteristics more common in blacks than whites, but we do it. Sickle-cell anaemia, for example, is more common in African-Americans. On the other hand, it is not a reliable differentiation and I seldom bother testing for it. Haemoglobin glycation is higher in black people than white, but we know the girl was diabetic, so glucose would already be heightened in her system. There is evidence of anaemia caused by destruction of her red blood cells."

"Cause?" Peter said.

"Thalassemia. It's a blood disorder. But again we were unlucky, since thalassemia is inherited."

Ehrlich stopped and both Henry and Peter waited for him to complete his account of the forensic tests.

"You're sure she's black?" Henry said.

"I'm sure."

But Peter needed an ironclad conclusion. "And not Asian? Not from the Subcontinent?"

Ehrlich didn't hesitate. "No, she's not."

Peter understood that Alice Nahri had attempted to obscure the race of the victim. She had succeeded to a degree, and now she had several days' head start on the authorities. But part of the delay in sorting out the racial issue had been due to Alice's luck. Even with the bloating of the corpse and the destruction of the soft tissues, the blackness of her skin in some areas would have been obvious in other circumstances. Peter looked at her exposed flesh. A cat-of-nine-tails had lashed the entire surface of the body. A web of marks, many of them infected, covered the skin. They resembled henna tattoos or baked-on lace and gave the body a perversely exotic look. Peter thought he knew the cause, not that he could quite believe it.

Dr. Ehrlich caught him looking. "Jellyfish stings. Accentuated by methyl mercury in the water. The Anacostia is a shallow river, and therefore warm in the summer. Some people think jellyfish only inhabit the South Pacific and Australia, but we get armadas of them in the Chesapeake and the Atlantic as far north as Cape Cod."

"Lethal?" Peter said.

"Not to her. Sorry, don't mean to be flippant. No, the sting is painful but not fatal to a healthy person. I was stung once. Treated it with baking soda and aspirin. Just more of her bad luck, I guess."

Bad luck, Peter thought, or a fifth cause of death.

CHAPTER 21

Peter Cammon and Henry Pastern spent an hour examining the Ford Focus, which the Bureau had left in a sequestered zone of the Quantico parking lot. The car was a disappointment. They found two small bloodstains on the headrest on the passenger side but the impoundment report had already noted these. Peter found a crack in the plastic bumper, a confirmation that the vehicle had hit Carpenter with great force. He took note of a round mark on the dashboard where a GPS device might have been secured.

Their visit to the banks of the Anacostia was equally pro forma. They found nothing useful in the yacht club parking lot. The two men stood on the grass fringe and looked out on the forlorn waterway. What hung in the air was the desperation of Alice Nahri, who had been willing to slaughter a woman, a stranger, in a storm of vicious assaults, just to win a few more days of freedom.

Peter had Henry drop him off near the Hoover Building. They pulled over on F Street and chatted. Henry was reluctant to let the chief inspector go.

"Henry, you'll need to call Inspector Deroche in Montreal. If you want I can telephone ahead and tell him to expect you, but you should be fine. Push him to take the girl seriously. She's the key to this. I wouldn't trust his opinion on the Booth letters but he's a good detective and he needs to know the details on the rental car and the latest forensics. The Sûreté has the lead on this, not Scotland Yard."

Henry nodded vigorously and drummed his fingers on the steering wheel. "Are *you* staying on the case?"

The question was simple enough but it startled Peter. He thought for a moment. Later, he told himself that his reply was meant to encourage the novice detective, nothing more.

"To the end, Henry," he said.

Peter strolled to Ford's Theatre, which happens to stand a block or so from FBI Headquarters. He joined a tour of the restored interior, which felt cool and hollow in its solemnity. Booth had chosen this killing ground to take out a president, firing a single derringer bullet into Lincoln's skull. While the National Park guide narrated the tale of Booth's attack, Peter hung back by the orchestra seats beneath the horseshoe of the balcony; here he gained a clear line of sight towards the presidential box and the stage below. The Lincolns had sat in the box on the right, which projected almost to the apron of the stage. There was the bunting on which Booth caught his spur. Peter applied his detective's eye to the scene. Booth's leap to the proscenium was foolhardy, and it was no surprise that he fractured his shin bone. Escaping through the rear of the stage never was a good plan, and bystanders almost stopped him. But then, melodrama was the young actor's stimulant, Peter knew. Renaud's book pointed out that Booth often confused stage drama with real life. In pain, the actor still managed to hit his mark stage front, and couldn't resist turning and declaiming "*Sic semper tyrannis!*" to the audience. Lincoln, slumping forward in his chair a few feet away, fell into a coma.

Peter took a minute to visit the small museum in the basement, where Lincoln's bloody coat and Booth's derringer and knife were displayed in glass cases. He took special interest in Booth's diary, the one he had jotted in during his ten days of desperate flight. The volume was more of a logbook, what would be considered a day-timer today, and Booth's frenzy and desperation, though not remorse, were evident in his scattered scrawl. Peter could see where pages had been torn out. He peered through the glass and looked for a Booth signature on the diary. The actor had not signed his final declaration of innocence.

Despite the searing heat, Peter enjoyed his walk back to the Willard Hotel, but as he lay down on the bed in his silent room, a wave of foreboding, of fatefulness, swept over him. The case was slipping beyond his influence. He had never been given a mandate and he had a slim chance of latching on to one. He was no closer to finding the girl or the letters, certainly not the killer. The pursuit of Alice Nahri, murderess, was entirely in the hands of the FBI, and it would never be Chief Inspector Cammon, retired, who would effect the arrest of the prime suspect, Leander Greenwell.

He was torn about where to head next. He was finished with D.C., but a return to England felt like a full-scale retreat. He was inclined to drop by Montreal on his way to London and visit Renaud for a few days. Deep instinct told him that Alice Nahri would also return to the City of Saints at some point.

And so Peter did what he often did to revive his spirits. He rang up one of the women in his life.

It was evening in England. Sarah picked up her mobile on the first ring.

"Dad! It's terrific to hear from you. Are you in Montreal?"

"No, I'm in Washington. On business."

Sarah giggled. Peter was taken aback. His daughter's laugh was like tinkling crystal. She was twenty-eight years old now but he always envisioned her as a little girl, his youngest child; she was also the one who understood him best. He felt affection sweep over him, a yearning for home, for Joan and the family.

"Sorry, Dad, but I'm never sure where you're going to call from. But, yeah, good. You're working again," she said.

For Sarah's part, her posture with her father had shifted about four years ago. She would never say so, but she used to fear him. She had grown up knowing that he had killed six men in his time with Scotland Yard. She had no grasp of what that was like. They had never discussed the shootings and as a result her doubts festered. He had been doing his duty, she knew, yet as the years passed she worried that her father had become inured to death. But four years ago, she had helped him on a murder case in Dorset. At dinner one night in the coastal town, he related the story of how he had discovered the body of a murdered girl in the Channel the day before. She listened with growing respect. The story was gruesome but was also permeated with her father's sadness. Luck had led him to the victim, he claimed, but Sarah noted that no one else had managed to bring the poor girl home.

"Dear, can you tell me something about jellyfish?" he asked Sarah.

Her laughter caused him to hold the hotel phone away from his ear.

"Sorry," she said.

"What's so funny?" he said, not really taking offence.

"You always take me by surprise, Dad. But as a marine biologist I am *always* ready to talk jellyfish."

"In particular, are there jellyfish in Chesapeake Bay?"

"Ah, well, the Chesapeake is one of the great ecological zones of the world. They have just about everything. Yes, there are jellyfish there. Why?"

"Would they be able to travel up the Potomac River, or a branch of it called the Anacostia?"

He could hear her moving about, presumably towards her computer. "Depends on tidal flow and water temperature. I'm going to go onto a database . . . Here it is. *Chrysaora quinquecirrha*. Sea nettles. They can be found all up the Atlantic Coast, the warmer the water the better. Classic-looking jellyfish, white or sometimes red, lampshade tops and long tentacles."

"What will a sting do to you?"

"Well, this kind of sea nettle won't kill you with its toxins, unless you are prone to anaphylactic shock. It will leave a red mark where its stinging cells inject you, and it will hurt, but you'll recover."

"Will they swarm a body, if that's the right word?"

"That's the perfect word. Multiple stings, the easier to bring down the prey."

"What else can you tell me? Would they swim up the river?"

"More likely they would float up on the tides. They're a serious nuisance on a lot of public beaches. I don't know about the Anacostia but people lobby to have them culled or eradicated. I wouldn't go for a dip off Atlantic City, for example. Might meet a moon jelly."

"Which is?"

"Guaranteed lethal if it stings you. But that's not your Chesapeake sea nettle."

"Last thing, dear, would they attack a dead human body?"

Sarah seemed elated that her father had called her, pleased that her dad's professional interests meshed with hers. She took this question perfectly seriously. "Sure. The jellyfish has no way of telling what's alive or dead. But it wouldn't enjoy dead human flesh."

"Thanks for all this."

"Call Mum. There's no change in Uncle Nigel or Aunt Winnie, but I think she'd like to hear from you."

"Right. Will do."

"By the way, there are lion's mane jellyfish in the Chesapeake system."

To this apparent non sequitur Peter could only say, "So?"

"I'm surprised at you, Dad. There's a Sherlock Holmes story, 'The Adventure of the Lion's Mane.'"

Sarah was laughing as she hung up.

Peter's gloom might have qualified as a premonition, for Sir Stephen Bartleben called him a few minutes later.

"What's happening in D.C., Peter?"

Peter took fifteen minutes to describe his journeys around the capital. "The Bureau should track down the girl pretty fast."

But both men knew all this was preliminary to the key question of next steps.

"Montreal," the boss said.

"Yes."

"I'm sending Malloway."

Perhaps it was the distance from London or Cammon's pique with the callousness of Bartleben's approach that made him reply, "That figures."

"What figures?"

"Malloway works for Counter. Frank would insist it be one of his own."

Peter's snideness was offensive. The choice of a Yard representative was the former deputy commissioner's prerogative, even if Frank Counter had nominal authority. "I need a regular man to do it, Peter. That's why Malloway."

Peter understood fully. There was a touch of sarcasm in the boss's retort. Bartleben was implying that Malloway could be relied upon to play his role conventionally, offending no one. Dunning Malloway would deal with Nicola Hilfgott with a degree of tact, unlike Cammon. Peter had met Malloway a few times. Peter recalled him as an ass-kisser who was not to be trusted.

"What does Malloway work on otherwise these days?" Peter said.

"He's on one of Frank's special squads. Worked on the phone-hacking scandal for a while. Showed good stuff dealing with the Palace on the alleged tapping of Prince Harry's account. Lately he's worked on the cricket-fixing incident with the Pakistanis."

"Just like Carpenter. That's just great," Peter said.

Sir Stephen ignored the taunt. "Also did counter-terrorism work a little in the Subcontinent office. I need a regular man, full time, with an international brief."

The deeper implication was that Peter was no longer authorized to deal with the Americans or the Canadians. Malloway would handle everything going forward. Peter barely held back.

"Stephen, Malloway should work closely with the Bureau here. A special agent named Henry Pastern. And he has to reach Deroche as soon as possible. I haven't told Deroche about the woman in the river and the ME's analysis, though Henry may have already called him. We need to square the circle."

"Peter, crikey, that's why mutual legal assistance protocols were invented. Malloway can handle Montreal *and* Washington."

Peter's rage grew. He tried one more time. "This isn't really an international problem. It's going to be an American manhunt. That's how we'll get the woman and, with any luck, retrieve Nicola's precious documents."

Prognostication was the wrong way for Peter to go. Sir Stephen paused, the silence implying that Peter had always been the wrong choice to handle Nicola's ego. "Complete your business in D.C., Peter, then head home. Skip Montreal."

Peter considered Montreal. Stephen wasn't wrong. He had no official business left in Quebec.

"Anything else?" Stephen said.

This was the moment to disclose his fresh plans, Peter knew, but resentment now poisoned any residual goodwill, and he only said, "Get Nicola to refine her draft of the three letters and send me a copy as an email attachment. That's it."

"Okay. I'll get them to you. Otherwise, Malloway can handle everything. I don't want you going to Montreal, Peter. We'll have lunch when you get back."

CHAPTER 22

Alida walked up to Independence Avenue and turned left towards the heart of Washington. The first glimmer of dawn brought the tidy, rich neighbourhoods east of Capitol Hill into sharp relief. She had by now painted her mind's-eye picture of her new home in America and although these houses were beautiful, she knew that they would never provide her with asylum. She saw a sign off to her right for "Lincoln Park" and reflected that the sixteenth president popped up everywhere. Alida otherwise ignored the sign but she might have paused had she known that Pierre L'Enfant, the capital's most important architect, originally intended that Americans should measure all distances in North America from that spot. She was at the centre of America.

But Alida kept walking. Her destination was four hundred miles to the north, in Rochester, New York.

It was ten minutes too early for the dog walkers and the joggers, but out of nowhere a taxi pulled up alongside and the passenger-side window descended.

"Mumbai," said the driver.

It wasn't exactly a gypsy cab but the driver, the brother of the owner, was unlicensed (which was why the police canvass of the taxi companies would fail to turn up Alida's fare) and for ten dollars and no questions beyond her telling him she was from Bihar he drove her to Union Station. She had the Mumbai man take a loop around the Mall so that she could glimpse the Washington Monument and the Capitol Dome. She wished she had a Kodak but she did not ask the driver to stop. Glorious as these landmarks were, she had no intention of living in the shadow of these heavily policed tourist monuments.

She remained calm. The trickle of passengers onto the vast communal floor of Union Station did not alarm her, nor did the security guards standing at posts around the perimeter. She had told the Mumbai man to leave her at the train station but her goal was the bus depot next door. Now she walked through the main building and across to the bus terminal.

Her booking proved straightforward, an eight fifteen ticket all the way to the downtown Cumberland Street terminal in Rochester.

The GPS was a problem. Walking up from the river, she had used it to plot the distance to upper New York State by road. The problem was the imprint left on the device. She could clear all records of previous trips but she suspected that the police had ways of recovering such data. She couldn't flush it down the toilet or break it up into little pieces. She had noticed a post office in Union Station. With an hour and a half to spare before the bus departed for Baltimore and points north, Alida returned to the railway lounge and bought a cushioned mailing envelope. She addressed it to Jack Dawson, Beverly Hills, California, on a fictional street; she wrote 90210 for the zip code. She took the GPS screen off its stand, slipped it into the envelope and paid for the postage. Returning to the bus depot, she transferred her meagre possessions to a dirty canvas bag she found in a trash receptacle and deposited her pink rucksack, making sure that Leo and Kate were lodged at the bottom of the bin.

The rhythm of bus travel soothed her. The Rand McNally sat on her lap as she alternately slept and gazed out the window. She could not get enough of the countryside of Pennsylvania as it rolled by. With the atlas as her guide to the wide-open future, she imagined, and compulsively recalculated, scenarios for her new life. The siren call of the blue interstates had marked her forever and she decided that she would buy a car as soon as she could. From her home base in Rochester — it sat at the very top of the country — she would explore everywhere to the west and the south. Alida was not the first young woman determined to visit all the states, but she believed she was.

While waiting in the Harrisburg depot for her connector to New York State, she saw a poster for Gettysburg that extolled the preservation of the famous town and Civil War battle site. Abraham Lincoln had given his celebrated speech right there on the battlefield. Johnny had told her about Gettysburg (and now she thought, for the thousandth time, of the letters she carried). She added the battlefield park to her list of places to visit.

Rochester, New York, turned out to be the first city that Alida learned to trust. As the Trailways bus passed the "City Limits" sign she mouthed the words "Welcome to Rochester, Kodak City, Pop. 214,231." This made her smile: Kodak was the universal term in Bihar for a tourist's camera. Simultaneously she saw from the elevated expressway the skyline of the city and the grey-blue of Lake Ontario in the distance. *If I had a Kodak,* she thought, amusing herself, *I could take a picture and pin it on my wall.*

At the bus station she disembarked and walked out to East Street, where she saw the top half of a tall black building in the distance, a modest skyscraper that nonetheless anchored the centre of the city. It welcomed her as a beacon to a new, exotic life. In the opposite direction she noted a sign and an arrow: "East Street Mansions" and below, "Eastman House." The pieces of her reverie began to slot into place with remarkable swiftness.

Her first task was to find cheap accommodations — with a landlord who lacked prying eyes. She understood that bus stations were often built in the downscale parts of town and she knew that rooming houses along the nearby streets would have adverts posted. She ambled down the street facing the main doors of the depot and in minutes spied a frowzy hotel that was nothing more than a brownstone walk-up with segmented by-the-day-or-week flats. It would suffice.

She walked past the rooming house, cut up to the right until she found a main street, and soon discovered a store that sold luggage. With her new navy blue gym bag Alida became the image of a graduate student. At least, that was how the pockmarked and warty landlady sized her up when she arrived at the rooming house. A cash payment got her a shabby rental on the second floor. Alida let herself into her room but left again to deposit the Booth letters and the remaining Canadian bills in a locker at the bus station. She bought a city map at the candy counter, returned to the brownstone, and spread out the map on the chenille bedspread. Within a few minutes she had located the visitor centre as well as the most direct route to Irondequoit Bay and the harbour. She plotted a rambling walk past the four tallest buildings in Rochester, which were helpfully identified by icons on the map. She concluded that the Xerox Tower, the tallest at thirty storeys, was the black skyscraper she had glimpsed on her arrival in town.

The Xerox Tower turned out to be grey, not black, an illusion of the early afternoon sun. She circled the lobby as if checking out the architecture but didn't bother going up the elevators; nor did she disturb the lone security guard at the information booth. She did note that there was only one exit door.

She walked on to the next skyscraper. The Times Square Building immediately caught her fancy. Although it was not all that big, at fourteen storeys, it was surmounted by four sculpted wings that, according to a brochure, had served as a beacon for new arrivals since the building went up in 1930; a plaque in the lobby asserted that each wing weighed twelve thousand pounds and together they were known as the Wings of Progress. She took an elevator to the fourteenth floor. There was no observation deck but she was able to spy Lake Ontario from one of the topmost windows. The building delighted her, like the rest of Rochester.

She traversed a park area labelled Washington Square, in the centre of which stood the Soldiers and Sailors Monument. At its apex perched a benign Abraham Lincoln. He was everywhere in America, it seemed, and she reminded herself to read the Booth letters again. She smelled the moisture in the air before she turned a last corner and saw the lake. Ontario was the smallest of the Great Lakes, the brochure stated, but it seemed immense. The view, as Johnny might have said, sealed the deal for Alida. The water stretched out like the floodplain of Bihar after a monsoon but for her the lake was "American" in every way, a vista to infinity and endless with potential, a highway for big ships, and a presence crouching like a beast by the edge of the city. Alida also liked the scale of Rochester, sprawling yet defined by its neighbourhoods and its waterfront. She walked the long way back to East Street and took in the façades of the preserved mansions, and had a very American thought: *someday I could own one of those.*

But the Xerox Tower remained her main focus. She knew that the rich man spent ten-hour days in his office and watched over the city and the lake from his windows on the twenty-eighth floor of the building. Sometimes he slept in his office. Alida prepared herself. She was in the mood to spend some cash.

The next morning she strolled around until she found a women's store downtown. She bought a white blouse, black slacks, and a black velvet jacket. She sprang for stylish earrings and a pair of Foster Grants at a department store on the same street. On the way back she went into a thrift shop and found a pair of knock-off Blahniks — no use squandering money. On impulse, she bought a briefcase to complete the picture of a modern businesswoman. It showed just the right amount of wear to prove her bona fides as a hardworking executive. She took it to a hole-in-the-wall shoemaker's and had the Pakistani owner polish it up to a high gleam. In her room, she changed into her complete outfit, except for the heels, and examined herself in the bathroom mirror. Coming downstairs to see how she looked in the natural light she encountered the landlady, who smiled with wonderment at this alien creature.

"How do I look?" Alida said, using her best British-schoolgirl inflection.

"I never, ever get to see one of my tenants dressed to the nines. Where are you about to head off to, young woman?" the plump lady said.

Alida smiled but instinctively drew back a step. She was grateful for the old woman's chatter but the more Alida befriended her — she had decided she might need to stay two weeks — the better witness the woman would make if the police interviewed her. She began to twitch as she stood posing in the hall. She regained control. She had decided on the long bus journey to put her ingrained paranoia behind her. A new life meant a new philosophy. She smiled now, smoothed her skirt, and kissed the landlady on the cheek.

"I have a part-time-job interview," she said. She had told the woman that she was a university student.

The landlady smiled back. "Don't forget your shoes, dear."

Alida went back to her room to fetch the Blahniks and when she came down, the woman told her she looked gorgeous. Alida thanked her.

She timed her return by taxi to the Xerox Tower for eleven thirty, hoping to spot her target leaving for lunch. She searched out a Kinko's down the block and copied the pages of the Booth letters. Returning, she passed the indifferent security guard and took the elevator to the twenty-eighth floor. Two businesses occupied half the floor space each. Lembridge had given her the man's name, Crerar, first name Ronald, describing the businessman as short and swarthy, and "not to be underestimated." One of the firms on the twenty-eighth was an insurance company and the other, so said the etched letters on the glass door, was Intrepid Regional Investments. She entered this office, marched directly to the receptionist and asked if Mr. Crerar had left for lunch yet.

"I'm sorry," the honey-haired receptionist said with a smile, "he's just finishing an appointment. Do you want to wait?"

Everything in America felt new to Alida. She reflected on the fact that this was her first encounter with an American woman her age. Alida was eager to please, to gain the feeling of sisterhood, even though she would never see the woman again. She grinned back.

"Thank you. I'll see Mr. Crerar at the restaurant."

Alida entered the insurance office and pretended to be interested in the promotional material. Five minutes later, a man who had to be Ronald Crerar came out of Intrepid Investments and pushed the button for the elevator. He was short, his hair thinning, but he wasn't swarthy or disagreeable. On the contrary, his expensive clothes and his self-confident way of moving compensated for his lack of height and hair. When she talked to him, she would reassess his charms.

She strolled into the elevator area and stood close to him. He smiled at her.

"These elevators take forever," he said.

"We call them lifts," Alida said. "And they do take forever."

"We're going to have lunch, did you know that?" Crerar said.

His intention was to startle her but Alice knew how to project cool. "All right," she said matter-of-factly. She introduced herself as Teresa Smith.

They settled into a secluded banquette in an upscale restaurant two streets away. As Alida anticipated, the maître d' was all artificial smiles in Ronald Crerar's presence. She had already surmised that Crerar always got what he wanted and the restaurant was clearly a staging area for his seductions, commercial and otherwise. She reminded herself not to underestimate her target. After all, he had instantly figured out that she was the woman who had mentioned the non-existent lunch date to his receptionist. He had acted to make their date a reality and that gave him an advantage. Besides, Alida was in mild shock at finding herself in such luxury after two days in grubby clothes on an intercity bus. She was nervous, although not so much that her twitch kicked in.

For his part, Crerar was anything but subtle. He turned every conversation back to his business enterprises, which, nonetheless, remained nebulous. At one point, just to force him to take a breath,

Alida made up a potted biography about being raised in England and attending business school in Manchester.

Crerar at once burst out: "I went to LSE for a year!" She wanted to tell him that the sons of half the dictators in the Middle East and Asia had degrees from the London School of Economics.

The whole interaction stayed coy. "You're in insurance, then?" Crerar ventured. She understood that he was drawing an assumption from her materialization across the hall on the twenty-eighth floor. When he ordered wine, she consented to one small glass (and only that so that he did not think she was a Muslim) and prepared to redirect the conversation.

When the sommelier left, Alice said, "No. You might say that I am in the non-insured business."

"Okay. What kind of business are we talking about? And why were you on my floor?" His voice had quickly turned hard.

"I'm in a cash business. I know you can appreciate that."

Lembridge had implied that Crerar was avaricious, a man with too much discretionary cash (unlike the academic himself), and Alida, during the long hours on the bus, had tried to guess how brutal and grasping the businessman would turn out to be. If anything, he was both shrewder and more lustful than expected. She decided to be forthright, in order to find common ground in their mutual greed, all the while dangling the chance of sex.

"I have something you'll want to purchase," she said.

"First, tell me what business you're in."

"Rare documents, artifacts that have come onto the market," Alida said.

"Or haven't come onto the market, young woman. From what sources do you get hold of these items?"

"Let's leave that for a moment. There's a proper order to do these things," she said.

"I need to know who referred you to me," he insisted, although the possibility of sex muted his tone.

"Put it this way. We will need an authenticator who is acceptable to both of us. Once we agree on that expert, you will know who gave me your name."

"I have to assess the risk. The trail of ownership must be validated," he said, leaning close to her. "I can't risk buying an item on the Stolen Art list."

Alida respected Crerar's spine. He outmatched Johnny and Lembridge both. She shifted tactics again.

"Nonsense," she said, mustering an edgier tone. "The risk-reward is based on your needing to own this item, even if you only visit it once a year in the safety deposit chamber of your bank. With that in mind, previous ownership is moot. The bonus, Mr. Crerar, is that no one knew this document existed until three months ago, so that listing problem is solved. The only issue is authentication."

"Call me Ron, Miss Smith, please."

For the balance of their lunch, she managed to control the negotiation. She refused more wine. She let drop that the two documents were Civil War–era treasures and then she linked them to the assassination. Within ten more minutes, she had him begging to know how John Wilkes Booth might be connected to them. She feared for a second that he had heard about the Booth letters already, but it was a natural question. When she informed him that she had photocopies of two letters in her briefcase, one signed by the assassin, he gave her a broad smile of admiration. If only he knew that the originals were slotted in her portfolio, too, right next to the copies. Ten minutes later, the duplicates, set out on the linen tablecloth, effectively closed the deal. She sensed his testosterone rising as the greed took hold.

They worked through the arrangements over the next hour. Alida ordered three desserts, but only because she was hungry. He seemed charmed, as if gluttony equated with self-assurance. The price came down from $85,000 to $50,000, subject to verification by the document expert. She said she had someone in mind. They discussed a mutually convenient venue outside Rochester. Summing up, Alida promised to call him within a week to confirm the expert's name and the locale for the exchange. It was all so reasonable. They would close the deal ten days hence in a safe spot a few miles back down the I-90. She refused his dinner invitation, saying she was far too full.

CHAPTER 23

Michael and Maddy drove down to Henley on a Saturday morning. He took the wheel. Jasper positioned herself in the centre of the back seat and served as a kind of moderator between husband and wife.

Michael, Peter and Joan's only son and their oldest child, couldn't believe his luck when Maddy came into his life. He worked in the parole system in Leeds and she was high up in women's services. He believed they were a complete match. The loss of the baby had sent her into a depression, from which she seemed to have recovered. Now, he found Maddy's passion for amateur sleuthing amusing and gratifying, for she was jollier than he'd seen her in months. He watched her sort her stack of lists and diagrams and he smiled, ready to give her his total support. His love for his wife didn't prevent him from indulging the family habit of edgy sarcasm. As they crossed into Oxfordshire he said, "This is a shot in the dark, if ever there was one."

"Thanks for that, dear. But you didn't see my clever dissection of the population of Henley-on-Thames. Your dad would be proud."

"Did you perform a regression analysis of the entire Oxfordshire demographic, then?" Each had a half dozen credits in social statistics.

"No, it's just a bloody list, my love. But I'm so confident of finding her, I'm doing this on a Saturday."

"Which means what?"

"The town registry is closed on Saturdays. Have to rely on my own resources."

They drove on in silence for several miles. "And I have my trusty dog," she added.

"What was the name of Sherlock's hound?" Michael said.

"Toby. He was in the story I was reading last night."

Michael looked over at her. "Have you been in dad's study?" It wasn't meant as an admonishment, and Maddy knew it.

"Peter okayed it. And your mum said it was all right to borrow the books. She's read them, too, she said."

Michael felt like the odd man out in a family of detectives.

Maddy had visited Henley-on-Thames as a child and vaguely remembered the bridge and the waterfront. The Thames, of course, gave the town its charm and its drawing power for those seeking a semi-rural retreat. The world-famous regatta was over for the year and the town had returned to its lazy, riverside calm. They arrived as the locals were descending into the core for Saturday shopping. The couple found themselves moving against the flow but within a few streets the traffic thinned. They pulled over to reconnoitre. Maddy had annotated her printout map of Henley with swooping red arrows.

"Are we invading the Falklands?" Michael said.

"We start from the centre and work out to the fringes, pausing only for pee breaks. Jasper, don't drool on the assault plan."

The maiden name of Alice's mother was Mabel Ida Parsons. By lunchtime, they had checked every "Parsons" on Maddy's list, starting with the directory entries that listed an "M. Parsons" and an "I. Parsons." They called ahead but if they got no answer, they drove to the address. They advanced from the core to the suburbs. Henley was not a big place and they finished their itinerary faster than anticipated. No one offered a connection to a woman who had spent time in India. The only "Nahri" named in the directory did not answer, either to a call or a direct visit. Michael and Jasper stayed in the car while Maddy knocked on the doors on either side of each listed address. There were no responses.

Back in the car, she said, "What a crappy detective I am. Your dad would find her in a split second."

"With the resources of the entire Yard behind him," Michael said. "We can keep looking, Maddy, but we don't know she ever had her own house. She may be sixty-five or ninety-five, or dead."

"She's not dead. I'm sure. Let's check the nursing homes."

He leaned towards her, ostensibly to look at her list but really to show solidarity. Jasper poked her head between the seats to see, too.

"Okay," he said, "we start at A and go to Z. What's first on the list?"

"Albemarle Nursing Home."

"What's last?" Michael said.

"Retirement Home for Superannuated Zulus."

There were seven old-folks' facilities in Henley with variations on retirement, care, and nursing in their titles. They visited five and rang up the other two. None of the administrators counted a Mabel Ida, née Parsons, Nahri among their occupants, nor did any recall a citizen of Henley by that name. Maddy sat in the passenger seat in a dejected slouch and Jasper poked her with her damp muzzle. It had begun to drizzle. It was already mid-afternoon and they were back on the high street. Michael looked up the road through the windscreen.

"I need one more variable in the mix," Maddy said. "I would bet the lotto Ida followed in the footsteps of Orwell's mom. I'm sure of it."

But it was Michael who experienced the moment of gestalt. While they sat there in the street in the rain, neither ready to head back to Leeds, he read through her printout of Eric Blair's Wikipedia biography. Michael had never read Conan Doyle but he knew who Dr. Watson was and that had so far been his role on this trip, providing support and occasional flippant suggestions. But for that moment he became the detective — not Sherlock, but Peter. Michael had once overheard Joan say that she thought Peter had psychic powers, a magical ability to put facts together and divine the truth. As a boy,

Michael had been scared of his father's putative gift. Now, on a quiet street in Henley, he came to understand Peter's secret, mundane as it was: the job of the detective is to persevere until small truths reveal themselves to his tuned-in instincts.

"Can you wait here?" He got out of the car.

"Can't we come?" Maddy said.

He turned and leaned into the car. "Would you say from the sign up the road that that might be the oldest tea shop in Henley?"

He came back in five minutes and scurried in from the rain. "Not only did I find her, I was swarmed by three women who demanded to know how she was, would I say hello, and could I please report back on her condition."

Maddy's look was almost feverish. "How did you figure it out? More important, where is she?"

"She's in a retirement place in Shiplake. You said Mabel wanted to be a British lady. Where would a British lady of limited means spend a lot of time? Tea rooms, of course."

"And Orwell spent a couple of his childhood years in Shiplake, just up the road from here!" Maddy burst out.

"She ran a hat shop in Henley for twelve years. Two streets over, but it's closed now. She had tea here every afternoon. But there's a reason they pestered me for information, Maddy. She's got cancer."

They decided to have lunch first — "Anywhere but that tea room," he insisted — before venturing to Shiplake. They ate sandwiches in the Saab in a park by the Thames, both of them a bit amazed at their detective work.

Mrs. Mabel Nahri, known locally as "Ida," was passing her latter days in what was billed as an "assisted living" flat in the only such facility in the village of Shiplake. The administrator of the home, a prim woman of about fifty, accompanied Maddy and Michael from the entrance up to the second floor. She halted outside a room that plainly was Mrs. Nahri's.

"You will find the room a bit strange. Assisted living implies a degree of independent capacity, to prepare one's own meals, for example. Ida no longer has the wherewithal. But she has been here for years. We maintain a more medically intensive service on the fourth floor but we didn't have the heart to move her. We brought the mountain to her."

"Is she fully aware?" Maddy said.

"She does not suffer from dementia but the cancer has weakened her," she whispered at the threshold. "If she becomes agitated, it's from worry over her two daughters."

"Do they visit often?" Maddy asked.

"Alice came by a month ago but her visits have been sporadic. She's the one who pays the expenses. The other sister, Avril, is mentally challenged and lives in a facility a few miles off."

"How are the payments made?" Michael said.

The question was impudent, Michael realized too late. They had already admitted that they weren't family members, but the presence of the dog had implied that they were friends of the family. The woman now pursed her lips and hesitated, prepared to defend her patient's privacy.

"What is your connection to the Nahris?"

Maddy and Michael each presented a business card. The woman seemed to have the impression that they were some kind of inspectors on a formal visit. She frowned and looked down at Jasper.

"We're hoping to find Alice," Maddy said. Her tone implied that Alice was in some trouble, unspecified.

Maddy watched the administrator weigh all the factors. Alice didn't visit often, Maddy could see, and it was never the woman's intention to be confrontational — she welcomed visitors and Ida had so few.

"A bank in Henley covers the invoice each month. Most months, anyway." The woman's demeanour softened as she glanced again at Jasper. "It will be all right to take the dog inside. It might cheer her up. By the way, always address her as Ida."

She opened the door for them. The flat was one large chamber that managed to combine sitting room, bedroom, and kitchen. Bookcases, a sideboard, worn Persian rugs, and landscape prints personalized the space but the hospital bed in the centre of the chamber spoke "critical care." Medical machinery surrounded the bed. Maddy found it impossible to guess the age of the woman in it. The wasting cancer had shrunk the skin around her face and neck. Her eyes widened when she saw Maddy. The tendons at her throat tightened like ropes as she struggled to speak. "Have you seen Ali and Avy?"

Maddy pulled up a chair next to the bed and reached for the woman's hand. Jasper lay down on the rug next to her; Ida did not seem aware of the dog. Maddy remembered that the woman wasn't suffering from dementia, and spoke to her accordingly.

"No. When was the last time you saw Alice?"

"I can't remember when but we had tea together, watched a movie together." Ida turned away.

While it seemed disrespectful to launch immediately into a cross-examination of the old woman, Maddy seized the opening. "Do you know where Alice might be?"

Her gaze swung back to Maddy. "She would never return to India! There is no possibility of that."

Maddy had dealt with hundreds of lonely women not all that different from Ida, and she knew when to back off. She remained quiet as the old woman lay back on her pillow. But there would never be another opportunity to trace Alice Nahri backward in time. Nor could Peter afford to wait for Alice to show up in Shiplake again.

"Where would she . . ."

"Alice is in London," the old woman whispered.

"Do you have a number where you can reach her? She needs to know about your health."

"My daughter will know."

Ida had exhausted herself. She closed her eyes but remained half awake. Michael circled the room, inspecting the framed pictures of Alice and Avril as children. Avril, unsmiling, was tiny and looked at the camera with sad, worried eyes, while Alice, much taller, projected impish confidence. Maddy continued to hold the woman's hand until she dozed off, then she joined Michael in his circuit.

Most of the books on the four-tier stand were bought-by-the-yard classics in cheap leather bindings, but Michael noted that well-thumbed copies of Orwell's *Coming Up for Air* and *Burmese Days* held pride of place on the eye-level shelf.

"Notice anything special about the items here?" Michael said.

Maddy allowed him his detective moment. "Not a thing."

"There are four videotapes on the bottom shelf. The television over there has a VCR attached to it. What do the movies have in common?"

Maddy knelt down and removed the four James Cameron films: *Titanic, The Abyss, The Terminator, Avatar*. The first three were videotapes but *Avatar* was a DVD, not playable on Ida's machine. The boxed set looked new, whereas the others showed frequent use, *Titanic* the most.

"Seems to me Ida is more the *Howard's End, Brideshead Revisited* type," Maddy said, her tone conceding that she had no real insight into Ida Nahri's tastes.

"Certainly not a Bollywood fan. *Titanic* and *Avatar* are the top-grossing pictures of all time. I wonder if they were as big in India when Alice lived there," Michael said.

Maddy examined the videos one by one and gained some understanding of Alice's visits to her mother. Ida had been ill a while. Maddy's own mother had died a lingering death in a hospital and she knew that the boring stretches — Mum dozing, Mum out of the room for treatments — expanded time itself. These were Alice's favourite flicks, not Ida's.

"If I tell you, will you find Ali for me?" the old woman called out suddenly. She struggled to sit up in bed. Maddy moved to her side and leaned in close.

"Yes. Can you help me?"

"How far along are you?"

"We think she went to America."

"No, I didn't mean that." Her voice grew stronger. Her focus became bright and direct. "You're pregnant, aren't you? I'd say three months gone."

CHAPTER 24

Peter was indulging himself in a full breakfast in the Willard restaurant when Henry Pastern caught him on his mobile. "Have you heard, Peter? Greenwell has resurfaced."

"Deroche has him in custody?"

"Yup. What are your plans?"

He had yet to book a flight anywhere. He took a sip of tea. As a public citizen, he had the right to go wherever struck his fancy. He thanked Henry for the news.

He managed to book the last seat on the United Airlines noon shuttle to Montreal. As the small jet descended to Trudeau International he scanned the beautiful old city below. It struck him as more exotic, more classically European, than before. He recalled Pascal Renaud's recommendation that he visit Quebec City and its Citadel, the great bastion on the St. Lawrence.

He had called ahead to leave Pascal his flight number, and to ask if he could stay for three days at the condo, but he had no reason to expect the busy professor to pick him up. Yet, at the Arrivals lounge, there was Renaud with a broad smile, seeming to have all the time in the world.

Pascal came over to take his valise. "So, Peter, why are *you* back in town? Have you found the notorious letters of JWB? Have you been in contact with the slightly less fanatical Inspector Deroche?"

For a second, Peter wondered if staying with Renaud was a good idea. It occurred to him that the professor might be near the top of Deroche's list of suspects. As well, each contact between Deroche and Renaud increased the chances that Bartleben or Counter would learn of Peter's presence in the city. Perhaps it was naive to think that he could stay out of sight. But Peter's reasons for embracing Renaud's hospitality were both personal and professional. He wanted a friend, someone he could talk to, confide in. Pascal had opened up about his sister and had welcomed Peter's own confidences. Peter had developed several theories regarding the Carpenter case just at the moment when Bartleben had shunted him out of the game. He had homed in on two components: the whereabouts of the girl and the location of the letters. He valued Pascal's perspective on the letters more than anyone else's. He hated sitting on the sidelines, and he intended to impose on Renaud as long as the professor would have him, at least while he figured out a path back into the case.

But Peter did not directly respond to Pascal's aggressive question. "Thanks for meeting me, Pascal. What's on your agenda for today?"

"I lectured this morning. My students were more *ennuyés* than usual. Must be the fine weather. I'm yours for the afternoon, and the evening, too. We can exchange our findings."

Peter grinned. Obviously Pascal was eager to disclose some new intelligence. Peter caught his mood of adventure; sometimes it was invigorating when no one knew where in the world you were.

Peter's mobile vibrated in his pocket. An email from Bartleben topped the index of messages; a paperclip icon indicated an attachment. "Do you have the capacity to download a text file from my cell to your desktop computer?" said Peter.

"Sure. No problem."

"I'll make you a deal," Peter said. "I have Nicola Hilfgott's latest draft of the three letters. Now, Pascal, strictly speaking, this is part of the murder investigation and confidential material. I'll review them with you, get your opinion on a number of things. But you have to respect the confidentiality of the evidence."

Renaud took the exit at Atwater too fast, causing Peter to tilt to his left in the passenger seat. "Absolutely! I agree. . . . Of course, they are forgeries. . . . It happens, Peter, that I have news along that theme. A copy of one of the letters may be in the hands of a university colleague."

"Which letter?"

"Williams's to Booth."

When they reached Renaud's townhouse, without delay Pascal hooked up Peter's cell phone to his desktop computer through a USB link and loaded the file onto the hard drive, and then copied the original to a USB stick for Peter's convenience. Sir Stephen had forwarded Nicola Hilfgott's reconstructions of all three letters. Pascal printed out a copy, one letter per page.

He turned to Peter. "Can I print a copy for myself?"

"Sure."

Pascal organized the printouts and retrieved two bottles of beer from the fridge. Peter caught him glancing at the text of the letter on top of the bundle. He had to smile. His friend was rabid to examine the replicated documents but hospitality came first. Also, Peter guessed that Pascal knew about Greenwell's resurfacing.

"Have you heard, Pascal, that Leander Greenwell has been arrested?"

Renaud nodded. "Yes! He's being held in the Bordeaux Prison." He was unable to resist a history lesson. "That's the provincial detention centre for men, famous for over eighty executions, though of course we don't believe in capital punishment anymore. But it means Deroche can close down access to him, except for his lawyer."

"Do you know if he's been charged? Has he applied for bail?"

"Yes. Charged, that is. I don't know how the bail process works."

Renaud appeared nervous. It occurred to Peter that his new friend might have an inside source for information about Leander Greenwell.

"Peter," Renaud said, "in the interests of complete honesty, I have to tell you that I once met Greenwell. It's not surprising, since academic historians sometimes need the services of antiquarians . . ."

"Is there something in particular I should know?"

"Yes. When I heard that Greenwell was back, I went to his store to see if I could talk to him, but he had already been taken into custody. I was just being nosey."

Peter let it pass. He was in the mood to relax, in spite of Pascal's fervour to get at the letters. And so Peter launched into his own update, keeping it light and sanitizing the forensic details. The professor listened patiently, content to serve as Peter's sounding board. He felt privileged to be invited inside a police investigation.

Peter punctuated the end of his story with a swig of beer. "Okay, Pascal, who's this nefarious colleague of yours?"

Renaud swished the last ounce of his beer around the bottom of his glass before setting it on the table with a thump. "Professor Olivier Seep, and what I am telling you is no more than rumour and supposition. He lectures in history at UQAM, the University of Quebec at Montreal, and he aspires to be the academic champion of the separatist movement. To some extent, he placed this label on himself, which tells you about his ego. Everyone expects him to run for a seat in the Assemblée in the next provincial election. You must understand that he and I teach at different institutions. He is not my rival in the movement, though we despise each other, to say the least."

"Why the hostility?" Peter said.

"In the separatist version of history, Peter, remember that everything is a grievance and nothing is forgotten. Professor Seep puts an intellectual gloss on the repetition of ancient grievances and that suits the purists in our movement just fine. As an academic, he should know better than to let old stories turn to engraved stone. But he musters up anger and false sincerity, and that plays well to the choir. Two nights ago Seep gave a speech to a small group — but not so small that the press refused to attend when he notified them — in which he asserted that the English government in Montreal in 1864 was prepared to summarily execute French-Canadian activists for treason, *la trahison*. He said that he had seen a letter. A colleague told me later that Seep claims to have seen three letters. The Booth correspondence?"

Peter shrugged, then smiled, knowing that Pascal couldn't wait any longer. "Okay, Pascal, shall we look at these imaginary letters?"

He ushered Peter to the dining room table. Each man sat with a copy of the reassembled letters in front of him. They read them in chronological order, although it soon became evident that it was the third one that Professor Seep had cited.

Number 1: October 23, 1864, John Wilkes Booth to Sir Fenwick Williams

Dear Sir:

My sincerest regards. As one who has traveled throughout the States, both North and the sovereign South, and is presently visiting Montreal . . . I write to you, this date, with important information. I am a son of the South dedicated to resist the oppressors from the North. Let me say, Sir, that there is yet time for Britain to honour its common ground with the Confederate States.

My attention has been drawn to certain agitators in your midst who have cultivated the seditious interests of illegitimate groups in the Canadas. I speak these truths as one representing the Government of the CSA in Richmond, Virginia. Please note that my brief has been to gather information only regarding sympathies in the Border States and in the Northwest, supplemented by reconnoitres of prisoner of war camps in New York.

While engaging certain figures in Montreal, which include Canadian patriots sympathetic to the aims of the Glorious South, I have been approached by French-Canadian "patriots" who claim to seek common cause with the Confederacy. These latter overtures interest neither me nor Jeff Davis, but they should concern your Office, as they are violent in their aims and executions . . . Plans are under way to launch violent . . . against your person, and to employ Greek Fire against militia barracks.

My reasons for this disclosure are honorable. The aim of the South has never been to undermine the stability of the Canadas, rather mine is to alert you to the impending threat from Separationists in your midst. I may be reached at the St. Lawrence Hall Hotel.

With Regards,
John Wilkes Booth

Renaud offered the first comment. "Many historians believe that Booth was plugged into the Confederate spy network but no one has ever suggested a formal mission from Jeff Davis. Otherwise, the tone is right: Booth is both arrogant and presumptuous."

One discrepancy amused Peter. Booth coined the term "separationists." In her first iteration of the letter, Nicola had used "separatists." Either way, Nicola was determined to paint them as extremists, even back to 1864.

They proceeded to the next letter.

Number 2: October 24, 1864, Jacob Thompson to Sir Fenwick Williams

Dear Sir,

I thank you for seeking my advice on the letter, inst., from one John Wilkes Booth, actor.

Please be advised that said Mr. Booth does not speak for the Confederate States, either the offices of the Secretary of War, the Secretary of State, or President Davis. I and the other Commissioners from Richmond exclusively serve as the csa's emissaries in Canada, as we have represented in . . . to Governor General Monck.

We do not encourage any division between England and any other legitimate country. Our instructions upon assuming our posts some months ago were to respect the neutrality of Britain in the continuing conflict, without abusing British and Canadian sovereignty. I will not treat with Separationists aiming to draw European powers into such factionalism.

Mr. Booth is a fanatical actor who is attending in Montreal for the first time. He is without a diplomatic mandate, and should be ignored.

Jacob C. Thompson

Peter pointed to the second-last paragraph and the historian picked up on his thought. "You can see how defensive Thompson has become. It's late 1864, the election is pending in the United States, and the Confederate commissioners have accomplished very little. The last thing Thompson cares about is French-Canadian revolutionaries. Certainly, Thompson's denunciation of French-Canadian national ambitions is hypocritical."

They moved to the last letter.

Number 3: October 26, 1864, Sir Fenwick Williams to John Wilkes Booth

Sir,

Your letter of October 23 has reached me. Without commentary on the merits of your asserted cause, though I feel compelled to point out it is in a situation of martial decline, the position of the Canadas and Britain is clear: neutrality in the conflict. Her Majesty's Command will not tolerate insurrectionist actions of French radicals in Canada at any time . . . I can assure you that revolutionary acts against the government may amount to capital treason, if verified as active, and I will oversee the expression of such a French secessionist cause here.

Yours respectfully,

Sir Fenwick Williams
British Military Commander, N.A.

"What do you think, Pascal?" Peter said. "There's that word 'secessionist' again."

"The third letter, Peter? This is thinner stuff. The prose, as Hilfgott writes it, doesn't ring true. The presiding general in British North America merely states the official position of the colonial government. It's a short letter. He brushes off the actor. The comment on capital treason is an abstract statement, phrased in the conditional. I am surprised at Olivier for making so much of it. But he is a true believer, capable of anything."

"I wonder if Seep might have seen the original of the Williams letter," Peter said.

Pascal's grin broadened. He was slightly drunk. "What do *you* think of the letters, Inspector?"

It seemed that they had fallen into the habit of rhetorical repartee, and Peter did not answer directly. "I agree we should be careful about Hilfgott's precision. In the Williams letter, the last one, he states, 'I shall oversee the expression' of the secessionist cause. Surely he said 'suppression.' I question Hilfgott's accuracy there."

"Madam Hilfgott's deliberate mistake?" Peter said.

Both Seep and Hilfgott were manipulating the letters, the words of dead men, for their opposing causes, the separatist and the federalist. How were these two connected to murder?

Peter began to pace the living room. It was time to face some tough questions. "The allegations by Booth of a terrorist plot aren't supported by real evidence. You give no indication in your book that he was knowledgeable about his host city. What could Hilfgott take from those unsubstantiated claims, Pascal? What agitators? What seditious interests? And what did Booth care about Canada's future, as you point out?"

"Booth was a crazy man," Renaud agreed.

"But I don't think that's why Hilfgott's so zealous about retrieving the letters. Rather, she's the matching, mirror image of Professor Seep. She's a troublemaker."

"Could it be that we're in the presence of two more fanatics, Peter?"

They needed a break. Pascal had overdone it on the beer and he went off to take a nap before his late afternoon seminar. Peter remained in the living room and mulled over his next strategic move.

He called the Bonaventure Hotel and asked to speak with Mr. Malloway. It was an educated guess that his colleague would be at the Bonaventure, and he was right; the desk clerk confirmed that Malloway had registered. But the phone shifted to voicemail. At this point, Peter lost his nerve and dissembled. "Dunning, this is Peter Cammon. I'm in Montreal for a couple of days, on my way back to London. Please give me a ring."

He left his mobile number. He sighed as he finished his beer in the silence of the townhouse. There was no professional justification for his presence in Canada and Malloway would have every reason to resent a call out of the blue.

CHAPTER 25

Peter napped for twenty minutes. The telephone jangled him back to full awareness.

"Peter, this is Dunning," said the caller. Peter immediately tried to interpret the man's tone. There was no evident hostility in those four words.

"Thanks for calling back, Dunning. How have you been?" He tried for a neutral tone himself, with maybe a touch of the elder statesman.

"Just fine. So, you're in Montreal, Peter."

"On my way home in a day or two," Peter said.

"I arrived yesterday noonish. Where are you staying?"

"It's called the Saint-Henri section. I'm staying with a friend."

"I'm at the Bonaventure, as you know. Same spot you stayed in, wasn't it?" he said, to show that he'd figured out how Peter had guessed his hotel.

"I'd like a chance to brief you on Washington," Peter said. He wasn't seizing the agenda; rather, he was prompting Malloway to tell him what he knew.

"I just hung up from talking to Henry Pastern," Malloway said. "Is he competent, do you think?"

Peter decided to drop a few names. "I think so. Rizeman is a good man at the top end and he will ride herd on Henry, as necessary. Ehrlich, the ME, has been helpful."

What happened next was either coincidence or the collision of two suspicious natures. Peter looked at the call display on his mobile and saw that the incoming number wasn't the Hotel Bonaventure, though the sequence was familiar. He realized that it was only one digit from the number he had been given for Nicola's office assistant. At the same moment, Dunning Malloway understood that the jig was up and he spouted, "Listen, Peter, I'm in a spare office at the consulate. I'm waiting for a meeting with Nicola Hilfgott in about an hour. Meanwhile I'm looking over her replications of the famous letters she's so hot to trot about. Can you join us?"

Peter didn't balk but was wary of the potential for scapegoating. "Let's be strategic," he said. "The consul general and I don't get along so well. It also may not work to your advantage. She'll have talked to Frank Counter by now and she'll know I'm off the case. *Persona non grata*. She won't welcome you dragging me along."

"She's a bit crazy, don't you think?"

"In what sense?"

"For one thing, I can't make head nor tail of these letters. Even less do I understand her obsession with them. Why don't you come as my invitee? We'll tag-team her."

"What are we aiming for?"

"I'll be open about it, Peter. I need to rein Nicola in. The retrieval of the letters is secondary and you can help me blunt Nicola's obsessiveness on that subject."

But the letters should be important to Dunning, Peter reasoned. Fraud, theft, and murder tainted those historical documents. Nicola's cavalier manipulation of several government agencies amounted to misfeasance. Possibly malfeasance, if she were somehow complicit in the purloining of the Booth letters. Peter was surprised by Malloway's dismissive attitude to the letters. He decided to push harder: "Why doesn't the High Commissioner yank her, send her home?"

"He may. But, ironically, the thing that makes her vulnerable also gives her a measure of protection. Extracting her, or openly cashiering her, would raise questions — the British consul general in Montreal suddenly hustled back to London. You remember the James Cross affair?"

Peter recalled his discussion with Pascal in the Russian restaurant. "In general terms."

Malloway was in a chatty mood, or else the small thrill of talking about his hostess on her own turf made him bold. "Were you involved, Peter?"

"Not really. Before my time, too, you understand. But the Yard was on alert. MI5 contributed and the SAS would have been ready to go if called upon."

"Cross was the commercial attaché and trade commissioner in Montreal, pretty much the same position Nicola Hilfgott holds. It won't do to have her pulled all of a sudden. By the same token we can't tolerate her out there denouncing separatists. Charles de Gaulle in reverse." Peter understood the reference: the president of France had famously chanted "*Vive le Québec libre!*" on a state visit to Canada, causing a major scandal.

Peter heard a voice in the background. Despite its faintness, he recognized it as Neil Brayden's. The words were unintelligible.

Malloway's side of the conversation was bland and self-conscious. "Okay . . . I'll be there . . . Right."

Peter heard a door shutting, and then Malloway again. "Sorry about that, Peter. I'll clear the way with Nicola for you to participate. I could really use your help."

Dunning Malloway had a narrow face and smooth skin that made him seem boyish, an impression that he tried to offset by sporting a thin moustache and an older man's suit. Peter, watching him enter the consul general's boardroom, was reminded of Malloway's sartorial pretensions: he wore a summer suit from Davis & Son, complemented

239

by a silk tie, Thomas Pink button-down shirt, and Italian loafers. Peter rose and they shook hands, just as Nicola Hilfgott thundered in.

Nicola and Dunning quickly took chairs across the table from Peter. He was surprised that she had excluded Neil Brayden. He saw that she was determined to take charge from the outset. She at once turned red, as if she had hit an arterial switch, and expostulated, "Gentlemen, there has been a distinct lack of progress in this case. Let me say, Dunn, that I am not criticizing your office and, in fact, I am grateful that someone has been appointed full-time on the investigation." *Did she almost say "anointed"?* "But we are no closer to finding the missing letters. I'm disgusted."

Peter immediately reassessed what was going on. Nicola must have delivered the same harangue at dinner the night before with Malloway, so why repeat it? Had she threatened Malloway? Had Tom Hilfgott served barbeque?

"Do we agree that Leander Greenwell knows more than any other person about this case, both the letters and the death of Peter's and my colleague?" Malloway said. His manner was smooth, but his query sounded rehearsed to Peter. Was he cuing Peter to express support, in effect, double-teaming Hilfgott using the professional interplay of two policemen? If so, Peter couldn't think of anything to say.

"If he has the letters, that's all I need to know," Nicola said. She voiced no sympathy for John Carpenter.

Malloway continued. "I spoke with the RCMP's 'J' Division in New Brunswick yesterday afternoon, as soon as I arrived. They paid a visit to Greenwell's family cottage and took a look around." He paused and looked over at Peter to make sure he was understood: Malloway was taking charge. "Greenwell's cousin welcomed them in. No evident sign of the letters, or any facsimiles thereof. And, of course, Greenwell is in custody here."

Peter weighed Malloway's judgement. Deroche would not react well to his calling in the Mounties. He remembered Pascal Renaud's admonition: everything is different in Quebec, everything is political.

Malloway must have known that his move could provoke the Sûreté. Peter concluded that he had called the RCMP as a sop to Nicola.

"Where do things stand with Greenwell?" Nicola said. "Has he revealed where the letters went?"

Already Nicola was growing tiresome; the interrogation of an accused was a delicate matter. Malloway and Cammon made eye contact, achieving unspoken agreement to limit their disclosures to the civilian in the room.

Malloway spoke. "He has been charged with second-degree murder . . ."

"Second-degree? Why not first-degree?" Nicola said.

It was to Malloway's credit that he did not overtly grimace. His manner turned formal as he diverted to another subject. "Peter, could you debrief on Washington?"

Peter roused himself and leaned forward, hands folded on the table. With a minimum of speculation he reviewed the Anacostia River murder, leaving out specifics of the jellyfish attacks and most of the forensics while making certain to convey the desperation Alice must have felt as she abused her victim and made her escape. He emphasized the teamwork that the Bureau was bringing to bear on the hunt for Alice. He summed up. "The young woman did all this to buy time. It's highly unlikely she'll return to Canada, so our best chance is the FBI. Dunning, you've talked to Special Agent Pastern. Anything more to add?"

Malloway shrugged. "The warrants are out there. Alice Nahri is a vicious piece of work, I'll say that."

"Where do we think the girl is now?" Hilfgott said with impatience.

Peter and Malloway fell into a rhythm. It was in no one's interest to overstimulate Nicola, to drive her to make any form of contact with the American government.

"The federal warrant has nationwide application," Malloway said. "It's in the hands of the FBI. I'll be going to Washington at some point to reinforce our interest in prompt action. Nahri and Greenwell may be in cahoots. Much depends on what evolves with Greenwell here in Montreal and I'll work with Deroche on that."

Nicola leaned forward. "Does she have any of the letters, for God's sake?"

Malloway took a deep breath and fixed his gaze on the consul general. "Alice Nahri is a stupid tart. How did she think she'd dupe anyone, killing a woman of a different race and dumping the body in the river, where it would be found easily? The Bureau will pick her up very soon."

Malloway's flash of anger shocked Peter. There was no need for it. And then another wild thought occurred to him. Was it possible that Dunning had a completely different take on the girl? Had John Carpenter showed her off at the office, and was Malloway now seeking some form of retribution? His entire focus was on Alice, it seemed.

"We have a file on her," Malloway said. "Nicola, this is part of the official inquiry, so I ask you to keep it confidential. Alice Nahri was born in Bihar of an Indian father and a British mother. The father is dead but the mother is in a home in Henley-on-Thames. Our people are visiting her to see if her daughter has been in touch. I have also met with the brother of the victim, Joe Carpenter, who is about the only person who has met Alice. It's a long shot but if there is any family contact, we will know. Now, here is the confidential stuff. I have contacted the Central Bureau of Investigation in Delhi. Alice Nahri is known to have had involvement with criminal organizations in India, Pakistan, and Nepal. She was seen with leaders of the Maoist rebels in Bihar State, where there have been numerous attacks on local politicians and gun battles with police in the Kaimur Hills. She is known to Nepalese authorities as a smuggler of gems and drugs across the Indian border. Bihar is adjacent to Nepal, and her hometown is on the main trade route to Kathmandu."

The briefing was winding down. Neil Brayden came into the boardroom, as if on cue. He nodded to Peter and took a chair on his side of the table as Nicola took charge again, avoiding eye contact with Malloway.

Nicola sighed dramatically. "The next issue is to be kept in absolute secrecy," she stated, her low tone implying that her fixations outweighed the policing concerns of the Yard's detectives. "Let me put the matter of treason and terrorism back on the table . . ."

To Peter's knowledge, terrorism hadn't yet made it to the table.

"Has everyone read the letters, as I reproduced them from memory?" The question was half-rhetorical, no acknowledgement expected. "The letter from Booth to Commander Williams indicates that in 1864 there were serious anti-government conspiracies operating in Canada East. Wilkes Booth made contact with the conspirators, it appears, and Williams promised to do something about them."

Dunning Malloway sat back and tapped his fingertips on the edge of the polished table. "As I recall, Williams's response was highly contingent . . ."

Nicola interrupted yet again. "Williams felt compelled to promise 'to oversee the expression of a French-Canadian cause.'" As Peter had mentioned to Pascal, he was sure that the original had promised "suppression" of the agitators; she had misremembered, perhaps consciously.

"Only 'if verified,'" Malloway said.

"Which Booth *does*."

Peter watched the flare-up and began to appreciate why Bartleben wanted Malloway to hammer on Nicola. She was relentless and unstable. She was even loonier than Peter had thought and that's why Malloway wanted him there.

"Nicola, do you believe the three letters are useful for anything in particular?" Malloway asked in an effort to move towards closure.

"Dunning, have you heard of Professor Olivier Seep?"

"No."

"Chief Inspector?"

"No," Peter said, looking away.

Nicola got up from her chair and paced. "Monsieur Seep is a prominent separatist. He's an adviser to the Parti Québécois. He supplies their rhetoric, although the PQ hardly lacks self-appointed

243

philosophers. He is a radical, make no mistake. The province has endured two referenda, which narrowly defeated the separatist option, and these radicals are waiting for the opportune moment to force a third. It all depends on fomenting the right atmosphere." She shook her head. "The independence movement is always on the lookout for a trigger, a *cause célèbre*."

"More like a *casus belli*," Malloway said, unnecessarily.

"The talk around town has been building, gentlemen. In recent days, Monsieur Seep, who is planning his run for a seat in the National Assembly, has been planting hints that he has seen the Williams letter, the one containing the reply to Booth. He made a speech this week, full of innuendo. He's likely, in my view, to launch more attacks accusing the government at the time of Confederation of suppressing legitimate French-Canadian interests."

"How do you 'plant hints'?" Malloway asked. Peter felt a moment of admiration for the man.

"I have no doubt that Seep has the letter or has seen it, or knows where to find it," she said.

There was an awkward silence. The meeting had served little purpose, other than to keep Nicola at bay. Besieged, she could only glare at the three men as the sun angling through her boardroom window caught her in its spotlight. Malloway had performed well. Still, Peter kept wondering why he and the consul general hadn't hashed out these issues at the mansion the evening before.

Finally, Dunning Malloway said, in a friendly tone, mostly for Nicola's benefit, "Well, Peter, have a safe trip home."

Peter walked back along Rue de la Cathédrale to the Bonaventure with Malloway. For several minutes they remained silent while they allowed the September sun to burn away the tension of the meeting. Malloway invited Peter for a drink in the bar but he begged off. They stood for a minute at the bottom of the stairs by the hotel entrance.

Malloway was aware that Peter would have to abandon Montreal soon and fly back to England. "Any more advice before you go, Peter?"

"If Frank hasn't already done so, hand Deroche a copy of all three of the recreated letters, even if Hilfgott keeps objecting," Peter said. "Better Deroche see the text from us rather than others."

There was one last question hovering in the air and Dunning posed it now.

"What role do you plan to play in all this, Peter? I don't see that you have one now."

Peter regarded the question as unanswerable and impertinent. If and when the time came to choose a part, he was pretty sure that Bartleben would back him up. For now, he didn't care how Dunning Malloway saw it. He shrugged but then on impulse, said, "No role for me, Dunn."

"I hear you pulled a gun on Carpenter's brother," Malloway continued.

"Where did you hear that?" Peter said.

"From the brother. I went to see Carpenter's family."

"Well, there were guns involved. No one was prepared to shoot it out."

"In a church? I should hope not."

Peter was unfazed but the comment sent his thinking in a new direction. Malloway's visit to the Carpenters in New Bosk hadn't been necessary. Yes, he might maintain that he had been paying his respects to the family but perhaps he had dropped by for the reason Peter himself might want to visit again: to learn more about the girl. Maybe Alice was important to Malloway for reasons that Peter hadn't yet imagined.

"Did you know they haven't held the funeral yet?" Malloway said.

This time Peter's puzzlement showed. Malloway looked victorious.

"Why the devil haven't they?" Peter said.

"Joe Carpenter says he won't bury his brother until his killer is convicted."

CHAPTER 26

Peter had a dream that night, a variation on what he called his Horror Dream. A stock cast of players populated the dream, all family, and this time, as usual, he was caught struggling to reach the roof of a large building to rescue Joan. He was alert to small alterations in the setting. His brother, Lionel, made a rare appearance this time; he stood to one side, tall, silver-haired, and patrician — a contrast to Peter. Sarah was there and Michael waited next to her dressed like a groom at a wedding. Curtains of water formed the walls; that was different. Peter, alone, climbed twisting Escher staircases up to the roof. When he reached the top platform, no one was waiting; Joan wasn't there. A black pistol, probably a .38, lay on the tarred roof. Peter rarely described his dreams to anyone, and for good reason. A listener would say that this one was a typical anxiety dream. Peter considered the water image. Alice Nahri was connected to water, having drowned one victim, perhaps two. But she didn't appear on the rooftop in Peter's nightmare. Peter knew that a dream is about the dreamer. Standing on the windswept roof, he himself was an isolated figure — no one's rescuer.

He awoke at 5 a.m. in Pascal's spare bedroom. The fan in the erratic air-conditioning system boomed air through the ducts and then shut down with a thump. It was the latter noise that jarred him awake. Earlier that night Pascal had insisted that they walk up Greene Avenue to a favourite café. Peter had accepted in good humour, for he had decided to end his Montreal sojourn — he could follow the two investigations, Washington and Montreal, from afar — and, with this feeling of finality, he had gotten drunk with Pascal. The booze had blurred a lingering sense of dejection.

And that was what the dream told him. His isolation had left him powerless to help John Carpenter, or anyone else in this investigation. He was no closer to finding the killer. He was still inclined to go after the girl, and in his mind he listed a dozen ways to find Alice Nahri. His dilemma was how to reinsert himself into the case, and when.

What Peter knew was this: the investigation of young Carpenter's demise was dragging because a crowd of lonely, self-absorbed men and women, one of them probably his killer, still haunted the Lachine Canal and refused to step into the single spotlight by the old factory.

He got out of bed and went downstairs to the kitchen, where he opened the well-stocked fridge and examined his breakfast options. The sight of stacked bottles of beer curdled his stomach. He poured a glass of orange juice and began to make phone calls.

"Hello. Frank Counter . . . "

"It's Peter, Frank. I'm in Montreal en route to Heathrow."

"Have you seen Malloway?" Counter didn't seem surprised by the call.

"Yes. He invited me to sit in with him at his session with Nicola yesterday afternoon."

"Crikey. How did that go?"

"Smoothly, I'd say. Malloway was masterful. You can tell him I said so."

Frank Counter liked people to get along. "I think he fills the bill nicely."

"Right. By the way, what else does Malloway have on his plate?" Peter wanted to see if Frank Counter's response matched Bartleben's.

"Well, he's worked on a few drug cases, some international liaison with Southeast Asia and the Subcontinent. He's on that group we set up on the Pakistani cricket scandal, the *News of the World* thing. That mess is exploding and I could sure use him back here now. You saw the *News* story?"

Peter ignored the question. "Did Dunning volunteer for the cricket thing?"

"Yes. With his exposure to India, it was a natural fit."

Peter used Pascal's phone to call Maddy while his mobile charged up. He found her in the kitchen.

"Tell me, what's happening? Have you found Alice Nahri?" she said.

"You sound weary," Peter said.

"Just back at work, that's all."

"Are you going to the cottage anytime this week?"

"Tomorrow, I think . . . Yes, Joan's off to Birmingham." There was an implication there that Peter should call his wife.

Peter reported the salient features of his D.C. visit. "Alice is alive."

Maddy in turn gave a full account of the trip to Henley.

"Could you do something for me, dear?" he said. He wanted to say "for us."

"Yes, certainly."

"Phone the All Saints Church in New Bosk in Lincolnshire and see if the Carpenter funeral has been scheduled."

"Won't it have happened? I thought the family was demanding the body back as soon as possible."

"I'll explain when I get back."

"Which is when?"

"I hope to get a ticket out tonight. Arrive the following morning."

"Wait a minute, Dad. I've got it . . . The John Carpenter funeral is set for tomorrow, early afternoon. According to the church website."

He marvelled at her facility with the internet. "Okay, here's what I'll do. I will try for a flight tonight and if you are available, we'll drive from the airport to New Bosk."

"Done and done," Maddy said. "See you at Heathrow."

Peter reached Deroche at the end of one of his all-night stakeouts.

"Greenwell hasn't confessed, but I will keep you informed, Peter," Deroche said, his voice weary. "Give me your coordinates in England and I'll report regularly."

"That's good of you, Sylvain."

"No, Peter, I *owe* you. The next time I go out on a stakeout of the Rizzutos, you're invited. By the way, I'm meeting with Monsieur Malloway this morning. Does that mean you're no longer on the case?"

"I'll keep my hand in, and I'll share everything with you, Sylvain."

"That's what I hoped you would say."

"I have another favour to ask."

"Shoot."

"Don't tell Malloway we talked."

Deroche guffawed. "Sure. And everything I share with him I will share with you first."

Peter waited another hour and called Henry Pastern.

"It's good to hear from you," Henry said, from somewhere in the J. Edgar Hoover Building. "Back in the U.K.?"

"Actually, back in Montreal," Peter said.

"Alrighty."

"Henry, I'm cleaning up loose ends. I . . ."

"Are you staying on the case, Peter? I hope you are."

Peter appreciated the special agent's directness. "I've been replaced, Henry. As liaison, that is. But you already know that, right?"

"I'm aware. Dunning Malloway contacted me yesterday."

"What did you think of the letters?"

"My learning curve on the Civil War is a bit steep. The letters *sound* real but we have to verify the text before we expand the search. I haven't put them on the international list yet."

"How are the warrants for Alice Nahri going?"

"Out there yesterday. Our Legal Department took its sweet time. A minor glitch: we still haven't identified the girl in the river. Federal judges don't like to issue countrywide, federal murder warrants when the victim hasn't been named. I asked Ehrlich to package the victim's clothes and the Metro vice squad is working on the ID. We all agree she's a local hooker. Metro isn't too happy that the Bureau's asserting itself in this case, but as soon as I mentioned the suspect was born in India, my local counterpart made it clear that D.C. Metro doesn't need that kind of grief. They'll cooperate to the full, but it's our baby."

"It's *your* baby. Good for you. You've been busy," Peter said. It took fortitude for Pastern to call Ehrlich again, whose cutting room he had sullied with vomit.

"Alice hasn't used the credit card. We searched every drainpipe and trash bin in that end of D.C. for the GPS but found squat." Henry's voice trailed off.

Henry must have been attuned to Peter's preoccupation with the girl, for he said, "Peter?"

"Yeah?"

"If we arrest Alice, I'll call you first."

"Thank you."

"Thank you again for the letters. Oh, by the way, there's an expert on assassination lore, lives in the Chesapeake area. Now that I have the draft letters, I'll put him on standby. His name is Lembridge."

Peter wasn't quite finished stirring the pot. Using Renaud's computer, he sent a long email to Special Commissioner Souma of the Indian security service. He requested a data bundle covering passport applications filed throughout India for the previous three years, females only. He added further parameters to narrow the search. Finally, he asked Souma to send the information to Peter's home email address, without copying London.

CHAPTER 27

If the book dealer intended to turn himself in, he missed his chance, for one of Inspector Deroche's men had been checking Greenwell's shop twice a day and nabbed him as he opened the front door. Leander Greenwell feared the police, which was not unusual among older gay men, but his initial alarm when the detective clamped his hand over the door key was tempered by astonishment that the authorities had failed to find him earlier. Over a period of two weeks he had been on the lam through four provinces and a half dozen borrowed rooms, none of them qualifying as a safe house. Leander took advantage of a brotherhood of dealers and conservators whom the police could have identified from phone records, had they made the effort. He ranged from a friend's above-store apartment in northern Ontario to a chalet in Nova Scotia to a farm in Quebec's Eastern Townships. He stopped at the family cottage in New Brunswick to pick up some clothes and a telephone Rolodex he kept in a cupboard. When he heard later from his cousin that the RCMP had visited the cottage, he decided to return to Montreal and organize his affairs before turning himself in. But Deroche's man put him in handcuffs on the spot and threw him into a cold cell in the Bordeaux Prison before he could call Georges.

For some time now Leander had professed to be content with who he was, how he had turned out. At the age of sixty-two his life was settled and, in his words, satisfactory. Being gay had become easier over the years. Montreal was a cosmopolitan city, largely tolerant of its gay population. Not that Leander participated actively or openly in the community. He linked up easily enough with younger men but these were individual connections; it did not suit his personality to climb the ramparts on gay rights or flaunt his sexuality. His round belly and black beard gave him a benign aura and customers accepted him because he was unthreatening. As Georges said, "They don't care if you're Freddie Mercury or Santa Claus."

His business ventures, like his life, had advanced in stages. He created the shop with a firm philosophy: he would always be professional, tough, and ethical, the best book dealer in town, with a front-of-the-store demeanour to match. Within ten years, he was able to buy the building and pay off the mortgage. He branched out into rare documents and marketing on the internet won him an international reputation. At sixty, he convinced himself that there would be no more great changes in his life. He had always wanted to be rich but had reconciled to making a good, if not spectacular living in the trade.

Georges Keratis transformed Leander. Georges gave him love. The young man was honest, loyal, and optimistic about the future. At first, it was unclear to Leander why Georges would want to love a rotund book seller twice his age and this pebble of doubt wore on him. Until he met Georges, Leander had done little other than trade books, make buying trips and attend conferences of the like-minded (regarding books, not sexual preference).

"Book collectors are a stiff-spined group," Georges chided once, and toasted Leander with a glass of wine.

Georges worked as a bartender, waiter, and sometime manager at Club Parallel, a large bar and dance club in Old Montreal. The venue brought in gay and straight clientele in equal numbers and was almost unique among local clubs in that respect. Management valued his easygoing charm with both kinds of customers. The relationship between Leander and Georges took a year to mature. At times, the younger man mocked Leander's profession, once saying in jest that Leander's dusty volumes and crackling parchments kept dragging him back from human warmth to cold pages. It was hard to change; Georges called him an antiquated antiquarian. The real change began when both men recognized that they were a fine match of complementary opposites. Part of the younger man's appeal was his intellect, although even here there were differences. He once asked which books Leander considered funny. He cited *Vanity Fair* and *Tristram Shandy*. Georges had *Catch-22* in mind.

Leander's affluence had never been on display in either his business premises or in his upstairs apartment but now he began to lavish money on Georges. Initially he didn't disclose his accounts to Georges, nor did the younger man ask about the funds that financed their regular trips to New York and Toronto. To Georges's credit, it was only Leander who obsessed on money. He imagined that their future depended on a higher level of wealth. Thus began the saga of the letters.

It took Leander three years to assemble the Civil War correspondence, the third letter, Williams to Booth, falling into his hands first. He was startled by the British commander's language in promising to suppress French-Canadian agitation in the Civil War period and realized that he had something valuable. Moreover, he had come across the prize fairly, as part of an estate sale in the Townships; his ownership was indisputable. He scouted for the right buyer, and in a flash of unorthodox inspiration, approached professor Olivier Seep with an offer for a quick sale.

Leander began to agonize over cash flow. Business in 2010 had tailed off from the year before, as much due to the inscrutable ebb and flow of the collecting trade as to the recession. He had been biting into his savings to cover his presents to Georges. His strategy in approaching Seep was inspired. Leander had never plugged himself into the separatist community, although he frequently sold rare books to academics across the province. He knew that Seep had family money — ironically, he lived in a big house in the Anglo enclave of Westmount — and that he was outspoken in his attacks on the federalists. Leander unfortunately overlooked a third factor. Seep was cheap. The professor balked at paying the $20,000 the dealer demanded. He would have had to sell one of his paintings, he complained, as if Leander should have any sympathy for the wealthy. For a month, Olivier Seep hounded Leander to lower his price.

Leander's timing was serendipitous, but not for the professor. Later that month, the other two letters landed in his lap. The Thompson–Williams note, bought for pocket money from a small-time dealer in Lévis, should have filled in the puzzle neatly but Leander had doubts about its provenance. There were also rumours in the trade about a document or two that had disappeared from the Quebec Archives. Seep rejected the new package price of $40,000 and thus it made sense for Leander to strike a quick cash-for-parchment transaction with Madam Hilfgott. The three linked documents were extraordinary historical treasures but he set a bargain bottom line of $30,000.

But it was the young woman who challenged all of Leander's complacent assumptions. A scant two hours after John Carpenter's first visit to set up the transfer on Nicola's behalf, the beautiful sylph wafted into his bookstore haven and tried to seduce him with a scenario of betrayal. It was that dramatic, he recalled. Her offer was simple: he could keep a third of the money and all three documents. Maybe he could resell them. He had laughed at her. The original deal was simpler, he stated in a patronizing tone. She waited until he finished. He laughed at her again. She took off her blouse and simply stood there half nude and waited a bit longer in the silence of the store. Leander was put so off-kilter that he almost reached out to touch her breasts. She seemed to challenge his sexual proclivities, as if there were another sexual choice for him, and in fact he felt lust creeping up from his groin. But he did not back down.

But it had only been her first offer. Before he could eject her, she buttoned herself up, then went and locked the front door, turning over the "Closed" sign.

Until Alice's invasion of his shop, Leander believed that he had played the consul general perfectly (that harpy), keeping the price up and locking in an under-the-counter cash sale. But now he worried that Nicola was behind the woman's manoeuvre. Nicola had seemed capable of anything, even sabotaging her own deal. The locked door roused panic in the book dealer. He felt a trap being sprung.

Alice spun out a fantastic plan to drug the young Scotland Yard officer, her boyfriend, and steal the letters before he could deliver them to Nicola.

He pointed to the obvious flaws. "How do I explain retention of *any* of the letters?"

"Hide them wherever you want. I don't care, I just want the money. I will keep you out of the dirty work. I will get Johnny so drunk he'll never remember the robbery." Her voice was cold.

"You said you were going to *drug* him . . ."

Alice's temper flared at his challenge and she took out a knife with a six-inch blade. She drove the tip into the nearest leather-bound book, which happened to be a volume of Trollope.

Before he could speak again, she removed the knife and unlocked the door. She repeated, "I'll keep you out of the dirty work."

If only.

Two nights later, Leander handed all three documents over to the Englishman at midnight for a package of hundreds, then retreated to the second-floor apartment above the store. He put the bills in his safe. To establish an alibi for the next several hours, he left the store and showed up at the Club Parallel, idly wondering if Georges would be willing to backdate his arrival to midnight. But Georges hated him sitting at the bar like a pick-up artist and sent him home.

When the bell downstairs rang at three fifteen, Leander assumed that Georges had left work early but it was the woman, and she had her knife in hand and a brand new story to tell.

"Johnny is dead but I didn't kill him," she said. Her face was flushed and tears made rivulets through her makeup. She calmed herself in a minute; her voice steadied.

"How the hell did that happen?" he asked, locking the door behind her and flipping off the front bulb. He now prayed that Georges would stay at work until four, past closing time. He grasped right off that he was about to become the logical murder suspect. How could he explain away the double-cross, *her* double-cross?

It got worse.

"I'm screwed," he stated, in despair, but she stared coldly at him.

"I need the money and I'm keeping the letters," she said.

Leander was almost relieved but this *was* $30,000. He thought of asking for half. His calculations swung like a pendulum. He wasn't sure that his visit to the bar coincided with the timeline of Carpenter's killing. He couldn't stop thinking about Georges — would he provide the necessary alibi? The woman appeared to read his every thought. She came up to him and, just like that, cut a shallow two-inch line along his jaw. It was small enough to call a shaving mishap but the trickle of blood sickened him.

That changed the conversation. Desperate, keeping the knife in view, Leander suggested they split the cash evenly.

"Two thirds for me," she said. "Go get it." She followed him to his safe and he retrieved $20,000. Something about her chilled him, cancelled any thought of resistance. Alice hadn't deigned to show him the recovered letters. It was closing in on 4 a.m. and he feared Georges blithely walking in the front door. He marshalled the last of his courage and suggested that she leave him one of the documents, perhaps the Williams–Booth letter.

"It's only fair," he said.

Alice laughed. She took a set of keys from her coat pocket. The car locks beeped outside and Leander saw the Ford for the first time. Had she run down the callow boyfriend? Perhaps she had drugged him and thrown him out of the car. How cold-hearted was this succubus? He looked at the shine in her eyes and was afraid.

Alice left before he could say another word. He stood in silence, short $20,000 and three rare pearls.

Georges did arrive home a few minutes early, having caught his lover's jittery mood at the bar. Leander's account of the Carpenter exchange was minimal. He lied, saying that he had heard on the radio that the buyer of his wares had died. He feared that Georges would stalk out, leave forever. In other circumstances Georges himself might have contacted the police — Leander's neck was bleeding — but the week before the young man had been roughed up outside the bar by a group of Neanderthal straights who took out their philosophy on his ribs. The MUC cops had been unsympathetic.

They decided to wait. Leander kept the "Closed" sign in the window.

Deroche and his men descended just after dawn. Leander, in a silk dressing gown, answered the door and let the two detectives inside. By now he had his storyline clear. Yes, he had made the deal with Hilfgott, done the exchange with Carpenter, and accepted the cash. Ten thousand dollars? Sure, here it is. Will I get it back from you, officer? I don't know any girl.

Deroche interviewed him again at the Sûreté offices two hours later and challenged him on the scar on his neck.

"Shaving," the book dealer said.

"You shave in the middle of the night?"

The morning was long but Leander's alibi held. The serving staff at Club Parallel all agreed that he arrived at the bar around the time of Carpenter's death. Leander returned to the store and by midday was on a bus to Toronto. He left no message for Georges, who took his lover's abandonment in stride. Georges closed the shop but maintained the upstairs apartment for Leander's return. He knew that Leander would not call. Both men understood the need to preserve Georges's deniability regarding the book dealer's whereabouts.

Leander's thin alibi was enough to delay his detention, but Inspector Deroche later regretted not arresting Leander Greenwell on the spot, and he miscalculated again when Leander arrived home from his wanderings. Almost as if to compensate for his earlier mistake, Deroche and his men threw the book dealer in jail and asked the attorney general to prepare a charge of conspiracy to commit murder. The lawyers were willing to add second-degree murder. All this was readied before taking Leander's full statement.

Leander's interrogators sat him in a chair in the centre of a featureless cube in the Bordeaux Prison and threatened him with beatings, prison rape, and the permanent closure of his precious bookshop. It was all too extreme, and Leander began to balk. Worse for Deroche, there was an anti-gay undertone to the threats by the police. Leander, initially in dread of prison, found his courage as the threats piled up. He concentrated on remembering every word.

His very sharp lawyer quoted those words back to the presiding judge at the habeas corpus hearing the next morning. "Conspiracy to commit murder!" he thundered. "What a convenient charge. But, your honour, the last time I checked the *Criminal Code*, you need another person to conspire with. Where is this chimerical second party?"

Deroche found no evidence confirming Alice's participation in the assault and drowning, and no connection at all to Greenwell. Late in the hearing on Leander's habeas corpus motion, the prosecution did allude to the exotic girl and presented a copy of her passport photo. The presentation rang hollow and desperate in court.

"Couldn't we have some evidence that is a little more *local*?" jibed the defence counsel, who went on to enumerate the police abuses inside the interrogation chamber. Even more damning was the Crown's failure to address Leander's alibi and that lacuna highlighted the vagueness of the conspiracy charge. The judge looked down his nose and suggested to the government's counsel that the Crown's chances at a preliminary hearing on any homicide counts were looking slim.

Deroche's people dug a deeper hole. Montreal Urban Community police arrested Georges Keratis on charges of lying to the police and kept him overnight in a drunk cell. A curled phone book was used to soften him up during questioning. But Georges wasn't soft and he kept his mouth shut. He fought off two assaults from other detainees before he was released the next morning. The young man's employment required him to be bonded; the owner of Club Parallel was sympathetic but he wasn't pleased, and he said so. But when the boss, who was a good guy, saw the blue bruise on Georges's zygomatic bone, he handed him a stick of make-up and told him to get back to work.

Greenwell dug in and clammed up. Deroche stretched the book dealer's stay at the Bordeaux to a sixth day, in spite of the habeas corpus ruling. In that time, Leander hardly got to know his cell. If he wasn't being shouted at by officers and guards, he was in court benefiting from his lawyer's stream of motions. Only a passionate pitch by government counsel won a postponement of the process, rather than outright dismissal of the charges.

The Crown wanted Leander kept on a short leash, and the judge granted a long list of bail conditions, which included his turning in his passport, informing police of any plans to travel outside Montreal, and avoiding contact with anyone with a criminal record. His lawyer filed a counter-bid to have the passport restriction voided, since the book dealer travelled to New York regularly to conduct business. He won that round as well.

Perhaps overconfident because of his alibi and the lack of witnesses at the Carpenter murder scene other than Renaud, Leander decided to say nothing to anyone, even his lawyer, after his release. Deroche, realizing that he had jumped the gun on the two heavy charges, let him be. No one seemed in a hurry to schedule the preliminary hearing.

Leander could not stop thinking about the woman with the knife. He called Georges to warn him off. "It's just till the legal stuff is over with. Stay away until then."

Georges, always direct, said, "Why?"

"I'm trying to protect you."

"I don't need you to protect me. I need you to love me," Georges replied.

"Just for a while," Leander said.

And so Leander continued to live alone in his shuttered store.

CHAPTER 28

There's no way to improve a red-eye, Peter grumped as he boarded the direct overnight flight from Montreal. This time he was on British Airways rather than Air Canada but the amenities were the same. An air hostess offered him a plastic glass of champagne the moment they took off; first-class seat, second-class champagne. He started to watch the in-flight feature, *Inception*, but found he wasn't in the mood to sort through multiple dream levels or listen to repeated explications of dream-world rules. He took off his earphones and ordered a good British ale from the woman.

The BA flight arrived twenty minutes early and this time Maddy was waiting at Arrivals without the dog.

"Jasper is home with Joan. She's off to visit her sister but'll be back for dinner."

Maddy wore a neat blue suit, appropriate for both court hearings and funerals, Peter thought. She looked beautiful but appeared tired and contemplative to him. "You didn't have to come all this way. Joan or Tommy could have fetched me."

She responded with a quick, judgemental frown. Clearly, she thought they were beyond such niceties. He smiled and she flashed her sly grin.

"I'm pregnant!" she blurted out, her smile widening.

For the next two hours in the car, they chatted about her and Michael's plans and their expectations of parenthood, and Peter, nodding frequently, played the role of protective father-in-law. Maddy had already told Joan about the baby but Peter felt that his daughter-in-law was confiding in him in a special way. After all, they were partners.

As they neared the town, Maddy said, "Is there something important we're looking for in New Bosk?"

"I'm not sure."

She allowed him this vagueness, knowing he would get to his theory. She sensed that Washington and Montreal had worn him down.

Eventually, Peter said, "Joe is pretty much the only one who can give us details about Alice Nahri. This time we'll be careful how we approach him." His comment was in part a signal to Maddy that he was relying on her; she had fully debriefed him on her visit to Henley, and her insight into Alice's relationship with her mother could prove useful.

Maddy and Peter arrived a few minutes before the scheduled start of the ceremony. Several mourners still milled around on the lawns beside the ancient walls of the Romanesque church, appreciating the warm day. Peter saw no one else from the Yard. Everyone was local, and dressed in black.

"Do you see any of the family?" Maddy whispered.

"They're inside, no doubt."

"We should find our places."

It was then that Peter balked from entering the church. He emerged from the car into the sunlight, and with no warning the memory of his brother blindsided him. He feared that death, not catharsis or forgiveness, held sway inside the old church. He had only one thing to offer the Carpenters. He would find their son's killer and lift their grief. But he could not, at this moment, enter this chamber.

He stood there in morbid contemplation. All the guests were

inside now. He took another minute. The old professional instincts were returning. He was in the sorting-out phase, what Joan sometimes called his mystical stage. There was something wrong with the Carpenter investigation. He probed in his mind for a way through the fog and as usual it was the women who came into focus, who offered a path: Nicola Hilfgott, Alice Nahri, Maddy, and Joan. And Carole Carpenter. Women were his salvation, the ones who made sense of his cases. Yes, finding Alice was the key.

But his brother's ghost displaced any optimism. Peter was a detective and should have been able to compartmentalize his grief. For now, he believed what Emerson said: "Sorrow makes us all children again. The wisest know nothing."

Maddy saw the pain of loss in his eyes. She had her own loss to mourn. And so she waited to see whether he wanted her to join the congregation inside. She would take on the role he'd assigned to her. She did not see what her father-in-law hoped to learn at the funeral, yet she had faith in him, and now she waited even longer, obediently. She believed that she had shown restraint when it counted, holding back on her wilder theories. Their partnership would proceed however Peter shaped it.

Peter took a moment to focus on her once more. He offered a wan smile of encouragement. He supposed that he was mildly in love with Maddy but what he craved above all was to protect her. Part of that sheltering required trusting her.

"I want you to go inside with the rest," he said. "I'll stay out here until the service ends. You probably have a few minutes, so see if you can diplomatically get into the annex, if there is one. I don't know about this diocese but I expect that the flowers of condolence are set up in a separate space. There's a renovated crypt underneath but I haven't been down there."

"Will they be holding the reception, food and the like, in the annex, do you think?" Maddy said, nervous. "There may be the local serving ladies to contend with."

"I can't imagine there'd be room enough for food and drink for all this lot. But on an occasion such as this, the flowers will be set up to be admired. Take a look at all the To-and-Froms on the bouquets. Let me know if any names strike you."

She knew that he was being slightly coy: there was at least one name he was searching out. "Am I to stay for the service?"

"If you would. I'll hide out in the car."

"I knew we should've brought Jasper. You could have walked her."

Maddy joined a cluster of mourners at the covered main doorway of the church. It began to sprinkle rain and the throng moved in more decisively. The church would be full. Her first sight of the Romanesque arches drew her eye upwards to the vaulted ceiling. The angle made her dizzy; these days, she interpreted her every feeling in terms of her pregnancy and now she steadied herself against a stone column. The delirium persisted and she turned to the entryway, halting by another pillar. The steps to the downstairs gaped on her immediate left. She had missed the stairs; the crowd had obscured them when she entered.

The scent of flowers wafted up from below. As she descended, Maddy wondered who had decided to gut the catacomb in favour of what was probably a linoleum-floored reno job.

But the compromise had been thought through. Off to the right, the subterranean burial chamber still stood, out of sight behind a locked oak door. She raised an eyebrow at the sign by the door: "Crypt. No Entry." The room on the other side was an excavated space, about thirty feet long, twenty wide. The room could accommodate a reception crowd, she estimated, but the steps were the problem, forcing single-file climbs and descents. With the fluorescent lighting, the atmosphere in the room was submarine-like. As Peter had predicted, no food was set out but she counted ten floral arrangements arrayed on two draped tables. She could see that most came from the same florist.

She started at the near end. One tag read "We loved you, Johnny."

Another said "We'll miss you, Fitz." There was no bouquet from Alice Nahri. In fact, none of the scribbled names meant anything to her until she came to the seventh bouquet. The tag read "Our condolences. Dunning Malloway."

"Malloway not here, then?" a voice said directly behind her.

Maddy turned, struggling to look innocent. She knew that this was the brother. His eyes were sunken and sad. He might have had a drink already.

"I don't know," was all she could manage.

"I guess if he's in Montreal with Johnny's killer, he can be excused," Joe Carpenter said. He was not being overly aggressive with her, perhaps because he was playing truant himself. He took out a pack of Nicorette gum and put a piece in his mouth; she noticed that it was a four-gram stick, the stronger dose. "You representing Scotland Yard?"

She sensed a tailing off of his hostility to her, although she knew that it was momentary and she must be careful. "I'm very sorry for your loss."

"My brother was the best. My mum calls him the best hope. How do you think that made me feel? They've charged the book dealer. Have you found the girl?"

Maddy walked over to him. The crowd could be heard above them. She reached out and touched his sleeve, a movement that surprised both of them.

"After you," Joe said.

The funeral lasted forty-five minutes, during which Peter waited outside the car in the lot. The local hearse stood ready twenty yards away with its back doors open but Peter paid it no mind. Most idlers would have wandered about the tombstones, some of which looked ancient, but Peter had little interest in them . He checked his phone messages three times; there were none. What he wanted to do was call Deroche at the Sûreté. If any part of the investigation felt underdeveloped it was the role of Leander Greenwell in all this: unless and until he disclosed an alliance with Alice or Nicola, then all the authorities had was guesswork about the deeper motives underpinning the murder of John Carpenter. There it was again, he thought: the women driving the case.

Mainly from restlessness, he made a call to Henry Pastern, who answered on the fourth ring. He was out of breath. "Hello, Special Agent Pastern."

"Did I get you from somewhere, Henry?"

"Peter Cammon? Where are you calling from?"

"I'm at John Carpenter's funeral."

"Always making interesting moves, Peter. But I'm surprised. Malloway said he talked to Carpenter's brother and there wouldn't be a burial until the killer had been found and convicted."

"News of Greenwell's arrest changed Joe's mind. It's happening as we speak."

"Then he didn't hear the latest news. Malloway tells me the case against the book dealer is faltering. I called Deroche, and reading between the lines of what he told me, there are problems with a lack of physical evidence. Maybe police conduct as well. Leander's all lawyered up."

"So you've kept in touch with Malloway?"

"Heck, Peter, he was *here* yesterday. Blew in for an overnight with a long list of questions. I spent most of the day with him. Showed him the car. He went home on a red-eye flight last night. He must be closer to you than me by now."

The sudden possibility that Dunning Malloway might show up at John's funeral made Peter turn towards the church. He recovered enough to say, clumsily, "What do you think he thinks, Henry?"

Peter wanted Pastern's overall impression of Malloway, and Henry's response did not disappoint him. "I was a bit surprised. He discounted Greenwell's role. He believes Alice Nahri killed your man. Theft is the only motive. And I'll tell ya, Peter, the opinion here in Art Crime is that those letters, especially the one with Booth's John Henry on it, could bring a hundred thousand on the auction market."

"Does he believe that Carpenter himself might have gotten involved in stealing the documents?"

Henry paused thoughtfully. "Didn't mention it. Didn't seem interested. Finding Nahri is his top priority, quote-unquote."

"I may have a line on Alice Nahri's latest alias. I'll be in touch."

"Thanks, Peter. Any news on the hunt for Nahri, I'll call."

When the casket emerged, Joe among the bearers, Peter faded back a step behind the car, although it did not fully conceal him. The hearse crunched down further into the gravel as the long box was loaded. Obviously, John Carpenter had been moved from the shipping container into the family's walnut coffin but Peter couldn't help imagining, however irrationally, that the three letters lay inside. It was to be a cremation.

The milling crowd outside the church did not serve to hide Peter, and so he made no more effort to conceal his presence. He waited by the parking area, knowing Joe Carpenter would find him. He could see that Maddy was chatting by the graveyard with Joe's sister, Carole; it was the kind of gesture Joan or Sarah would make. He watched as the sweet girl brought Maddy over to introduce her to the mother. Peter was pleased that his daughter-in-law was at ease with these people; she even won a smile from the sister.

The business with the hearse complete, the crowd moved to their cars and began to fall in line behind the hearse. Peter remained by Maddy's vehicle, the only person in the car park not on the move. Peter knew that Joe had seen him the second he came out of the church. He watched the brother approach, saw him calculating his confrontation so that he could say his piece in one dramatic outburst (and who cared if everyone heard), and hop into the trailing car with his mother and sister.

"You must think I'm thick."

Peter Cammon's policy was to let aggressive witnesses burn themselves out. He kept silent. He wasn't afraid.

"Bring a gun then, did ya?" Joe added.

This was the natural point for Peter to offer condolences but he judged that even kindnesses would provoke Joe. Peter hardened his look.

"Did Malloway send you? You and the woman bein' the token mourners from London?"

"Malloway's looking for the girl," Peter said.

"So? You've given it up?"

"I'm here of my own accord to pay my respects and to ask you about Alice Nahri."

"She and the book dealer were in it together. We can agree on that."

Peter hesitated. "Yes, she was involved."

"You're representing Malloway, or what?"

Carpenter knew that he was being tiresome. Peter replied, "You know I'm not. Not on any count. I owe your brother my best effort. I'm here because you're one of the few people to meet the woman."

"And if I get my way, I'll be the last one she'll ever see."

"You know the Canadian police and the FBI are looking. They've the best hope of finding her."

"She has a mum and a sister over in Oxfordshire. Mother's white, I'm told. Father's from India." Dunning Malloway had revealed more than he should have done, Peter thought.

"The father is dead."

"I know that. The bitch has a long criminal record. How'd she get into Canada and America with a criminal record? Into this country, for that matter?"

Peter let Joe run on but now he nodded towards the stalled procession. "They're waiting."

Joe Carpenter walked back down the line to the last car as Maddy arrived at Peter's elbow. Perhaps it was a Lincolnshire custom to place the family at the back of the cavalcade, Peter guessed.

Peter was unsure how much Maddy had overheard. They got into her car.

"Did you get what you wanted?" Maddy said.

"Yes, I did," he said.

Maddy sat back and put on her seat belt. "Okay, what *exactly* did you want to know from Joe?"

"I realized he wouldn't give me much. But I confirmed what I suspected, that Joe Carpenter knows an awful lot about the girl, and about Malloway's efforts to find her."

"He got to know the girl well, then?"

"That's not what I mean. He knows about Alice's mother and sister, where they live. Dunning Malloway is the only possible source for that information. Why did Malloway give him so much background?"

"You're right," Maddy said. "It's not information he has any need of."

"Malloway is obsessed with Alice. That's becoming clear."

Maddy started the motor. "I talked to the mother and the sister. The sister is very nice. I wrote down my number — not on my business card — and said to call me sometime."

Peter looked over at her. She was like Sarah, able to make friends so easily. She was pretty effective with witnesses, too, he reflected. It had been shrewd, not giving the sister her business card; Joe would not have an excuse to overreact to "Director, Women's Services."

"Joe's a man at odds with his life," Maddy ventured. "He thinks that—"

Joe rapped on the passenger door. Reluctantly, Peter lowered the window. The mechanic said, in a surreal tone, a mix of a whisper, a cough, and the artificial projection of a ventriloquist, "Find her or I'll come and fucking kill you instead."

They fought traffic and heavy rain all the way to the cottage. The challenge of the elements provided an excuse for not talking, for Maddy was in a state of shock. Peter regretted bringing her so close to murder, especially now that he knew she was pregnant. At her job she had seen husbands and boyfriends threaten beatings, but murder, and its counterpart revenge, were too much. Joe Carpenter had issued an unequivocal warning. Maddy understood that he would kill Alice if given the chance. *The dead bite back*, Peter had heard more than one policeman say.

Maddy recovered by the time they reached the cottage. She touched his arm as he turned off the motor. "Don't say anything to Joan to make her worry."

She composed herself and agreed to stay the night. While she went upstairs to wash up for dinner, Peter and Joan stood on the veranda. Joan turned and kissed his cheek.

"There's more happening, isn't there? Go with it, Peter. Trust Maddy. You've been doing the right thing so far. Keep her involved and keep her safe."

Peter stood in shock, marvelling again at the women in his life. Joan had seen the core of everything without his saying a word. But then he turned the conversation into a detective moment by articulating Joan's crisis.

"Your sister's fading quickly, isn't she?"

Joan's look confirmed it. "She won't last the week."

The three of them sat in the dining room, Jasper under the table, and reviewed the investigation. Peter violated a half dozen Metropolitan Police rules of confidentiality but he hardly hesitated. He was only on contract with the Yard. His retirement status gave him some latitude. He told himself that he was positioned at just the right distance from Stephen Bartleben and his big desk.

There were so many threads to the case that Peter didn't try to channel the discussion towards any particular thesis. Once Maddy and Joan got going, he had no chance of asserting discipline. Both women inevitably returned the conversation to Alice. The young woman was the touchstone for how they felt about the case; she embodied the mystery of it, and all three of them agreed that she was the solution.

After three hours, Maddy looked exhausted. Joan told her to go upstairs and to take her time in the morning. As Maddy got up from the table, Peter recalled, "At the funeral today, dear, you said that Joe Carpenter is at odds with his life."

Maddy turned back; her face glowed in the light of the chandelier. "Yes. An older brother, respected for staying at home, loyal to the women in the family, sure. But that storyline only holds together as long as there's someone to sacrifice for. The family's move up the ladder depended on John Fitzgerald, the young Kennedy, their hope for the future. He's dead now. Topsy-turvy."

Joan and Peter sat on the veranda for another hour. They listened to the crickets and saw the occasional bat swoop by the shed. The outside lights were off, making the close night air seem a bit cooler. Both were amused by Jasper's decision to bed down with Maddy, but as a result, they felt especially alone.

"Staying up all night isn't good for her," Joan stated.

"She's young, and she certainly is enthusiastic," Peter said, in the kindliest of tones.

"The baby's due in the spring. Probably April. She's healthy, but just be sure to hit a balance. Make sure she gets rest. She and Michael are happy, so let her help you. I don't know why she's so passionate about the case, but there it is."

Before bed, Peter checked his messages on the desktop computer and found that Commissioner Souma in Delhi had sent him a huge data packet derived from the Indian passport office. It encompassed long lists of recent passport applications across India. There were thousands of names. Peter jotted a note to Maddy and taped it to the monitor.

Peter wasn't surprised that Maddy was up and alert long before he roused himself and padded downstairs. He found her at the computer station off the living room, Jasper at her feet, the dog's head resting on the tangle of cables under the table.

"I've found her! The new Alice Nahri, I've found her." Maddy

270

said. Jasper looked up at Peter as if she might claim credit for the discovery.

Peter was instantly wide awake. "What have you discovered, *ma chère*?"

"You've got lists from India coming out your ears," she began, "but it only took a while."

He brought a chair over to her side. "Have one of these," she offered. A gift box of Canadian maple sugar, pressed into maple leaf shapes, sat on the table by the computer. He had forgotten buying them at the Montreal airport. Five pieces were gone. Maddy handed him one, and he nibbled at it while she fed another to Jasper, who would have eaten a cricket ball if Maddy had presented it to her.

Maddy pointed to the screen. "I copied the names to a subsidiary file, not just to preserve the originals but to take the lists out of PDF format and make them more searchable."

"Okay."

"I put the names in alphabetical sequence. Then I took out all the Sikh surnames and anything oriental, not to be bigoted about it. I took a chance and deleted names like Smith and Evans, since they seemed anomalous. There were no 'Nahris,' no 'Parsons,' and no, no 'Orwells' either."

She paused for effect. "But has the name Alida Nahvi ever come up?"

"No."

"I had no way of matching individual names to Motihari or Bihar. The details simply weren't there. Neither was age, although the application forms must undoubtedly list sex and age. We just have a catalogue of names. For a long time I just stared at the revised list. I went back to names that might resonate with Alice's home state. Well, Nahvi is close to Nahri and I added it to my new, shorter list. Even then, there were hundreds of possibles. I needed some reason to settle on one name or any other. I fell asleep in front of the terminal and in my dream it came to me."

"When did you have time to sleep?" Peter said. He realized that his daughter-in-law had probably been up since dawn.

"Early. I nodded off in my chair. It was one of those half dreams. In it, I found myself talking to Alice *Nahvi*. The girl in my dream didn't look like Alice Nahri but she called herself that, repeatedly. So, I went back to the lists."

"And you figured something out through your dream?"

"No. Michael did. I called him."

Peter couldn't help himself. "You called him at *this* hour?"

"He's used to it. So, I asked him on the phone, did the name 'Nahvi' mean anything to him, and he knew immediately. The Na'vi are the blue people in *Avatar*. They're a virtuous native tribe on a distant planet. I asked him why Alice would choose the name and he reminded me of the videos on the bookshelf in Ida Parsons's room in Henley. All of them were films made by James Cameron, including a boxed-set thingy of *Avatar*. He even figured out the first name. Take Alice and her mother's name, Ida, combine them, and you get Alida Nahvi."

"Brilliant. My son as sleuth. Maybe I should call Michael in as consulting detective."

"Not a chance," Maddy said.

They reviewed the material for an hour more, until Maddy grew weary again and went back to bed. Peter took Jasper for a walk. When he returned, Joan and Maddy were both up. He agreed to go with Joan to see Winnie in Leicester while Maddy continued her research and minded the dog.

In the afternoon, Peter made a quick call to Henry Pastern to reveal Alice Nahri's new alias.

"Good work. I'll amend the bulletin on the girl," Henry said.

"I have reason to believe that Alice — Alida — is a fan of the movie *Avatar*."

"Great. I'll put out an APB for a ten-foot-tall naked blue woman. Sorry, too much coffee."

"She seems to be a fan of all of James Cameron's films. Do you want a list?"

"No thanks, Peter. I'm celluloid literate."

An hour later Henry called back. "Something you said triggered a memory. I checked the inventory of items found in the trash cans and in Lost Luggage at Union Station. We found a pink knapsack with images from *Titanic* on it. We're checking it for prints."

"No chance there was a GPS inside it?" Peter said.

"Not likely. But every little bit helps, I guess."

"Every little bit helps," Peter confirmed.

CHAPTER 29

Over the next three days, Peter attended to life at the cottage. He accompanied Joan on poignant visits to Leicester and Birmingham. He and Maddy spent a long afternoon in the shed organizing their files on the big trestle table.

Peter began to realize how easy it was to lose contact with a formal police investigation. He had no mandate and thus no easy premise for unprompted phone calls to colleagues, old or current. He wanted to reach out to Deroche in particular but Bartleben would immediately learn of it and demand an accounting for Peter's meddling. In the boss's thinking, Peter would have to choose: fully in or fully gone.

The one person who would always give Peter a sympathetic hearing regarding the case called him on a late Wednesday afternoon.

"Pascal, it's good you rang. How are you?" he said, not restraining his pleasure.

"I'm heading into battle, Peter." Pascal was semi-drunk.

"I can return your call later."

"Ah, Peter, you need to be here to see what's going on. Come over for a visit. I'm locked in a series of debates with Professor Olivier Seep that would amuse you. Tonight is Round Two. For the record, I did not initiate these academic duels."

"Then why, pray tell, did you agree to them?" Peter said, as lightly as possible.

"Because I am a Quebec academic. We debate the sun coming up in the morning and going down at night. By the way, it is possible that sunrise and sunset are Anglo conspiracies to restrict our sovereignty. We must take clear positions on all things."

Peter saw that his friend was rehearsing, setting his posture for the evening's debate, at which, presumably, he would catapult Greek fire across the stage towards Seep's lectern. There was nothing more vicious than the academic battlefield, he knew. He guessed that the debate would touch on the Civil War and further understood that Pascal would be on the defensive: the reasonable separatist arguing against the true radical.

"I doubt that I would understand the nuances," Peter said, encouraging his friend.

"In Quebec, the Parti Québécois has adopted a policy of extreme rhetoric and a strategy of confrontation. It is still in opposition, so that is all it can do while it waits to be elected. The population does not want another referendum on independence, so the PQ must be careful. It is all words, words, words, to quote Hamlet, that Danish equivocator, and I have said so in public. Typically French, isn't it, that I speak to tell others they are chattering too much? But now Seep has come forward with a new approach, a strategy of provocation."

"Has he quoted again from the letters?"

"Sort of. In our first debate, he postulated that the English have always been ready to use violence against the French majority, that the British administration at the time of Confederation promised to actively suppress the French, and he can prove it. This is consistent with the British actions in the 1837 Rebellion all the way up to the two referendums, he argues. I am expecting him to shoot his mouth off tonight about the text of the Williams letter, which he appears to have seen. And there is more, Peter."

"Oh?"

"I have inside knowledge that Seep will mention Nicola Hilfgott's name during the debate tonight."

"Raising the ante and making her the villain," Peter said. "He may have copies of one, two, or all of the letters."

"Perhaps."

"But how did he get them? Surely not from Hilfgott, who hates Seep and everything he represents. Do you think Deroche could have disclosed them?" Peter silently counted the individuals who had copies of the reconstructed texts: Hilfgott, Malloway, Pastern, Deroche, Pascal, Maddy, and himself. And maybe Neil Brayden.

"Not to Seep," Renaud answered. "Deroche hates separatists *and* academics." His voice turned anxious, a bit self-pitying. "You need to understand something, Peter. Seep and I may despise one another but we are on the same side. I am doing battle with him because I don't respect him, and he's adopting the wrong strategy. I don't know how long I can keep it up. You need to break this case open."

A breakthrough of a different kind swept over Peter. He saw as clearly as he saw the postern light on the entrance to the cottage lane that Pascal had put his career in jeopardy to help him. His only purpose in the debates was to draw out Olivier Seep and in so doing get the radical professor to reveal his involvement in the theft of the Williams–Booth letter, and by extension the murder of John Carpenter.

It was a moment to show trust and Peter could only think of one gesture he could make in return. "I have a favour to ask, Pascal. I expect that Leander Greenwell has been released by now. Do you think you could you try again to make contact with him? You can't phone and you have to be careful when you knock on his door. Deroche's people may be watching. I want you to ask him about everything that happened that night."

"Ah, Peter, you haven't heard the latest." Peter sensed Renaud's mood lighten. *Skulduggery can often do that,* he thought. "The rumour is that Deroche blew it. Got a little rough at the Bordeaux Prison and Leander's lawyer called them out on it. The judge released him with a reprimand to the Crown, even though the prosecutor argued he was a . . . what is it?"

"A flight risk?"

"Yes. And there is even more news."

"Out with it."

"There has been an incident. Leander Greenwell's boyfriend. His name is Georges Keratis."

"I remember."

"They sort of live together. Georges is not a bad fellow. He works at Club Parallel downtown. Deroche's soldiers have abused him a few times, so he doesn't like the police any more than Leander does. Deroche accused Georges of giving a false alibi. *Bien*, last night someone attacked Georges on his way to visit Greenwell's store. It was the kind of beating that enforcers apply to their victims. You understand? Collectors for organized crime, that kind of thing."

"What could they possibly want from Georges?"

"I have no idea. I'm not even sure it was a mob attack. Georges won't talk to the police, apparently."

"Someone was sending a message."

"If so, they were sending a message to *Greenwell*." Pascal suddenly laughed. "Seriously, Peter, why the hell else would anyone beat up Georges Keratis?"

The point was rhetorical. Peter wished him well in the debate and expressed the hope that he would be back in Montreal soon.

"You know," Pascal said finally, "I told you my name is spelled with a 'd' and not like Inspector Renault in *Casablanca*. Did you know that Claude Rains is buried in a small cemetery in upstate New Hampshire? We should drive down there sometime."

Peter smiled at his end of the line. It was Renaud's way of saying this could be the beginning of a beautiful friendship.

Peter understood that he could not avoid London much longer, yet he hesitated. He wanted Bartleben's support on a number of fronts — a continued flow of information from the Yard, for example — but he had little to offer in exchange. He owed HQ a written report but he wasn't ready to posit firm theories about the sins of Alice Nahri or Leander Greenwell. Bartleben would also demand a meeting. Peter had no desire to sit in a room with Frank Counter, or worse, Dunning Malloway.

Serendipity forced the issue in a morbid way. Peter put off the call for three more days. He used the time to sketch out a report, although he found himself leaving out key facts — the whole subplot of Olivier Seep's intrigues, for example. That Saturday night, Michael and Maddy formally announced the baby was due in mid-April and everyone toasted the family's good fortune with flutes of Schweppes ginger ale on the veranda. A few minutes later, the hospice phoned to report that Joan's sister had died.

They convened the funeral in Chelmsford, Winnie's birthplace. A large crowd, most of whom exceeded Peter in age, gathered for the dignified funeral in a local church that, though more Gothic than Romanesque, reminded him hauntingly of the church in New Bosk. Winnie had died without children; Peter and Michael joined in as pallbearers. At one point, Peter caught Maddy's eye and surmised that she was thinking of New Bosk, too.

Sir Stephen came up behind Peter as he stood talking to Maddy on the church lawn. Peter hadn't seen him inside the church earlier.

"I'm glad I could make it," Sir Stephen said. He wore the most stylish black suit among the whole crowd of mourners. Peter looked over at the Mercedes in the parking lot; Stephen's driver stood by the door. Tommy Verden hadn't been enlisted as a chauffeur.

"Thank you for coming," Peter said. "Joan will be pleased."

"Yes, I already conveyed my condolences to her. By the way, Inspector Verden asked me to deliver his condolences, too, and his regrets that he couldn't come today. I have him off in Islamabad, helping out Frank Counter's people on this *News of the World* cricket thing."

Peter took Sir Stephen's sincerity at face value. There was nothing suspicious in Tommy's absence. The day before, Tommy had called Joan to offer his apologies for not attending the funeral.

"I owe you a report," Peter said.

"We need a meeting."

"We don't need a meeting."

"I'm here to make peace, Peter, but if you're telling me you want totally out of the case, then everything will move onto Frank's plate. All things American and Québécois."

"Has Dunning produced an interim report?" Peter said.

"No, but he briefs Frank daily. And he's active. Plans to fly to D.C. next week for an update from the Bureau on the search for Alice Nahri."

"I don't see the need. She could be in any of fifty states. Henry Pastern is on the ball," Peter said.

"Nevertheless . . . Malloway talked to Inspector Deroche yesterday. It seems the inspector believes that someone hired a couple of mob goons to beat up Georges Keratis. Malloway agrees."

Sir Stephen's ramble was meant to show that he was on top of the cast of suspects and witnesses.

"He does?" Peter could not see a mafia-Greenwell link but he let it go. Still, he couldn't resist saying, "Malloway told me in Montreal that his main brief is to size up Nicola Hilfgott. Do you think he can handle her?"

Sir Stephen Bartleben never allowed himself to blush but his pursed lips told Peter that he had hit a sensitive point. Malloway's mission to Montreal had been as much Bartleben's idea as Frank Counter's. Sir Stephen didn't answer for a full minute. "Nicola is a goner. The separatist obsession. Can't shut up."

"Let me guess," Peter said. "The James Cross factor keeps her in place."

Bartleben shook his head. "Not really. There are plenty of excuses we in the Mother House can invent, whatever she imagines is protecting her. Maybe her husband will hit her with a golf club." Peter noted the reference: the world was currently preoccupied with Tiger Woods and his marital troubles, and golf jokes were in fashion.

But Peter understood why Sir Stephen was being so flippant. He was dodging his own exposure to Nicola's nonsense. The act of recalling her from Montreal would reverberate within Bartleben's own fiefdom. Frank Counter would depart under a cloud, almost simultaneous to Nicola. Stephen had to manage this mess carefully.

Bartleben shook his head again. "She's been sleeping with her assistant."

"Neil Brayden?"

"Do you know him?"

"Yes. But I didn't know he was shagging her. So what?"

"Just piling up justifications. Who knows what goes on in the Hilfgott household." He exhaled loudly to indicate the bureaucratic weight on his shoulders.

Peter suddenly got Bartleben's insinuation. "Are you suggesting Brayden is the one who attacked Georges? On Hilfgott's behalf? Whose theory is that, Stephen?"

"Oh, I don't know. That's why I want you back on the case."

The octogenarian crowd on the lawn showed no signs of moving to their cars. Peter looked at Stephen. *We old people love to prattle*, Peter thought. "Does Malloway buy into this theory?"

"Why don't you like Malloway, Peter?"

"I don't trust him. He's jumpy. Alice Nahri is central to the case and it's becoming clear that he's obsessed with her. At the same time, he shows no faith in Deroche, who, whatever his weirdness, at least has the prime suspect in custody. Almost."

"Frank speaks highly of Dunning's work on this Pakistani cricket business. He did a stint at the High Commission in Delhi, so he has tentacles where we need them."

"And Hilfgott?" Peter said.

"Spit it out, Peter."

"I think he cares more about finding the girl than about Nicola's fixation."

"I will be . . . watchful."

The funeral was over and Peter's family had gathered by the car.

"I'll have an interim report to you next week, Stephen."

"Then we can have a meeting."

"No. I don't want to meet."

"What is it you do want?"

"I want Washington."

"Why?"

"Because that's the last place anyone saw the woman."

For the next week Peter continued his intensive research on Bihar and Old Montreal, the Lincoln assassination, jellyfish, James Cameron movies, and the mafia. He became something of an expert on the Rizzuto crime family. Deroche was right to be concerned. Someone was exploiting the long-term imprisonment of the ruling godfather, Vito Rizzuto, and killing his soldiers. Peter found fresh rumours that the ageing grandfather, Nicolo, would come out of retirement to reassert control. Peter had never worked in Organized Crime at the Yard but he knew that shootings in urban streets and firebombings of bakeries and cafés presaged a classic consolidation of mafia power. Ultimately, he saw no reason for any of the Cosa Nostra factions to assault Leander Greenwell's young lover, Georges Keratis.

Peter bought a map of the United States and tacked it to the wall in the garden shed. Peter liked puzzles and he stared at the map every so often, ranking Alida Nahvi's hiding places among the fifty states. At intervals Maddy joined him in his sanctum and they daydreamed together.

Henry Pastern called at the end of the third week. It was about time for them to check in and Peter expected a routine mutual update.

"Has Malloway visited recently?" Peter began.

"A bunch of calls, that's all. But I have news."

"I'd welcome it."

"We've found her," Henry stated.

Peter wasn't in the shed at that moment. He conjured up the big multicoloured map of the states.

"Where?"

"Buffalo, New York."

PART THREE

Twenty-Twenty

Perfect understanding of events only after they have happened. The ability to understand afterwards what should have been done or what caused an event, and therefore based on information that was not available at the time a decision was made. Perfectly normal visual acuity, i.e., 20/20 on the Snellen eye chart.

CHAPTER **30**

2009

"You would defy me?" the Sword expostulated from his side of the glass-topped desk in his vast Piccadilly hotel suite.

In fact, I would, was Alice's immediate thought. She had no doubts that the Sword would kill her if she rejected his next assignment. I have paid for your loyalty in British pounds, he was saying, no bonuses to be expected. But it wasn't all that many pounds or rupees or Euros, she thought. She had worked for the man for four years, indeed had been constant, never turning down his wishes, yet her reward hadn't been personal wealth. She lived inside *his* wealth but the cash had never flowed in any volume to her Hong Kong account. And she often took risks for him, travelling the notorious National Highway 28 to Kathmandu with gems, drugs, and other contraband. Asking for five days off was reasonable and would not get her killed. *Taking* five days without prior approval would not cause him to kill her either, although that was admittedly moot, since she had never sneaked off before. She felt caught in a sticky trap, her minor request showing how hopeless it was to dream of earning her escape.

"You want a five-day vacation?" said the Sword.

"Attending my father's funeral may be your idea of a vacation, but it's not mine."

She knew how to read his moods. If her master had intended to refuse he would not have sat at the desk. The Sword, half-Vietnamese and half-Pakistani, had a thing about status. He wanted respect, but more than that, he craved *business* respect. He had made a lot of money fast but remained a junior player in the demimonde of football and racetrack betting. His passion remained the horses and Alice knew that he was negotiating to buy a five percent share in the Sha Tin track in Hong Kong. She had been there on his arm many times.

The desk, rendered absurd because of the formal poses the Sword and the girl were forced to strike in the slippery steel-framed chairs, was his attempt at looking like an executive. She wanted to laugh at him but didn't dare. The Kashmiris and the Malaysians and the Chinese would never welcome him into their clan operations. He was the Rodney Dangerfield of sport touts. *That's why we click*, Alice thought, *we're both mongrels salivating for prizes at the dog show.*

Alice had never fractured the Sword's trust, for good reason. He was violent and insecure and she was often the closest object to his rage. She always flattered him, since the more insecure he acted, the more important it was that he be conciliated with displays of loyalty. Actually, he wasn't doing badly. The Sword was a talented criminal. His biggest success, the one that might catapult him to the penthouse rooms of every European and Asian luxury hotel, was his recent alliance with organized crime interests. The future of sport gambling lay in the match-fixing syndicates, she knew, and he was connected.

"I have done all the things you've commanded," Alice said. She had, too, including sleeping with football stars and Hong Kong moguls. "Give me the time."

He frowned. "There will be a price to pay."

"For taking five days of non-vacation?"

"You haven't heard what the price is."

"What is it?"

"Cricket wagering. We are entering the gambling trade big-time starting next month."

Cricket-match fixing was the most lucrative and the most corrupt of intrigues, and thus the most dangerous. The clans guarded it jealously. She had dozed through several cricket matches in her youth — Motihari was as obsessed as every other town in India — and had no interest in the sport. But she knew exactly why the Sword was interested in this gentleman's game where the players wore white and the contest moved at a stately pace. The Sword hungered to belong to this classy enterprise.

"What is my role?" She imagined having to coddle up to the overpaid, overpraised cricket stars while the boss slipped them cash bribes in U.S. dollars.

"The game is growing and changing," said the boss, rapping hard on the desk. "Have you heard of Twenty20? It is the new form of cricket. Have you heard of spot-fixing? We are about to get into that in a big way."

"What do you expect me to do?"

"You will play a major role. Help me with the teams. We will operate everywhere in Europe and Asia, but especially London. That should please you."

"There's more, I'm assuming."

He paused. "The danger is that the authorities, the police agencies, and the cricket regulators have the gambling syndicates in their sights. Scotland Yard has formed a task force. I want you to infiltrate it."

Alice could not resist some sarcasm. "That's a lot for a week off."

"Ah, now it's a full week?"

"No, only five days for the funeral."

The Sword survived by observing details. He knew that Alice's father had been buried two days ago. Why did she need five days? He decided he would monitor her more closely from now on.

They agreed that Alice would report on the sixth day, upon which he would educate her in the game of cricket and the shadow world behind it. Alice recalled a review by George Orwell of the novel *Raffles*, in which the hero is said to be a fine cricket bowler as well as a cat burglar. The point, Orwell perceived, was that cricket is one of the few sports in which the amateur can exceed the professional. She astutely saw that the game risked destroying itself: in the twenty-first century the players were becoming corrupted by their professional status. Match-fixing attracted the aggressive criminals, the ones willing to bribe or blackmail players without compunction. The Sword saw an opportunity but Alice believed it to be too dangerous. As she planned for her flight to Delhi, she decided to use her week at home to plan her escape, too.

"Do what I tell you or I'll shoot you in the head," Alice said to the journeyman mechanic, which was precisely what she would say to her uncle five minutes later.

"I will call the constable," the boyish apprentice said, his first act of resistance in years, bursting out now only because he thought he could foil a scrawny girl.

If Hashi, the junior mechanic, holds the same status as he did ten years ago, Alice concluded, *then he lacks a backbone.* "No, you'll give this letter in person to the police commissioner," she replied, confident that the mention of the chief of police would intimidate him. He began to protest but she stared him down and, gripping the note, he fled the garage.

Alice strode the length of the old garage to the office, where Raji Bosh was playing *Carmageddon* on his computer. In response to her threat, indignation spread across his face, although he said nothing. Alice held the .32 to the bridge of his nose, and said, "I'll take your eyes."

Raji Bosh calculated that she wouldn't shoot, but the gun gave him pause. It appeared deadly and new, the bluing still on the barrel. She saw him looking. "I bought it in Darra." He understood; in Darra, Pakistan, the gunmakers would fashion any kind of firearm one needed overnight, and at a cheap price. Instead of speaking, Raji Bosh sat back in his swivel chair while a carjacker destroyed his avatar on the computer screen.

Alice forced him to drink the bottle of Thums Up Cola that

contained four percent gamma-hydroxybutyrate acid. It was three times the dose he had inflicted on her ten years previous, enough to knock him unconscious. Before the GHB kicked in, he managed to get out, in English: "I delivered very fine funeral honours to Father Aamon."

He did not plead, remaining arrogant. He made it sound as if he had beatified a Catholic priest — Father Aamon — in a cathedral. She had visited her father's resting place an hour ago, a sorry gravesite in a Motihari suburb. There had been no ceremony at the banks of the Ganges, no garlands of flowers.

Alice worried that the junior mechanic would abandon his resolve and bring the police around anyway. She needed fifteen minutes to search. Raji Bosh lay helpless on the office floor, knocked out by the drug but not dying. She opened the storage room at the rear of the garage and stood back to examine the pyramid of detritus within. She knew that her uncle was a pack rat, a cheapskate who never discarded anything. She considered torching the junk, shutting the windows, and allowing the smoke to suffocate him. She pondered running over him with a Tata inside the garage. Feeding him battery acid. Dropping an engine block on him using the chain pulley over the work bays.

The wheelchair lay at the back of the jumble of trash. She pulled out each item, as if she were untangling the Gordian knot. Finally, she yanked a snarl of junk out into the room, heedless of the mess. The chair, she could see, had a bent left front wheel but when she tried it out, the thing rolled well enough on the cement floor. Using an oily rag, she wiped the dust from the top of the mahogany frame; the rest of the chair would be covered for her journey.

It took a half hour to fill out her inventory. She found sufficient rope in the storage bin, and her uncle's sunglasses lay, as expected, in the desk drawer. She discovered a blanket in the boot of a customer's sedan. Hoisting her uncle, who had grown plump over the decade, proved the tougher task, but she eventually had him tied to the chair. She draped the blanket over him.

287

Poor invalid.

At last ready to abandon the garage, and her life in Bihar, Alice took down the portrait of the god Mithra and propped it on Raji Bosh's lap.

Alice remained calm as she wound her way along the potholed roads to the bridge. The sunglasses obscured most of her uncle's face. She encountered a half dozen locals, some of whom she knew. None displayed recognition of Alice Nahri or the invalid in the old-fashioned British wheelchair.

Such a dutiful daughter.

She reached the bridge in less than an hour. The heat of the noon sun failed to revive Raji Bosh, who drooled on his blanket. Even on the bridge, deserted at this hour, the light breeze that had floated down from the Himalayas did not rouse him.

Alice headed for the centre of the span. From the far end of the bridge, a woman came towards her pushing a baby stroller that mocked her uncle's chair. Alice could clearly see the curiosity on the mother's face, even though they were a hundred yards apart. A baby blanket hid the child from the baking sun and the woman hurried to gain the other side of the exposed bridge. Alice had stopped in the middle by now, as if to admire the view. The mother thought it odd that the figure in the wheelchair lay wrapped in a throw rug. And why did he hold a portrait of Lord Krishna on his lap? She moved on.

It was important to Alice that her uncle be awake before she toppled him into the Motijheel. She folded back the car blanket, now soaked in his sputum and puke, and slapped his jaw to revive him. Raji Bosh groaned, fighting to wake up, which he did after two minutes. She removed his sunglasses. He opened his eyes but failed to absorb where he was. He managed to turn his face up to her and recognition oozed into his teary eyes, a question flashing across his clammy face.

"The Motijheel," Alice said. "The water trough."

A four-foot concrete barrier lined the state highway bridge but Alice easily found the strength to unstrap the body and lever him over the rim. She was lucky that no traffic entered the bridge from either end. Raji Bosh realized what was about to happen and a reflex made him clutch the framed picture before it could fall.

"Mithra," he whispered.

"No," said Alice. "You always had it wrong. It is Mithridates, inheritor of Mithra. Mithridates was a real king, Persian, not Zoroastrian." She had discovered more in her research: mithridatism was a cult, premised on the masochistic habit of building up toxin resistance in the body by steadily ingesting small, non-lethal amounts of poison. The practice was supposed to attract power to the user of the poison-cum-drug. Raji Bosh turned his face to Alice, who removed her own sunglasses. The massive dose of GHB had crippled the man, sealed his fate. He possessed no power and was beyond salvation.

His body hit the floating island of green hyacinth and plopped right through to the depths of Moti Lake. The chair followed, sat a while on the loose bed of weeds, and sank.

The police commissioner read through Alice's letter, which succinctly chronicled the attempted rape. She stated that she demanded justice and if the commissioner decided to come after her, he might first give some thought to his own "complicity." The letter noted that the jumper cables had been affixed to the battery of his yellow Scorpio.

CHAPTER 31

On the third day, wearing a new set of casual clothes from a Rochester consignment shop, Alida hopped a bus to downtown Buffalo.

Without straying far from the terminal, she quickly found a print shop that offered internet stations and spent an hour perusing a list of every downtown hotel. She ran MapQuest routes to those that were within walking distance of the bus station. Six in total; and another eight if she broadened the radius by a mile. She needed just the right place in the city core. From her recent travels, she knew that most of the old, independent hotels located by railroad and bus stations had vanished from the American landscape. She narrowed down the list. The hotel should be no higher than ten levels, with multiple ground-floor exits, a freight elevator, and preferably a sleepy, slowed-down atmosphere.

To save time, she returned to the bus depot and looked around for the oldest employee in the place. She spied a grey-haired, dignified man in an office by the ticket window; darting around the front counter she wandered in, smiling and apologetic.

"I wonder if you can tell me, are there any of what they call 'young women's hotels' around here?" Alida was surprised at how she had mastered American inflections.

The man smiled. "No one calls them that anymore. They don't exist. But I recommend the Gorman, three blocks over. It was originally an old railroad hostelry. Safe and clean and basic. I could take a break and guide you." The man's gaze was wistful but Alida wasn't in the market for a grandfatherly date.

The Gorman Hotel stood eight storeys tall and sat among rows of modest office buildings, like the oldest relative at a sleepy family gathering. She reasoned that this place could be perfect, or would be if her other requirements panned out. The Gorman was known as a "traveller's hotel" and had been built in the 1920s for drummers travelling by train. It was now patronized by their modern equivalent, lonely sales reps on one-night turnarounds. Alida entered through the main doors. Business appeared to be slow. The lobby was small, no breakfast room or internet stations, and with only two rumpled armchairs to idle in. It was not the kind of lobby where anyone waited for long, and the three customers observed by Alida over the next five minutes walked directly from the clanky elevator to the street without making eye contact with her or the desk clerk. By then the clerk had noticed her, which was fine with Alida, and as he looked up from his motorcycle magazine, she was pretty sure that one of her remaining criteria had been satisfied. He was young, with excessively combed blond hair that made him resemble Alan Ladd in *Shane* but without the charisma.

Suspicion is bred in the bones of desk clerks and his half-second glance sized her up as a hooker, but that all changed with her smile, which moved his thinking along to another cliché, the girl in the big city for the first time.

She approached the desk.

"I don't know Buffalo. I just came in on the bus and I guess a place close to the station will be the best thing."

He was shorter than she was. She remembered hearing that short cowboy stars sometimes stood on platforms to appear to be the same height as their leading ladies. She didn't know why she kept flashing on western movies. She wasn't nervous.

291

"Did you want a single or a double, and how many nights?" the boy said, his voice cracking on the last word.

"A large single, I suppose," she said, in an effort to throw the initiative over to him. "I'm an aspiring actress. I have an audition in the Theatre District tomorrow."

"So, one night, then?"

"Yes. Unless I get the part. Then I'll be back!"

"Okay. Good luck. Do you have a credit card?"

The young clerk began to check his computer screen. Absorbed in her play-acting, she almost forgot her final prerequisite. "Could I see the room first?"

"Let me get my master key," the boy said. Without registering anything on his computer, the he picked up a plastic card — Alida wondered if they still called them skeleton keys — and gestured to the lift. She went ahead in order to give him a chance to check her out.

He pressed the button for "3" and she immediately said, "Anything on the fourth?"

He stabbed at "4" and as he stepped to the back of the lift she turned and looked him in the eye, saying, "Sorry to be a nuisance. You have a nice baritone voice, like you should almost have an English accent."

Her flirting deeply disconcerted the boy, she saw. They chatted about the weather and the bus ride, but nothing that would identify her later. She jumped from topic to topic, until he was completely off base, and red-cheeked from her sly flattery. The elevator moved slowly; it stopped with a shudder on the third level, almost upending them before it restarted. She recorded the useful fact that the doors took a long time to close, even longer for the ascent to recommence.

He opened the thick composite door to 402 with the key and stood back to let her enter. Alida knew instantly that this would be perfect. The décor was ordinary: a double bed, a desk and chair, and a full lavatory with white subway tiles and a heavy old porcelain sink. At once she noticed a bonus feature, the inter-room doorway, and her heart raced. She looked him in the eye; a lick of blond hair drooped across his forehead. She nodded her approval of the room.

"What's your name?" she said.

"Jeff. Some people try to call me 'Jeffie' but I won't stand for it."

This pleased Alida. He was the kind of boy who measured his manhood by his victories in imaginary arguments. His follow-up effort at seduction was a watery smile. Alida had to force her own enthusiasm.

"Are these rooms joined?" she asked. The connector door was typical, with a turn lock on her side and, she assumed, the equivalent in the adjacent room.

"All the way down the corridor. Use 'em for families or for convention parties, though it can get out of hand, business types carrying their whiskey from room to room. Some of them get so pissed. Then they find a connector locked at some point and they figure something's wrong, and they . . ."

"You want to show me the Theatre District later, Jeff?" she said, interrupting in a new, smoky voice that he could not misinterpret.

He gulped. "My shift's till nine."

"That would be great. I don't know . . ." She almost forgot where she was. "Buffalo at all. My luggage is at the bus depot. I'll sign in, take a walk around the town, and be ready by nine. Bob's your uncle, Jeff."

At the registration desk, Alida made a show of counting bills from her change purse to cover the seventy-three dollars for the night. It was against the rules for Jeff to take cash without a credit card backup but Alida knew that this wouldn't be his last infraction of the night. She insisted on cash and gave him a false address in Troy, New York. She could see his mind churning: What risk was there with no in-room movies or mini-bar to drive up her tab?

She wandered the downtown for an hour, happy to be a tourist. While she had already committed her heart to Rochester, she sought out the sights of downtown Buffalo on the map. She dutifully stood in front of Niagara Square and admired City Hall, and then took in the buildings up and down Ellicott Street. The two female statues on the pinnacle of the Liberty Building nearby reminded her of the Wings of Progress in Rochester. She read the plaque on the obelisk that was centred before City Hall and discovered yet another American president: William McKinley, assassinated in Buffalo in 1901 at the Pan-American Exposition by Leon Czolgosz using a .32 pistol. Presidents and assassins lurked everywhere in America.

On her way back to the Gorman Alida bought a mobile phone with a hundred minutes of time. The sales girl assured her that her number wouldn't register on anyone's caller ID system. In room 402, she showered and put on knickers and the glitter T-shirt she had bought in upstate New York. She went to sleep above the covers.

About 6 p.m., she got up and called Lembridge in Chesapeake Beach. It took some fast talking, mixed with threats, to prevent his hanging up but once she told him what she wanted — including sex again — they talked for an hour. It took only that long to seduce him. Minute by minute, she felt the sleaze seeping back into his voice, forming a slurry of greed, lust, and professional arrogance, leading him to say, "Miss Cameron," — Alida still used the false name from their Chesapeake encounter — "we both want the same things, don't we?"

"Sure we do," Alida said.

She knew what resided at Professor Lembridge's core: he was bored with his life, and this was an adventure he couldn't resist — if she pitched it properly. She promised him half the proceeds and all the sex he could handle. The professor said he had met Ronald Crerar before and when she dropped a number into the conversation, he replied that the businessman was good for it.

Precisely at 9:01, Jeff knocked on her door.

"Ready?" he called from the hallway.

She opened the door and as soon as he was fully inside, she stripped off her shirt. The window faced west and she passed the next hour on her back guessing when the last vestige of sunshine would be gone from the sky. When there was no more light, she would have two choices: to flee ever westward into the blackness, or to wait here for the sun to come full circle and find her again. The city turned cold for a moment, and she shivered. Her chosen home was just up the highway, but could she ever hope to conceal herself in Rochester, which one brochure called the City of Photographs?

Still, the stay-put option appealed to her, even if she knew there was a good chance that the next sunrise or the one after that would bring the Sword to town.

CHAPTER 32

Peter landed at Buffalo International Airport on a late September afternoon expecting to be met by Special Agent Henry Pastern but there was no one at the gate, and so he continued outside into the cool air. The FBI maintained fifty-six regional offices and it was unlikely that Peter would be acquainted with any of the agents who were gathering in Buffalo for the takedown, other than Henry. Yet, leaning against a police-issue sedan in the pick-up lane outside the building was an old friend.

"So, Chief Inspector, they're importing the Coldstream Guards to help me do my job," said Price Murdock. The FBI detective stood six-foot-four and had bulked up since Peter had last seen him at Quantico in 1999.

"They gave you one of the fifty-six, Price. Congratulations." Murdock, who had sent a card when Peter retired, was now approaching retirement himself.

As they headed downtown, Peter filled Price in on most of what he knew about the Booth letters and Alida Nahvi. Price explained that Henry Pastern, who was coordinating the operation, had scheduled a meeting of all participants later that afternoon in anticipation of the sting to go down the next morning.

Price waited while Peter checked into the Marriott and then the FBI man took him on a tour of the area around the Gorman. The hotel appeared to have only two avenues of escape: the main entrance and a small safety door at the rear. Peter was puzzled by Alida's choice of an old hotel like this, since a larger building like the Marriott would appear to offer more places to hide should flight prove necessary. Even odder was the acceptance of this shabby meeting place by the buyer, Ronald Crerar, who according to Henry liked to travel in style. He noticed that two blocks over stood a fashionable boutique hotel, the Pharos, which likely offered more amenities.

"Who do we have at the strategy session this afternoon?" Peter asked as Price drove the downtown zone.

"Your colleague Dunning Malloway is coming in today. He'll be there. Some of my people. Henry Pastern is running the operation. We'll be joined by Dave Jangler from Buffalo Police. Jurisdictional protocol has to be respected. Jangler's worry is that the operation might spill into the streets of Buffalo. But he's a good man, a veteran, and Henry figures we need local manpower to supplement our crew. My team, all special agents, can monitor the ground-level exits. The guy putting in the microphones is my guy, too."

"Do we know the room number where the exchange is to take place?"

"Not yet. I know, I know, Peter. Not much use having a techie when we don't know the room. But the girl scheduled the exchange for tomorrow at 10:30 a.m., somewhere in the hotel. We were able to access Ronald Crerar's schedule and he's pencilled in for that time. He lives in Rochester and will be driving down in the morning. Now get this. We know the girl's room number — 411. Registered under the name Alice Parsons. Lembridge says the girl told him she was in that room. We approached the hotel manager on the pretext of searching for a felony fugitive and there was your girl, paid in full and in advance, room 411."

"Can we wire *that* room?" Peter said.

"We're trying. Problem is, there isn't much concealment for a camera but at least we can place a microphone in the ceiling fixture or the door jamb. My guy says he'll try."

"Then we'll have the same problem with the meeting room."

"Agreed. A double problem, since we won't know till the last second where it will be."

"Let's play it by ear, then," Peter said, trying to sound like one of the team.

Murdock looked uncomfortable. "Peter, excuse my asking but I'm not sure why we're graced with the presence of *two* Scotland Yard detectives. What's the story on Malloway?"

Peter went on at some length explaining Malloway's brief in the Carpenter investigation, and his own limited, loose status. He grasped that Murdock was making a point, although not making a big issue of it: neither British detective had any real authority and they would have to defer to the leadership of the FBI and the Buffalo Police throughout the takedown operation.

"Do you want a weapon, Peter?"

Peter did not hesitate. Transporting a registered police weapon of his own on the flight would have been a pain, he knew, even with personal and official weapon permits to show. He had by now reconciled himself to remaining unarmed during the sting. Besides, Price wasn't really offering: it was a nod to Peter's reputation in the Bureau. "No, I can't see needing one."

"Good, because I shouldn't be offering you one." Murdock laughed. "Just so you know, your colleague Inspector Malloway has requested a gun, small arms."

"Are you supplying one?"

"Not unless you insist, my friend."

Peter could only offer a sardonic laugh.

The planning session began at four thirty in a boardroom in the FBI's local office. In attendance were Peter, Dunning Malloway, Henry Pastern, Price Murdock, two of Murdock's young special agents, and the technician. Peter was surprised that local police weren't represented after all. Dunning and Peter exchanged nods across the room.

The dynamics of the meeting were likely to be bizarre, Peter thought, as he took a seat at the big table. Murdock's people would fret over Malloway's need to be there at all, Scotland Yard's participation further muddled by the shaky premise of Peter's own attendance. He expected Dunning to put his well-shod foot in something. There was also a danger that Henry, who was chairing the meeting, might overstress the value of the Booth letters while underplaying the lethality of Alida Nahvi. But Peter was curious about Henry's cultivation of Professor Andrew Lembridge, who had alerted the Bureau to Alida's location.

As the discussion evolved, Henry showed a maturity and determination that surprised both Peter and, he noted, the other veterans in the room.

"Lembridge was the key," Henry said.

"What kind of professor is he?" Price Murdock prompted.

"American history. Also an expert on Civil War documents. Adviser to the National Archives. Authenticator to the stars."

"You don't seem to like him much," Price said.

"What's to like?" Henry said. "I've spent a long day with him. When I first contacted him by phone, he said he could provide authentication of the Booth correspondence, if it emerged. He didn't tell me at the time that he'd already *seen* the letters. Before we could meet, Nahvi called him about the Crerar deal. Lembridge lost his nerve. He walked into the Hoover Building and talked to another special agent. But here's the thing: he lied twice. Claimed he checked online and saw her wanted poster — his words, not mine. Said the mug shot, by the way, based on her British passport, didn't do her justice. Wondered if she should be elevated to the Ten Most Wanted List. Complete bullshit. The agent called me in and it took us half the day to straighten out his story."

"Where and when did Lembridge first run into her?" Murdock asked.

"He lives on Chesapeake Bay in Maryland. Teaches at George

Washington University in D.C. She came to see him out of the blue, he says, at his home a few weeks ago. The same night the hooker was killed."

"Did she bring the letters to him that night?" Peter said.

"Yes. Copies. Two of the three, including the one with Booth's signature on it. He looked them over, thought they might be authentic. He says he offered to buy them. She wanted to sell, but at the last second she bailed and took the letters back."

Peter understood that Lembridge was still telling lies. Nicola Hilfgott had paid at least ten thousand Canadian dollars for the three letters, and Peter guessed the letters were worth much more on the underground market. Alida wasn't stupid. She'd been in a hurry that night but Lembridge wouldn't have had enough money lying around to buy them from her. She had a different plan and something went wrong at Lembridge's house.

One of the agents asked the logical follow-up question: "The night she met Lembridge was the same night she offed the prostitute. What really happened between him and Nahvi? And why didn't he contact the Bureau before now?"

"It finally came out," Henry said, sighing. "They had sex that night. She took snapshots on her cell phone. Then she threatened to send the pics to his wife. He says he was shocked when she called him again a few days ago. At first he agreed to her plan to sell the letters to a rich Civil War collector in upstate New York — his words — but he decided to do his civic duty when he saw her on the FBI website. Who knows what to believe."

"And you believe this will go down tomorrow, Henry?" Peter said. He wanted to compliment Henry for his solid work.

Henry, citing Andrew Lembridge's signed statements, briefed on Alida's arrangement to sell the Booth letters to Crerar. Missing from his explanation, however, was the number of the hotel room where Lembridge, Crerar, and the woman would be assembling. She hadn't informed Lembridge of that yet. Peter could sense the FBI team's frustration.

Price Murdock orchestrated the next part of the briefing. His technical expert, hitherto silent, explained that he had ruled out installation of video in any of the rooms but he had succeeded in hiding a sound feed in the interior door frame of 411, and another in the outer frame.

Peter interrupted. "Was there any trace of the woman in room 411?"

The techie looked startled. "Not that I noticed."

Lembridge had arranged with Alida to authenticate the letters on the spot. The agents would wire him for audio before he took his taxi to the Gorman. Since no one knew where the money-for-letters exchange would occur, this was the best way to monitor the meeting room.

The men moved to a roundtable critique of the plan. This was a practical stage in the finalizing of every FBI tactical operation, a democratic and motivating process that allowed all participants to identify problems or offer solutions. Murdock's team members were eager to get it right. It became clear that the danger of exposure from too many agents wandering the halls of the Gorman was inhibiting their set-up. Each time one of them entered or exited any of the rooms the task force had rented, they risked bumping into the woman or Crerar. Resolved: only the techie, dressed as a businessman, would be allowed to move freely through the lobby and the upper corridors.

Dunning Malloway spoke for the first time. "What about municipal police? They aren't here. What will their role be?"

Murdock fielded the query. "A reasonable question. Dave Jangler couldn't attend, but his people will monitor the outside of the hotel beyond the exits. They know the streets in the area. But they are under orders not to stop Nahvi or Crerar until and unless I give the signal to Dave."

Alida, they expected, would install herself in 411 but it was unlikely that the transfer would occur in her room. Henry surmised that she had stashed the letters somewhere else; otherwise, he stated, they might have seized her right away. The police team wouldn't learn the room number of the meet before Alida conveyed it to Lembridge on the spot by cell phone; the same applied to Crerar. Additional concerns were raised about the weaselly professor. Would he sweat? Would he lose it upon seeing the girl who had threatened his marriage?

"Leave him to me," Henry said, with a smirk. "I've bonded with him over our mutual interest in Civil War autographs."

"Henry, will Lembridge be able to give a definitive ruling on the spot on the authenticity of the Booth signature?" Peter said.

"Hopefully. But whatever documents the woman provides — or doesn't — we have to effect an arrest. At least we'll have *her*."

The answer was feeble but Price Murdock, in part to lock in a sense of camaraderie, jumped in to bolster Henry's point. "It seems to me very possible that Crerar will demand an adjournment so that further tests can be performed. Modern document analysis employs digital image processing, electrostatic detection apparatus testing, known as ESDA, and various photographic and chemical tests of materials, all of which require a cartload of equipment."

There were no more questions. Peter saw that the plan was a go, even though most of the officers had reservations. The fundamentals were there: Alida was selling stolen papers and a rich client was here to buy them. It should be an easy takedown.

"That clinches it," Murdock said. "We'll send Lembridge in, wired."

Henry Pastern evidently remained nervous about Lembridge's ability to play his role. He reiterated his firm instructions to the professor to sing the praises of the rare Booth letter and talk up the price with Crerar.

Peter had serious doubts. Alida might have a gun, and who knew what Crerar would be carrying. And an old hotel? It would be tough to avoid attention, no matter how unobtrusive the police tried to make their presence. The typical takedown, most commonly used in bribery cases, involved FBI watchers monitoring mini-cameras from another hotel room.

Malloway apparently shared his fears. In the hallway, he whispered to Peter, "No cameras?"

"None," Peter said.

The police officers took the elevator in twos, so as to avoid attracting attention. Peter made sure he wasn't paired with Malloway on the way down.

To Peter, the plan seemed lax and untethered. It was easy to think that they could seal the hotel, watch the exits and nab the woman whatever moves she made. That was the root of the problem: they had no idea what Alida Nahvi would do. Alida hadn't been particularly smart but she possessed an instinct for survival, manifested in relentless sociopathic behaviour. It bothered him that none of the police had yet seen her, but if she saw them — Murdock and his agents looked like the veteran cops they were — she would run. And the ten grand (Or was it thirty? Or fifty? Or a hundred?): what would Alida, Crerar, and Lembridge be willing to do to keep their shares?

On the way down to the lobby, Peter made a decision to stay outside the Gorman Hotel while the sting went down. The FBI listening post on the second floor would be crowded. In addition to Pastern, Malloway, the technician, at least one special agent from the Buffalo office, and perhaps Price Murdock himself, they could also expect Buffalo police to demand a spot in the room. Peter wasn't needed inside. If everything went down as planned, fine, but if not, Peter would try to be ready on the street.

For the first time, he wished he *did* have a gun. But a second later, he retrenched; he had always imagined that his final confrontation with the elusive Miss Nahvi would happen without gunplay. Maybe it would happen in a different country. Maybe back in Montreal.

Peter considered how to deal with his Yard colleague. It seemed perverse to keep his distance in the middle of a joint police operation but that was what he would do. Malloway had his orders from Frank Counter and Peter did not much care what they were, although he was sure that Counter had told him *not* to defer to Peter on anything. The easiest approach was to ignore the man and hope he would reveal himself.

Back at the Marriott he checked the bedside telephone in his room but there were no messages. He slept for a while but suddenly woke up sweating, his mind churning. He decided against calling Bartleben: there was nothing new to report. It was well past midnight in England but he tried Maddy in Leeds. Michael answered and told him that she was awake but was having nausea attacks. For a few minutes Peter talked amiably with his son, who seemed to know all about the Buffalo trip. To Peter's surprise, Michael ended the conversation by urging him, twice, to stay safe.

Peter poured a glass of water and stood by the window, taking in the view of Lake Erie. He thought that Lake Ontario must be off to his right; the east-west sequence of the Great Lakes stymied him. The silence was interrupted by the phone: it was Maddy. She sounded fine and Peter didn't ask about her morning sickness. He gave her a brief update on the situation in Buffalo but played down the risks of the Gorman game plan.

"I wish I could be there at the endgame," Maddy said, divining his nervousness.

His appreciation of his daughter-in-law had increased steadily since their first session at the cottage. Maddy had become his partner. At the same time, he felt protective. He didn't share his fears about the next day.

"I'll call tomorrow evening, your time," he promised. "If you want something to do, maybe you could look up all the cross-border bridge and ferry boat routes around Buffalo and the Niagara area?"

She said that she would do that and would be dropping by the cottage the following afternoon to see Joan and to pick up Jasper. He sensed her hesitation. "Are you taking a gun this time, Peter?"

"No. There will be more firepower there than the gunfight at the O.K. Corral. My job will be to stand out of the way."

CHAPTER 33

Alida had let slip to Lembridge that she was booked into room 411 but this was a bald hoax. She was out of bed by 4 a.m. — but in room 402. Jeff lay beside her; he was out cold, and had been since 1 a.m., when she had drugged him with GHB. She ignored him now as she went to the window and checked the alley behind the hotel. Satisfied, she dressed in jeans and T-shirt, and because it was almost October she put on her new wool pea jacket.

The hallway on the fourth floor remained empty, as it bloody well better be, she thought, and she waited in the quiet for the elevator to start its clanking ride up to her floor. The woman in 411 was a fiction; Alida had never been inside the room. In his besotted state, Jeffie had inputted the misleading name, Alice Parsons.

The computer downstairs also listed the other units on the fourth as rented to Messrs. Adams, Stanley, Jamal, Costigan, Redman, Prior, Sanderson, Mannering, Listowell, and Khouri, which is to say, nobody; the names were made up and all the rooms stood empty for the night. She had the fourth all to herself. She had even managed to get Jeff to delete Alice Parsons from the computer before the night man came on shift, so as to stymie any further inquiry.

She took the elevator down and strode through the lobby, out the door, and along the block to the all-night coffee shop. Ten minutes later, she returned with an oversize macchiato and six donuts; they were cheaper by the half dozen. Not a soul emerged to share the streets with her, no police cruisers or street sweepers; if she had seen a hooker she might have freaked out a little but there was no one. She ignored the decrepit clerk and went back to her room.

The drowsing night man, a dyspeptic old husk, had noticed on his arrival that the hotel had been exceptionally quiet all evening, odd since all of the north and south sides of the fourth were booked. There were only a few other guests, some of them long-term residents, sprinkled through the other seven floors, and traffic had been minimal since he came on. Business had been slow during the autumn shoulder season — too early for the Christmas trade, too late for conventions — and he didn't fret. He didn't care if the hotel was half empty.

The general manager almost never showed up in the dark hours and the night clerk continued to doze. The girl brought him awake — not by any noise she made but merely by the change in atmosphere in the lobby as she passed. He glanced up and judged her to be a guest, perhaps a student. He roused himself and, out of curiosity, checked the guest list on the computer. He concluded that, after all, occupancy was about average for a midweek day. It was strange, if only statistically, that every one of the guests on the fourth was a one-night booking, but he did not delve into the list any further. He thought he smelled jasmine.

Alida locked the door of 402 and immediately called Ronald Crerar on her burner phone. The entrepreneur had boasted that he usually got up before sunrise and began his day with fifty push-ups and two cups of coffee, but when he answered all Alida heard in his voice was sleep. When she issued her instructions, he snapped awake, refusing to admit any slackness, and swore that he would be at the Gorman by ten twenty-five.

"No," Alida said. "*At* ten twenty-five, on the dot. Have your limo driver drop you off at the Pharos Hotel and walk the last two blocks."

It was too early for Lembridge. She decided to wait until 10 a.m.

to contact him on his mobile with the correct room number. That way, she would likely catch him while in transit from his hotel. If either of her guests decided to install a backup friend in another room, he wouldn't know the rendezvous spot until the last minute.

Down in 206–208, a logistical problem bedevilled the FBI: the placement of the monitoring station itself. With no intelligence on the location of the exchange, Price Murdock and Henry Pastern had settled on a double suite on the second floor. Murdock had his technician bring his gear through the back freight entrance. Alida was in 411 and they would take up a position two levels below, the stairs and elevator providing quick access to the fourth. The team was in place by 8:30, except for Malloway and Jangler, the Buffalo cop. The listening post immediately felt crowded and airless, despite the double room. The detectives began to whisper nervously to one another. In their blindness, they tossed about ideas. Without a voice trigger from 411, they didn't know if the technician had set the microphones correctly. Someone suggested sending up a policewoman dressed as housekeeping staff, but it was pointed out that they hadn't notified the manager or front desk of the sting, and a strange face could spook both the morning manager and the cleaners, as well as Alida Nahvi.

Reconnaissance over the past two days had established that the night clerk handed off to the morning shift at seven forty-five. The morning guy was a sallow blond kid, judged by Murdock's men to be "dopey and unobservant." They agreed not to do anything to alarm him.

On his way into the Gorman, Detective Dave Jangler remained nervous. Murdock had asked him to join the special agents in the surveillance post but he hated the idea of waiting in an enclosed space where the FBI ran the show. He felt alienated and he didn't like it. Their technical guy had been unable to install surveillance cameras in room 411; the best he had managed was to place a sound mike in the hallway. Local police should be in charge, Dave Jangler felt. The Bureau was cramping his style.

Jangler's experience coming into the hotel accentuated his unease with the sting's loosey-goosey organization. He figured that he was the last of the team to arrive. It was exactly seven forty-five, the time for the changing of the guard, and he was disconcerted to see the older clerk still behind the desk. Jangler expected the old fellow might challenge him — a stranger, no briefcase — and so, coffee in hand, smiling, he preemptively approached the desk.

"Just my imagination, or are you working a long shift?"

"Should be gone by now. Kid on the day shift, his mother called in, said he was hung over. Asked me to stay on until noon. Said he'd kick back four hours' worth. Fine with me, if I don't fall asleep."

Jangler was about to move to the elevator when he thought to ask, "Say, you see a young woman, maybe Pakistani or Indian here recently? I saw her here yesterday."

"Yeah. A looker. But we can't give out room numbers. You understand why."

Jangler took a fifty out of his wallet, and as he handed it over said, "I won't knock on her door, just want to slip a note under it."

The clerk split the hairs nicely; they didn't allow hookers to work out of the hotel but a mild hustle should be harmless. He called up the relevant screen. "Gotta be 402."

"Room *402*? Why 'gotta be'?" said Jangler.

"I personally checked in all the current guests on the second, third, and fifth. None of them's your girl. Every tenant on the seventh and eighth is a long-term renter. Sixth floor is under construction. The fourth floor is fully booked and the only female name I have on that floor is 402. Judy Jones. Must be her."

"What about 411?" Jangler said.

"Nope. Room is closed up for fumigation. Bed bugs. Shouldn't disclose that to a customer, either . . ."

No Alice Parsons in 411, thought Jangler. *Not unless she has six legs.*

It was Alida's first piece of serious bad luck and Jangler seized on it. He thought over his next move. There was still time to consult the team now gathered in 206–208 but their leader, Murdock, wasn't in that room; he had resolved that he should be the one to nursemaid Lembridge to the Gorman. Instead, Special Agent Pastern had taken charge inside the hotel. This was a potential screw-up, Jangler feared; Pastern was a novice. Murdock had ruled that Pastern was a document expert and stationed him in the monitoring room in case they needed a quick call on the validity of the Booth letter. But wasn't that what the Maryland professor was there for?

Dave Jangler was put off by the FBI's high-handed displacement of the Buffalo Police in this takedown. He knew his turf and he knew the Gorman and the neighbourhood around it. If the woman happened to be in 402 right now, he could personally end this in minutes. And so Jangler, without authorization from the team or its FBI commander, turned towards the elevator. It was 7:59.

Before he could enter the elevator, he bumped into the Scotland Yard fop, Malloway, whom he had encountered the afternoon before in a last-minute caucus with Price Murdock. Jangler saw the participation of Scotland Yard in this sting as one more unnecessary component. The Englishman, like the other participants, was faking a businessman's persona and carried a paper cup full of hot coffee, which he managed to spill over his shirt cuff.

"Shite!" he cried.

Startled by the English accent, the elderly desk clerk looked up.

Jangler vamped. "Hello, Walter. Catching an early start?" He pushed Malloway ahead of him into the elevator. "After you."

The two detectives remained silent on the way up, but whereas Malloway prepared to exit on the second, where the observation post was located, Jangler stabbed the button for the fourth. He smiled and kept mum as Malloway, visibly puzzled, got off the elevator.

The hallway on the fourth level was quiet when Jangler emerged. The elevator was in the centre of the corridor and the detective glanced down to the right; 402 must be at the end. He noted that the door to the stairway beyond was windowless. There were twelve rooms in total on this level and every doorknob displayed a "Do Not Disturb" placard. Padding along the hall, he eased his gun from its holster and stopped by the door of 402. Gone were the days of the keyhole; a programmed plastic card activated the lock. The door provided a peephole for the occupant's use, however, and Jangler kept out of view to one side. He considered enlisting a chambermaid to rap on the door with some excuse but it was too early for the cleaning staff to have arrived. He hoped to take the girl alive. He had to act now or else fall back on what he thought of as the "convoluted FBI plan."

Jangler reached out and tapped smartly on the door. "Manager."

He hadn't thought it through. Why would the hotel manager knock on a guest's door with a "Do Not Disturb" sign (adorned with a glyph of a finger and "Shhh!" clearly displayed)? It took him only a second to realize that he was inviting a bullet through the door.

He waited five minutes in the hush of the shabby corridor. He heard nothing from the room, though he thought he smelled coffee. Giving up, he walked away from 402 and descended the stairwell to the second level.

Inside 206–208, the FBI technician reported that his microphone had picked up Jangler's footsteps and the rap on the hotel room door. The techie was proud of his work but Jangler at once deflated his ego. "I was at the *other* end of the hall from 411."

"Super-sensitive mike," the techie said defensively.

"What about cameras?" Jangler said. "Is there one in that hallway?"

"No," said the technician. "I wasn't able to place one."

Jangler exploded and pounded his fist on a table. The technician retreated.

Henry Pastern, who until now had believed that he was doing a good job, stood up. "What the hell were you doing on the fourth?"

"Why the hell don't you know that the only perps in 411 are bedbugs?" Jangler said. "The woman is in 402, not the room at the other end of the hall."

CHAPTER 34

Alida had heard Jangler's knock but she was in room 404 at the time. Fifteen minutes after entering 402 in the predawn with her cup of coffee, a seizure had overtaken her. Her twitch had begun halfway into her call to the front desk to say that Jeff would not be in on time. She used her mobile to call the general number for the Gorman Hotel and reach the ancient clerk. Even in her distress, she managed to simulate the flattened inflection of an American Midwesterner. As soon as she hung up, she fell to the floor and began to shake. The dizziness hit her in disabling waves.

Her plan had always been to abandon 402, in part because Jeffie had registered it under Judy Jones that first day, and who knew what some snoop would deduce from a female name. Now she barely succeeded in crawling across the carpet through the passage that connected 402 to 404. But then she remembered that Jeff occupied the double bed behind her, and she crawled back. She struggled from the floor to the mattress, battling nausea. to reach her knees and meeting the slack face of the naked desk clerk; his breath was foul and his skin was clammy with sweat. She placed two pillows on the floor at the end of the bed and with a supreme effort dragged Jeff by the feet off the end, his face thumping into the pillows. Between spasms, she drew his leaden body through the connecting doorway. She got partway across the room and dumped him. In all, it took fifteen minutes and she had to halt every foot or two. Jeff's face was raw with rug burn when she finally left him by the bed in 404.

Alida staggered back to 402 and managed to locate her purse; her other clothes were already in the closet down in 406. When she closed up the connectors from 402 through 406 she left the crullers and the now-cold coffee on the desk in the end room. Several hours later, the tapping sound reached her in 404 and pulled her slowly out of her sweating, dreamless sleep; she thought she heard the word "manager" but wasn't sure.

Peter remained out of sight with Price Murdock at the back of the hotel. It was a good place to be, he thought, low-risk — let the FBI run this caper inside — and, even better, distant from Malloway, who was somewhere within the Gorman.

Their problem was Lembridge. At 9:30, Murdock had shepherded the professor to the Gorman without incident but he remained far too nervous. Peter and Price ordered him to wait in the lobby for Alida's call. He was to write the number of the rendezvous room on a piece of paper and leave it with the desk clerk. Murdock's people had wired Lembridge for sound. The professor wore a light blue summer suit and a black shirt, which appeared odd to Peter until he realized that Murdock had made him change to the darker shirt. The colour might better conceal the wire, as well as Lembridge's perspiration. Peter could see that the professor was fighting panic.

Murdock left Lembridge by the front desk to wait for Alida's call, and rejoined Peter outside. Peter began to worry that the meeting wouldn't happen. Alida could have been monitoring the streets and become suspicious.

"Where the hell is her phone call?" Murdock said. The detectives had moved closer to the hotel at Murdock's suggestion but Peter felt exposed in such proximity to the back entrance. He was about to suggest that they move a block away when Price's mobile chimed. It was the FBI agent assigned to watch the façade of the hotel. Peter waited as Murdock talked to her. Crerar had arrived. The agent had not only seen him take a call in the lobby, she also remarked that Lembridge picked up his own phone a minute or two later, after Crerar entered the elevator.

"Did Crerar acknowledge Lembridge?" Peter said to Price, who passed the query on to the agent.

Peter caught the woman's answer. "Don't think so. They studiously ignored each other."

Alida got up fast, opened the connector and returned to the bathroom in 402. She was running late. She cleaned up her sweaty face and neck as best she could. Swiftly now, she dodged through the open interior doors to 406 and, for the dozenth time, inventoried her clothes and her blue gym bag, which held the two Booth letters; she suppressed the memory of her pink Jack-and-Rose rucksack. Almost as an afterthought, she checked the useless and discarded Jeffie in 404. She had lugged him onto the mattress; he was alive but he had thrown up over the side of the bed.

Alida peeked into the hallway and verified that nothing had changed along the corridor. Telling Lembridge about "Alice Parsons" had been a smart bit of deception, if not without risk. She had managed to get Jeff to delete the name but now the house computer showed 411 to be empty. The police officers might notice the change.

She called Crerar, verified his arrival in the lobby, and told him to take the lift to room 310. The door would be left unlocked and he should wait. Two minutes later she called Andrew Lembridge and gave him the same information, adding that she would arrive in 310 six minutes after he did.

"I will not have the letters with me. I will fetch them when and if Crerar shows the cash."

Lembridge answered her cell phone call as the technician was

313

testing Lembridge's wire. The technician clearly heard the professor's acknowledgement of Alida's instructions. He reported to Henry Pastern that Nahvi would be arriving in 310 without the original documents.

Finally, Alida went back to the bathroom in 402 and did a last check of her blouse, skirt, and jacket, and finished applying her makeup. She strutted through to 404 and on to 406 and began opening more doors.

Henry Pastern felt blinder than he had expected. After only two hours in the observation room — an inaccurate label, since they could *see* nothing, only listen to Crerar and Lembridge making uncomfortable chitchat in room 310 — the suite was dank with human sweat and rising tension. Although it was an illusion, the sound transmissions seemed to increase the heat in the cramped space.

Henry strained to hear the conversation in 310 and detected increasing irritation in Crerar's voice. Nahvi was two minutes late. Everyone in the observation room seemed to be on a cell phone and it was hard to concentrate. Dave Jangler, who had reluctantly stayed in the monitoring room, and who had the worst cabin fever of all, tried to reach Murdock outside.

Only Malloway, Henry Pastern, and the technician remained focused on the eavesdropping receiver. Henry felt little in common with these tough detectives, never having pulled his weapon on the job. As for Malloway, their initial connection over the Booth letters had soured as Henry came to understand that the Scotland Yard man's obsession was with Alida Nahvi and not the Booth letters. Malloway had inserted himself in the takedown operation as the designated liaison man with New Scotland Yard but Henry much preferred to work with Peter Cammon on all matters. Henry's thoughts buzzed. If the sting crashed and burned, he would earn the blame. He had argued for a cautious strategy, considering it fifty-fifty that the woman had the material hidden off the premises, to be retrieved and revealed at the last minute. Now he was willing to concede that the papers probably were somewhere within the hotel. They should have arrested her hours ago. He said nothing but listened with Malloway as her voice emerged, staticky as an old radio.

On the even-numbered side of the fourth floor, every connecting door stood open, creating an odd receding perspective from 402 to 412. The .380 pistol fit awkwardly in her jacket pocket. The echo of the knock on the door returned to her, and so did the single word "manager." There had been no reason for the manager to visit. She worried that this room was being monitored somehow, perhaps through a spy hole drilled in from the stairwell, and so she played the part, just in case, and did nothing unexpected. Leaning back into the bathroom doorway, she could see all the way down to 412 through the doorways. She thought she could run the length of it in ten seconds, if she had to.

Jeff remained unconscious next door. With the drug she had injected in his thigh, he would sleep all day. The manager, according to Jeff, seldom arrived before noon and by then she would be on her way back to Rochester. That left only the elderly night clerk to worry about, but unless he bothered to check for credit cards for the imaginary tenants on the fourth, he would be content to respect their late-sleeping habits. Alida knew from Jeff that the hotel had one chambermaid assigned to floors one through three, another to clean four, five, and six; a third maid took care of the upper floors. Alida's maid would not arrive until eleven thirty and when she saw all the placards on the doorknobs on four she would move on to the fifth floor.

Just before locking up 402, Alida checked the back alley from her window. An overweight man in a suit stood with a cell phone to his ear while he smoked a cigarette.

Alida had no intention of sticking around to rob Crerar, or even withholding Lembridge's share of the payment, although he deserved to be cut out of the transaction. There were times when speed and decisiveness were crucial. She had learned that much from the Sword.

She entered room 310 without knocking. The two men stopped their argument, and Crerar managed a smile.

"We're discussing the fact that the professor has no equipment with him, no fluoroscope, for example, to authenticate the signature," Crerar said.

The men in the observation room fell silent as they heard Alida speak, except for Jangler, eager to get to 310, who continued to call Murdock in the parking lot.

"Professor," Alida Nahvi said in BBC newsreader tones, "haven't you told him about the tests we performed already?"

Lembridge managed a clumsy murmur. Alida threw him a suspicious look but he recovered and began a tepid affirmation of the authenticity of both letters. The Booth letter was the gem, the other thrown in as a bonus, he said. Alida did not alter her confident expression, although she was desperate to get moving. All this blather took less than five minutes. This had to be wrapped up super-fast, Alida reminded herself. She knew that the deal was a lock, everything before the exchange just banter, whatever the skittishness of Andrew Lembridge. Crerar knew too that the time had come to move to the next stage. He stood and went over to a boxy attaché case on the desk and opened it, revealing bundles of cash.

"Where are the letters?" he demanded.

"I'll go and retrieve them," Alida stated. "They're in a safe on another floor. It will take me no more than *seven* minutes. When I bring them up, you can examine the material as long as you want — you have seen photocopies — and if Professor Lembridge pronounces that they are the same ones he saw before, we conclude the transfer."

The common sense of both men may have been temporarily occluded by lust. In her tight skirt and with her efficacious manner, Alida beguiled them. They both thought they were clever in glimpsing the gun in her jacket pocket. That was a real aphrodisiac.

In the observation room every agent prepared for action. They all

316

heard the word "up" — Alida would bring the letters *up* from floor one or two. For his part, Henry Pastern's excitement flared at the chance of reclaiming the precious documents, his yearning mixed with the thrill of finally becoming part of a successful field operation. Only Jangler, champing at the bit, saw that she was planting a diversion. Only he had seen Room 402, albeit from the outside, and instinct told him that Alida was keeping the letters there. Jangler drew his gun and opened the door to the second-floor hallway.

"I'm going up to monitor the fourth floor from the east stairs," he said. "Nobody follow. I don't want the stairwell filled with officers."

Malloway, to Jangler's clear annoyance, called him back and complained that they didn't know whether the girl would use the lift or the stairs, and there was a chance that she would run into Jangler. The American merely cursed at the Yard detective and moved into the hall. The remaining agents in the room rushed to make their phone calls to colleagues outside. Malloway disappeared into the corridor, as if to follow the Buffalo cop.

Alida was pleased with Crerar's firm response to her little speech. She gave the thumb-and-forefinger okay sign, went over to the briefcase full of cash, and swiftly closed it. It wasn't a necessary or logical manoeuvre but it sealed their understanding; she was trusting that the money would still be inside when she returned. As she rotated from the window back to the men, she glanced at the scene in the alley; she was one floor lower than the first time. She saw the fat businessman answer his phone again. The man hung up in a few seconds and began to jog, almost dangerously given his bulk, to the back end of the alleyway. *Why is he there?* She watched until he disappeared from view.

As she turned to the door, Lembridge said, "We'll wait here." It was an innocuous, unnecessary assertion, even considering that the professor might be catching the mood, anticipating completion of the deal. Alida assessed the man she had seen from the window. This time he had been standing out in the alley for no good reason, no cigarette in sight. And now Lembridge appeared more nervous than the circumstances warranted. She remembered the knock on the door earlier. She thought she knew the voices of all the desk clerks and the hotel manager. The word "manager" had been spoken by a stranger.

She understood now. The man in the alley was a cop.

Alida said nothing more and closed the door to 310 behind her. She walked the short distance to the east stairwell. Taking off her clumsy knockoff Blahniks, she tiptoed up one level and into the hallway, at the same time taking out her room keycard. Jangler, who had crouched down on the sixth floor landing to ensure that he was well out of sight, heard the fire door onto the fourth open and close.

Alida walked to the end of the fourth floor and punched the button for the freight elevator. She was now in front of the room farthest from 402. Not pausing for the arrival of the lift, she turned about and opened 412 with the universal keycard she had stolen from Jeff. Had the corridor camera been installed, the "watchers" on the second would have seen her. As it was, the monitors heard only a light click as Alida gently shut the door.

Inside, all the connecting doors stood wide open, like a painter's study in perspective, creating a long inner corridor. Not hesitating, she walked through the passageway as far as 404 and locked the connector to the Judy Jones room. Room 402 was now a hollow, locked box, the only detritus linked to Alida Nahvi a bar of used soap in the shower and two stale donuts on the desk.

She waved goodbye to Jeffie as she locked the door to room 404 behind her.

In 406, she stripped off her skirt and discarded her shoes. Within two minutes she was outfitted in the maid's uniform.

Alida then made an impulsive decision that paid off nicely. *I want them wasting their time in 402, while I'm doing my thing at the other end of the hall,* she decided. Someone had betrayed her and she suspected Lembridge. Certainly Jeff hadn't been the turncoat. He had compliantly reserved all of the fourth-floor rooms on both sides in fictitious names, doing nothing to alert management. She had fulfilled his sexual fantasies, that was for sure; horniness had made the boy keep the faith.

Evidently the police hadn't figured out which room she occupied on the fourth. If the cops were waiting, she reasoned, and if they had their act together, they would have obtained a universal key of their own. *So why haven't they used it to enter 402?* Because they didn't have one.

Hurrying out of the room and into the corridor, she went to the door of 402, unlocked it, and jammed a wad of paper from a bedside notepad into the lock mechanism.

Detective Jangler, hunched down in the stairwell, wondered what the hell was going on. He was sufficiently seasoned not to take literally her promise to return in seven minutes, but he was willing to grant no more than three extra minutes before breaking down the door of 402, his gun drawn. He moved down to the fourth level and prepared himself. He heard nothing from beyond the windowless fire door.

He was still pondering the puzzle when he came from the stairway out into the empty corridor. In fact, he had just missed Alida in her maid's outfit. No sound came from any of the rooms up ahead but he was sure that the game was up; she was somewhere on this level. Kicking in the door to 402 would be difficult, and so he stepped to the door panel and leaned in to listen, wondering what to do next. As he nudged the door it swung open slackly.

As he entered, Jangler knew the room would be empty.

He took about a minute to confirm the self-evident. The bathroom had been used but it told him little. Had he been looking for evidence of sex the bed sheets would have provided it, but he ignored them on his first pass. He also failed to twig to the lump of paper on the carpet. He checked the connecting door, opening his side, but found the other firmly secured.

While Jangler was rummaging through 402, Alida was composing herself in 412, adjacent to the freight elevator. Satisfied, she picked up the plastic bucket of cleaning supplies and hoisted the blue gym bag over her other shoulder. Quietly opening the door to the hallway, she wheeled to the right and stabbed at the button of the freight lift, praying it hadn't moved. The heavy doors opened right away. At

the other end of the corridor, Dave Jangler sensed something, perhaps a mild shift in air pressure in the corridor, and darted into the
hall. Alida's luck held as Jangler caught a flash of the blue skirt of a
chambermaid who appeared to be carrying a bucket — sufficient to
confirm that she was staff but not enough to make him suspicious of
her coincidental presence on the fourth.

Alida took the freight elevator to the main floor rather than the
basement. She had earlier considered going to the laundry room but
inevitably she would have to ascend to the ground floor and risk one
of the exits. Carrying the blue bag in one hand, she hit the panic bar
on the exit that opened onto the west delivery bay. Stepping into the
bright morning sunlight, she scanned the paved areas for police and
quickly determined to keep to her original escape route. She turned
away from the Gorman. The immediate goal was to reach the Pharos
two blocks away; she would have to pass through two office buildings and a few hundred yards of open streets to reach the taxi stand
in front of the boutique hotel.

Peter had chosen to remain across the alley by the Gorman's main
entrance, and thus missed Alida's exit. Murdock had decided to monitor the back of the hotel, but Peter had received no calls from him,
heard no shouting or gunfire. All was quiet where Peter stood in
the shadows. There had been no foot traffic whatsoever through the
lobby. He had lost sight of the special agent who was working the
front of the Gorman. Mostly from boredom, he edged another few
feet to his right to give himself an angle on the east face of the hotel
and one small corner of the back parking lot. Perhaps it was instinct,
but he magnetically moved a few more feet to improve his view. Only
a few seconds later, he caught sight of a chambermaid partway across
the delivery bay behind the building.

Peter recognized the woman at once but was so astonished that
the sight momentarily fixed him in place. He estimated that the
fastest route to her lay around the long way, to the east, avoiding the

chain-link barrier to the parking lot. He began to work his way to the rear of the hotel, and for a minute he lost sight of her. Rounding the last corner, he approached the receiving bay and the single rear door. She was now three hundred yards away.

For a few more seconds he did not move, even though Alida saw him and stared back, making eye contact. Peter understood where he had seen her before: not just her passport, but her picture somewhere else. It occurred to him, irrationally, that this phantom could disappear into the air at will. She was beautiful even at this distance. Her smooth face showed anger and sadness in equal parts — and fascination with him, he fantasized.

Peter could now see the full expanse of asphalt and parked cars, all seemingly fixed in place by the glaring sun. His trance shattered as Price Murdock came out of the hotel, huffing and straining as he burst from the delivery door. Price immediately saw Alida in the distance.

Peter moved towards Price and almost collided with the special agent as she came out the back door, gun out. While all three understood that the woman in the chambermaid uniform was their target, no one shouted at her retreating figure, or said anything. They merely stared. Murdock, wheezing heavily, took out his Glock and slowly raised it at Alida, likely trying to intimidate her, Peter judged. Price would not risk injuring bystanders. The other special agent raised her Glock 17 in a parallel line and waited for the boss's shot.

Price Murdock delayed to see what the girl would do and that extra few seconds gave Dunning Malloway time to come out the back of the hotel. His gun was already in his right hand. He saw Alida and fell into position next to the other two shooters and Peter. The four mocked Wellington's thin red line, or a ragged firing squad, Peter thought. Murdock threw Malloway a questioning frown and stared at the gun in his hand.

Malloway stiffened and sighted along the pistol.

"No," Murdock said, and he and his fellow agent pulled their weapons back.

Peter understood that Malloway would disobey; he wanted the

woman dead. Instinctively, Peter reached out his hand and forced Malloway's arm upward. It was a fast and simple gesture. The gun went off and the bullet disappeared into the sky.

Alida looked back at Malloway and then at Peter. Peter could not make out her expression, but he knew that she somehow had taken in every detail, even at that distance.

A few seconds later she was gone.

This did not end the confrontation. Murdock, anger turning his face deep red, glared at Malloway, adding a sidelong glance at Peter. "Where the hell'd you get that weapon?"

Before Malloway could respond, Murdock sat down on the pavement and fell onto his back. His faced puffed up and he turned a darker red as he fought for breath and clenched his arms against his side in an effort to quiet his heart.

CHAPTER 35

Murdock's people, working with Jangler, later figured out that Alida scooted from the parking lot through two buildings, crossed the street to the Pharos and jumped into the first cab at the stand. She was out of the zone in three minutes. The driver took her to the Portage Road Transit Center, where, appearing to know precise schedules, she hopped a series of buses that eventually deposited her in Rochester, New York.

At the scene, recrimination against the Scotland Yard detectives was delayed as the special agent beside Price Murdock used her cell to call for an ambulance. Peter knew that he himself was of no use in these circumstances. FBI agents are superbly trained to deal with emergencies such as heart attacks and he backed off and watched until he heard the ambulance siren grow loud. He noticed that Malloway had vanished. With Price attended to, Peter walked around to the front of the Gorman and over to the next intersection, seeking a line of sight up and down the urban streets. Peter was standing exposed in the intersection when Jangler ran up, out of breath. He explained that a search of room 402 had come up short on the Booth letters, leaving as evidence "only a pile of useless fingerprints."

Peter joined Dave Jangler, the two FBI agents and a squad of uniformed police officers in searching the streets and buildings around the Gorman. Noting that Malloway was gone, Peter guessed that he had taken off after the suspect and was unlikely to return. If and when he did, Peter was determined to let him tough it out with the FBI. While he might be able to explain away possession of the weapon, his firing the gun in a public area was unacceptable, and could lead both Henry Pastern and the Buffalo Police to register a formal complaint with London. The abruptness of Malloway's vanishing act told Peter other things: Dunning must have fled before hearing confirmation that the letters weren't to be found within the hotel; his immediate pursuit of Alida Nahvi reinforced Peter's suspicion that it was the woman and not the documents he was after. Malloway must have known that the chances of finding the woman on his own were slim, yet he was making the attempt.

After an hour of searching, Jangler took Peter aside. "You noticed, Chief Inspector, that I wasn't at the planning session yesterday."

Peter, who was as tired and frustrated as any of the special agents and police officers scouring the area, said, "I wish you had been."

"You bet. But the reason I was absent was that my team and I were busy checking with cab drivers, restaurants, and shops in the city to see if anyone had encountered the woman. I can tell you, if we had found her that way, I would have arrested her on the spot. In retrospect, I wish we had. Water under the Niagara Bridge, as we say. But someone at the downtown tourist office, presented with Nahvi's description, identified her and said she asked how to get to Grand Island." Jangler described the island and its location. "I sent an officer out there yesterday to look around. He happened to check the Holiday Inn and he found a reservation in the name of Alice Nixon for one night, tonight."

"I don't suppose she's shown up," Peter said.

"Nope," Jangler said. "I just called. But I could use some help checking it out. I can have a constable with a cruiser drive you."

Once there, it took Peter only a few minutes to ascertain that Alida had never arrived to claim her reservation at the Holiday Inn. He told his police chauffeur that he would stick around to watch for the fugitive. As soon as the cruiser departed, Peter flagged a cab at the front of the hotel, handed him a fifty dollar bill, and asked him to drive to the best spot for viewing the western arm of the Niagara River.

Peter stared across the water to the Canadian shoreline. The current created an effective barrier to anyone thinking of swimming or paddling across the international line. He erased that scenario from his list. But would Alida find another way to sneak into Canada? He clung to the belief that she had unfinished business in Montreal. She was truly on the run now and Peter knew most of the reasons. Not only was she implicated in the Carpenter murder and the savage death of the Anacostia hooker, he now knew that the beautiful creature he had seen behind the Gorman Hotel was the girl in the photograph in the *News of the World*. He seldom read the *News* but that afternoon on the flight to England he had scanned its exposé of the cricket scandal, with its candid shots that included a party scene in a luxury hotel, booze spilling from raised glasses (even though the players were all Muslims), drunken faces in the camera lens, and party girls in the background.

He hadn't made the connection before, but that was Alida Nahvi in that London hotel.

And now she was being hunted. Malloway was hunting her.

His mobile vibrated. It was Jangler, who reported that Murdock had been taken to a hospital and was now stable. The woman had evaporated. Recalling that the old night clerk had been forced to extend his shift through the morning, Jangler had his men call on the day shift clerk, but it wasn't until they thought to check every room on the fourth floor that he was discovered. Young Jeff could not yet be awakened because of an elephant-crippling amount of drugs in his bloodstream. Jangler wasn't happy about anything.

The river was mesmerizing and Peter gazed at two boats tossing in the channel, while the taxi driver smoked a cigarette back by the car. Peter worked to figure out what Alida Nahvi wanted. The beautiful young woman was searching for safety far from London hotel rooms and Pakistani cricket pitches. She retained no fealty to Motihari, hometown of George Orwell, or to Orwell's British childhood home in Henley; Alida loved her mother but she must know that her old life was irretrievable. On her jagged path to her El Dorado, wherever it might be, she had killed, probably twice, possibly more, and had spoiled all her chances. Peter would not, could not cut her any slack. He saw no equivocation in her decisions to murder. John Carpenter's death had occurred within a few days of arriving in Canada; she must have swiftly improvised and carried out the plan to steal the letters. Then Alida had murdered the hooker, a blameless victim of her panic to get away. Alida Nahvi remained erratic and dangerous to the general public.

Peter continued to stare at the channel. His phone's ringtone made him jump. It was Maddy. He was sure she could hear the river and the bridge traffic in the background as he answered, but she refrained from asking where he was.

"Dad, you said you'd call." There was both apprehension and relief in her voice.

Peter summed up the fiasco at the Gorman, knowing it was a scattered, unsatisfying narrative. He mentioned the guns levelled at Alida in the street and the way she looked back at him with . . . disappointment?

Maddy replied blithely, "I don't know. How would I like looking at three coppers pointing their guns at me?"

The question made him realize that he owed his daughter-in-law a better report. For the next thirty minutes the saga poured out of him, a mix of facts and educated judgements, lacking an ending. She let him tell it without interruption. He stood close to the current as he related the story, while the cabbie smoked another three cigarettes and let the meter run.

"At least she didn't kill the desk clerk," Maddy finally said.

"My battery is running out, dear," he replied.

She rushed to tell him why she had called. "Three bridges cross to Canada from where you are. The Peace Bridge goes from Buffalo to Fort Erie in Ontario. The Rainbow runs from Niagara Falls, New York, to the equivalent town in Canada, and you can walk across that one. The Whirlpool Bridge is a smaller crossing but you need a special pass to use it. There's also the Lewiston Bridge along the river from the Falls."

"Thank you, dear," he replied. "That's very useful. Could you do some more computer research for me?"

She remained silent while he told her about the cricket scandal and its disturbing connections, and the kind of information he needed now.

"I'll get right on it." She sounded more cheerful and enthusiastic. Peter worried about her pregnancy but he could think of nothing to say that wouldn't patronize her.

There was a further pause. "You're looking at the bridges now, aren't you?" she said.

"Yes." He was more certain than ever that Alida would head north. He promised to call Maddy within a day.

Peter watched the river for a few more minutes. He could see two of the bridge spans from where he stood but he no longer cared which one Alida might have taken.

CHAPTER 36

Peter stayed one more night in Buffalo after the disaster at the Gorman and then shuttled up to Montreal. He would have abandoned the Nickel City faster but he felt an obligation to Henry Pastern. He would do what he could to paper over the crisis Dunning had caused with his smuggled gun. Henry took the brunt of the blowback from Jangler and from Price Murdock's people, who argued that his vacillation had allowed the girl to escape, even if she had fled without the money. Murdock himself remained in hospital; his heart attack was judged a mild one. In those first hours, there was muttering from Washington about an official complaint to the commissioner of New Scotland Yard. *Americans take guns seriously. And they take other people's guns even more seriously,* Peter thought.

Peter made enigmatic promises to file a report on the incident with London but in truth he was in no hurry. Let Malloway and Frank Counter, his supervisor, wear this one. Peter called neither Bartleben nor Counter. For the time being, he informed no one of his itinerary other than Pascal Renaud, who invited him to stay at the townhouse once more.

Pascal understood immediately. "Tell me, Peter, does anyone but me know you're coming up here?" he said over the phone.

"No," Peter confessed. He would tell Maddy in a day or two, and then Joan and Michael. Joan would forgive him if he delayed calling.

"Reminds you a bit, doesn't it, of Sherman's March, cutting off your supply train and disappearing into the thickets of Georgia? When do we lay siege to Savannah?" Pascal remarked.

When Peter arrived at the condo early that evening, Pascal immediately opened two bottles of beer and they picked up the conversation where they had left off.

Peter repeated, "I think Malloway is coming back here. I just don't know when."

"Then why not call your *chef*?" Pascal remarked, nodding encouragement. He meant Bartleben.

"For one thing, he'll demand I come home but I'm staying, for reasons I see no point in explaining to him. Out of spite, I'm likely to announce my permanent retirement to a country cottage in the Laurentians." Peter took a long swallow of his pint. He relaxed. "I hold at least a few cards, Pascal. My *chef* doesn't understand yet what Malloway's up to and I want to pick the right moment to tell him. Malloway may have returned to Britain for a bit. He has to explain his cock-up to management. But one way or another he'll come back here."

"And it will be soon?"

"It will be soon."

Renaud processed Peter's train of thought. Still, he hesitated, not sure that his new friend was ready to disclose his ultimate deduction. He ventured, "Are you saying he's coming back for the girl?"

It was Peter's turn to pause. "Yes."

"Okay," Pascal continued, "But why would *she* return? For the money?"

"In a way," Peter said. "Alida Nahvi tried for the big score but failed. Her plan was to take the money and run, literally."

Renaud fell into his Socratic rhythm. "But she is coming back to demand the money from . . . Greenwell? Malloway? Hilfgott?"

"Her priorities have shifted. She'll return because of Malloway and Buffalo."

"Ah, for revenge," Pascal said.

"Yes. Revenge for John Carpenter."

"Pretty risky, Alida going head-to-head with a Scotland Yard policeman."

"I don't know, Pascal, which one do you think is deadlier?"

About midnight, the two friends agreed that they should stop drinking — each with several beers under his belt — and Pascal went outside. As the professor opened the front door of the townhouse, already in a cloud of Gauloise fumes, Peter heard the chatter of the bar crowd over by the Atwater Market.

"Where are you off to?" Peter called.

"A last drink on the patio. Care to join me?" He winked.

Alone, Peter took the empty bottles back to the kitchen, then settled in to read his email traffic at the computer in the living room.

But first, he checked his phone and text messages. He had silenced his mobile, knowing that Frank Counter, Sir Stephen Bartleben, and Owen Rizeman likely had already phoned to hector him about the Buffalo incident. There they were: no message from Bartleben, but voicemails from Counter and Rizeman, and another from Henry Pastern; all were brief, Rizeman's annoyed and Counter's and Pastern's plaintive. Tommy Verden had also left a "call me" message.

There was only one item of urgent interest to him. Maddy's text message read, "Oodles of stuff on Cricket shenanigans. Call Thursday a.m., no matter how early (and before I leave for work)."

It occurred to Peter once more that Maddy, like Bartleben, never slept. She picked up on the first ring with a sprightly, "Hi, Peter."

He thought about her morning sickness but he was determined not to ask. "How are you?" he said.

"Where are *you*?" she said.

"Just in Montreal."

"Just?" She laughed. "So, did Alida cross that bridge when she came to it? You're on her trail?"

"I'll explain later. Let's talk about cricket."

Maddy responded in kind to Peter's businesslike approach. "Do you want me to send the clippings? There's a ton of them."

"Send everything."

He could sense her preparing her notes. "How long have you got now?" she said.

"As much time as you need. Let's go."

Peter had asked her to compile a chronological summary of the salient facts from any and all news sources. Without any interruption from her father-in-law, Maddy related the sorry tale of the Pakistani cricket stars and their fall from grace.

The last week of August 2010, in its Sunday edition, the *News of the World* published an explosive exposé headlined "Caught!" claiming that members of Pakistan's national cricket team had taken bribes on the order of £150,000 to throw a test match at Lord's against the English team. This was the issue Peter had read on the airplane. Images from a surreptitious video and lurid still photos of the cricket stars bolstered the tabloid's allegations. The pivotal figure in the grainy video was an evidently untrustworthy player's agent from India, the Fake Sheikh, who agreed to participate in the newspaper's sting by gaining the agreement of the team's captain and six prominent players to what is known as "spot-fixing," in this instance three intentional "no-balls," whereby Pakistani bowlers would foul by deliberately stepping over the bowling crease. Pakistan lost the match to the English and the no-balls were recorded on film for all to see.

In response, the International Cricket Council suspended the players, pledging a full investigation. The Pakistan Cricket Board promised its own quick inquiry, while the president of Pakistan and its ambassador to Britain assured the world that none of this conduct was typical of Pakistan's cricket culture. The sting having occurred in London, New Scotland Yard announced an inquiry into the cricket scandal. As far as Maddy could tell, the Yard was proceeding gingerly, perhaps content to let the disciplinary processes of the ICC and Pakistan roll out before laying serious charges against the implicated players.

As the sport of cricket has evolved, so has the pressure to suborn the game. Cricket gambling generated over £250 million in wagers in 2009 on teams in the Indian Premier League alone. Peter recalled Frank Counter presenting similar numbers. Maddy dredged up one report that estimated that $300 million U.S. had been wagered on the test matches between England and Australia earlier in 2010. Her research confirmed that cricket betting has grown in lockstep with the burgeoning price tag of professional teams: teams in the Indian Premier League are valued collectively at $4 billion, the richest of the many cricket compacts. The traditional wager in cricket, as in other sports — whether a country allows legal wagering or not — has been the "match bet," hinging simply on the outcome of a given contest. The newer forms of wagering include the "spot bet" — on the outcome of a single action by a bowler or batsman — and the "fancy bet" — betting on the scores of a batsman, or the number of runs within a given number of overs.

"No surprise, then, that 'spot-fixing' and 'fancy-fixing' have flourished," Maddy added. "More opportunities to bet."

If the fan appeal of cricket's structure is vulnerable, it is the length of the traditional game, often five days of frequently interrupted play, that makes it so. Most of the innovations aimed at tightening up the game have caught on nicely, particularly with the exploding novelty of Twenty20 cricket: a streamlined match that can be played in a few hours. The new game has grown in popularity with every season since its inception in 2007.

Since Pakistan won the World Cup of Cricket in 1992 and Imran Khan emerged as one of the greatest bowler-batsmen in the sport, cricket has been a matter of national pride in Pakistan. The *News of the World* scandal hit the country particularly hard, in a year of terrible floods, worsening border tensions with India, and international suspicions of the government's sincerity in the fight against al-Qaeda and the Taliban. (Maddy mentioned YouTube videos of Pakistani fans weeping in the streets at the news.) Most of the players identified in the sting video were prominent participants in Twenty20 cricket matches, including the championship round earlier in the year in the Caribbean. In the glare of the headlines, the International Cricket Council appeared ineffectual, not only as regulator of all cricket internationally, but as the promoter of the relatively new Twenty20 final. Rumours that the Fake Sheikh represented a Far East gambling cartel further sullied the reputation of cricket.

Peter, cognizant that both Carpenter and Malloway were connected to the cricket investigation, said, "Any sign of charges being laid?"

"You'll see in the clippings that pressure is on to bring fraud charges fast."

Peter added, "In the Subcontinent, the sport of cricket is a relief from bad times — war, famine, terrorism. Scandal involving their national team hits especially hard, even though gambling and bribery are rife across several continents. The Yard must tread carefully."

Peter reiterated his promise to call her back tomorrow with his reaction to the cricket material. By the time he hung up and checked his email again, a message with a number of attachments from Maddy had arrived.

CHAPTER 37

Peter slept for only three hours but awoke full of energy. It gave him the courage to finally call Bartleben.

Sir Stephen was eating sushi at his desk when the phone rang. His assistant knew that calls from Chief Inspector Cammon, retired or not, were to be put through immediately, and she interrupted her senior without hesitation.

Sir Stephen put down his California roll. He picked up the receiver and tried for a lofty tone. "Hello there, Peter. About time you called."

"I'm in Montreal."

"Why are you in Montreal?"

Peter ignored the edge in Bartleben's voice. "I could ask why Malloway isn't here with me. Wasn't he put in place to handle Nicola Hilfgott?"

"I'd call that rhetorical, Peter."

For his part, Peter had decided to be as aggressive with his old boss as he had ever been. He didn't regret returning to Montreal. If Sir Stephen shut him down, Peter would fight back. Overnight, he had felt a shift in the case and in himself. He was prepared to freelance until forced home to England by Her Majesty. The Rogue Game, as some within the Yard culture labelled it, was universally despised for its implied disloyalty but Peter never worried about obeisance to the Crown; thousands of years of law provided all the ethical reference points he needed.

As for Sir Stephen, he wasn't blind to the advantages of having Peter Cammon stationed in North America, whether in Washington or in Montreal: Cammon often saw what others did not. Sir Stephen waited for Peter to speak.

"There are things you should know," Peter began. "The debate over the letters is on the brink of going public and if it does, you're in trouble. Nicola will go head-to-head with the separatists. She will be loud and intemperate."

"Jesus wept."

"An academic here with close links to the *péquistes* has already mentioned one of them publicly. On the other side, I'm sure that Hilfgott is ready to throw the Booth letter back in his face, with or without possession of the original with Booth's signature on it."

Sir Stephen let out a sigh. "I'll take care of Nicola. But you're really calling about Malloway, aren't you?"

"Yes. Is he in London now?"

"He came back and reported to Frank the same day. What *are* the facts about Buffalo, Peter?"

"He brought a weapon across the border and told the FBI he was joining the operation unarmed. Then he drew a gun and pointed it at the fleeing suspect, and fired it even though the FBI agent in charge told everyone to hold back. Have you talked to Malloway?"

"No, but I've been fully briefed by Counter. Malloway admits all you say about events in Buffalo, in general terms. Frank gave him a thorough dressing-down. He reports that Malloway is abjectly apologetic but remains focused on finding this Alida Nahvi."

"I bet he is. Has Frank done anything to clean up this travesty?"

This palaver should have involved Frank Counter — it was bad policy to back-channel a colleague — but they both pressed on. Peter could hear his boss sorting through papers on the big desk. Sir Stephen paraphrased from a document. "Frank contacted a

Detective Jangler in Buffalo, who is furious at us but angrier with the FBI for fouling up the operation. Then Frank contacted Special Agent Pastern in Washington and promised full cooperation. . . . Hoped that this wouldn't spoil Anglo-American relationships."

"That's helpful to know," Peter said, trying to keep the disdain out of his voice. He had another thought: if Counter was out, then Bartleben was well on his way back in.

"Anyway, Peter, you asked me to keep track of Malloway. He hasn't yet booked passage to Montreal, but he tells Frank that he'll be there as soon as there are any developments."

At first, Peter gave no reply, until Sir Stephen finally said, "Well, *are* there any developments?"

"How much do you know about the cricket business?"

"Endured it in school. My son got pretty good at it. Never watch it on the telly myself."

"Dunning Malloway and Alida Nahvi are both connected to the *News of the World* scandal. Dunning is on Counter's sub-task-force on the Pakistani sting in Mayfair."

"I know about it. Very political, cricket's become."

Bartleben was sounding more like Noël Coward every day, or a cut-rate Yoda. Peter explained how he had twigged to the picture in the tabloid.

"What do we know about the syndicate behind this one?" Peter said.

For the first time in the conversation, Sir Stephen showed enthusiasm. "We are starting to believe that the organizer behind the bribery is not the Fake Sheikh, but a Pakistani citizen named Devi, whose nickname — did they learn this from the movies? — is the Sword. All I can say is, if this comes out, he'll be executed in the town square in Islamabad with his *own* sword. A Pakistani shorting his own national cricket team, bribing its star players to throw a vital game? That won't be tolerated."

They were just chatting now. It was a step on Peter's circuitous path back into the investigation and Bartleben welcomed it. "It seems to me Malloway was after Alida from the jump," Peter said. "I think he knew her identity early on. I think he's connected to the match-fixers."

"You don't need to pitch me, Peter. Malloway will be pulled from the case today."

"No. Let out some slack. Where is he now?'

"At the office."

"We owe Carpenter this much. We have to allow Malloway to reveal his motives in all this. We're not there yet, Stephen. When he books travel to Montreal let him go. But have your assistant call me at once."

Peter did something he never managed to finesse at the cottage: he went back to bed and slept soundly until the afternoon. He lolled in the bed in Pascal's spare room, dozing in and out.

Content, he padded down to the kitchen, where Pascal had aligned the coffeemaker and the toaster beside a rank of jam jars and coffee mugs. The computer was his to use and he checked his email, discovering a large bundle of articles from Maddy. In the spirit of fully immersing himself in Renaud's hospitality he printed out most of the clippings and stacked them on the coffee table. With coffee and croissants balanced on the computer stand, he began some research of his own, then sent off a long missive to Special Commissioner Souma in Delhi, asking about a criminal called the Sword.

At four thirty, Pascal returned from the university and they went for a walk along the far side of the Lachine Canal, where the housing was somewhat downscale from the Atwater condos.

"How would you like to see Olivier Seep in action?" Pascal asked.

Until this interruption, Peter had been stuck inside a replay of the Carpenter murder, entranced by the nearby Lachine. But he immediately embraced the idea. "I've been wondering whether Nicola or the professor would be the first to release one of the letters. Two sides of the same coin."

"Two sides of the same counterfeit coin, knowing that pair," Pascal said.

Renaud had finished his trio of debates with Professor Seep, and Peter knew that the only reason he would endure another diatribe would be to hear or see a verbatim version of the Williams–Booth letter Seep purported to have.

They took a taxi to McGill University. Afterwards, they could walk down the hill to Old Montreal for a drink in a *boîte* somewhere and discuss Seep's harangue, and the world of separatist politics in general.

Renaud threaded his way through the lecture halls and they arrived at a below-ground theatre that was only half-full. There was no security in evidence and everything appeared low key; this assembly would not be mistaken for the Oxford debating society, Peter judged. He scanned the audience and found no police officers and no one varying from the student template. This was neither a rally nor a press occasion, although Pascal had hinted that it would serve as a platform for a political screed by Seep. Pascal appeared to be enjoying himself and Peter tried to relax, unsure what to expect from the speaker.

Ten minutes after they had taken their seats, a tall middle-aged man wearing a rumpled tweed jacket strode to the lectern to applause from a few students. Seep wore his hair long, perhaps, Peter reasoned, so that he could sweep it back from his face for dramatic, punctuating effect. He wore cowboy boots to boost himself to the six-foot mark. He almost bounced onto the stage. His expression was fierce and his survey of the small crowd a severe judgement that commanded the attention of every student.

He was an effective speaker with a strong baritone, yet he did not quite have the charisma needed to move a small and scattered audience in a big space. As a result, he had to try harder to shock. He had rehearsed his spiel, Peter could tell. The prof shifted his Olympian gaze to each part of the room like a politician, and bestowed a smile on a cluster of female students. Peter doubted that he captivated anyone but the most radical or the dewy-eyed among the company.

At first, Peter had trouble with the language, which mixed Parisian diction and local *joual*. He began to absorb full sentences, and then the rhythm of the themes as Seep developed his argument. The rights of the French in Quebec had historical roots that paralleled in lockstep their suppression by the British. The professor avoided the obvious chicken/egg trap by anchoring French rights even further back in the history of French America, predating the arrival of the English. A loss in battle to the colonial masters in 1759 did not obviate the entrenched rights of the French, nor did it snip the resilient thread of French culture. Academic references peppered the speech in a kind of code, familiar to the students and Renaud but not completely grasped by the Scotland Yard detective.

Seep's exploitation of the Williams letter fit nicely into the flow of enumerated grievances. He quoted directly from the draft reconstructed by Hilfgott, in English:

"To Mr. John Wilkes Booth:

. . . be assured that revolutionary acts against the Government amount to capital treason, if verified as active against the legitimate British governing body in Lower Canada, and I will oversee the suppression of any such French secessionist cause."

Seep looked up to see whether his student audience had taken in the full import of the quote. He turned towards Renaud and smiled. Then he marched off the stage.

Peter and Renaud found an al fresco café on the downhill slope from the university.

"What did you think?" Pascal said.

Peter surprised himself with his own indignation. "Professor Seep is capable of hatred. I doubt that Sir Fenwick Williams actually accused any Québécois of 'treason.' Too provocative to be believable, Pascal?"

Pascal indicated agreement. "Do you think he was talking to Madame Hilfgott, and only her?"

"I didn't find him all that effective at the end. Was anyone even listening?"

"Let me say this, Peter. Olivier Seep's ego always runs away with him. You're right, he completed three debates with me in a similar way. All he has is that tiresome refrain: 'The English have always been ready to suppress the French using force.'"

What do both Nicola Hilfgott and Olivier Seep know about all three letters? Does Seep possess the original of the Williams–Booth missive? Is that why he rushed off the stage after his diatribe, fearing that one of Deroche's people might run up from the audience and arrest him for murder?

At 4:45 a.m. Pascal Renaud roused Peter with a heavy knock on the door.

Peter jerked awake and had the odd thought that he should have brought his old Smith & Wesson pistol with him to Montreal.

Renaud hissed, "There's been a fire."

They gathered in the kitchen and neither talked until Pascal had assembled the coffeemaker. "I just heard it on the news," he said. "I couldn't sleep. You remember Georges Keratis, Leander Greenwell's companion?"

"I never met him but, of course," Peter said.

"He works at Club Parallel. Someone torched it about two hours ago. It's still burning, though radio reports say the blaze is almost under control." Both men suppressed the urge to drive to the scene. Peter had met more than a few arsonists who liked to attend their own conflagrations but that wasn't the real motivator: both of them were frustrated with waiting, and a fire was something approaching action.

"Your estimate?" Peter said.

"It must have happened less than an hour after closing. They shut down at three forty-five on Thursdays and Fridays, earlier the rest of the week."

"Do they open late the next day?" Peter said.

"Yes, noon. The arsonists knew that everyone would desert the place fast after a long night. Somebody waited around. That means either an unhappy customer or the mob. First they beat up Georges, now this. However you look at it, a Molotov cocktail through a back window sends a message."

Peter felt himself slipping back into his investigator's frame of mind. "How do you know it was a Molotov cocktail?"

"Reports said it looked like someone tossed a gasoline bomb in through the back window."

"So soon after closing? More likely that someone went inside and ignited the gas feed," Peter said. "One way or the other, it sent a message to Leander Greenwell."

Pascal remained uncertain. "Leander has people who don't like him very much, but the mob? They have no connection that I can imagine to the Booth letters or the death of the sad Monsieur Carpenter. And Greenwell has no link to the commercial world of the clubs — the protection rackets."

They scanned the radio for updates. The air in the kitchen was warm and redolent of coffee. Peter looked out on the empty street and reflected that it was a night like this that saw his young colleague murdered. His duty to Carpenter weighed on him more oppressively than ever. He turned to find his friend standing backlit in the kitchen doorway listening to a French station. Peter reminded himself that Pascal had tried to rescue Carpenter from the water, and he suddenly felt that he had taken advantage of Renaud. He also knew that very soon he might ask him to help again, in a different way.

"Pascal, you've met Leander Greenwell, am I right?"

"Casually. As a book dealer, he courts the academic community."

"Would you be willing to try again at his shop tomorrow? I don't

341

think he'll talk to me." Pascal had found the store shuttered the first time he had investigated. The professor raised his coffee cup in a form of salute. He was in a good mood now that he was being formally invited into the investigation.

Peter enlarged on his request. "I don't believe Greenwell murdered Carpenter. Whether he was involved in the scam, I don't know."

"I agree. Leander is not a killer," Pascal said.

"Keep it as light as possible. Slip in a question about the fire-bombing of Club Parallel."

They looked at each other and sipped their coffee. Peter saw that the academic understood what he really wanted.

"The girl, Alida, tried to sell the letters to an American collector. You think maybe she'll try to sell them back to Greenwell?"

"Possibly. But I'm interested in *any* theories Greenwell may have. I think she got to Greenwell that night. If she's made contact with him since, I need to know. Only Greenwell can tell us what happened."

The street lamps down at the end of the road blinked off in anticipation of the sunrise.

CHAPTER 38

Renaud's meeting with Leander Greenwell never happened. Friday afternoon — it must have been about 2 p.m., Peter and Pascal agreed — the book dealer committed suicide by slashing his wrists in the bathtub in the lavatory above his shop. Pascal came into the living room, where Peter was grinding through the latest email of clippings from Maddy, and even before Pascal spoke Peter read the tragedy in his face.

"Greenwell?" he guessed.

"Cut his wrists."

Pascal had tried to visit the book dealer that very morning. A morbid thought now occurred to Peter: Renaud might have been standing at the entrance to the store about the time Leander was preparing to slit his veins.

"I could have stopped it," Pascal said.

He walked over to the front window, where the sun was streaming in. Peter recognized his need to enter a bright space; it was a common reaction to the claustrophobia of guilt. Later, grief would drive the guilty into the shadows.

"How did you hear the news, Pascal?"

The transcript of the three Booth letters, which they had planned

343

to review again in light of Olivier Seep's recitations, sat at the end of the table, an unpleasant memento mori.

"Someone called me just now. Georges Keratis found Leander about an hour ago in the bathtub, bled to death. There was no saving him."

Peter approached quietly. "You tried to see Greenwell. Let's talk about it. I want you to tell me exactly what happened this morning."

Peter spoke as a friend, only peripherally as a policeman. He was thankful that Pascal hadn't been drinking; the professor now eyed the tray of liqueurs on the sideboard. Peter moved aside the papers on the table and sat his friend down on the chair across from him.

Pascal composed himself. "Step by step? I left here at ten o'clock. I walked over to his store, arriving at eleven or so. It's a long way but I like to walk. I found everything locked up, the blinds upstairs pulled down . . ."

"Did you try the doorknob?" Peter interjected.

"Yes, I did. Locked. There was also a sign in the window saying the store was closed. The feeling of the house was cold. I'm not saying that nobody was in there but the building felt as if it had been shut for a long time. The bookshop is on the main floor and the top half is one apartment."

"You rang the bell. Did you knock?"

Peter remained patient, watching the horror of Pascal's timing sink in. "I rang the bell but you know, Peter, I didn't hear it ring inside. I should have knocked. I should have knocked *hard*."

"Leander disabled the bell," Peter said.

"I watched the store from across the street for about fifteen minutes."

"Did you see anyone else approach the shop?"

Pascal focused but his concentration turned to puzzlement as shock skewed his memory. "I guess not . . . No, no one."

"No. You couldn't have known."

Pascal looked up, in tears. "But it's what I did next, Peter." There was a pause. "Peter, you know that I'm gay?"

Peter seldom lied but he did so now, telling himself that lying was the tribute one paid to friendship. "Yes, I know."

"I'd met Georges casually. I know, I should have told you earlier in the interests of full disclosure. It hadn't been my intention to make contact with him, but I guess I was excited. I went looking for him after I left the store."

"More likely you were concerned about Leander," Peter said sympathetically.

"I thought he might know where Leander had gone. He also might have a theory on the Club Parallel arson, I thought. I walked over to his apartment on St. Denis."

"What did Georges say?"

Pascal leaned back in the chair. He exhaled loudly. Tears coursed down his face. "That's the thing, Peter. He said hardly anything. Wouldn't speculate on what happened at the club. Just said the owner is determined to reopen. He said he would drop by Leander's shop to check on him. You see, I'm the reason Georges went over there. If I had arrived at Georges's place earlier, if I hadn't waited across the street or if I'd taken a cab, he might have reached Leander in time."

Peter wanted more details but there was a proper pace at which to debrief a witness, he well knew. He went to the sideboard.

"You need a drink."

The front doorbell rang at seven thirty and instinct told Peter that it was Deroche. His arrival at the townhouse had been just a matter of time.

Renaud was upstairs taking a shower — Peter had allowed him only two shots of brandy — when Peter opened the front door. Deroche did not smile.

"When did you arrive in Montreal?" Deroche said, as Peter led him into the living room.

"Yesterday. I have no official status."

"Oh, really? That's not what Mr. Counter tells me."

Peter gave a strained laugh. He wondered if Sir Stephen had told Frank Counter to give Peter some slack — enough to hang himself? "What did he tell you, Sylvain?"

"Not a lot. You're here under orders from Monsieur Bartleben? I have the impression Counter doesn't like you much. I tried to tell him you are pretty good with a Taser . . ."

"Lord, I hope not." Peter imagined Frank Counter recoiling as the Sûreté inspector related the saga of the shoot-'em-up at Caparza's. They had agreed to downplay the story.

Deroche looked around the room. He was restless, as usual. He kept his long raincoat on and paced the living room. A mischievous look came over his face.

"Counter said he would 'be in touch by email' with you soon."

Peter went over to the computer and found Frank Counter's fresh message: "Malloway left for Montreal this morning."

When Peter turned back he found Deroche slumped in a leather chair. As usual, Peter couldn't tell whether he was beginning a shift, or just ending one.

"I came to interview Professor Renaud."

"He's upstairs. He told me he saw Georges Keratis earlier today."

"I know. Keratis told me. I want to hear Renaud's version. It was definitely suicide but why would Greenwell do that, Peter?"

"If you want, we can wait for the professor to come down. Avoid repeating ourselves."

Deroche frowned. "We won't be repeating ourselves, Chief Inspector. I simply want to talk to you first."

"Did he leave a note?" Peter said, hoping to control the discussion. He wondered if Deroche suspected Pascal Renaud of foul play.

"No note, Peter. It was an act of despair. I like the French word better, *désespoir*. He bled to death in his bath, alone."

They were talking policeman-to-policeman. Both men had encountered suicides and there was nothing sadder. Deroche wouldn't be repeating the bathtub details to Renaud.

Peter saw that Deroche was waiting for something.

"Sylvain, it's the arson at Club Parallel that's bothering you, am I right?"

"Do you mean, did I get my wish?"

"All mafia, all the time," reflected Peter. "Are you saying it's the same bunch that's been attacking the Rizzutos?"

"I don't know. Even the mafia needs a reason to torch a business. I see no connection between the mob and the death of Mr. Carpenter."

"Or Greenwell?"

Deroche's demeanour turned secretive and grim. "Whoever torched the place, they were sending a threat Greenwell's way, and he knew what it meant. This was a mob attack, Peter. He obviously feared they would kill him. Do you see a connection to Carpenter's death? Something to do with those Civil War letters?"

"Doubtful." He had reached a Rubicon with Deroche. Crossing it would mean that he wanted to be a player in Deroche's epic obsession with la Cosa Nostra. All mafia all the time. Peter hedged. "But there might be some link to gambling syndicates in Europe and Asia."

Deroche wasn't stupid. "Asia? The Indian woman is the connection?"

"Too soon to tell."

"Where is she?"

Peter gave a brief summary of Alida's travels to Washington and Buffalo, and the sting operation at the Gorman. He wondered if his account jibed with the story furnished by Malloway and Counter.

"I don't know where the girl is. I wish I knew," Peter said.

Sylvain continued. "Leander wanted, above all, to protect Georges. He was removing himself from the picture. For some reason, the mafia is — was — after Leander."

They heard Renaud moving about upstairs, so Deroche finished his private questions.

"Peter, I read the copies of the three letters you provided. Were they important enough to kill for?"

"I think that Carpenter was murdered for them. They could bring fifty to eighty thousand or more on the market."

Deroche grunted, dissatisfied with everything.

Pascal came downstairs and the inspector's interrogation moved briskly. Neither man seemed to mind that Peter remained for the interview. The few new facts that Peter learned were significant, although he did not yet know how they fit in the puzzle. Coincidentally, minutes after Pascal gave up his vigil at the bookshop, Georges Keratis called Leander but got no answer. When Pascal arrived at the flat and explained his efforts to find Leander, Georges rushed over to the shop. Both Pascal and Georges had reason to feel guilty, for persistence by either of them that morning might have interrupted Leander at a fatal decision point.

Deroche disclosed that Club Parallel had never been bothered before by the mafia, and the owners were not paying out protection money. Pascal remained contrite but could add little more.

The inspector delivered one more surprise at the end of the half-hour interview. "As you probably know, someone beat up Georges Keratis a few days ago. His boss went to the police on Georges's behalf. In effect, we didn't offer much help at the time. I owe something to Georges and Leander."

CHAPTER 39

The next morning, Peter rose to find that Renaud had already gone out. His scrawled note on the kitchen counter said that he had been invited to brunch by a university colleague, but to Peter it sounded like an excuse. Pascal had become as restless as Peter. He had drunk a third of a bottle of Johnny Walker the night before, which would have poleaxed Peter. He just hoped that his friend wasn't out there playing detective.

Peter had his own difficulties, although a hangover wasn't one of them. Greenwell's suicide had clarified nothing. He began to pace from the kitchen to the living room and back. No brainwave arrived. He had finally mastered Pascal's coffeemaker and he prepared a large pot in anticipation of a long wait for something to break. He booted up the desktop PC. Although Maddy had sent no new clippings on the cricket scandal, he still had plenty from Friday to read. It was Saturday and he imagined Michael ordering Maddy (if that were possible) to cease and desist for at least one day.

When he finished scrolling through the morning's news, he minimized his browser and saw that a new email had arrived. He shut down the web page he was reading and saw that Special Commissioner Souma had sent him a message. The subject line read, "Info Request:

349

Regional Profile." Peter knew that the heading was intentionally meaningless. Souma had understood that he was sending intelligence to an unsecured mail server and had reframed the information to make it seem innocuous.

The chap known as the Sword was a Pakistani national of Vietnamese heritage and was familiar to police in the Far East and India. He ran an international gambling operation, which indiscriminately exploited football, cricket, field hockey, and horse racing. No nation had managed to convict him but he had a police record in several jurisdictions. The problem was that he was everywhere and nowhere, flitting around a dozen countries. Souma's in-house conclusion was that the best hope for trapping the Sword was probably a corruption charge, based on a mix of regulatory and criminal violations. The email made no explicit connections to the Mayfair Hotel caper. The Sword was still small time but coming up faster than the police liked to see. The most disturbing thing, Souma appended, was the Sword's proactive efforts to hook up with European syndicates, including the Sicilian mafia.

Peter shut down the computer and contemplated another stroll along the canal. He ruminated on the chances that Malloway had arrived in Montreal, and a fresh idea came to him. Before leaving the condo, he Googled the website of *Le Devoir* and found Olivier Seep's speech. Peter had failed to spy a reporter in the audience. He'd thought Seep's lecture lacked fire and was hardly worth highlighting, but Pascal had commented presciently that, with mounting political tensions leading up to the Parti Québécois convention in the spring, the press would attend. Apparently they had been trawling the rhetoric of the ambitious Professor Seep for escalations of his favourite theme, the perfidy of the Anglos. The news report provided a verbatim quote from the Williams letter. Peter wrote it down, intending to compare this version later with Nicola's.

He wandered down to the Atwater Market for a *pain au chocolat* and another coffee, and ended up finishing his snack on a bench by the canal. He realized that he was becoming obsessed with Dunning

Malloway; he told himself that there was no professional rivalry involved. Peter had earlier surmised that Malloway was after Alida Nahvi because he was convinced that she had the letters with her. But was the flipside true? Did Malloway believe that Hilfgott and her precious letters were useful because they offered a path to Alida? Was Alida the only target here?

At the edge of the canal, Peter looked down and imagined Renaud jumping into the dark pool. Water was everywhere, Peter mused: the Lachine Canal, the Anacostia, the Niagara, and now the self-inflicted death of an old book dealer in his bath.

Peter's first mentor at New Scotland Yard, so many years ago, was an old hand named John Case. Case had recruited Peter. He was acerbic and never became flustered, but his self-control wasn't icy or dismissive. He was elegant and his instruction moulded gentlemen policemen, investigators who were polite and kept the exact distance from witnesses required both to win their confidence and slightly intimidate them. At first, Peter found this posture unfeeling, but as Case himself was a consistently upbeat, warm companion, Peter adopted the model and came to learn that empathy with witnesses was tactically useful.

On this subject, John Case had once told him, "There will come a time when witnesses may start coming to *you*. Count yourself lucky when this happens. Some will be pleading, some will claim to have solved the case and still others will be on your doorstep demanding that you arrest one of the other witnesses. Nobody knows why this happens. It doesn't always. Don't let it inflate your ego. And don't be too frigid with your supplicants: they want something from you and they may arrive despising you for not solving the puzzle faster. To them, you are a bureaucrat and when has a bureaucrat ever moved fast enough?"

Case had paused at this point. By now, he would have hung up his suit coat on the rack, shot his cuffs, and snapped his braces, all preliminary to lighting up his thin, burled walnut pipe and delivering the punch line: "And don't forget this, Peter. They may have dropped by with the intention of killing you."

Returning to the condo, Peter caught sight of Neil Brayden standing on Pascal Renaud's front steps. A visit from Deroche, or even Malloway, was one thing, but Brayden was truly the Unexpected Guest. He wore a narrow-lapelled suit, a thin black tie, and a white shirt that made him appear more than ever the chauffeur. Peter couldn't imagine why he had come. The roles had been cast. Brayden had thrown in his lot with Nicola Hilfgott, and whether or not Nicola was doomed, it was too late for shows of disloyalty.

Peter recalled John Case's lecture: be cool, not cold.

Brayden offered a plangent smile, something Peter hadn't seen before. "Nicola and Malloway were up all night," he said.

"And you were, too?" Peter said.

"Yeah, well . . . Can I come in?"

Peter led the way into the living room. He shut down the computer while Brayden waited. In the kitchen he poured the last of the coffee into a mug for Brayden; he was pretty sure he took it black.

Peter didn't trust him. There was a type of witness who always told the truth but not enough of it. This was Brayden. He had yet to lie to Peter but the problem with him was his notion of loyalty. Neil Brayden was chauffeur, point man, and adviser to a woman who would run over her husband's grandmother with a golf cart if it helped her career. Brayden was also Nicola's enforcer and her lover.

"Nicola has gone too far," he said, after taking a chair.

"When did Malloway arrive?" Peter said.

"Yesterday afternoon. She insisted on picking him up herself at the airport. Came back straight to the house in Westmount, closeted themselves in her study until 2 a.m."

Peter did not ask how Brayden knew all this. If Hilfgott had shut him out and presumably dismissed him, how did he end up at her mansion that late in the evening? The answer was clear enough: Brayden, feeling betrayed by his superior, had found an excuse to watch from the shadows of the residence, monitoring his boss and Dunning Malloway. Jealousy was in play.

"I'm in a bind and I'll admit it, Peter. Now, I won't put *you* in a bind by telling you things that you might have to report back to London."

Brayden was whining. Peter's first thought was: *Thinking what I'm thinking about you, I won't turn you in to London. I'll shoot you right here myself.* But he was unprepared for the grim farce that followed.

"Nicola came to me this morning, a couple of hours ago, and gave me an order. I swear that I don't intend to obey it. She wants me to beat up Professor Olivier Seep."

"Why would that serve her purposes?"

"She wants to know where the girl and the original letters are. She thinks he knows."

Peter then realized what had panicked Nicola. She had seen the *Le Devoir* report with its direct quote from the Williams letter, and she understood that there were only two ways Seep could have obtained the authentic original: by making a deal with Alida or by taking it from Carpenter himself.

Brayden turned his palms up in wonderment and frustration. "It gets worse. This morning she ordered me to drive Malloway back to his hotel."

Peter marvelled at Nicola's gall, shutting out Brayden and then forcing him to kowtow to Malloway, whom she had just slept with. There was only one explanation: Dunning requested that Neil drive him.

"He wanted something from you, am I right?" Peter said.

"He asked me to approach Georges Keratis and force him to tell me where Greenwell hid the letters, especially the letter from John Wilkes Booth to the general. That's the one that implies there was a French plot to get the Americans into a war over Canada."

Brayden's talents as an enforcer were in high demand. Peter decided to up the pressure. "Did Malloway know that Nicola wanted you to go after Seep?"

"Yes, but he said the hell with what Nicola wants. I'm caught in the middle, Peter. Malloway thinks Georges knows, via Greenwell, where Alice Nahri went. But don't you get the irony? Nicola wouldn't care if I went after Georges. She's tunnel-visioned where Seep is concerned. Meanwhile Malloway is slandering Nicola to me. Keeps saying she's toast, saying that all that counts is finding the woman, your man's killer."

Frank Counter had used the same words: Nicola was toast. This was getting to be like the fox, the duck, and the grain crossing the river, Peter thought, with no one to be trusted in the boat with another.

In Peter's reasoning, two deductions could be justified. First, Olivier Seep had one of the three letters in his possession. Otherwise, Nicola would be unlikely to press so hard. Second, Malloway told Neil to interrogate Georges about *Alida's* whereabouts, not the letters. Why? A benign interpretation would be that he wanted Carpenter's killer, a noble and simple goal. Peter didn't believe that.

He considered Brayden and his plea for sympathy. The man might have committed the earlier assault on Georges, and he might have been the one to torch Club Parallel, although Peter doubted that; both attacks smelled of the mafia. Peter could make no promises of immunity from prosecution, or even a sympathetic report back to London on his conduct. As John Case had advised, the witness often wants something the investigator can't bestow.

Unlike Sir Stephen Bartleben, Peter was never proud of his Machiavellian urges. But from time to time he indulged them.

"Here's what I think you should do. You can't go near Georges Keratis for any reason. Inspector Deroche has offered him police protection. Stay away from him."

"The firebombing?" A look of gratitude came over Brayden's face.

"Yes. Deroche feels guilty about police treatment of Georges, and probably Greenwell, too. His people will be watching him. Inform Malloway you can't get close to Georges. That is absolutely all you tell him. And don't tell him I said hello."

"And what about Nicola?" Brayden said.

Peter fixed him with a hard look.

"Be sure of this. Nicola is officially in the bad books of Foreign and Commonwealth Affairs. The High Commissioner finally agrees that she's gone too far in this pissing match with Seep. Her instruction to you shows how far she'll go. You will have to tell her you refuse to approach Seep. The worst thing she can do is send you home. Nicola thinks everyone should hunger for those letters, so let her blather on."

The discussion came to an end. They both felt like gossips tattling on their colleagues.

After the very chastened Brayden left the townhouse, Peter killed time by reading and sorting the stack of clippings that sat by the computer, hoping the effort of mindless classification might produce some gestalt.

The busywork was also his way of delaying an update to Bartleben. Peter was Sherman, on his own in hostile Georgia. But it wasn't a bad feeling.

Deciding on yet another walk to the canal, he brought along one of Pascal's cigarettes. As he smoked, he paused at the spot where Carpenter had tumbled in, noting that the crime scene had reverted to former uses, with cigarette butts clumped at the edge of the waterway and candy wrappers flattened on the grass. Oil from the twice-daily passage of the short-haul factory train continued to leech up from the rail bed. Peter looked around and tried to conjure up the murder scenario. He walked around the empty fringe of lawn and along the asphalt path; the farther he got from the canal, the more ominous the watery trench loomed behind him. The wrappers, the discarded plastic bottles, and the crumpled smokes formed a pattern, he did not doubt, but one that only a physicist would dare to compile. He had read in a magazine about how the Lego company had set up a website that allowed a child to submit a design for, say, a castle or a dinosaur or a petrol station. The Lego people would convert the mock-up to a Lego structure and send back a package of blocks so that the kid could build his fantasy. Peter liked the idea that the final structure — dreamed up by a child — presaged the gathering of its elements. He wanted to submit the design of this killing and have someone send back all the pieces. He waited for the wrappers, the cigarettes, the plastic bottles, and even the shine on the rails to draw themselves together spontaneously, predestined into a natural, if warped, whole; a Frank Gehry castle or a trash dinosaur — or a murder. He turned around to the water and nodded a respectful acknowledgement to John Carpenter's spirit.

Pascal stamped into the house that evening and announced that his previous night's consumption of scotch had caught up to him and he was taking a nap.

"Wake me at six," he instructed.

Peter, with no desire for alcohol, went back to downloading and sorting. He was closing in, he felt, but he remained tentative, guarded about next steps. It was not like him to delay in this manner: he could simply have Malloway, Hilfgott, and Brayden airlifted out of Montreal in the morning. Bartleben would respond, if he pressed hard enough. They would be sweating in an interrogation room within twenty-four hours. One or perhaps all three knew who had killed Carpenter. Forget the documents, the letters had become a mirage, slipping out of view the closer he got.

The townhouse was silent; with the weather having turned, even the air conditioner refused to fill the emptiness. He needed a stimulus, but not booze; he could use a spur to break through the last mental obstacle. *Actus reus* and *mens rea*, both remained out of focus.

He began to understand his own irresolution. He would have to wait for the girl. She was his spark. She had travelled half the world, fumbling towards some dream that Peter had little hope of understanding. She had killed wantonly along the path to . . . where? Where would Alice Nahri, born Indian and British, tied into corruption in Pakistan and Nepal, on the run in Canada and the U.S., find any peace? The world of blue people, Pandora, was a fiction. He knew she would keep moving, perhaps in a circle back to Montreal, the City of Saints. She had a restless twitch.

He yearned to call Maddy but it was the middle of the night in Leeds. She and Michael had found the *Avatar* connection and Maddy had an instinct for the young woman's movements and motives. He wanted their advice. And he needed Joan, too. She had ordered him to finish the case — he owed it to the Carpenter family. But he owed her, too. Her brother wouldn't last much longer and he ought to be home when it happened.

CHAPTER 40

Peter stood by the window for at least fifteen minutes as the sky above the street outside lapsed into blackness. He was alone again. Renaud had woken up to say that he lusted for a drink, and he knew a tavern up on Greene Avenue. From an angle by the window, Peter could almost see where young Carpenter had been struck by the Ford sedan. The sodium bulbs on the light standards buzzed and flickered into life, creating round stamps on the streets and the medians, like flashlights pointed from heaven on arbitrary spots. If Seep had the original of one of the three letters, then he had either killed Carpenter to get it or was implicated through Greenwell and the woman. It was a sign of Peter's frustration with the Carpenter case that he considered phoning Deroche and having Professor Seep arrested. Deroche would do it if Peter insisted; he despised the separatist.

Peter put aside thoughts of Alida. The young woman was driven by devils he could never understand. He retreated to the kitchen and opened a beer, resolving that it would be his only drink of the evening. Olivier Seep remained a wild card. Peter couldn't see him firebombing the club, nor physically attacking Georges Keratis. If he latched onto an original of one of the letters it was most likely through direct collusion with Greenwell himself.

Blithely insulting the entire province in a few keystrokes, he revived the PC and Googled "corruption" and "history of Quebec." The Google algorithm spewed out page after page of references to government commissions of inquiry into graft, as well as sites featuring scabrous incidents of corruption over the years. He read for an hour, trying to understand how the nationalist movement regarded the mafia presence in the province.

Of course, the history of corruption in Quebec, and Canada more broadly, was hardly unique and it reflected the growing pains of an expanding society. Perhaps it was inevitable that the country's first great public works project, the building of the Canadian Pacific Railway, spawned contracting scandals during the rule of the first prime minister, Sir John A. Macdonald, or that in the twenties rattling cases of harsh whisky were smuggled across the border to the Prohibition-constricted American market.

At about ten thirty Peter shut down the computer. He circled the main floor, cranking shut two casement windows and checking the front door; he smelled frost in the night air. His ritual mimicked the cottage, where he performed the same circuit each evening. As he made his rounds, it occurred to him that perhaps he had settled too far into Renaud's domain.

His mood turned him obsessive-compulsive. He squared the ream of blank paper next to the monitor and did the same again with the stack of printouts on the other side. Leaving his research exposed was a vote of faith in Renaud. He trusted his new friend. Pascal might come home slightly debauched from the Atwater bars and if he woke Peter up, that was fine. He turned off every inside light but the kitchen overhead and the night light in the upstairs bathroom.

He went upstairs to the guest bedroom, which felt close and airless. He kept on only a singlet and shorts, lay on the bed, and tried to doze. Several rows of town homes separated Renaud's place from the Atwater Market; babble from the outdoor cafés bounced intermittently off thermal layers into the room. The sound reminded him of an old tube radio unevenly tuned in.

He failed to sleep. He had had fewer dreams since his brother died. All those waking hours spent thinking about Lionel had supplanted his dream life. If only he could work out the meaning of his passing. He had had no opportunity to say goodbye. About a month after Lionel's death, Peter had a very bad night. Waking up in the glow of the spring sunrise he felt guilt wash over him. He had climbed out of bed and come down the stairs to the kitchen, where he stood for a while staring at the floor. He hated the taxonomy of the Stages of Grief but there was no doubt that he had entered the Bargaining phase. He would have traded his own life to have Lionel survive. He sat on the front steps and wept for ten minutes or more; he let forth uncontrollably. If Joan heard him she chose to leave him alone. He went for a long, solitary walk up the nearby country lanes. The next day he went out and brought Jasper home.

In his will, Lionel had asked Peter to retain his personal papers. Peter had stored them in the air-raid shelter at the cottage. He now recalled an odd phrase in the will that contrasted with the dreary legalese: "There may be material therein, brother, that will help you fill in the lacunae regarding Father." Staring at the ceiling in Pascal's condo, Peter smiled to himself. He had a new mystery to solve, a family one. He would open up the air-raid cache when he got home and find what his brother wanted him to find.

Peter fell into a dreamless sleep.

She's sleek in the zipped black pantsuit that makes her look the elegant party girl but not cheap. Montreal girls know how to dress, she thinks. The only problem is no pockets, and she has brought a clutch bag for the gun. She walks along the canal but then shies back from the water. She slows her pace as she gets to the section where John crawled into the death pool. She has given up hope of proving anything and now she keeps on, without contemplation or a look back. She heads towards the railroad tracks and the edge of the spill of light from the annoying flood lamp by the factory fence. She marks the plastic bits and wrappers and cigarette papers

strewn about at random, and recalls the scene in Terminator 2
*where the shattered drops of silver alloy flow back together and
reconstitute the unstoppable robot villain. Keeping to shadowed
zones, she reluctantly makes her way to the road, where there is no
choice but to enter the unforgiving light.*

*The townhouse stands a street back from the water. She takes
one glance behind her and sees how truly opaque the verge beyond
the lit-up asphalt is. The whore stood in a pool of light like that,
on the edge of blackness. There is no one about. She walks up the
steps and takes a key from under the flowerpot, and hesitates only
to verify the silence.*

An unfamiliar motor and a change of air pressure raised Peter from
his slumber. At first he assigned the whirring sound to the air-
conditioning unit but he quickly perceived that the gas furnace had
kicked in. He rolled over to the edge of the mattress. If he had failed
to dream, was the after-image of a dream possible? For that's what
had imprinted itself on his mind, an old-fashioned photogravure.
Alice Nahri and John Carpenter in a cheesy wedding-cake portrait,
into-the-sunset figurines holding hands. But those joined hands were
transmogrified into an electrified fibre, and the after-dream symbolism
became clear to him. He understood then that the strongest link on
his chart of suspects and victims was the fibre that carried Alida's sins
and her remorse towards Carpenter, in a quest for forgiveness.

Peter had slept solidly for four hours, and now he was alert to
any threat the darkness might bring. He did not jump out of bed;
what was the point if you didn't have a gun? Rather, he lay back on
the coverlet, half-cool, half-warm; he heard nothing but the rush of
tepid air from the ducts into the chilly room. Silently, he slipped out
of bed and stood on the carpet, backlit by the window in the bathroom. He felt ridiculous. He wouldn't impress anybody in his creased
undershirt and plaid shorts. He prepared himself for the presence in
the hallway.

The girl slid into the bedroom — it seemed just the right spot to strike a pose — with her hands displayed to show that she lacked a weapon. Peter wondered if she owned one; the FBI found no gun in the Focus or on the body of the hooker pulled from the Anacostia, and Alida had left nothing in the Gorman Hotel. He noted that her pantsuit left no place for a concealed gun, or even a blade. She was beautiful.

He wasn't afraid of her, armed or not.

They stood six feet apart. He tried to think like a constable facing down a suspect. He could rush her or try to intimidate her. His mind raced. Maybe she did have a pistol in reach; it would be in the hallway, if anywhere. Chief Inspector Peter Cammon had no illusions left about any human being's capacity for violence, and he was brave, but he was content to see what Alida wanted from him.

"I didn't kill him," she said. He understood that she had waited a long time to make her case to him. Her voice was smooth liquid. Her words were genuine, unaffected, meant only for him.

With that one statement, Peter's perspective on the investigation shifted again. He at once understood what he cared about in this case and what *he* wanted from it. Facing him was the one person who knew what had happened. Peter Cammon, retired chief inspector, had parked himself in that stuffy London office in the Mother House while Bartleben patronized him, and he had flared back at the boss's attitude. But Bartleben might have been accurate in his flattery; Montreal had been what Peter needed and it was a shame that he'd slipped away from the Grand Game. Peter was good at crime. He had also been right: from the beginning he'd seen that the woman was key. There was evil in her betrayal of Carpenter, but he believed her when she said she hadn't killed him.

"Are you here to tell me what happened?" he said.

"Olivier Seep killed him."

Peter needed more from her. "Why did you come to Montreal with John Carpenter?"

"I had to leave. There is a man. The Sword. He's a heavy player in organized crime in Pakistan."

"The cricket bribes? The photos in *News of the World*?" Peter said. "You know about that?"

"I still don't know why you came to Montreal."

She adopted a confessional tone. "The Sword forced me to get close to Johnny. I had no choice. He ordered me to infiltrate the task force."

Peter's surprise was evident. "You know about the task force?"

"Yes, the cartels know all about Scotland Yard."

Peter's thoughts jumped to that day in Sir Stephen's office. Had the boss suspected the infiltration of Counter's unit? Had he brought in Peter because he was an outsider, and Bartleben's man?

Peter had to ask his toughest question now; there would be no other opportunity. "Was John on the take?"

"No, never. He was honest. And Johnny never had a chance to work on the cricket investigation. So ironic. He focused on the telephone-hacking. The Sword knew that the people who worked on the hacking crimes worked closely with the ones assigned to the cricket bribery. He thought he was being subtle by getting me to hook up to the cricket investigators through Johnny. But Johnny's work on the match-fixing was minimal. As soon as we got together, I saw that he would never be a good source. I tried to tell the Sword but he did not believe me. He kept pressing me for information. Said I wouldn't be paid unless I delivered."

It occurred to Peter that much of this had happened before the incident in the Mayfair hotel and the splash in the tabloids. "Tell me about the Sword."

"The bribery of the Pakistani stars was the Sword's chance to make his own mark in the world of match-fixing. The party in the hotel came about suddenly. The Sword actually called me at Johnny's flat and told me to go. He instructed me to watch the cricket players. And do other stuff. If only I'd known that the *News* was paying the Fake Sheikh for pictures. I eventually saw that the Sheikh was setting us up in the hotel And I knew it was time to bail. I waited for the whole thing to blow up. And it did."

Peter wasn't about to let her off without a deeper admission. (He wondered how he would ever write his report to Bartleben.) "It was your idea to come to Montreal, wasn't it?"

"Yes." The air in the bedroom was smothering. Alida took a step in from the doorway. She was beautiful, seductive, with the poise of a practised model. "Johnny and I met at a club in Soho. I liked him well enough and we might have made a go of it anyway. But I knew from the day the Sword gave me my orders to attend the party with the cricketers that I'd never be off his leash. There was a lull in the phone-hacking work and so I urged Johnny to take this silly job in Montreal."

"Tell me how you decided to steal the letters," said Peter.

The young woman took a step to her right and then back; it was her version of pacing while she considered his query. He could still make out her expression in the dim light. It wasn't a case of deciding whether to confess, Peter knew, but how much detail to provide. He further realized that this visitation was meant to be her last stop before vanishing.

"Johnny was as bad as me in some ways. In Montreal we both felt we had escaped from jail. It was sex and fun. He thought the whole Hilfgott thing was crap."

"You went to Leander Greenwell on your own?"

She hesitated. "Yes, I did."

"What did Leander say?"

She glowered at him and held up her hand. "Forget about Leander. Don't you understand? Hilfgott is crazy. The real amount of the payment was thirty grand of her husband's money. Greenwell was as greedy as anyone. He made the deal only because Hilfgott was willing to pay more than the other bidder."

"Seep."

"Yes. Seep was crazy as a bed tick, too. My mother would say that."

"But you went to Seep and made a deal."

Alida shifted her weight to her other foot; she took a step backwards into the hall and regrouped, ending up mostly in the dark. She came forward again. The look on her face showed that he had missed something. Peter discerned that she was deciding how much more to reveal; but he knew there was a key point she wanted to get across.

"Seep wanted a particular letter, he told me. If necessary, I was willing to leave one with Greenwell, a three-way split. I didn't care which one I got but Johnny had already mentioned Lembridge and I figured I could get some quick money for it with the American's help. Greenwell told me there were private collectors in the States. I started thinking I could follow up with that kind of deal. I needed money."

But Peter saw that Seep, out of anger and avarice, changed everyone's plans by turning robbery into murder.

"We made a deal. My job was to get Johnny drunk. Not too hard to do. Seep said he had a drug we could mickey him with. He gave the dose to me but I didn't use it, since the booze seemed to be doing the trick, and the drug, in combination, might have killed him. We were celebrating in the market after the handoff and I led Johnny towards the dark place over here. He was stupendously drunk and fell behind. I had already handed Seep the rental keys. Seep was supposed to wait in the car and after Johnny passed out, he would collect his letter, while I would take the other two, and he would let me off at the hotel."

Peter was wary of being too direct again but he asked, "Were you gone when Seep drove up?"

"I was almost at the tree over by the factory. I turned and saw Johnny fall down on the grass and then get to his feet. He staggered onto the road."

"It's important for me to know what happened next with the car."

"You want to know, Inspector? Something true and clear and simple in this mess? The professor saw him and deliberately accelerated. Sent him flying onto the grass. Johnny got partway up and crawled; got up, fell down, and crawled some more. I ran over to him. He was bleeding, dying. No one came out of the houses. Seep got out of the car and ran at me. Then he started to attack Johnny.

I threw one of the packets at him to slow him down. Then he did something odd. He picked up the letter and read it and smiled."

"Coincidentally," said Peter, "it was the letter Seep wanted in the first place, the one with Williams's signature."

"Yes. Seep would have killed me, too, but when I ran he didn't follow. I didn't see him throw Johnny into the water."

"The car?"

"I ran all the way to Greenwell's place — and there was the car already outside. Seep was trying to set both of us up."

"Seep abandoned the Ford to implicate you. The keys were in it?"

"Yes," Alida said. "Leander thought it was me who had driven it to the store."

Peter filled in the rest. Alida had threatened Leander and kept both remaining letters. With most of the cash as well, she took off for Annapolis.

He saw that she still wanted to talk. "Why me?" he said.

She looked down at the carpet. The distant furnace had run through one cycle and come on again. "I wanted you to know I didn't try to kill the kid in Buffalo."

"Jeff? No, you didn't. He survived the drug you gave him."

"Horniest kid I ever met."

Her statement added up to a mix of irony, wonder, and a plea for credit for refraining from murder. Peter hadn't forgotten the prostitute, ravaged by jellyfish and lice, lying gutted in a D.C. morgue. He played along.

"You didn't kill anyone in Buffalo."

Alida backed towards the corridor. He was talking to a shadow. It was the oddest confession he had ever heard.

"Why did you stop Dunning Malloway from shooting me?" she said.

"You saw that?"

"Oh, yes. He aimed right at me. I saw his eyes."

"Not the right time and not the right move, Alida. What more can I say?"

"But there was more. I saw the look on his face, the shape of his mouth," she said. "You also knew he would have fired until the gun was empty. Is the American policeman alive?"

"Mild heart attack. He'll be okay. His recovery will be steady."

"Thank you," she whispered. "Thank you." The space around them had grown cool; Renaud's furnace did not seem very efficient.

Alida stepped back into the archway of the bedroom.

"One last thing you should know. Malloway works for the Sword. He's being paid to kill me."

She became invisible.

Peter stared at the dark. He had been full of calculation, down to the feet and inches between them. She was a murderess, he reminded himself. Special pleading ultimately wasn't enough. He had tracked her from country to country, state to state and except for a glimpse in Buffalo hadn't come close to catching her. Now she had come to him, unarmed and desperate to explain. He had to decide whether to let her go.

And he was sure that there was something else she needed to tell him.

Her retreat into the hall was strategic, leaving him to make the next move. Should he follow? He stood for a full minute by the bed in the silence. His slippers were lined up on the floor, six feet away. The furnace had stopped. He heard a drunken shout from outside somewhere.

As he turned to the window, the girl walked back into the dimly lit room, completely naked.

She held a small gun in her right hand.

"Christ, Alida!" Peter said, jumping back. He hadn't heard any zippers opening, any clothes falling. She stopped, the gun angled away from him. "What are you doing?"

His words were preposterous, as if he were a father expressing opprobrium at finding his daughter *déshabillée* after a date with a boy. Fatherliness wouldn't have been a bad posture to adopt with the girl, he thought, had all else been equal. She was a killer, yet Peter had made his decision: at that moment he was prepared to let her run. She was the most beautiful woman he had ever seen. Her perfection was a rebuke to an old man's sorry state.

She could have seduced him in a minute. For that first moment, his hopelessness matched hers. Her nakedness was her confession, telling him she had nothing more to hide. As the seconds passed, a distance began to grow between them; she felt it, too. He had Joan and his family. What did she have?

He stared back at her calmly, trying to ignore her gun. It was difficult to do. Her body was smooth, with perfectly moulded proportions. The flaw, the small burn marks under her breasts made the rest of her riper, and spoke of the strength of a survivor.

Peter's mobile rang. Absurdly, he was glad that he had changed to a sensible ring tone, not Big Ben. Was there a man in a thousand who would not have checked the display, even with a naked woman standing in front of him? It was Maddy. It was 9 a.m. in Leeds. He stabbed the button for his voicemail to kick in and turned to face Alida.

The mood was broken. He waited for the gun to move or for her to speak.

"I have the last two letters," she stated. Her words held no hostility or defensiveness, certainly no hint that she wanted to return the documents.

Peter watched as Alida raised the gun and pointed it at him. He still wasn't afraid. He tracked her eyes and her measured movements as she checked the safety. He wasn't tempted to rush her, even as she glanced away.

She twitched.

Very slowly she lowered the small pistol to the carpet and placed it on its side. She stood straight and began to back out of the room. Without the gun and fully naked, she seemed neither lethal nor innocent. She disappeared into the corridor.

She had said, "I have the last two letters." Peter had listened to her jumble of confessions, pleas, evasions, and prevarications. That last statement did not mean that she had only two letters. She had all three now.

He picked up the gun.

CHAPTER 41

Peter dressed and rushed downstairs. He had little chance of finding Alida in the maze of suburban streets, and he wasn't going to try.

He knew where to go next.

He could have rationalized taking a minute to call Maddy but first he had to figure out where the hell Olivier Seep lived. The address wasn't in the phone directory. He booted up the computer and was searching the website for the Université de Montréal when Pascal came back in.

For the moment, Peter refrained from telling Pascal about Alida's ghostly manifestation in his townhouse. Pascal seemed alert and vigilant, and Peter looked at him with a degree of puzzlement. Why hadn't he spied Alida in the street?

His friend tossed his ring of keys on the credenza by the front door. "What are you doing up at this late hour, Peter?"

Peter tried the university online directory but no residential addresses came up. Pascal went into the kitchen. He seemed not to notice Peter's distress. Peter could see him from the computer station, and watched him consider pouring a glass of wine and then think better of it.

Peter jumped from his chair and reached for Renaud's keys.

"Where are we going?" Pascal said.

"Do you know where Olivier Seep lives?"

"Naturally. In Mount Royal. Imagine, here's this dyed-in-the-wool *indépendentiste* living with the English . . ."

While Renaud drove, Cammon peppered him with questions: How was Seep's house laid out? How many entrances? How was the exterior lighting positioned?

Pascal described what he could remember about the house, but turning onto Sherbrooke Street he pulled over to the roadside and demanded, "Who are we expecting to find there?"

"Seep himself. Hopefully alive."

"The girl, too?" said Renaud.

Peter opened his phone and began to call up Maddy's message. While it kicked in, he turned back to Pascal. "I don't know. How far away are we? Let's move."

Pascal pulled back onto the street. "I'm moving, I'm moving."

Peter listened with growing dismay to Maddy's voice. "Peter, it's Maddy. Five minutes ago I received a call from Carole Carpenter. She was in a panic. Her brother, Joe, is on his way to Henley, she says. He's been talking about Alida and the lack of progress in finding her. He was extremely overwrought, she said. He thinks the sister, Avril, can be forced to tell where Alida is hiding. Michael and I are on our way. Should be there in three or four hours. Michael is driving and I'll try to reach the local police from the road."

Peter tried Maddy's mobile but encountered a busy signal. A second call to the house in Leeds invoked their standard message.

Peter was wearing a black windshell over a T-shirt, and he was cold. Pascal ignored the weather. Relaxed by booze but stimulated by the night air rushing in through the driver's window, he launched a stream of questions back at Peter. "Do you know what a *monte-en-l'air* is?"

"A second-storey man?" Peter replied, struggling with his cell phone directory as they passed in and out of the glow of streetlights. "Very good! It is a cat burglar, yes."

Peter stabbed at the speed dial. "Great. Does Seep's place have a second storey?"

"Oh, yes," Pascal responded, but he noted Peter's preoccupation and backed off for the moment. Peter had no time to guess what point the professor was making.

Peter was desperate to reach his son and daughter-in-law but further calls to her mobile failed. He flashed on Malloway's image and the angry face both Peter and Alida had reacted to in Buffalo outside the Gorman. Malloway would do anything to get to her. If Joe Carpenter had the address of the home where Avril Nahri was living, Malloway had been the one to provide it, along with a not-too-subtle hint to seek revenge.

He tried Maddy's cell again, and this time her crackly voice responded. "Peter, we're only a few —" The signal abruptly faded.

Rather than fight through the ether to reach Maddy again, Peter called his oldest friend, Tommy Verden. He imagined Tommy drinking coffee over his crossword puzzle or on some errand for Sir Stephen.

"Verden." The voice was distant but clear, and it warmed Peter.

"Tommy, it's Peter here, in Montreal. How fast can you get to Henley-on-Thames?"

No yachting jokes, no complaints about the hour. Tommy simply stated, "Two hours twenty."

Peter filled in his old friend on the developments in the pursuit of Alida Nahvi, without describing her visit to the condo in detail. Tommy knew the basics of the manhunt from their mutual boss. He was all business. "A crucial decision has to be made. Carpenter might go after Nahvi's sister but Avril won't know anything. The mother, Mabel, is the more profitable target."

"Agreed," Peter said.

"He'll soon realize Avril knows zilch and he'll move on to the mother at the nursing home, though he might do harm to the sister first. I'll go to Avril first. I presume that is where Michael and Maddy will head."

"Yes, I think so. Malloway has Joe pretty confused. Joe thinks he's helping to find the girl but he's got no patience. It's a short leap to retaliation for Johnny's death."

Tommy and Peter hadn't worked hand-in-glove for nothing. Verden detected the *other* urgency in Peter's voice. "You wouldn't be on the girl's trail now, would you, Peter?"

"Something like that."

"Malloway?"

"He's turned, Tommy. And he's after Alida."

"You want me to mobilize our people?"

Peter hesitated. He wondered what instructions Bartleben might have already conveyed to Tommy or Frank Counter about Malloway. "It's complicated. I'm not keen to alert Frank to anything yet."

"Don't worry about that part. I can call in anyone you want. We do have assets in Montreal outside formal channels, if that's your fancy."

"I'll keep that in mind. Whatever you can find out about Malloway's itinerary would be useful. I've lost track of him here."

"I'll talk to his secretary. Anything else?"

"What are you going to do, Tommy?"

"I'm trying to decide whether to take the Mercedes."

"Stay safe."

"You too, Peter. I was prepared to point a gun at Joe once. I guess I can do it a second time.." He hung up.

And just as he did, Renaud announced — for some reason, in a stage whisper — that they were one street away from Seep's house. Peter ordered him to park right where they were and turn off the motor. Pascal knew enough to defer to a professional policeman, but he watched in amazement as Peter confirmed his cat-burglar persona by taking out a pencil flashlight and holding it between his teeth while he examined Alida Nahvi's gun.

"*Câlice.* What are you going to do with that?"

"Very likely nothing," Peter said. By the weight of it, he could tell that the cheap Lorcin pistol was fully loaded. He guessed that Alida

Nahvi had taken it from the hooker, or perhaps bought it from a street dealer somewhere in the States. It was unlikely that Alida had done any maintenance, but nor were there signs that the gun had been dunked in the Anacostia River. Peter removed a round and saw that it contained a standard-calibre load. He did not like the fact that the pistol was chrome-plated and would reflect light. It would fire if he needed it to, but hitting anything vital with the .380 was sketchy beyond a few inches.

"What do you want *me* to do?" Pascal said.

The weapon excited the professor. *A good reason to keep civilians away from a potential crime scene*, Peter reflected.

"What's the address?"

"It's 336 Carleton Way. What can I do to help?"

Peter pocketed the gun and got out of the car. He ignored his friend's question and began ambling down the sidewalk. Pascal hissed, his voice loud enough to alarm any dog walker, "Should I lock the car?"

Peter spread his hands palms up; he had no time for rhetorical questions. Pascal clicked the locks with his remote and they walked in tandem along the street. Pascal might have been familiar with the house and the neighbourhood but he acted like an amateur. He looked around nervously, goofier than a lost tourist. Peter feared a patrolling police officer or private security guard noticing them. He picked up the pace.

As they arrived at the gate to the big house, which Peter judged to have been built in the early 1900s, Renaud faltered. "Shouldn't we wait for Deroche and his cavalry?"

In a flat voice Peter said, "I didn't call him. Between you and me, I'm not giving the inspector an excuse to shoot a separatist and then claim he thought he was a mafia hit man." The last thing he wanted was Deroche's entire organized crime squad descending on Seep's home.

Pascal Renaud saw that his companion was determined to handle this situation solo, and that rescue by the local *gendarmes* was far from his mind. To his credit, Renaud suppressed his fear and merely said, "Is the girl in there?"

"I'm guessing not," Peter replied. "She was there, for certain, but she would be crazy to stick around."

"Do you think Seep is dead?" Renaud persisted. "Why did she come here at all?"

"For the third letter. And other reasons."

Peter could make out Pascal's face by the diffuse glow of a street lamp and marked the concern and confusion in his eyes. Seep was his enemy but violence wasn't an acceptable tactic in academic wars.

He eased past the iron gate and started up the long path to the stone front steps.

"What do you want me to do?" Pascal whispered. Darkness veiled the professor's face but Peter sensed his rising panic.

"I'm going to try the front. If it's locked, I'll use the back. You stay here."

Pascal's antennae were fully engaged and he understood immediately why Peter was taking the bold approach: he expected that Alida Nahvi had left the oak-and-iron front door unlocked.

They were on the top step now. "When we get inside," Peter said, "point me to the living room, the dining room, and the kitchen. I need you to do that."

Instead of responding with another stage whisper, or some hand signal, Renaud reached around Peter and turned the knob. The door swung inward.

Peter gestured to Pascal to take off his shoes. He did the same and they tiptoed down the hallway on the runner, Peter leading so that he could be the one to choose which of the several rooms to penetrate.

The house was what estate agents in Britain called a strict centre-hall plan: the corridor they were in ran almost to the kitchen at the back of the house; the living room waited on their right, the dining room on the left. Peter lingered, listened, heard nothing; he began to absorb the layout of the ground floor. Alida had left the front door unlocked. She had meant him to enter this way.

To the left or the right? The next provocation would come soon and he would have to be in position. Peter had no plan to use the gun. It had feeble stopping power at any distance. The girl had left it for him to show that she was *not* returning to Seep's mansion.

Yet the question still haunted him: could Alida be inside? How much danger waited in the farthest rooms? Peter's thoughts roiled in anticipation of what he might find. Did her gift of the gun mean that she wasn't leaving him a corpse? He kept the weapon in his pocket. Seep could be anywhere in the house, tied up in the master bedroom, perhaps, although Peter didn't think that was Alida's style. Alida Nahvi had a sadistic streak but sexual humiliation was not her way. A criminal psychologist, he knew, likely wouldn't have bought into that distinction.

Peter waited another minute. Pascal was no help, crouched on the hallway carpet behind him. Peter stared down the corridor and started to gain clarity. He projected his thoughts like tracers into each of the three rooms ahead and grew certain that he would find Seep tied up in one of them. Peter was seventy-one years old and had seen everything. He had killed men (about one-and-a-half per decade of service, Bartleben had once ventured). The moment he picked up the weapon from the rug in Pascal's bedroom, he admitted to himself that he would use the pistol if necessary tonight.

Either to save Professor Seep, or to kill him.

There in the cold hallway, protocol and jurisdiction — all the rules — faded to the background. Alida had savaged and executed another woman out of desperation. Unlike Maddy, who was loved and was about to have a child, Alida had lived her short life in a looking-glass world populated by men who wanted to exploit her and hunt her. By her standards, holding back on killing Seep was progress, however perverse the calculation. Peter did not forgive her, and did not conjure up a scenario of redemption, but for tonight he would let her run.

Peter concluded that the pencil torch would alert the neighbours faster than the regular lights in the mansion. As Peter, with Pascal right behind him, turned into the living room, he heard a moan from across the hall. They crossed back and Peter hit the first switch that his hand met. The central chandelier in the dining room flared on in full glory, illuminating a mahogany table and twelve chairs. Expensive flock wallpaper was almost obscured by dozens of paintings that reminded Peter of the chockablock displays in the Palazzo Pitti in Italy. There were precious works by Lemieux, Borduas, and Riopelle. Pretension was the aim but the blood-soaked fellow at the far end of the room tied to the immense mahogany sideboard destroyed the effect.

Olivier Seep sat with his back against one leg of the sideboard, to which he was tied by what appeared to be a dog leash wrapped several times around his torso; it was knotted where he could not reach. Darkening blood formed a long 'V' down his torn shirtfront. He was missing several front teeth and it looked as though he had vomited the blood. A bruise had welled up on the right side of his forehead. He was semi-conscious and evidently had been drifting in and out. He could have snapped the leg of the sideboard with a forward lurch but the action would have brought the furniture and a hundred pounds of valuable china and flatware down on his trussed body.

Renaud's moan almost matched Seep's as he moved around Peter to untie his helpless rival. Peter stopped him.

"Pascal, I want you to go to the kitchen, turn on the lights, and see if any dog dishes are sitting on the floor."

"Dog dishes?"

"He's bound with a cord that might be a dog leash. Do you know if he owns a dog? The thing we don't need is a Doberman launching itself at us."

"A dog? No bloody idea."

The cascade of blood from Seep's mouth made it difficult to check for a pulse under his jaw but Peter tested his left wrist and found a strong beat. He would live. Peter worried for a brief moment that Alida might have killed the professor's pet but concluded that this wasn't her kind of perversity. Monitoring the entrance to the dining room, he shot a glance towards the kitchen, now brightly lit by over-head neons. Renaud looked back and shook his head. When Pascal made to return to the sideboard, Peter held up a traffic cop's palm then moved to join his friend in the kitchen. Peter noted that the chain was on the back door. The attack would come from the front of the house. Peter crouched at the kitchen entrance to the dining area, less than six feet from the wounded man.

The centre hallway did not connect directly to the kitchen, so the two men could not be seen from the front vestibule. The light from the chandelier in the dining area would lead the attacker that way, Peter hoped. He motioned to Pascal to extinguish the overhead in the kitchen. A further hand motion kept him quiet, although Pascal continued to watch with distress the bloody figure bound to the sideboard.

This time Peter kept the gun at the ready. After a short while, he saw Pascal, his knees cramping, slump to the floor, back against the kitchen cupboards, inadvertently mimicking Seep in the dining room. It would only be a few minutes. There was no point in shut-ting off any lights; they didn't matter now. Another five minutes passed. Peter was content to wait but he could detect his friend's growing agitation. He had a point: calling an ambulance was the responsible thing to do.

Peter took the moment to revisit Alida's appearance at the town-house. He understood Alida's cryptic parting words: "I have the last two letters." Alida had stolen the Williams–Thompson document from Greenwell the night of the killing. She had tracked down Seep and stolen the Booth–Williams letter to complete the set. Now she possessed all three letters.

Peter heard the sound from the direction of the front door. He stood up in his stocking feet. He waved to Pascal to remain still. Peter shifted to the dining room from the kitchen and took a position in front of Seep's crumpled figure. He concealed the gun by holding it below table level.

Dunning Malloway, pistol in his right hand, squinted against the chandelier's glare as he entered from the hallway. Peter remembered the two pairs of shoes in the vestibule; the intruder would be fully alert to the threat from *two* men. Malloway was sweating but otherwise was composed. He seemed puzzled by Peter, but not angry or particularly focused on him.

Peter knew that the massive dining room table and his own upper body blocked Malloway's view of Seep. Perhaps the younger man heard a sound or smelled the blood, but he did not hesitate further. He raised his .38 and, striking a duellist's stance, aimed it down the length of the polished table.

CHAPTER 42

They sat in the car in the rain and stared at the back of the Violet Care Home.

"Joe hasn't been here," Maddy said, almost disappointed.

The crumbling asphalt parking area contained only a few staff cars, including a Vauxhall, which displayed a "Visiting Chaplain" card in the side window. The rear door of the institution appeared firmly locked, the whole building tranquil.

"We guessed wrong," Michael said. But he wasn't entirely displeased. Husband and wife had argued about whether to come down to Henley at all. "If Joe Carpenter is spinning out of control, the Thames Valley Police should handle it," he had said.

"They won't consent to posting a constable here for hours at a time," was Maddy's retort.

Michael refrained from asking whether he and Maddy themselves would end up stationed outside Avril Nahri's place the whole day. His wife was playing detective and was determined to impress her father-in-law, though Michael kept that opinion to himself. Instead, he deferred to her obsession with the Carpenter case, as Maddy knew he would. An hour after the panic call from Carole Carpenter they were on their way from Leeds to Henley-on-Thames.

They agreed that Maddy would investigate the Violet Care facility while Michael took Jasper for a pee on the grass fringe of the parking lot. Maddy had to walk around to the front of the home in order to gain access. She returned in twenty minutes. The drizzle had increased and Michael was waiting inside the car with the damp dog.

"There's been nothing," she reported. "Security seems pretty good. A lot of it to keep the residents in, but they're confident that anyone intent on causing a disturbance will be stopped at the door. A buzz-in is required to get past the first gate. And all the security stuff we both know well."

They both managed difficult people, inmates in his job, wife batterers in hers. He had been through two hostage-takings at regional prisons; she had been present the night a vengeful husband broke into a hostel where his wife had taken refuge and stabbed two staff members.

Maddy rushed out the passenger side, went over to the grass verge and threw up. Back in the car, she said, "I'm calling Peter."

Michael's action was counterintuitive, a bit unreal to him. He reached over and covered Maddy's cell phone with his hand. "No."

He had been the cautious one until now, ardent to protect his pregnant wife, while sceptical that they would find anything at all in Henley or Shiplake. Ambivalent, he had even agreed to bring Jasper, thus making the trip a family excursion. But now he saw that Maddy, who had spent so many hours chasing down Alida, remained serious. She sat next to him, holding back nausea, her hair soaked. If she was this obsessed, let this husband-and-wife adventure play out, Michael ruled.

Besides, Jasper, panting in the back seat, was proxy for her master, Chief Inspector Peter Cammon, father and father-in-law. She leaned forward between the seats, ready for their next adventure. Peter would have been proud to know that Michael and Maddy felt his presence in the car.

"No, Maddy, we're going to Shiplake."

The rain seemed to be on a cycle; it returned in shimmering veils, as if bent on submerging cars and pedestrians alike. At the assisted living home the story repeated itself: only a dozen cars in the car park and no recent in-and-out traffic. The building seemed battened down to the Cammons. Residents of old-folks' homes eat early and without doubt the elderly residents had already been led off for their afternoon naps. Maddy had her husband drop her by the side door so that he could take the sedan somewhere out of plain view. The rain faded again as Michael pulled over by the long, curving driveway and let Jasper run off leash in the nearby copse of sumacs and poplars. The home was out of sight around the curve. He spent fifteen minutes looking without much interest at the sodden trees. Jasper, free at last, ran through the mucky forest bed until Michael was forced to enter the wood to find her. He dragged her out of a ditch and bundled her into the back seat of the sedan. Her stench forced him to wind down the driver-side window a few inches.

Michael got out and strode along the mucky access road towards the residence. Still out of view of Maddy, he heard someone say, distinctly, "I've seen you."

He halted. There was no one on the roadway or in the woods. Some strange thermal inversion had caused the voice to bounce off the underside of the cloud bank and reach him seventy yards away. As he crept around the final curve, the clouds broke and allowed a shaft of sunlight through. Fog steamed off the asphalt and hung three feet from the ground. Outside the side door of the residence, Maddy was standing still, facing Joe Carpenter through the haze. Joe was pointing a large handgun directly at her breastbone.

Tommy Verden lived much closer to Henley-on-Thames than Michael and Maddy did but he had to fight his way out of the London suburbs that morning. He brought the Mercedes, the company car and the one he savoured driving. It won some respect from other vehicles and he made progress through the morning rush. Peter's message had been a little too brief in that it left Tommy unclear about what Joe Carpenter hoped to achieve by threatening Alida Nahvi's family. Like Michael and Maddy, Verden set his Sat Nav for the sister's place first — having obtained the location from Bartleben's assistant — since Avril was supposedly Carpenter's primary target. By late morning he reached the car park of the Violet Care Home. Peering through the pelting rain he sized up the situation, and without stopping the Mercedes decided that all was normal here; the car park was a still life and the building an adequate fortress. His sense of urgency grew. He quickly reset the Sat Nav for Shiplake. On the last stretch before the nursing home he took his Glock out of its special case and positioned it on the passenger seat.

The long driveway up to the building appeared quiet but the heavy rain had given way to a hovering blanket of steam and it was impossible for Tommy to discern the layout of the grounds, let alone be sure that no shooter was skulking about. There was a familiar figure up ahead, just at the curve, but it wasn't Joe Carpenter.

Michael turned at the purr of the approaching Mercedes. He hadn't yet seen the car, but in a state of uprooted amazement recognized the purr of the engine. It was a sound from his childhood at the cottage, the floating chariot — or its modern replacement — driven by the man they called Uncle Tommy. For Michael and Sarah, Tommy had always been the family protector. Michael crept back around the curve, sure that Joe Carpenter had not yet seen him. He waved to Tommy to halt, worried that Joe might hear the big car. The older man caught the fear on the other's face; he immediately got out of the Mercedes and beckoned to Michael. When Jasper, in the Saab, saw her temporary master walking away, she began to whimper. Tommy opened the back door of the Mercedes.

"Bring the mutt back here," he hissed.

Though there was little time, Michael followed Tommy's instructions and opened the Saab to let Jasper into the road. The retriever vaulted over the front seat and scampered onto the muddy path before Michael could grab her. Tommy, his disgust ill concealed, ushered the dog into the luxurious interior of the E-Class Mercedes and closed the door.

"Tommy —"

"Who cares about upholstery?" Verden said. The Mercedes stood farther from the nursing home than the Saab, and maybe a barking dog wouldn't be audible at that distance. He shook his head and put the Glock in his jacket pocket. Michael was supposed to be the moderate, sane one in the Cammon family and now here he was bringing his mutt to a potential shootout. The Cammon girls were usually the wild ones. Sarah was so independent that every move in her life seemed made out of contrariness. Joan ruled the roost and was tougher than Peter (Tommy liked that very much). Maddy was cut from the same cloth and he had no doubt that she was the leader in this adventure. Michael, in his view, was lucky to have her; she was family now and no different than the other "kids."

"Tommy . . . He — he has a gun," Michael said finally, dispelling Tommy's ten-second reverie.

"Where's Maddy?"

Michael explained.

"Michael, she's pregnant! How could you let her . . . ?"

Tommy headed silently up the muddy lane, the Glock at the ready. Michael followed.

Maddy saw Joe the second she had emerged from the building. The staff inside had encountered nothing unusual, and she surmised that she and Michael had arrived first. As she exited the side door of the home, there he stood under a tree, his clothes and hair soaked. He held a large, battered gun in one hand.

"I've seen you," he said in a daze.

"We talked," Maddy called to him. "At the funeral." Joe was several yards away and it felt awkward conversing at this distance. "Your sister called me. What do you hope to gain here, Joe?"

"That bitch killed John. It wasn't the book dealer."

"How do you know?"

"From a solid source. There's a murder warrant out for her. She's killed other people."

"She won't come back for her mother or her sister . . ."

"She keeps in touch with them."

Maddy thought it significant that Joe hadn't rushed inside. He had hesitated, but if he chose to shoot her, he would to try to breach the side door and probably continue shooting his way up to Ida's room.

"She's gone, Joe. Harming these women won't lure her back."

Tommy Verden, with Michael trailing, appeared on the path. Maddy saw them first and then Joe turned as he followed her gaze through the fog. Michael moved to one side, prepared to interpose himself between the gunman and his wife. Tommy stayed in place and held his weapon straight out towards Joe Carpenter, who looked in awe at the figure with the gun.

"This isn't going to happen," Tommy said.

"This is the *second* time, fella," Joe said. He started to whine. "Why shouldn't I find out where she is? I've the right."

"Are you sure she killed John?" Maddy asked, but it sounded like the delaying tactic it was. Joe swung his gun towards Verden.

Tommy spoke: "It was Dunning Malloway who told you she did it. Malloway is on the take. You can't trust him."

"I have the right," Joe repeated. He held his weapon pointed at Tommy's head. "Malloway told me Greenwell is dead. The girl killed John."

Maddy knew a standoff when she saw one. She watched Michael, in an agony of fear, edge forward to block Joe Carpenter in case he swung his gun back towards her. Maddy knew that his intervention would set off the duellists. She moved between the two armed men, altering the trigonometry.

"You can't kill three people."

"Why not?" Joe said. "You're protecting that bitch."

Maddy took another step towards the mechanic. He couldn't miss at this range. "Because I'm expecting a son," she said.

Joe Carpenter took a long time to lower his firearm, and Tommy did not move. Even when Joe relented, the veteran detective kept the Glock trained on him. Maddy came even closer, ensuring that Tommy would have no clear shot, and began to talk softly to the Lincolnshire man, who now seemed forlorn and pitiful. Tommy gave Michael a frustrated look but Michael could only shrug. Neither of them could hear the conversation. The older man kept his aim steady.

Tommy's mobile phone rang. Maddy continued speaking to Joe, who began to cry. The caller could have been anyone, but Tommy's decades of experience had made him slightly psychic and he flipped open the cell, all the while keeping his Glock trained on Joe Carpenter.

"Hello, Peter," he said, as evenly as possible. He listened for a minute before walking over to Carpenter and handing him the phone in exchange for Joe's weapon.

Maddy insisted that Tommy Verden release Joe Carpenter, who stepped backwards, now unarmed. While the three men stood apart, like western gunfighters who had missed their moment, she disappeared into the rest home.

Fortunately for Maddy, the facility administrator hadn't heard the confrontation outside and she let her upstairs to the old woman's room. Mabel Ida Nahri snored peacefully in her bed. Maddy kissed her forehead. Then she went to the bookshelf and took the boxed set of *Avatar* DVDs, still shrink-wrapped in its plastic, and tucked it under her sweater. No one would challenge her; a pregnant woman had her privileges.

When Maddy emerged, Joe Carpenter had gone and the other two men were standing guard at the door. Down the long driveway, they heard Jasper begin to howl. The dog was hungry.

CHAPTER 43

Like Joe Carpenter, Dunning Malloway had too many targets, but he wasn't displeased to find Peter Cammon standing in his direct line of fire. He had been waiting a long time to shoot someone — waiting for a hundred thousand pounds sterling to kill the right someone. Dunning had never shot anyone, but he had no qualms. He hadn't faltered in the Buffalo parking lot when he had a good bead on the girl. The old detective had jogged his arm and now his interfering had come full circle. Dunning would wade through any number of bloodsuckers and bureaucrats and old men to get to the girl — he was sure that she lurked somewhere in the house — and Cammon provided that little extra motive.

It did not appear to Malloway that Peter was armed, but he might have something in his hand hidden by the table top. It was often said around the office, mostly by Counter, that "Old Cammon hides things." Once, when a junior colleague pressed the matter, Frank Counter had said, "Cammon goes rogue from the get-go. Doesn't share. There's a dozen ways he hides things."

Dunning waited a few seconds longer. He took an extra moment to analyze his situation, and thus, unwittingly, planted a seed of doubt in his own mind. Did Cammon really have a gun? Why didn't he move? Dunning shifted to his right to flank the dining room table and saw Olivier Seep on the floor behind the detective. At the same time, he caught sight of another man in the kitchen. He was confused. Cammon still wasn't moving; it was almost as though he had been struck mute by the pistol in Dunning's hand. Simple arithmetic told Dunning that he now had three times the witnesses to eliminate. But none of them was armed. He began to debate with himself. His gun should have produced clarity of purpose: kill them all and find the girl. Unfortunately, Cammon's stoic refusal to move provoked Malloway's indignation, and outrage is the enemy of judgement in a man who has never killed.

Peter Cammon made his own calculations and decided to wait his opponent out. The Lorcin pistol, held just below the table, lacked the stopping force of Malloway's weapon, although Peter was close enough to take a decent shot. He held to his plan: he would use the unreliable gun only under extreme duress. He could hear Tommy Verden now: "Let's see, you shot a colleague with an unlicensed popgun probably stolen from a hooker by the hooker's killer. No gold stars for you."

Peter hoped to make this a negotiation, otherwise known as buying time. *Time burns off impulse*, he thought. *Talk leads to rationalization. Wait him out.* As long as Malloway and Pascal Renaud didn't panic, the man who spoke first would lose.

"Is the girl here?" Dunning Malloway said.

"No," Peter said. "She was, but not now." Malloway was staring at the bloody bundle strapped to the sideboard. Peter registered his confusion at the sight of the blood-soaked near-corpse.

"She did that to Seep? Why?"

"You've forgotten in all this, Dunning, that the girl always knew Seep killed her boyfriend. She's always had that in her mind. This is payback."

"But she was complicit. Made a deal."

The more he whinges, the weaker his resolve to end this with gunfire, Peter estimated. "This is over, Dunning. Alida is gone."

"I don't believe you."

The fading of Malloway's hopes might well spark him to shoot, Peter knew, and his objective became to keep him arguing. Peter decided to prod from another direction while looking for an opening. "The cricket syndicate is going to be rolled up, Dunning. We know about the deal with the gamblers and the Pakistanis. We know the head man."

"You can't touch him. You don't even know his name."

"His nickname is the Sword," Peter said mildly. "Real name Devi. Alida told us. Souma in Delhi confirmed it."

"She wouldn't dare tell. And if she did talk to you, which I doubt, she can't be far away. She'll show up," Malloway replied. He was justifying himself, and that was fine with Peter.

"She *did* show up. She was here and she won't be back. Face it, Dunning, you can't shoot all of us."

"A gunfight can be staged."

It happens sometimes that an innocent civilian facing a gun barrel can't stand the tension any longer and tries to interact with the gunman. Peter had seen this form of instant Stockholm Syndrome before. And so Pascal Renaud chose that exact unpropitious moment to satisfy his curiosity.

"Don't you want the Booth letters?" Pascal blurted, now positioned near Peter. "They're worth a fortune. If you kill us, they may never surface."

"I couldn't care less about the letters," said Malloway.

"He cares about the girl," Peter said, trying to keep his voice even. He shifted to block the gunman's angle of fire on Pascal, while continuing to shelter Seep on the floor behind him. He held the pistol motionless under the table. "His patron, the Sword, wants her dead."

Seep began to revive, exhaling deeply between groans and whimpers. He struggled against the cable that bound him to the sideboard. Malloway took two steps to the right and fired a shot into Seep's right foot. The professor screamed and flailed, his left foot slamming against the floor. The blast caused Peter and Pascal to jump, even as Peter noted the accuracy of the shot. He fought to stay in position. Fortunately, Malloway still failed to see the tiny pistol under the table.

"Where's the girl, Professor Seep?" Malloway said.

Peter risked a step to his left, so that he half-shielded Seep. "Dunning, you don't get it, do you? He doesn't know where the girl is planning to go. If he did, she would have killed him rather than just beating him. She's covered her tracks."

Malloway's dilemma was evident to Peter and Pascal. *Guns transform men, it is said.* Malloway, having fired once, felt the authority of the pistol, Peter could see. Malloway turned to Olivier Seep and started to crouch down. Peter took the opening to raise his weapon.

The back of Dunning Malloway's head exploded in a way that morbidly recalled to Peter the Zapruder film of JFK's assassination. The right rear quadrant of his brain burst from its cavity. Minute pieces of the carapace carved like shrapnel into thirty expensive paintings, while brain matter and blood re-coated the artwork in arterial red. The paintings rattled with the discharge of the .45.

Peter clutched the unfired pistol in his hand. He looked from the gun to Neil Brayden, who seemed as if he might fire the .45 again.

Cammon saw what Brayden saw, that a second bullet would be unnecessary. Brayden pointed his gun slightly downward but did not immediately move from the far doorway. His left arm hung at an odd angle. Peter noted that like himself and Pascal, Brayden had tiptoed in without shoes. His big toe was sticking out through a hole in his sock.

"I saw all your shoes in the entrance," Brayden said, his voice hoarse. "It's like an effing mosque out there."

Pascal Renaud leaned against the kitchen doorway with relief, Malloway's brain spray not having quite reached him. But Peter knew that the crisis wasn't over. For one thing, Brayden wasn't moving and it was a short segment of a circle to a new deadly vector. Peter made sure the safety on the Lorcin was off.

"Neil, why did you do that?"

Brayden's eyes were glazed. "I killed him."

Peter grasped that he wasn't referring to Dunning Malloway. "Who?"

"An hour ago. Tom Hilfgott."

Of all the people Peter had encountered lately, Tom Hilfgott was the least connected to violence. "What happened?"

"He thought I had slept with Nicola last night. He got it wrong. Any other night, sure, but it was Malloway who slept with her. Tom thought I had screwed his wife. Ironic, isn't it? He must have heard something going on in her bedroom. He came after me with a golf club."

"Self-defence," Pascal whispered. Peter wasn't sure if his friend was trying to comfort Neil Brayden or reflexively offering an academic's observation.

"Shut up, Pascal. Neil, what made you come here?"

"Nicola tried to stop the fight," Brayden said. "She told me Malloway was on his way here."

"Neil, you have to put down the gun."

"I have to go," Brayden said. He was out of the room in five seconds. Peter moved quickly to Seep and checked his vital signs. His breathing was harsh and his pulse was elevated, signalling shock. Peter wadded his jacket and jammed it against the foot wound. He had Renaud unhook the bleeding man from the sideboard and check for major cuts and bruises while Peter went to the telephone in the kitchen and dialled 9-1-1.

As the emergency operator answered, in French and English, Peter heard a shot from outside. He tried to gauge the direction of the sound. If Brayden had fired the .45 again, it logically should have come from the front of the house, his escape route, but Peter remained unsure. He had no idea of the size or configuration of the backyard, and doubted that he could easily gain access. But however illogical it seemed, Peter was confident that Neil had fired the gun at the rear of the residence. Peter had no idea who the target might be.

"*Attends,*" Peter said and passed the phone to Renaud, who accepted it with his blood-smeared hand. "Give them directions.

Police *and* ambulance. Tell them one gunshot around the back. But stay here, Pascal."

Peter slid the patio door open about two feet and got down on his hands and knees. He crept across the threshold and onto a wooden porch, where an opaque panelled railing shielded him from the lawn. He paused to check the small pistol. The dining room chandelier cast a faint glow through the window but otherwise the backyard remained in shadow. He heard movement from the end of the property but could see nothing. Peter had no choice but to stand if he wanted to evaluate the danger. Whoever Brayden had shot at likely had the house under surveillance front and back. Brayden must have seen the men waiting at the front and dodged around the side lane to the backyard, firing a shot as he ran. Too late Peter understood his own mistake. Brayden was still at the side of the house and thus had not triggered the photosensitive floodlights at the rear. But Peter did so now by standing up. Below him emerged Neil Brayden in stark blue-tinged light at the edge of the lawn. He turned to Peter in agony, and then looked back towards the far reaches of the lawn, which remained in darkness.

A shot came from the dark but missed Brayden and slammed into the base of the porch, launching splinters everywhere. Peter had encountered death-by-cop before. He vaulted the railing and landed hard, just behind Brayden. He kept the gun in his hand as he jumped.

The figures hiding in the back bushes saw only two agitated men with weapons in their hands.

Another shot went over Cammon and Brayden's heads.

Peter shouted, "Deroche!"

Brayden, taller than Peter by several inches, aimed the .45 at a noise in the hedge in front of him. If he let loose with the big pistol he would blow apart everything in range. Peter began to raise his feeble weapon.

Sylvain Deroche rushed out of the shadows directly at Brayden in a foolhardy bid for glory. It was a suicidal tactic and it drew a second policeman from the hedge, pistol drawn. Brayden had both officers in his sights. Deroche's man fired at Brayden but missed. The bullet struck the picture window in the dining room and imprinted a spider web pattern in the glass. Peter was now pointing his weapon at a slight upward slant at Brayden's skull. As the pistol touched the man's hairline Peter pulled the trigger.

Brayden got off one shot. Another policeman fired twice, bullets zinging over the heads of the men on the grass. Peter fell to the ground. Deroche launched himself to his right and onto Brayden's crippled shoulder, but the man was already dead. Peter saw the .45 fall from Brayden's grip.

Deroche turned over to look at Peter, who in all the chaos still clutched his pistol. One of the officers gently wrested it from his hand. Peter turned to the inspector and both men instinctively gazed back at the one thing that had struck both of them as not making sense. The dining room window had not shattered. Olivier Seep had installed bullet-proof glass in his residence.

Sylvain Deroche got to his knees. "Let me guess, Peter. We won't find any old letters inside."

Peter nodded. "Not even one."

CHAPTER 44

Eight men laid into the oars, five on at the down-current gunwales, three to the upstream side. They rowed into the unwelcoming fog. The wind had abated and the surface of the St. Lawrence lay flat as a table, at least until the crew and passengers lost sight of it entirely in the enveloping mist.

The Marylander moved back from the bow and took shelter from the drizzle with the horses at the centre of the vessel, which was as much raft as boat. He marked his large trunk stacked in with the other luggage at the stern. To pass the time, he read the notice tacked to the tethering post. It advertised the Queen's insistence that excise be paid on imported goods and boxed liquors at the Montreal landing. He smiled his actor's grin, but only for a few seconds, for he felt a rush of loneliness as he floated between invisible shores. The South lay far behind him.

The fog might have stood for young Booth's single-minded lack of interest in the Canadas, and in both the river and the anticipated city on the coming shore. He listened to the crew cursing in French but understood none of it. Montreal was a mystery to him, except that the Virginia papers called it Little Richmond for all the Confederate agents and escaped prisoners who had taken up residence there. But he had his own special mission in the City of Saints. He cautioned himself to display his usual charm, if only to remain anonymous and unchallenged while in the town.

The fog dissipated like a rising proscenium curtain to reveal the bustling harbour a hundred yards ahead and the giant mountain beyond. Booth believed in icons of good luck and he marked the spire of an old church poking above the retreating mist.

It was the 18th day of October in the year 1864 and it seemed to John Wilkes Booth that all of the city was descending on his hotel, the St. Lawrence Hall. Men in Richmond had called the hostelry "Confederate Headquarters" and by far the best place to stay in the city. His wagon driver had to wait in a long line of similar wagons and stylish carriages. The actor instructed him to leave the trunk inside and meanwhile made his way through the traffic to the front door, only to be swept inwards by a crowd of soldiers, deliverymen, and merchants and their wives, all gathering for grand festivities. British regulars in scarlet and blue uniforms clustered in the lobby and for a moment Booth worried that his presence would be challenged; Union spies regularly reported the arrival of their Confederate opposites to the authorities. But he realized that the crowd gave him the invisibility he wanted, and he proceeded towards the registration desk.

Booth wearily crossed the expansive outer and inner foyers of the Hall while the raucous buzz of conversation flowed around him. Off to his left, through the rotunda, music and the clack of billiard balls emanated from the main bar. Farther on he noted a grand staircase leading up to a second-floor salon; on his right he marked a reading room with newspapers hanging on wooden racks.

Booth was used to being recognized, so he wasn't surprised when one man in the throng did. Henry Hogan, a thickset hotelier with Burnside whiskers and a friendly, all-knowing smile, had run the hotel since its opening in 1852. He often used a peephole in his office to monitor entrants to his place but this afternoon he remained at the front desk. His practised eye sized up the visitor as something more than the usual salesman. The arrival exuded a worldliness merged with youthful arrogance, while his long coat with the astrakhan collar and his high riding boots, now splattered with Montreal mud, set him apart. The jet-black hair was striking, too, and he was blessed with smooth, pale skin; Hogan found a resemblance to Edgar Allan Poe, the Baltimore poet and journalist. But the initials "JWB" tattooed on the man's hand gave him away. Hogan now had a decision to make, whether to acknowledge the customer's identity or let him be. As it turned out, the famous actor solved the dilemma for him.

"I would like a room for the week," the man said, in a pleasant, modulated voice. "I have a trunk."

"I will give you room 150, at the back of the hotel, away from the worst of the noise," Hogan replied, and rotated the register towards him.

Booth, without hesitation, signed "John Wilkes Booth."

Hogan smiled and, still uncertain as to Booth's business in Montreal, kept his voice low. "I saw your brother, Edwin, perform in New York, and your father some years ago in Philadelphia. Are you appearing on stage in the city, perhaps?"

The dark young man looked up and his expression intensified. "I have given over my theatrical activities for more important drama."

It was an intemperate thing to say. Henry Hogan was a Union supporter and known to pass information on his guests to colonial officials. But Hogan remained star-struck and continued, "We have two grand theatres. The Crystal Palace, alas, is closed for repairs but the Theatre Royal boasts fifteen hundred seats, gas lighting, too. I am sure you might arrange one of your nights of readings, 'The Charge of the Light Brigade' and 'Beautiful Snow,' perhaps."

Before either man could address Hogan's question, a figure intervened at Booth's left elbow, causing him to turn. The man was short, ruddy-faced, and earnest; had Hogan been asked to label his profession, he would have replied "Southern agitator," and he would have been correct.

"John Wilkes?" the *intervenant* said, keeping his voice low. Booth called up his actor's smile.

"If you would see to my traveller's trunk, Mr. . . ."

"Hogan. Of course I will." Hogan turned to imagined business as Booth and the new man left the desk.

They hustled towards the entrance to the hotel, and the man introduced himself in the same low tone. "I am Patrick Martin. From Baltimore. We share friends in Maryland and Virginia."

"I wish to be introduced to more of your friends," Booth managed to say through the din of the crowd.

They retreated to a tavern up the block near the Place d'Armes. Most of the patrons in the gloomy bar, Booth noted, spoke French but the barkeep was bilingual and Martin ordered rum for himself and brandy for the actor in English.

"We're both from Baltimore?" Martin began.

"I'm from Bel Air, just to the north," Booth said. "Our estate is called Tudor Hall. But, yes, consider me a Baltimore man. What is going on at the hotel? Is it wise for me to stay there with all that military about?"

Martin grinned. Booth saw a man comfortable in himself. "You don't want to stay at the Donegana Hotel," Martin stated. "That's where the escaped CSA soldiers who don't have any money put up. Now don't give me that look, Mr. Booth. You will meet plenty of our military men at the Hall. The Hall is where the important folks stay."

"And you know the important people?" Booth sneered, flaring at the insult to Southern prisoners-of-war.

For his part, Patrick Martin took note of his companion's volatile reaction and immediately wondered at his stability. He held back judgement.

"You asked about the multitudes in the city. The Confederacy is not the only colony on the edge of independence, my friend. As we speak, the Canadians are in conference at Quebec, upriver, and reports say that they have reached consensus on the articles of nationhood. This Canadian movement is a juggernaut, I can attest. A celebration is being prepared for their arrival in Montreal after the conference."

"Will they keep the Queen as their ruler?"

"Oh, yes," said Martin amiably. "This will not be our republic nor the haven of states' rights believers."

"Then I want no part of it. Kingship is to be reviled."

"Not so harshly, Mr. Booth. Victoria is well loved here. Within memory, the Prince of Wales came here on a Royal progress to open the Victoria Bridge across the St. Lawrence, a mighty feat of engineering. My own sloop is christened the *Marie Victoria*. This is a country on the move."

"Are *these* men so fervent for a British dependency as their future?" Booth said, indicating the French-Canadians surrounding them.

"Don't be so sure they want independence from the British at this stage of their history. Don't forget, if the damned North wins, they may turn their armies loose on the Canadas and the result for the French will be a greater threat of assimilation."

"It might be the moment for their own revolution," Booth riposted.

"Don't talk drivel, Mr. Booth. There are eighteen thousand British regulars stationed in the five colonies."

"Yes, and they all seem to be staying at the Hall," Booth replied.

Martin laughed. "That is certain, and they include Sir Fenwick Williams, commander of all Her Majesty's Forces in North America. You'll see him. Look for the bald head; always sports a gold-hilted sword."

By then Booth was on his third brandy, although Martin had barely sipped his second tot. The cagey blockade-runner looked at the young actor and worried. Still, Southern manners won out.

"I received your letter of introduction from our mutual friends. What can I do for you, sir?"

Booth leaned forward. "You can give me space for my wardrobe trunk on your sloop. I understand that you will soon embark on a long sail to Portsmouth across the Atlantic?"

Martin kept his voice low; their faces were inches apart. "I am indeed leaving in two weeks for England. You want your baggage transhipped? To where, Charleston?"

"First to the Bahamas, then on to Charleston," Booth said.

"That isn't a problem. The British tolerate our traffic to England. Beyond there, it will be someone else's problem, and there has been little hazard running goods through to Nassau. But I believe you want something else from me, Mr. Booth."

"I understand that government commissioners are present in Montreal and that their leader, Jacob Thompson of Mississippi, is resident at the St. Lawrence Hall. I would like to be introduced."

Martin shook his head. "You haven't heard, then. There has been an incident, a provocation. Earlier today, a group of expatriate soldiers, Army of Northern Virginia men, carried out a raid across the border into Vermont. They robbed the bank in a town called St. Albans and killed a local citizen, then fled back to Canada. The Union's provost marshal in Vermont has demanded their extradition and has already threatened to send his troopers onto Canadian soil, although what they would do here is unclear to me."

"And Thompson sponsored this enterprise?"

"Indirectly. The organizer is the second of the commissioners, Mr. Clement Clay, an Alabama man, who tends to be behind most of the schemes these commissioners attempt. He's about the most querulous fellow you will ever meet. But, yes, Thompson is now the focus of investigation by the colonial security people. The commissioners will not have time for you this week."

"That is disappointing."

"Why? What can they do for you?"

"I have ideas," Booth said.

"The commissioners are overflowing with ideas. Corner the gold market. Send Lincoln foodstuffs infected with smallpox. Inflame the Northwest against Lincoln in the election next month."

Martin tried to estimate how much Booth knew about clandestine efforts against the Union. Most behind-the-lines plots had failed and managed merely to irritate the British. If Booth were to meet the governor general, Lord Monck, he might grasp that the British were not to be provoked into war with Lincoln and Seward. The

St. Albans raid would test everyone's patience but Martin knew the crisis would pass like the others. He hoped that Booth understood that this was a time for discretion.

Patrick Martin escorted the slightly drunk John Wilkes Booth back to the hotel. The crowd had moved to the ballroom, which at present did duty as the dining room. Henry Hogan watched from his spy hole as Booth entered.

Over the next seven days, Patrick Martin did his best to entertain Booth, who showed little gratitude or patience, the exception being his suppers with the Martin family in their rooms at a boarding house in Rue Saint François Xavier, where he turned on his charm with Mrs. Martin and played the heartthrob role with their daughter, Margaret. Otherwise, the sailor kept his guest busy with visits to several banks in the Square Mile. The transactions mystified Martin, for the actor proceeded to buy sixty pounds British sterling, using gold coins for the purchase, and then obtained bank drafts against his account balance at the Ontario Bank in a similar amount. Booth appeared to be clearing the decks for action. In the afternoons the actor drank heavily, mostly brandy, and he often grew argumentative, spewing bile at Lincoln in the presence of anyone who would listen. Some days, disgusted, Martin abandoned him at the St. Lawrence Hall bar, pleading family commitments.

The actor settled into a routine that approached idleness. At the hotel, he took to examining the English papers, taking his drink across the foyer to the reading room, which was frowned upon. The *Gazette*, with its pro-South leanings, became his favourite of the dozens of papers published in Canada East, although he also read the pro-Union Toronto *Globe* for its tracking of the war. He learned of General Early's defeat at Cedar Creek, the manoeuvring of Hood and Sherman in Alabama and the declaration by Lincoln of Thanksgiving as a national holiday.

Each afternoon, Henry Hogan posted news of the Quebec conference on Confederation and the planned celebrations at the Hall. October 28th had been declared a public holiday. The fancy ball would welcome eight hundred guests. "Tickets: $6 for a gentleman accompanied by two ladies, $4 for a gentleman alone," the advertisement said. The next day, Hogan pinned the menu to the dining room door frame: "October 29 Gala Dinner: Oyster soup, viands and game, ice cream and fruit. Champagne, claret, lemonade, sherry, and ale." On the following afternoon, Hogan displayed the itinerary of the Colonial delegates, who were scheduled to arrive in Montreal by boat and train. The governor general, Lord Monck, would review the Canadian Volunteer Force on the Champ de Mars, while the local fire brigade would put on a demonstration.

In truth, Martin was bored with self-important patriots who talked big but lived in luxury in Montreal. On the fifth day, he asked Booth whether he could be of any additional help. It was his way of drawing out the younger man on his plans for Washington, where Booth intended to travel — "soon." Over drinks in the same French tavern, Booth laid out his plot to kidnap the president and carry him overland to Richmond, where Lincoln's release would be negotiated for that of thousands of Confederate prisoners-of-war held in Northern camps, the very inmates that the Confederate commissioners were unproductively scheming to liberate.

Patrick Martin considered Booth's project and quickly thought that it held as much promise as anything the commissioners had bruited about, publicly or privately.

"How can I help?"

"You can provide me with letters of introduction to anyone who lives in south Maryland who might assist. I know several good men in the Signal Service who have apprised me of clandestine mail routes to Richmond, but I need safe houses along the route, and I may need fresh horses once I cross the Navy Bridge and the Potomac southward."

"I know two men," Martin immediately said. He gave the names of Dr. William Queen and Dr. Samuel Mudd, and promised letters of introduction.

His ready agreement was in part diversionary. Let Booth essay a kidnapping. Martin would assist but he was not about to hook Booth up with professional Confederate spies in the Signal Service without Jeff Davis's approval. Queen and Mudd fell into the category of useful sympathizers, amateurs.

Patrick Martin was not there to experience Booth's transition from kidnapper to assassin. Martin delivered the letters of introduction on October 26th but did not tarry at the Hall for drinks. Booth's feelings on his own plan oscillated. Although Martin's letters gave momentum to his kidnapping plot, at the same time the plan had seemed hollow, and possibly impractical, when he voiced it. For the first time, John Wilkes wondered if assassination might be simpler. That evening, he drank alone in the bar and to the clicking of billiard balls and drinking glasses, he sank into a depression. At that moment he felt adrift. The idea of an alliance with the commissioners had spun away from him with the Vermont raid, which occupied their every moment and which had been a failure. Martin had in any case told him that Thompson and the others were impractical men, and that in late 1864 the Confederacy was no closer to recognition by Britain than it ever had been. "Why would they send thin-skinned men from Alabama and Mississippi, men who have never seen snow?" he had said.

Was there a better way to convince Britain of the hostile conspiracy of the Union against the emerging Canadian state?

By his last day in Montreal, Booth's thinking began to crystallize, aided by two unexpected incidents. While drinking at the Hall he caught Sir Fenwick Williams striding in from the rotunda, resplendent in his uniform. He seemed to Booth to move in stiff-backed slow motion, and as he passed Booth's table the two men made eye contact. The actor detected sympathy in the other's look.

A half hour later, while nodding off in the billiard room, Booth was awakened by a brazen voice over by the long mahogany bar.

"To Lincoln and the end of the bloody war!"

"To Lincoln!" seven men agreed, and the sound of bumping steins woke Booth fully.

He bounded from his chair and struck a pose by the billiard table. He picked up the white ball and rapped it down on the felt, leaving a small indentation.

"This Lincoln is a false president yearning for kingly succession! No good can come of his re-election. Tyrants like Napoleon and Caesar must fall before the rights of men and the honour of the democracies to which Athens and the British parliament gave life."

The oration went on like this for five more minutes. The room fell silent. Afterwards, Booth retreated from the lounge, sobered as much by the effort of declaiming as by the frosty response from the crowd. Booth climbed the staircase to his room, where he took out a leaf of paper from the desk and began to write. The letter seemed to compose itself but as soon as he read it through, a wave of drunken nausea struck him. Barely finishing the one-page missive, he let it slip to the floor. The next day he checked out of the hotel and bought a horse to carry him south.

Henry Hogan came to work early — the Colonial delegates were about to arrive — but he was not early enough to catch Booth, who had already paid the night clerk for his stay. The maid sent to clean the room, Irish and energetic, changed the coverlet on the bed and supplied a basin and a pitcher with fresh water for the next tenant; she swept the floor and polished the one window. She picked up the page of hotel paper from the floor and read the salutation: "To Sir Fenwick Williams." Reasoning that this must be important — and knowing that Sir Fenwick kept rooms at the far end of the hotel — she placed the sheet of paper in one of the envelopes supplied on the desk and dropped it in the in-hotel post.

Booth hides in the woods as the dew collects on the matted leaves around him, seeming to refuse to dry in the emerging sun. He turns to the next empty page in the diary that he carries and begins to scrawl, and as he does he remembers his week in Montreal, irretrievably far to the north of this cursed swamp. "For six months we have worked to capture," he writes. Some time ago he learned that his wardrobe trunk, containing his favourite theatrical costumes and an authentic Confederate sword, was lost when the Marie Victoria *sank in a storm in the St. Lawrence. Patrick Martin was reported drowned. Booth pauses for a long time, then continues to write. He ponders how to finish, for he knows that from now on he is unlikely to be given respite.*

"I bless the entire world. Have never hated or wronged anyone. This last was not a wrong, unless God deems it so, and it's with Him to damn or bless me . . . I do not wish to shed a drop of blood, but 'I must fight the course.' 'Tis all that's left me."

PART FOUR

Twenty One Fifty Four

Year in which the Na'vi rise up against the Earth invaders on the moon Pandora.

CHAPTER 45

No one emerged with laurels from the Carpenter Affair, as it came to be known around Sir Stephen's office. A police force owes a debt to its fallen and Sir Stephen, dissecting everything in the file (even Peter submitted a complete report), concluded that only two of his people, Peter Cammon and Tommy Verden, had kept that principle uppermost in their thinking and their conduct. Or, as he unloaded onto his assistant, Lorelei, that young woman of surpassing efficiency whom Peter and Tommy both liked for her tempering effect on the boss, when she asked about the wrap-up to the case, "There was a murder to solve. It got solved, my dear."

"But Cammon freelanced all over the place," Frank Counter squawked in Bartleben's office subsequent to their boss effectively sacking him three months to the day after the death of John Carpenter.

"When you trust somebody you let them freelance, off the leash," Sir Stephen retorted. "If it bears results, you don't call it freelancing."

Counter's antennae should have perked up when Bartleben started coining aphorisms but he was lost and sweating in a jungle of self-pity and he missed the signal. "Stephen, Cammon exceeded his mandate. And he let the girl escape — *twice.*"

Sir Stephen merely stared at Counter with contempt. John

Carpenter, Dunning Malloway, and Neil Brayden had all met ugly, lurid deaths but Sir Stephen was confident that the tabloids and the politicians wouldn't make a connection between Cammon's role and the phone hacking and cricket bribery scandals, as long as no one in the hierarchy lost his or her nerve. New Scotland Yard had announced a fresh investigation into the *News of the World* mischief and parliamentary hearings into the matter were on the calendar. Cammon would be safe and Frank Counter should know it.

In his bitterness, Counter persisted in his denunciation of what he called Peter Cammon's "meddling in Canada."

Sir Stephen's bloody-mindedness expressed itself in clipped sentences. "The deaths of our people won't come out in the inquiry. Nor hopefully in the cricket mess. Peter saw the risk of all this exploding. You didn't, Frank. And Peter did his best not to kill your boy, Malloway."

"Didn't succeed, did he?"

Class distinctions endure in Britain for a number of reasons, but one is often overlooked: members of higher echelons from time to time insist on the right to speak their minds brutally to those one step down in the hierarchy. Frank Counter liked to believe that he moved round the same circuit as Stephen Bartleben; he attended the right parties, belonged to some of the same clubs, and knew many people, a few of them inside the intelligence elite. But none of this held up when it mattered. Sir Stephen was no longer on the shelf, having graciously accepted the invented title of Coordinator, Special Projects.

Bartleben didn't restrain his cruelty. "You failed to understand that the Minister has to be shielded at all costs. Nicola's man went bad. Malloway turned. Wouldn't have occurred if you had occupied Malloway with keeping Nicola Hilfgott under control, and kept your boy on a tight rein. It was your decision to send Carpenter and then Malloway to Quebec. You're out, Frank. For now, at least. I'm putting Tommy Verden in charge."

"What?"

"Only of the investigation into the deaths of our officers. The phone-hacking business is moving to a new phase with the announcement under the *Inquiries Act*, and I'll handle that. I want the police investigation regarding Canada contained. Containment requires making sure the Sûreté and the FBI are happy, and maybe the municipal forces in D.C. and Buffalo as well."

"I have solid contacts in the Bureau and with Deroche in Montreal," Frank pleaded.

"Yes, but Tommy is especially good at the street-level stuff. Speaks their language. He will liaise with the Canadians and the Yanks. Mend fences."

Frank unwisely took a different tack. "But Deroche can be myopic in his own way, I hear. What interest does he have in helping us?"

"Only that Cammon saved his life on two occasions."

"So?"

"I've asked Peter to give an assist to Tommy."

"But Verden aimed a gun at Carpenter's brother inside a church. And again in a car park in Henley."

Sir Stephen lost it completely. "Tommy Verden maintains self-control at all times. Unlike yourself in this confabulation. So Tommy and Peter are being put in to clean up your failures. Then we'll see. By the way, as your final act perhaps you can find someone to go over and fetch Malloway's remains back to England."

When Frank Counter went to see Tommy Verden later that afternoon, the veteran inspector was already grinding away at the files. Sir Stephen had shown zero sympathy, but Frank had higher hopes for Verden. Counter walked into Verden's tiny office, which was located one floor down from Bartleben's sanctum. The orderliness of the room should have alerted him, for it betrayed a self-discipline and asceticism far from his own work habits. Tommy received him politely but coldly and listed the thirty or so contacts he had connected with in the first day and a half, just to make a point about who was on the ball.

Frank tried for an opening, slathering on a false concoction of collegiality and superiority of rank. "I think, Tommy, I can help you pin down the extent of Dunning Malloway's sabotage of the cricket investigation. *Mea culpa*. But I understand a lot about this character the Sword, and the way he operates, and I have great contacts in India . . ."

At first, Tommy said nothing. He knew that a burgeoning file existed on the Sword and woe betide Counter if he had held anything back from it. Counter hadn't got his head around the salient, stark fact that the Sword had promised Malloway £100,000 to execute Alida Nahvi. Someone in the Yard had to be sacrificed, even if out of public view. Tommy also respected the strict limits of his own mandate. He wasn't to take control of the Yard's public responses to the *NOTW* feature on the Pakistani cricket players but together with Peter, he would interact behind the scenes with all the operational players in four countries; he had already called Souma in the Indian police and Rizeman in D.C.

And so Tommy said nothing in response.

Frank Counter looked disconsolate. He leaned forward. "Tommy, I have contacts you don't . . ."

Tommy's raised eyebrow stopped him.

"Jesus, you know, I feel just like Napoleon exiled to that island," Frank continued.

Tommy's muscled body hulked forward. "Do you like palindromes?"

It was well known that Tommy Verden loved word puzzles, a habit picked up during long stakeouts in unmarked black sedans.

"Palindromes? Sure."

"Well, able was *I* ere I saw Elba. Why the fuck weren't you?" Tommy said.

The first of Tommy's thirty calls was to Peter, now back at his cottage. They talked for two hours. Peter followed up with a call to Sir

Stephen in support of Tommy's appointment. But it was Peter who suggested that he himself take on a special troubleshooting role in the match-fixing investigation. He preferred to leave the hunt for Alida in the Bureau's hands, but what he could do was help to track down the Sword before another gunman was sent to execute the girl. He explained his thinking to Tommy on the phone.

"Malloway never cared about the three letters. The Sword was paying him to find Alida Nahvi and kill her, and the documents were Nicola's sideshow. The Sword may continue to chase the girl. You'll discover that no one but Henry Pastern in Washington still cares about the letters, though that will be enough to keep him looking for Alida."

"Will Pastern look hard for her?" Tommy pressed.

"I don't know. Inspector Deroche won't. Oh, she'll stay on the wanted list, but not his personal ten-most-wanted. I don't think Deroche even believes that she exists. She's a will-o'-the-wisp to most of us, I admit."

But very real to you, Tommy wanted to say. He had caught the undertone of wistfulness whenever Peter discussed the young woman.

Peter changed the subject. "How is Tom Hilfgott?"

Nicola's husband had survived. Tom Hilfgott and Neil Brayden had duelled with irons and woods until a No. 2 drove Tom to the floor, unconscious. Nicola had found him and called an ambulance.

"Put it this way, Peter: the Hilfgotts are back in England. She was quietly recalled and apparently he recovered enough to travel. Foreign and Commonwealth have been working overtime to keep all this out of the press. I talked to a fellow over in Whitehall yesterday, at Sir Stephen's request, and they count themselves lucky that the media haven't latched onto the story."

"Better get *News of the World* onto it," Peter said.

"Quote-unquote: 'Tom Hilfgott's wounds were so serious he may not play golf again.' On the other hand, I hear he's already angling for an appointment for Nicola as high commissioner to Gabon, since Gabon's a full member of the Commonwealth, and apparently has some fine golf courses. Two of which Tom Hilfgott immediately queried by email, according to my sources."

The death of Neil Brayden was covered up, because neither the Quebec authorities nor the British government saw any benefit in publicizing it. The inquest was perfunctory, with no questioning comments by Dr. Lowndes in the autopsy report this time. Even the separatist groups in Quebec found nothing to exploit when they learned of the death of an employee at the British consulate. Foreign and Commonwealth Affairs shipped Neil Brayden's body home to his family in Bournemouth.

Peter's report to London ran twenty pages but he failed to mention Alida's naked apparition in Renaud's townhouse. The omission made it difficult to explain why he hadn't summoned Deroche that night. In Peter's report, he merely stated that Alida had coerced Seep into summoning Malloway, promising that he knew Alida's whereabouts.

Scotland Yard's failure to confront Nicola Hilfgott early on was more condemning. Sir Stephen had made it clear from the beginning that she was his *bête noire*. Her fixation on the Booth letters obviously was a personal fetish, well outside the mandate assigned by Her Majesty. Even her unreasoning hatred of Olivier Seep should have been evident from the outset. For his part, Dunning Malloway should not have been surprised that Nicola would find a way to manipulate Brayden into going after Seep. Unfortunately, Brayden had arrived at the Seep house with his own lethal agenda. Dunning Malloway paid a heavy price for his one-night stand with the consul general.

CHAPTER 46

Olivier Seep survived the assaults by Alida Nahvi and Dunning Malloway, but only by about two weeks. Chief Inspector Cammon pieced together the facts from the Sûreté and his own recollections, and added them to his report.

That night at the professor's house, Inspector Deroche, having confirmed the death of Neil Brayden in the yard behind the mansion, rushed to the dining room to investigate the blood-drenched scene. He left two men to minister to the professor while he secured the house. The officers struggled with kitchen towels to staunch Seep's bleeding; it was touch and go for the ten minutes they had to wait, but the medics quickly assured the police officers that Seep would live. The ambulance attendants bundled him off to the closest hospital, the Jewish General, where Seep was aware enough to take umbrage when the emergency room staff began talking to him in English; by the time they switched to French to accommodate him, he had passed out. His foot was put in a cast and his bruises and multiple abrasions were treated. Two cuts on his chest, one under each nipple, were minimized on the chart as non-life-threatening injuries. The resident gave him Demerol, which had the odd effect of both reviving him and sickening him. He threw up three teeth.

The professor's wounds stabilized rapidly, so that by the beginning of the second week he began to agitate to be sent home. By then he had also scheduled dental surgery.

Inspector Deroche visited the hospital every day for the first week. Peter advised him to lay charges immediately but Deroche hesitated. Finally, at the end of week one, the inspector concluded that Seep had no connection to organized crime, and turned his full focus on the Carpenter murder charge. Seep clammed up. Confession was not in the separatist's curriculum plan. Deroche proceeded with the paperwork based on charges of second-degree murder and criminal negligence by drowning.

As time diluted Deroche's momentum — the *procureur général* referred to the body of evidence as Swiss cheese and was reluctant to proceed — Seep improved enough to be shuttled home to his house with a private nurse. He broke into tears as she wheeled him through his hollow dining room, the floor stained with his own blood, the table gone for cleaning, and his valuable paintings stacked in a restorer's studio. Seep ached to hold a press conference to somehow denounce the Anglos — and, he fantasized, the British, too.

The private nurse quit on the third day, and though in pain and alone in the house, Olivier Seep fell into a peaceful sleep that night — an extra Seconal did the trick — for the first time since the attack. In the early hours, two hooded thugs attempted to burn down the mansion with gasoline. Their intent wasn't to kill the professor, since they had no idea that he had checked himself out of the hospital, but rather to send a warning so that Seep would reveal the whereabouts of the elusive Alida Nahvi. The fire gutted the downstairs (and thus began the sub rosa legend — for anyone who still cared — of the lost Civil War documents) but the firefighters saved the frame of the house. The professor perished of smoke inhalation. The arsonists were arrested at the scene after a neighbour called in the disturbance and were at once identified by Deroche as mob underlings. He vowed to prosecute the mafia soldiers to the maximum.

The morning after Malloway's death, Peter, still in Montreal, gave a sworn statement covering everything he knew about the Carpenter case and the lead-up to the shootout, although again he held back the image of Alida Nahvi *au naturel* in his bedroom.

A fortnight after the fire at Seep's place, Peter was surprised to receive a call at the cottage from Inspector Deroche, who offered a few new insights.

"Peter, I now understand who set fire to Club Parallel. It was not the Rizzutos."

"And it was not Seep, Malloway, or Brayden," Peter said.

Peter had figured it out soon after Leander Greenwell's suicide. The club wasn't owned by a mafia affiliate, and management denied paying protection money. Even the Rizzutos needed a good reason to torch a business. The mob soldiers behind the two arson incidents had to be part of a different, rival clan. Strictly speaking, their motive was removed from the internecine wars for control of Montreal.

"But, my friend," Deroche said, "I don't know why they would harass Seep or Greenwell."

Peter responded to Deroche. "The same reason for both attacks. Intimidation. You remember I mentioned the Sword, the East Asian gambler who hired Malloway to kill Alida Nahvi? It appears that he didn't trust Malloway to track her down by himself. Malloway failed to catch her in Buffalo. The Sword then hired some goons in Montreal to visit Greenwell and Seep both, to get them to reveal her location. Neither man knew where she was but the gang was being paid to locate her at all costs. After the Club Parallel fire Leander feared a second visit and took his own life."

"Yes," Deroche said, "but the attacks were also a display of power." Peter granted Deroche his moment.

"Which clan were they, then?" Peter said.

"We believe they're part of the 'Ndrangheta. Mob sects never make public shows of their strength unless they are sending a message to their rivals, and in this case the upstarts were issuing a warning to the established Rizzutos. The 'Ndrangheta took this hire job to show they can operate in Montreal under the noses of Nicolo and Vito. Things are just getting worse for the Rizzutos."

Once the mafia connection was made, Deroche cooperated more in wrapping up the killings of Carpenter and Malloway, and the demise of Leander Greenwell. Tommy Verden pledged Scotland Yard's fullest collaboration by providing the Sûreté with a complete briefing on the continuing investigation of the cricket scandal. Deroche was flattered. In London, Peter and Tommy spent several long days focusing on the career and perfidies of the man known as the Sword. Deroche joined in on two conference calls, thrilled to be included.

In the second week of November, Deroche was proven right in his prediction that the Rizzuto clan was doomed and would be eaten up, month by month. Sitting down to dinner one night, the patriarch, Nick, was assassinated by a rifleman waiting in the yard behind his mansion; the gunman's first shot penetrated the plate glass window and terminated the ancient mafia leader. Deroche sent an email to Peter: "Nicolo should have hired the guy who installed Seep's back window."

In Washington, Henry Pastern struggled to decide whether to add the three Booth letters that Greenwell had worked so hard to assemble to the FBI's Stolen Art list, but he eventually decided to hold off; he had never viewed the originals and was unsure which version of the letters, if any, was authentic. Once a month he checked all the databases relevant to the Alice Nahri / Alida Nahvi hunt. There was never anything new.

Back in Montreal Georges Keratis didn't care where the letters might be. He inherited Leander's shop, which he renovated and turned into a successful hair salon. He tore down half the bookshelves, sold some of the volumes, and gave away a lot of the rest; the rule was that any customer celebrating a birthday could select a book from the remaining pile and take it home. After a while, Georges felt guilty and he stopped trashing his benefactor's collection. He began to read some of the fine Quebec collection on the shelves. He eventually enrolled full time in the history program at McGill University.

Peter Cammon and Pascal Renaud worked at sustaining a long-distance friendship. From the moment of Peter's return to England, they bombarded each other with emails, all connected to the Carpenter case and its aftermath. Peter remained grateful for Pascal's openly offered hospitality and the even-tempered welcome into his home, a place that had served as a kind of headquarters for Peter's investigative kibitzing. Nor did he forget that Pascal was the one who had risked his life to attempt to aid John Carpenter the night he died.

Once in a while the professor would call the cottage from Montreal, just to chat. The Cammons planned a vacation to Quebec once the cricket inquiry subsided. The two men always seemed to work their way back to the "case"; it was as though both had yet to find their way to the end of the saga. One such call entailed a comprehensive report by Pascal on the highly politicized funeral of Olivier Seep.

"Madame Hilfgott will be outraged if she hears of the tributes paid to him," Pascal said. "You'd have thought Jean-Paul Sartre had mated with Che Guevara."

"No mention of the Booth correspondence?" Peter said. "Or is it all legend now?"

Renaud laughed. "The stuff that dreams are made of."

"*The Tempest?*"

"Last line of *The Maltese Falcon*," Pascal riposted.

Their transatlantic alliance went into decline as the weeks passed.

The deaths and funerals of both of Joan's siblings occupied the Cammons through much of November, and Christmas brought with it Maddy's advancing pregnancy, which began to preoccupy the whole family. By then, Peter was busy with Tommy Verden in the hunt for the Sword, a matter which Peter wasn't free to discuss with Pascal.

Other worries ate at Peter. He had led Renaud into the danger zone of Olivier Seep's house, where Pascal had been forced to confront the humiliation of his rival, trussed and bloodied on the floor. Peter should have considered Pascal's ambivalent feelings towards his separatist colleague and separatism generally — feelings entwined with his sister's death. Peter didn't dare ask him if he resented Peter's drafting him to drive to the mansion that night.

One question nagged at Peter more than any other. It seemed odd that Pascal and Alida had missed each other when she fled from Pascal's condo. Peter supposed it was possible. He conceded that she could have guessed the location of the door key under the flowerpot. But wild scenarios spun through his reinventions of that night. *Did Pascal spy Alida while he was monitoring the façade of Leander's shop? Did they perhaps talk in the cobbled alley around the corner, voyeurs agreeing that Seep had murdered Carpenter — Pascal must have figured it out by then. Did Pascal make a suggestion . . . ?*

Peter, ever the rational detective, came to understand that his suspicions were unfair. Renaud had consistently been an amiable host. He had gone easy on the politics, had confided the painful story of his sister's death; his empathy with Peter's own loss had helped pull Peter out of his depression over Lionel's passing. Distrust was no way to treat a friend. Peter owed him more than that.

Peter wasn't a devotee of New Year's resolutions but the first of January provided the perfect opportunity to exorcise his unfair speculations. He made the call, enjoying the intrusion into Pascal's hangover. As usual, the professor recovered within minutes and they launched into a cheerful post mortem on 2010. They inevitably wandered into a review of the night of Alida's ghostly arrival. Peter was careful when he finally said, "You know, Pascal, I can hardly believe it. One minute she was there, naked, the next . . ."

"A deadly ghost."

"Tell me, did you see her outside the condo that night? Even a glimpse?"

Pascal thought for a minute, and said firmly, "No, Peter."

CHAPTER 47

She keeps the letters in a strongbox under a false floor in the closet.
Banks ask for personal data on every application for a safety deposit
box, and so she keeps her money in cash and her valuables at hand.
From time to time, she takes a key, removes the letters, and reads
them through. It becomes almost a monthly ritual and eventually she
starts reading books on American history, the Lincoln assassination,
and so on. She reads Renaud's book on the Civil War. She figures that
this is good, honest preparation for the day she becomes an American
citizen, however that plan might work out. One day she picks up
an old *People* magazine and sees that Gloria Stuart, the actress who
played the elder Rose in *Titanic*, has died at the age of one hundred.
She likes to stand on the edge of the lake; from there, with her 20/10
perception, she can see every detail of the far shore. She remains
vigilant. She regrets not being able to return to Rochester but this
will do. Walking out to the pines each morning, she looks around
carefully and repeats to herself that this will do.

It was Maddy who made the educated guess. Or guesses. She did
not tell Michael about the shrink-wrapped package, for she wanted

its secrets to be hers, at least at first. It was all she could do to hold back from opening the *Avatar* box set but she resolved to go about this task one careful step at a time. On the weekends after the Henley confrontation, she enlisted Michael to drive around to garage sales and junk shops, where she rooted out used copies of VHS tapes of the *Terminator* series and *The Abyss*. She ended up buying a fresh copy of *Titanic* on DVD. She trusted that they were identical to the ones Alida had viewed. Maddy reminded herself to take it slowly — she would not be travelling to North America before the baby came. *Do things in the right order,* she told herself. On a late November weekend when Michael was working double shifts she got out all the films and lined them up by the television. Mimicking a forensic detective, she rotated the new DVD box set of *Avatar,* held it up to the light and compared the plastic wrapping of her new *Titanic.* They looked about the same, hermetically sealed by machine. With a paring knife she slit the plastic on the *Avatar* box and opened the flap. She took out the DVDs and the other materials, and stared at them for a long time. She placed the disc in the player and watched the film from the beginning; the clue was in there somewhere, she was confident.

In *Avatar,* the tall blue creatures never refer to any geographical coordinates for Earth, nor, according to internet searches, is there a town in the United States called Pandora. *Avatar* takes place on a mythical moon in the year 2154. *Is there a future world out there that gives you hope, Alida? Or does your sanctuary derive from the past, from the world almost exactly one hundred years ago, when hopeful men and women attempted the ocean crossing from Southampton to New York?*

She watched *The Terminator,* which ends with the heroine fleeing to the mountains of the American southwest, but Maddy couldn't imagine Alida doing that. It occurred to Maddy that Alida Nahvi was connected to water; it was her theme, her motif. The Lachine Canal, the Niagara River, the Anacostia, and the wide St. Lawrence. *Look for a place near water,* Maddy reasoned. It did not matter that the girl came from Bihar, one of the driest places in India. Maddy cued up Kate Winslet and Leonardo DiCaprio in the ultimate water movie. She watched it twice. None of the scenes was set in Buffalo or in Rochester, and none of the characters hailed from an American, British, Indian, Canadian, or Pakistani city that rang any bells. She fell asleep on the sofa as Céline Dion sang over the closing credits the second time around. She dreamt of water, and of her baby boy. The next day, she skimmed through *Titanic* four more times, fast-forwarding through many scenes. Nothing struck her until the sixth viewing: the scene where Jack Dawson — Leo — lucks into an invitation to dine with the upper crust in a borrowed tuxedo. When questioned by the nobs, he reveals that he was born in Chippewa Falls, Wisconsin. Maddy retrieved an American atlas from the shelf and opened it to the second-last state map in the book. She circled Chippewa Falls in red marker. Then she turned to the *Avatar* materials arrayed on the table.

There was a brass key that didn't belong with the movie materials. Alida must have placed it inside the DVD box — Pandora's box — and somehow resealed the container. Maddy had no doubt that it opened another box, in which the secrets of the Sword and his crimes would be found. *But where?* Maddy placed the key in the centre of the red circle and contemplated it for a long time.

EPILOGUE

Peter bought Jasper without papers but no one could doubt her pure breeding, and that she was his dog, loyal and true. He liked the distance she kept from other people, Maddy excepted; it was not an aloofness but rather an even-temperedness that suited him. Joan, when Peter and Jasper started up their dog-and-master walks, silently falling into rhythm, said to Sarah on the porch one day, "Those two are too much alike. They'll never have to talk, they're already telepathic."

"You'd understand about that," Sarah replied, and Joan swatted her.

He could only guess the dog's age but when he threw a stick she gambolled after it, and she never seemed to tire. Every morning and early evening they traipsed along varied routes through the downs and farmers' lanes until it seemed a logical time to return. It was seldom necessary to keep her on the leash. He would only hook her up when there was a prospect of traffic, or when they headed onto unfamiliar paths. Someone had trained her to heel; even then, her obedience appeared to be natural, a sign of intelligence. The dog would occasionally meet another and her response was always the same: she sat down and waited for the new friend to come to her.

On a weekday afternoon in May, Peter took Jasper for a long hike into new territory more than two miles from the cottage. These days

Peter brought with them a mobile phone, dog treats, and a leash; he didn't bother with a walking stick, though he might need one soon. The spring weather had ushered in a rare phenomenon: more sunny days than rainy ones. The pair had become explorers with a shared taste for new vistas and chance encounters with farmers, hikers, and birdwatchers. And so it was that day.

Their morning walk had been postponed by two phone calls from Bartleben seeking advice. The Carpenter and Malloway deaths had largely been cleaned up thanks to Tommy Verden, and public scandal averted. The cricket sting and the interminable voicemail-tapping incidents hung on in nasty ways. The press criticized the Yard daily for its dilatory approach to laying charges against the Murdoch tabloid in the face of clear invasions of privacy. What seemed straightforward became complex, with the parliamentary inquiry chronicling every alleged voicemail invasion, their hearings peaking with revelations that the *NOTW* had abused the privacy of one grieving family of a murder victim. As for the cricket transgressions, the sport's regulatory bodies stumbled along in the face of Scotland Yard's criminal inquiries. The potential for British prosecution of the Pakistani bowlers receded. Peter helped out by running liaison with Indian and Far Eastern police authorities but the infamous Sword went to ground.

Their sojourn took them to rolling countryside that Peter had forgotten. Joan had hiked with him to this part of the county ten years ago, he recalled. The sudden memory of his relative youth lured him farther than he might have gone on a normal day. Jasper never faded; Peter gave her water from a plastic bottle and she was fine. After two hours, they found themselves on a straightaway section of a wide country road that he didn't recognize. A rank of linden trees, dark-leafed and freshly in bloom, formed a windbreak that obscured the fields ahead, while dense hawthorn bushes hemmed in the immediate edges of the road on both sides. The thick growth darkened the path, a bit of Constable overlaid with Brontë gloom. The lane curved out of sight to the left about two hundred yards along.

The air was still. Peter heard a plaintive voice calling "Brute!" Or perhaps he heard "Brit!" or something else entirely. From around the turn a purebred Doberman galloped into view. He was young and unrestrained, as well as collarless, and he stopped in the middle of the dusty road when he saw Peter and Jasper. Peter had hooked the retriever to her leash in case a farmer's lorry suddenly appeared. Now, she did something he did not expect; instead of sitting and waiting, Jasper pulled away from him towards the young dog. Peter unsnapped the clasp. Jasper walked to the exact centre of the dusty path but did not sit down. She showed no panic; her positioning was strategic. He watched her go into a crouch, no deference given to the Doberman. Her posture left no doubt about what was going to happen. The young dog, in feral mode, trotted to within seventy-five yards and began to range back and forth, always returning to the centre of the road.

The Doberman barked twice and fell into a deep growl. Judging the coming fight, Peter sensed that the opponent, lithe and muscled as he was, was not trained to the pit. Peter had encountered pit fighting — a surprisingly widespread criminal activity — where the dogs are driven by bait and prods to attack ceaselessly until one combatant is dead or maimed. On the other hand, he had never heard of a brawling golden retriever.

Peter could have deterred the battle by re-chaining Jasper but for the moment, feeling the anger of the dogs building across the seventy-five yards, he simply walked over to the retriever and paused. In the silence Peter sought clarity of purpose. On other days, he had chosen reason in the face of violence, the law as his response to savagery. But his beloved dog was decided, had been from the first sight of the Doberman.

Peter leaned down to Jasper's ear and said in an inflection that was almost American, "Go get 'im."

Peter knew that dogs let into the pit run straight at each other like jousters in the lists. To the touts observing, they often appear to start spinning in a vortex of chaotic biting. The animals are seeking the hold, the body part that can be seized to effect in their powerful jaws. The trained attacker will latch on and shake the victim, seldom changing grip until the opponent becomes exhausted or bleeds away. The defender does the same. The best targets are the vulnerable throat, leg arteries, and underbelly; these are taken out by choking, hamstringing, and evisceration, respectively. A dog will sometimes be taught to go for the snout, a carryover from the unmourned days of bull baiting.

The body of a dog contains most of the same functional organs and skeletal features as a human and it is not too much of a stretch to compare a dog fight to a knife fight, with sharp teeth and claws serving as the blades. Jasper should have been at a disadvantage. She was smaller than the Doberman and no one ever bred a long-haired retriever for the pit. Her one defensive virtue, her thick fur, was diminished by the season; her coat was not as thick as it would be in the autumn.

She held her ground as the Doberman launched himself.

The attacker made the mistake of first seizing Jasper at the shoulder, where the fur was thickest. Canines differ from people in an important respect: their shoulders consist of flexible joints held in place by an articular capsule anchored by ligaments that allow them to stretch and torque their bodies in ways impossible for human physiology. At the same time, they remain vulnerable to tearing and separation of the joint. A clamping grip at the shoulder keeps the victim out of position, while potentially ending the fight on the spot if the teeth bury themselves too deep. Jasper's crouching stance prevented the Doberman from getting at her stomach or throat. The shoulder attack was the only lethal course open to the young dog. Jasper was ready. Though his teeth did puncture her shoulder fibre, the Doberman had made a tactical error. She moved under the adolescent dog and planted her teeth in his femoral artery. The pain caused the Doberman to give up his purchase.

The dogs rolled and fought for a disabling bite. Jasper did not let the Doberman retreat. The young dog seemed surprised that she kept coming. Jasper's strategy was to avoid being pinned by the

Doberman's superior bulk and Peter could see that she had fought before, although he had never found scars on her body. As they spun, the other dog's left haunch seemed to drag by a millisecond, although Peter saw that its power to slash and in-fight remained impressive. Jasper took bites to her right forepaw, which was the same leg the attacker had gripped at the shoulder, and to the skin on her forehead.

She broke off the fight, not in concession but to see if the younger dog was limping or bleeding out. And then they were back at it. Jasper's new approach was to snip at the extremities of the younger animal, inflicting painful punctures on toes, ears, and chest until the dog yelped and retreated. They regrouped. Blood flowed into Jasper's eyes, like a cut boxer. The Doberman surprised Jasper with a third attack on her front leg, holding on and trying to shake her to the ground. But this was a frontal attack and Jasper, with her right leg askew, dipped under her opponent and put her teeth into his throat. She pulled, ripping out the jugular so swiftly that the Doberman's rictus grip held fast to her leg and only released when Peter intervened and pried open the jaws.

The owner of the dog, a young man with sandy hair, came around the corner and stopped ten feet from his dead pet, while Peter cradled the retriever and held her apart from the canine corpse. All three of them were coated in red. The young man, confusion on his face rather than anger, meekly approached; he seemed stunned. Peter, glancing at him, saw that he could hardly tell which dog was which. The blood kept him back from the tableau.

Two farmers who had heard the fight came out from an access trail behind the stand of linden trees. Practical men accustomed to animal blood, they both understood that the Doberman was lifeless. One farmer put a hand on the other owner's shoulder. The one comforting the young fellow looked over at his mate, who nodded and went back down the trail in silence. Peter took a handkerchief and mopped blood from Jasper's face. The remaining farmer, needing to do something, proffered his own kerchief. Peter requested the bottle of water sitting by the roadside by Jasper's leash. As the farmer retrieved the water, Peter saw him look at the lead and then at the sandy-haired man, who carried no leash. He kept silent.

In a few minutes, the second farmer appeared with a small lorry with an open bed. Peter hoisted Jasper onto the back and climbed in with her. The farmer headed up the country road, while the other man stayed behind to deal with the stunned owner of the Doberman.

As best he could, Peter counted Jasper's pulse; he roughly estimated 120 beats per minute and he guessed that his dog might be going into shock. The wounds on her legs and forehead were beginning to clot but the blood at the shoulder joint continued to ooze. The best sign was her steady breathing.

The country vet smiled kindly when he saw the dog and his owner, both saturated with blood, enter his reception room. Living in the middle of hundreds of farms, he had seen every kind of animal wound, and so perhaps he was allowed to be philosophical. Even now, he maintained his affable nature. Peter sized him up as the kind of cheerful vet would some day self-publish his cheerful memoirs.

"So, what we have here is the winner," he said as Peter carried Jasper into the surgery at the back of the farmhouse. In a perfect imitation of Bruce Willis, he added, "You should see the other guy."

"The other one is dead," Peter retorted.

"And what breed was he?" the vet said, not contrite at all.

"Doberman."

"Not the one I would expect to win. For that reason, I will save your dog."

The veterinarian asked Peter to assist. This wasn't sentiment; his assistant was out dosing a horse for colic and he judged Peter to be in control of himself.

"You're a policeman, aren't you?" the doctor, who was about Peter's age, asked. Peter, exhausted, grunted. *Why does everyone peg me as a copper?*

Peter later described the vet as self-possessed, obviously a man of immense experience. In fact, Peter thought, he was a lot like a good policeman: *when you have seen every kind of tragedy, you compliment the victims by being good at your job.* They washed Jasper with a small hose and swathed her in towels. The evident priority was the shoulder injury, which the vet stopped from bleeding with antiseptic and masterfully quick sutures. He injected her with amoxicillin. The bigger problem, he proclaimed, was the knee joint and the carpus of her front leg, where the other dog had bitten through to the bone.

"The shoulder will heal but the broken leg can result in a bad limp. Choices to be made, Inspector."

In the midst of this chaos, Peter could not help asking, "How did you know I'm a policeman?"

"Inspector, you have lived in this county a long time. Not as long as I, but never mind. Everyone knows you by reputation or from seeing you on your strolls. The famous Chief Inspector Cammon and his dog. Now, here's what we are going to do. We will repair the cruciate ligament . . ."

Peter's mobile rang in his blood-soaked pocket. He flipped it open while the veterinarian began the procedure.

"Dad, It's Michael. Maddy's in labour, short contractions. We're at the hospital."

"I should be there," was all Peter could manage.

"The nurses say it may be hours, or it could be fast. You don't have to rush to get here."

"I promised her, Michael. I said I would be there."

Peter broke down in tears in the middle of the clinic. The vet pretended not to notice, but to signal the urgency of Jasper's condition he pulled out an apron and draped it over Peter's shoulder.

Peter recovered sufficiently to explain to his son about the dog fight.

"Stay with Jasper, Dad." Michael's voice was firm and implied that Peter needed instruction on his priorities. Five times, Peter promised to drive up to Leeds as soon as possible.

He hung up reluctantly and told the doctor about the baby. The man nodded, not so much in sympathy but to get Peter back to the table. Peter struggled into the apron as the vet tossed a clean towel to his new assistant.

"Swab the wound whenever it floods."

The veterinarian had put Jasper under anaesthetic but he talked to her, rather than Peter, as he worked. He leaned close to the dog's ear. "I could say something about the Lord taking away and giving back. . . . Bark once if you agree."

The two men worked steadily through to late afternoon. Putting down his instruments, the vet turned to Peter and grinned, but this time it was a proud smile. "This dog will fully recover. You can take that to the bank."

The mobile rang again. "How's Jasper?" Maddy said. Her voice was raw.

Peter glanced at the doctor, who was bandaging the dog's right leg. Peter said, "She'll be perfectly fine. I'll be up tonight, maybe. There's a lot of blood but . . ."

The vet glanced at Peter. The "famous" Chief Inspector Cammon was afraid of a little blood. His daughter-in-law and the vet seemed to achieve a form of psychic connection at that moment. The silence at Maddy's end and the look on the vet's face were judgemental in the same way.

Peter reverted to his fatherly persona. It was the best he could manage. "How frequent are the pains?"

The vet shook his head, with the opprobrium of a man telling another man that he didn't know what he was talking about.

Maddy shouted at him, so that he had to hold the mobile away from his ear; even the vet could hear her. "I'm at the door of the delivery room. Peter, if you abandon Jasper to come up here I will never talk to you again. I have to go."

"Wait! What are you calling the child?" the vet shouted back from his side of the operating table.

"Joseph Peter Tommy Cammon," Maddy called back through the line.

HISTORICAL NOTE

John Wilkes Booth travelled to Montreal in October of 1864 and conspired with the blockade runner Patrick Martin. This much is known. Whether he also made contact with British officials or the Confederate "commissioners" from Richmond remains a matter for speculation, and perhaps further historical research. One of the best academic studies of Canada's reaction to the "War of the Rebellion" remains *Canada and the United States: The Civil War Years* by Robin W. Winks (Baltimore: Johns Hopkins Press, 1960).

DAVID WHELLAMS spent 30 years working in criminal law and amending the Criminal Code in such areas as dangerous offenders and terrorism. His first novel in the Peter Cammon series is *Walking into the Ocean*. He lives in Ottawa, Ontario.

At ECW Press, we want you to enjoy this book in whatever format you like, whenever you like. Leave your print book at home and take the eBook to go! Purchase the print edition and receive the eBook free. Just send an email to ebook@ecwpress.com and include:

- the book title
- the name of the store where you purchased it
- your receipt number
- your preference of file type: PDF or ePub?

A real person will respond to your email with your eBook attached. And thanks for supporting an independently owned Canadian publisher with your purchase!

Get the
eBook free!*
*proof of purchase
required